REVELATION

by

VINCENT COBB

AN M-Y BOOKS PAPERBACK

© Copyright 2007
Vincent Cobb

A CIP catalogue record for this title is
available from the British Library

ISBN-978-1-909271-04-3

Published by
M-Y Books
187 Ware Road
Hertford
Herts SG13 7EQ

www.m-ybooks.co.uk

Front cover and prepress by David Stockman
www.davidstockman.co.uk

PROLOGUE

I was still shaking my head after Jim Robbins had left me at Warwick University. To my astonishment, he had offered me a position as detective chief inspector with the newly formed National Serious Crimes Unit at Scotland Yard. I still couldn't believe it, especially after the fiasco in Manchester, where Pauline, my lover, had unleashed her barbarous crimes on a serial killer.

After that terrifying episode I had virtually decided to end my career with the police force; I was even considering withdrawing my application to join Jack Crane at the FBI in Quantico as a profiler.

It was a devastating experience to accept that my lover was a murderer. On top of that, I was confused about my own sensitivity to psychic phenomena, given my recent exposure to it with Danny O'Brien. It had crossed my mind that, potentially, this was a gift that should be explored. What was puzzling me, though, was how to do it.

* * * * * *

So, there I was, in the cafeteria, sipping from a cold cup of coffee, and wondering how I should react to Jim's offer; he had given me two weeks to make up my mind. It was, of course, flattering – there was no doubt about that. But did I really want to leave the comfort of the cloistered environment of the university for the cold, inhospitable world of the career criminals – the rapists, the paedophiles, the serial killers? At that moment I really didn't know.

I strolled through the courtyards of Warwick, immune to the chill air of the cold snap that was successfully penetrating my inadequate clothing, and gave serious thought to Jim's offer.

My mind was in turmoil, struggling between the horrors of Pauline's plunge into the depths of criminal insanity and the plaguing thought that I too might have some psychic insight. Before I decided on anything this was something I had to resolve. I also had the feeling that it would determine which direction I should take in the future.

CHAPTER ONE

A few days later a thought came to me. I would try to arrange an appointment with Edith Morrison, the psychic aunt of an old friend from the West Midlands force, who I had met during the Connie adventures. This was assuming that, after all this time, she was still alive...

I was in luck. Not only was she still very much alive but also she announced that she had been waiting for me to contact her since our last visit. I was tempted to ask her why, but then I had second thoughts; I would wait until I came face to face with her before I asked the question.

I made my excuses with the dean, and a couple of days later I was setting off for Stourbridge to meet Edith. It was, once again, a cold winter's day: the sun was shining, but it was almost as if it were bidding us goodbye, it was so watery. It gave way to a sharp wind that threatened to blow in some snow.

The avenue in which she lived had hardly changed at all during the intervening years. The detached houses were well kept and the trees looked as if they had been cultivated to ensure their survival; well-kept lawns sweeping down to the pavements hugged the trees, comfortable in their environment.

Edith met me with a smile and a friendly hug. Her face had aged since I last saw her and the lines had deepened around her mouth. I guessed she must be closer to 80 by now.

"I'm so glad you decided to come," she said. "The years have passed us by and I thought you might never come back."

"But...but...how..." I was shocked at her announcement.

"...Was I expecting you?" she asked, as she escorted me through into the parlour.

"Well – yes!"

She led me into the same comfortable lounge that I remembered from my last visit. It too had hardly changed, apart from a carpet that betrayed its age in signs of wear, and curtains that, though they no doubt had been expensive at one time, were now showing their years.

After we had sat down she said to me, "Do you remember, when we met, I told you that psychics do not suddenly wake up one morning to discover we have the gift presented to us, ready to deploy? Do you remember that, Angie?"

"Well, sort of... I mean, we were talking about Connie – so I thought that whatever it was you were saying to me was related to her."

"At the time it was. And I was sorry to hear about her terrible misfortune. But, what I was really saying to you was that this gift we have been endowed with is an evolving blessing that can take years to reach maturity.

"I wasn't talking about Connie at the time, Angie; I was referring to you."

"Me?!" I said, surprised. "But my name didn't even come into it."

"Not at that moment it hadn't. But I knew I was in the presence of an emerging invocation. There wasn't anything I could say that might have encouraged its manifestation, but I knew, in my psychic self, that one day in the future you would come back to me. Isn't that why you're here – to seek the answers to your puzzle?"

"I…I don't know, Edith. It's true I wanted to ask you if I might have the gift – perhaps explore the possibility together. But it never occurred to me that it was preordained we should meet. I mean, I'm astonished – I just wanted to talk to you…"

"And isn't that what we're doing?" she asked in a gentle voice.

"Yes. Of course. But you've anticipated me." I shook my head, unable to accept the reality of what she was saying. This was not what I had expected: talking about it – yes; discussing how, if the psychic gift was present in me, we might develop it – yes. But to have something like this hurled at me was pretty bloody frightening. I got up from the chair, following the impulse I had just to run away.

"And now you want to escape – is that it?"

"I can't deal with this, Edith," I exclaimed. I rubbed my forehead with the back of my hand as if I were trying to clear my thoughts.

"Yes. I know, Angie. It's made you afraid, hasn't it? It isn't surprising, you know." She laid her hand on my shoulder. "I'm sorry if I startled you. So why don't we sit down again and try to talk about it. See if I can't give you some reassurance. I'll make us some coffee."

I didn't reply. I was almost in the same state of shock that had consumed me at the university. All these years and Edith had waited, patiently, knowing that at some time in the future I would return to her. But what would she expect me to do now? I mean, here I was as she had foretold, but how on earth could I seize this gift and turn it to my advantage? That's if she was right. I was still shaking my head in disbelief when she returned with the coffee.

"Feeling better, my dear?"

I wasn't sure, but I nodded all the same. The coffee was strong and hot – just what I needed.

"Well, when we've finished our coffee I would like you to come with me."

"Come with you? Where to, Edith?"

"To church. It's only down the road."

"I don't understand. What has this gift to do with God?"

"Where do you think it emanates from, my dear?"

"I...I don't know," I gasped, astonished at her suggestion. "What I do know is that I am not the least bit interested in religion."

She smiled. One of those perceptive and all-knowing smiles that used to freak me out. "You might have no interest in religion, as you say, Angie. But it certainly does have an interest in you. So what I would like us to do is to attend a local church, where you can pray to God for guidance in how you might best evolve His gift."

I stood up, almost spilling the coffee.

"Not fucking likely, Edith! I don't really know who you are or what your objective is, but there is no way you're going to get me inside a church. So, if you don't mind, I'll take my leave of you."

"What?" Her face expressed surprise at my outburst. "You've come all this way to see me and now you want to leave? To run away?"

"Too right I do," I said moving towards the door. "You're not getting me inside a church."

She didn't try to stop me. All she said was, "Angie, please. If you won't listen to what I'm saying will you at least take it away with you? And when the urge – the compulsion – causes you to question who or what you are, will you please remember what I have said and try to say a prayer to help you? I too will pray for you that you might see the light."

* * * * * *

Was I glad to get out of there? All this business about praying and going to church, and seeing the light, was way over my head. I didn't really know what she was after – perhaps to get to do a presentation to the Spiritualist Society. And I might or might not be a psychic; perhaps only time would tell. One thing I was convinced about was that Edith Morrison may have had some insight into my ephemeral qualities, but if I had followed her then God only knows where it would have led me.

I hastened my way back to Warwick University in the cold of winter's day, still unsure about my decision to rejoin the police force. I had the feeling that, if I were to sleep over the events of the day, I might be able to come to a momentous decision by tomorrow.

I was troubled and spent a sleepless night, worrying about Edith Morrison and her beliefs and my own confusion about my supposed psychic qualities. Then, during the course of the night I experienced a dream. Not one of those dreams in which you try to unravel the events that took place – it was a dream of such clarity that I clearly remembered everything that happened. A young teenage girl appeared to me. She was smiling and urging me not to worry. I didn't know what she was talking about until she said her name was Katy and she was the twin sister of Danny O'Brien. Danny had helped me out recently on a case in Manchester, when he deployed his 'sensing' abilities. I could recall him telling me that his deceased twin sister Katy helped him quite a lot. And here she was, suddenly appearing to me in my dreams.

I asked her how she might help me. She repeated that I was not to worry, that she would lead me into the Way, and all would become clear to me if I had a little patience.

I awoke feeling strangely refreshed, as if someone was now there to support and encourage me. It also cleared my mind, and I decided which direction for the future I would now take.

CHAPTER TWO

I used to love London on the rare occasions I visited the city. The museums, the shops, the theatres – they all held a fascination for me. But that was when I was merely a visitor, spending a day or an evening in the town: seeing a show, dining at a restaurant, and then returning home exhausted.

This was different, though. I was now living in the place. I had a small, almost bed-sit flat, just over the river in Battersea. If I peered out of one side of a window I had a glimpse of the Thames. The place wasn't even comfortable, and it reminded me of the apartment that Pauline used to have on the outskirts of Manchester: a tiny lounge with a kitchenette at one end, and then a small bedroom with a squeeze-in bathroom just off it. But it was – I suppose I would have to call it that – home, and it wasn't far from New Scotland Yard. Besides, I couldn't really afford anything more expensive; even a detective chief inspector's salary hardly warranted the rent that owners were asking these days.

I had already spent a few weeks at Hendon on a refresher course, mixing with all the youngsters. One of them, a serious, well-intentioned young man, made an approach to me, probably unaware that I was a detective chief inspector, much less that I must have been about ten years older than he was. I tried to hide my scepticism and politely told him I already had a serious partner. Still, it made my day. I wasn't what you would call pretty; but I was, even so, quite attractive. I had dark auburn hair, which I kept well maintained with regular visits to the hairdressers; brown eyes; and a rather plain face that would benefit from a nose job – that might make me more attractive. At 31, though, I still had a figure that most men would like to get their hands on.

Other than that my life had become a desert of loneliness; I had no immediate friends, no one to share my bed with, no colleagues I could even talk to. I could feel the hints of depression that had haunted me after my experiences with Connie start to settle in my subconscious. I wasn't even sure if I wanted to fight them. I began to question my decision to join Jim in London.

And then I thought of my life at the university. I didn't really have any friends there either – at least, not anyone I could share my innermost thoughts with. And what would my life be like if I continued to lecture at Warwick? Dull? Boring, probably, and hardly a boyfriend in my sights. But possibly, though (and this was a matter of speculation), I might have gone to America to join the FBI. Had I wanted to I could have received a work permit over there, because my father was a US citizen – but maybe this was just fantasy.

* * * * * *

The day before I started at New Scotland Yard I had another dream with the girl in a red dress – the same child who had appeared to me a few weeks earlier. She gave me the same enigmatic smile and reached out for my hand. Instinctively I allowed it to happen.

I then underwent a visionary journey in which Katy (I am assuming it was Katy) allowed me to witness a gang of armed robbers hold a family hostage in their own home whilst a man, I assume the manager of the bank, was escorted to his branch to wait for the timer on the safe to open it.

It was weird, and I had no idea what it was all about. I could see the montage on the top of the bank, depicting its name, and underneath was the heading: Thursday/Friday – soon. I woke up startled when I realised that the manager had been shot and killed. Jesus! What was that all about?

Then the vision disappeared and I was left wondering if this was to be my ethereal dream world in the future. I must admit that this experience did shake me up, and confused me. I awoke perspiring at the savagery expressed in the hallucination – the armed gang, the brutal treatment of the hostages, and the murder of the manager.

Was it a portent of something that had either happened or was about to happen? I didn't know, and since there was no one there to ask I tried to dismiss it from my consciousness.

* * * * * *

New Scotland Yard was a curious piece of nomenclature. I had always had visions that the central head office of the Metropolitan Police Department would be the epitome of luxury: spacious accommodations, fine fixtures and fittings, windows overlooking Whitehall. To my horror, I now discovered that I was accommodated in a basement office, with no windows and hardly any heating, and seated at my desk in a crowded space with some 30 or 40 staff nudging ever closer to me. There was also a computer I had problems accessing because of the mountain of files invading my desk.

And here I was, supposed to be a DCI – with a salary that had little or no improvement on my previous position at the university and with none of the trimmings.

I sighed as I realised what I had allowed Jim Robbins to talk me into. He, as a commander, was comfortably ensconced on the third floor of New Scotland Yard, with the kind of scenic windows I had been hoping for, and a secretary to go with his position. And to cap it all a superintendent, Charles Glasson, who got up my nose from the word 'go', now supervised us. Perhaps it was chemistry but we each took an instant dislike to each other. He was a black man, slim, around the mid-40s, balding (in fact, there was hardly a hair left on his scalp, and he compensated for this with an ugly chin beard), and his voice reminded me of a teenager struggling to become an adult.

By all accounts, though, he was very talented. At least, that was what Jim had told me – but then, he would have to say that, wouldn't he, after I discovered he had had no choice. Apparently the superintendent was imposed on him by the powers that be.

"I don't like him, Jim," I said to him one morning a few days after had I left Hendon. "I'm not sure whether or not he doesn't like females in general but he certainly doesn't like me."

He shrugged. "Maybe you'll have to give him time. He's only just made superintendent."

"Why did you appoint him to the Serious Crime Unit?"

"Well…to be truthful, I didn't. I was forced to give him the job by the top brass. I don't like to say it but it could be because of the colour of his skin. So, I don't really know him any more than you do. Look, Ange, why don't we wait and see what happens? I'm told he's very talented."

"I'll have to take your word for that. So, tell me, commander, what is it you want me to do? I'm supposed to have a staff of six in that overcrowded office; I still don't yet know who they are; you and that plonker Glasson are the only people I know in this building. My desk is spilling over with files that I haven't had time to read, so I don't know what they're meant to be about, and no one has given me any instructions on how to set up an intelligence department."

Jim gazed at me, an understanding expression on his face. "I'm sorry about the offices. We were meant to fit into the third floor here – where I am – but we're going to have wait a while for that. As far as your staff and your department are concerned, I'm going to introduce you to Inspector Layton this afternoon; I've had him transferred from

Paddington Green, where he headed up the Intelligence Unit there. He'll show you the ropes. I'll also introduce you to your staff."

"Good. At least something makes sense. And these files? What do you want me to do about them – become a filing clerk?"

He laughed. "They are the cases that so far have been referred to us. Try to read them, and then ask your staff to input them into the computer. We don't have to accept them, which really isn't up to us. Under the new legislation, regional offices are duty-bound to refer their crimes to the new division; we read and digest them, discuss them with the area concerned, and see if they do wish us to involve ourselves."

"Isn't that a little different from what you outlined to me earlier? I thought it was going to be up to us to determine whether or not we took the cases over?"

He sighed, the proverbial defence. "So it was – and it probably still is. However, I wanted us to have the time to settle in, organise our resources, before we took on something we couldn't really handle at this stage of our development."

"I see?" I said cryptically. "And what if something comes up that we feel is too important to be left to a divisional office?"

"Then you refer it to me and I will make the decision." Then, with his inimitable style, he changed the subject. "These files you're reading – you'll realise they are all either open or unresolved crimes. They'll give you a flavour of what we might be up against. You might even have some thoughts of your own."

"And what happens if I think they don't deserve our attention?"

He shrugged. "Initially that will be up to you and your team, but you'll still have to pass on to me a shortened brief of the cases. Then I'll decide if I agree with you."

It was my turn to sigh. "This is all very confusing, Jim. First you inform me that we will be the ones making the decisions; now you've either changed your mind or someone else has done it for you. Why can't you be straight with me?"

He leaned forward on the desk, cupping his chin in his hands. "I'm sorry, Ange. But those are the instructions I've had handed down to me. At present we're in no-man's-land. You'll have to leave it with me – I'm working on it."

I shook my head. This certainly wasn't what I'd expected. "There is one thing we haven't discussed yet, Jim," I said, trying to change the subject before I exploded.

"Really? And what is that?"

"My so-called extra-sensory perception. Have you any thoughts on that – or perhaps I should ask Glasson. He's made the odd comment or two."

"I see. Well, I might have told him that you have an incredible insight into profiling. But he doesn't know anything more than that. I mean, he doesn't know anything about Manchester or the earlier traumas…"

I looked at him levelly. "No. But he could have made his own enquires and formed his own opinions."

He sighed again. "You may be right, Ange. I wouldn't know. But why don't you give him a break? As for what I'm expecting of you – the answer is 'nothing'. Well, nothing I can readily identify. It's something you'll have to work with – you know…wait until something occurs to you that escapes the rest of us.

"When Sam Layton arrives today you can use him to head off the superintendent. And if he causes you any further grief I'll have to have a word with him. Now, would you like some coffee?"

"Sure. Why not?" It wasn't very satisfactory but I was sure there was nothing he was going to do about it at the present. And the coffee was good. After a little while I pointed at him. 'Tell me, Jim, will you have to wear that uniform every day? I mean, you do look kinda smart, but isn't it uncomfortable?" He actually looked like someone who was about to appear on television as a police spokesman.

He grinned. " I hope not. We have a meeting this morning with the deputy assistant commissioner so I have to dress like this. This afternoon I'm hoping to be back in my old jeans."

"Yeah. Well, I doubt that. So when are you going to put in an appearance downstairs? You know, inspect the troops?"

"Very funny. I'll be with you this afternoon and I'll introduce you to Sam Layton. I think you'll like him."

* * * * * *

He was right. Jim was dressed in his old jeans, a loose top and casuals. Sam arrived just before him. He was an early 30s detective inspector, good-looking, with a nice head of dark hair, deep brown eyes and a healthy tan that made him look like an athlete. He dressed not unlike Jim, with a designer set of jeans, a T-shirt and trainers. He had a quick and ready smile that I warmed to, and neither was he sycophantic with his superiors. He readily shook hands with the commander and called him by his first name, Jim. He then introduced himself as Sam, and called me Angie, but I had to turn away when he wanted to call the superintendent 'Charlie'.

"You can either refer to me as 'superintendent' or 'sir'," the boss growled at him.

"Yeah. Well, you'll have to remind me, 'cos neither of those titles sit right with me."

He turned away, a furious look on his face. "So, where do you want to start, Jim? Or should I ask Angie? Oh, and do I have to call you 'ma'am' or 'chief inspector'?" he asked flippantly.

"Come on, Sam," I said, smiling. "We'll both have to pretend to ignore him."

Sam turned and pointed at the superintendent. "Well, just as long as he sits there on his fat arse I think we'll get along fine."

The superintendent either didn't hear him or he chose to ignore him. Sam came over to my desk.

"Let me introduce the others, shall I?" Jim said, grinning. "This is Sergeant Sally Walker – expert on the criminal mind. Used to work with Sam over at Paddington in the early days.

"Hi, Angie."

She was around her mid-30s, small with a blondish type of hair – or it could have been dyed. She wasn't very pretty and there was an aggressive look about her that I came to recognise. I shook hands and smiled.

"And this is Inspector Reed – Mark Reed. He and I have crossed paths before. He comes with a good reputation in Serious Crimes."

Mark was on the burly side, or was he heavily built? He was a serious type who no doubt would be like a dog shaking a bone. His hand came up first to shake mine.

"Hi, Mark. Glad you could join us," I said. He nodded.

"And these are our two DC's. Meet DC Laura Metalski – you'll just have to remember to call her 'Laura', 'cos most of the time I can't recall her surname. And the other one is Peter Wadkins. Shake hands with the boss, you two."

They were both young and rather eager, not the type to let loose on their own. Laura was in her early 20s with short dark hair – she was the only one who gave me a short bow, which made me profoundly uncomfortable. "The name is Angie, Laura. Can you remember that?"

"Sorry, ma'am…Angie. Yes, of course I can."

"Pleased to meet you, Angie," Peter said with a firm voice.

He was about the same age as Laura but didn't have the same maturity about him. I wondered how I would get on with my crew, not having been the one who had selected any of them.

"So, I'm sorry about the offices," Jim was saying. "We're supposed to be moving up to the third floor but I think I'll be drawing my pension before that happens. You'll just have to make yourselves comfortable in this corner of the building. You'll find we share the computer systems with the rest of the gang but you will have your own direct telephone lines. So, if you want to get hold of one of us we can do it without having to go through the main system. And we each of us have our mobile phones, which I suggest you exchange numbers now. Try to remember the numbers, will you?"

CHAPTER THREE

After Jim had left I turned to the group and said, "Now, I've been given a set of files" – I pointed to my desk – "which I haven't yet read. And I have to tell you that I have no idea how I set up an intelligence department. I'm told, Sam, that that is something you can help with. Am I right?"

He nodded. "Sure. It's no great sweat. First, we set up the cases that have been referred to us, or at least the ones we decide are too important to be left with the local divisions, and then we correlate the information these people" – this time he was the one who was pointing around the room – "will feed us with from to time. Then we crosscheck them with the various intelligence sources available to us – there is already a list of databases we can interrogate. Occasionally, if the case is local, we can question whoever the grass happens to be. In other words, we build up our intelligence from the basics: databases, interrogations, whatever we can find from local sources.

"If we're able to arrive at a conclusion, or recommendations, whatever the case may be, we formulate plans for the executive staff – the strike team – to implement.

"Ther'ya – I told you it was easy. Any questions?"

"There is one point I don't believe you're aware of yet, Sam," I said almost chastely. "The commander has informed me that as of now we are not in a position to make a decision about these cases. Our brief is first we input the info in the files onto the computer, do whatever we have to do from an intelligence point of view, and then we transpose that onto a formal briefing to the commander. Either he will then make a decision or else it will have to be referred back upstairs."

"What?!" they all echoed in unison. "Hey, come on, Angie," Sam said. "This is not why I joined this outfit – not why I was persuaded to leave the Murder Squad and join Jim Robbins in this new set-up. You're sure you have it right?"

"I'm sure," I confirmed. "I was informed this morning."

"Well, the hell with it," he snapped. "I'm off to see the commander right now, and if he confirms what you've just told us then I'm off."

As he turned I laid my hand on his arm. "Whoa. Slow down, Sam. I've talked to Jim about this and he assures me he is working on it. So why don't we leave it with him for now?"

He hesitated, and then Mark said, "Have any of the cases referred to us been important?"

"Not that I'm aware of, but I guess these files are here for a reason," I replied. "So in the meantime I suggest we each of us read them.' I handed them out amongst the group "Every one of them, as you'll realise, is still open, and we may be able to provide an input. But in any event we have to log them into the computer. So, let's get to it, shall we?"

"And what are these guys going to be doing?" Sally enquired, gesturing around the crowded room.

"Evidently they're here as a filter; they sort out the cases and pass on to us the important ones. I don't think Jim has yet informed them of the changes."

Sam grinned. "I can see that – the super-arsehole over there still looks important."

* * * * * *

The first file I opened was a report of a serial rapist. The detail was pretty sparse and there was little evidence other than the MO; it did appear to indicate that the same offender was at work.

He attacked young girls late at night coming home from the local Met station. The route appeared to be haphazard; in other words, he travelled on various Met lines, seeking out his next victim. It seemed likely that his attacks might be spontaneous. In all probability he travelled on the same train as the girls, selected his victim and then got off at her tube station.

He must have followed the girls until he spotted a quiet pedestrian road, at which point he grabbed them and held a knife to their throats, threatening to kill them unless they submitted. Then he sexually assaulted the girls and raped them. None of the girls was able to give an accurate description because he invariably wore a hood concealing his features; on the one occasion when his face was exposed the girl refused to try to identify him because he said he would return and kill her. What had really frightened her was the blood trickling down her throat where his knife had pierced the flesh when she tried to resist.

So far eight girls in their early 20s had been raped across a circumference that circled the local suburbs around London. It was a classic serial rapist case: very little in the way of clues, no DNA samples because he obviously used condoms (which he probably disposed of locally: something to look into?), and shocked, distressed young girls who would take years to get over the assaults, if ever, and who could remember very little of their assailant other than his threats of violence.

What concerned me was that a typical rapist wasn't satisfied after a while with extracting vengeance on the unsuspecting female by violating her; at some time, assuming he wasn't stopped, he might venture into butchery of a more terminal nature. In other words – murder. So far, these eight young girls, probably unknowingly, had been lucky to escape with their lives.

I placed the file to one side, allowing myself time to digest it. I would think about it further before making a recommendation to Jim. It was not something we could ignore, especially as the Met had asked for our assistance.

Laura interrupted my thoughts – whatever her surname was.

"I think you should have a look at this – er, Angie."

She passed over the file she was reading. It was a murder investigation. Again, a young girl, 19 years of age, who had been raped and then strangled, and dumped in an active tip; she had severe bruising around her neck and some bite marks on her throat – a possible forensic ID. One of the employees discovered her body a few days later after the attack, when their bulldozer was shifting some debris. Whoever had killed her had been very careful to try and hide the body. She could have lain there forever but for the bulldozer.

"It's a tragic case," I commented. "But why do you think it would attract my attention?"

"Because I knew her – well, I know her family. They live in the same road as I do. In Kilburn. Her name was Kathleen – Kathleen Fisher. She seemed to be a nice girl but I knew her parents more."

"Did you know she'd been murdered?"

"No. I had no idea. I don't believe the police have announced it yet."

"Strange. And yet here it is in the file as an open case of rape and murder. I think you're right, Laura. This is something we should check into. I'll ask Sam to contact this…Detective Inspector Summerville at Kilburn? He's in charge of the case; ask him for some details – like why hasn't it been announced yet?"

"Are we allowed to do that – I mean, after what you said this morning?"

I smiled and gave her a knowing look. "We're still allowed to ask for further details, Laura. We're not asking him to hand the case over to us."

"Oh. Right. Will do. Shall I ask Sam to enquire if they've had any similar cases in the same area?"

"Good idea." In the meantime I asked Mark Reed to list the full names and addresses of the raped girls from my own file – where they worked, and any contact numbers – and pass them on to Sam.

The rest of the crime unit was busily making contacts throughout the various police forces. Some of the more senior CID officers had been recruited from the outlying districts and were busy communicating with their old pals. I wasn't the senior figure in the group so it was none of my business.

* * * * * *

I went back to another file to see what it might contain.

It came as a real shock. The dream I had experienced some time ago was brought back vividly into my consciousness.

The file contained the description of a gang of armed bank robbers operating around the Hertfordshire towns. It was almost exactly what I had dreamed about, with the exception that there was no little girl in red.

The format might have been one that had been tried before, but it still seemed to work. What the gang did was to storm the home of a bank manager late on a Sunday evening and hold the family hostage. Then they allowed the manager to go to his branch with two of the gang on the Monday morning, worrying about his family, waited until the time switch on the safe opened it, and then proceeded to steal the contents. I was looking at the fourth branch that had been raided this way, and each time it was in a different town and in a different bank. So far they had hit St Albans and taken close to £100,000 there, followed by Hatfield with over £200,000, then Hemel Hempstead with about the same amount, and most recently Berkhampstead, where the take was much smaller. It appeared that word had got around and, as it was accepted the police couldn't protect the homes of each and every manager, the various banks' head offices were now making sure that all the safes were emptied on Friday nights.

Why it had come to our desk was a mystery; this was something for the Armed Response Unit.

I left my desk and went to the toilets to think. What the hell was happening to me? First I had the dream in which Katy appeared to me. That had been comforting and had given me some reassurance. Now, I felt as if the rug had been pulled from under me. I had visually experienced prescience, as if I had been in the house watching the family being tied up, and then been following two of the robbers as they escorted the manager to the bank the following morning.

Or was this some kind of a revelation? Was this something that was going to occur whilst I was sleeping? Or – and this was something that really scared me – unless I was able to resist these apparitions would they eventually begin to manifest themselves to me while I was awake? As they did with Connie, my teenage friend, who was now hospitalised in a penal unit.

I rinsed my face with cold water, hoping it might clear my head. It didn't. As I had been away from my desk now for some time now, and realised that people might be asking questions, I decided I had to get back.

I was still pondering the dreams when Sam came to my desk – it wasn't a difficult thing to do, as he was sat only three feet away!

"There's one here we might take a look at," he suggested.

I was still shaking.

"Are you alright, Angie? You look as if you've seen a ghost."

"No. I'm fine, Sam. So what's so interesting about your case?" I was just remembering then that, in my dream, the bank manager, whoever he was, had been shot and killed.

"Well, I was talking to Laura, and she said you wanted me to speak with Detective Inspector Summerville in Kilburn about the young girl murdered from her street – well, raped and murdered. This case here is a second girl who was raped and murdered, and it's in Maida Vale, not too far from where the first girl died. She also had bite marks around her neck. It seems to me they could be connected?"

I frowned at the news. "Hmm. I'm surprised the two police districts haven't contacted each other."

"I'll ask the super … maybe they already have."

"In which case they should have told us. But ask him anyway."

"If I'm right we could have a serial killer on our hands."

I paused before replying. This was one of the questions I had asked myself before I agreed to join Jim in his new crime unit. Did I really want to immerse myself in the sordid world of the psychopaths, the dysfunctional, the sociopaths, and any other type of deviant who would cross my path?

At that moment I really wasn't too sure. It was only after my experience with Edith Morrison – I stopped myself then. No, that wasn't true. It was after my reality dream with Katy that I had decided that this was the way I wanted to go.

I sighed. This, then, was my decision, and I would face it head-on.

"You could be right, Sam. How were they found?"

He checked the file he was holding. "More or less the same MO. Came off the underground late one night; whoever killed them must have been on the same train, following them; caught them in a blind spot and dragged each girl into an alleyway. Then tore off their lower garments, raped them, and strangled them with a pair of their own tights. With the Kilburn girl she was dumped in a nearby tip – as you already know. As yet I'm not sure where the Maida Vale girl was found. I'll have to enquire – it isn't in the file."

"So there's no way of knowing if this a pattern?"

"I guess not. Both girls were identified because their purses were not touched and the addresses were inside."

I shuddered. God only knew what they must have gone through.

"Check through the other rape files and see if there are any similar connections." I pointed to Inspector Reed. "Mark there has a file listing a case of a serial rapist who has attacked eight girls during the last 12 months – around the railway stations circling London. Let's check into this. Ask the superintendent if he'll put some of the others onto it. Tell him we're concerned that in essence sadistic offenders, as this one appears to be, almost invariably become serial killers if they're not caught."

* * * * * *

After he had left I had a sudden inspiration. I decided I had to speak with Jim.

Another senior officer was with him when I entered; I was about to leave when he said, "Wait a sec, Ange, the commander was just leaving."

It was a nice office, a great improvement on the basement, and it had a clear view of the rain! He had a large desk in front of his own desk where he would be able to conduct meetings. This was where he was sitting when I entered.

I explained to him about my dream and how it now appeared to have come true; I showed him the file I'd been reading about the bank robbers. In particular, I emphasised that the bank manager in my dreams was dead.

"What do you think I should?" I asked him.

He rubbed his chin thoughtfully. "Do you know where the next attack might take place? Or when, for that matter?"

I shook my head. "Not really. Except it will be in the same area."

He looked at the file and studied it for a few moments. "Do you mean in the county of Hertfordshire?"

I nodded. "I seem to remember from my dreams that it will be in Watford – and soon."

He shrugged. "I'm not sure what we can do with that information. I can hardly ring the Herts police and warn them the next attack might be in Watford and soon. Can I?"

I had to agree with him. Then I said, "Why not inform them we have received an anonymous tip that the next raid is likely to be in Watford? We don't exactly know when but it will be soon."

He leaned forward on his desk, frowning. "You know, Ange, these bloody dreams of yours might well become our nightmares."

"So what do you want me to do about them?" I snapped. "Keep them to myself? Would that make you happier?"

"I don't honestly know. But you have to admit you've given me the flimsiest of information." Wearily he raised his shoulders. "Okay, I'll do as you suggest. Leave it with me."

I thanked him; at least my conscience was clear now. I returned to my office and the duties of the day.

I was turning my attention to the serial rapist who might or might not have become a murderer when a bellowing voice interrupted my thoughts.

"Crossley."

A finger was pointed at me from the far aside of the room. It was Glasson gesturing at me. I could almost hear the growl from where I was. I decided to ignore him.

"Crossley." The voice boomed out again.

I kept my head down but, over the top of my eyes, I could see that everyone in the room was looking at me. There was a deathly silence all around me.

Suddenly he was standing in front of me. "Are you deaf, Crossley?" he roared.

"No. I am not deaf, superintendent. But if you wish to communicate with me then either you address me as Chief Inspector Crossley – or you may call me Ma'am. Now, which is it to be?"

I looked at his face and I thought he was going to hit me. "How dare you talk to me like that? Do you know who I am?"

I maintained a stony silence, and then I allowed my voice to rise so the officers in the room could hear me. "I will talk to you, superintendent, in exactly the way you inspire me. You're abusive and you treat me with contempt, so that's how I will treat you. Is that clear enough for you?"

Glasson just stood there, unable to speak. His face was flushed and he genuinely looked as if he were about to have a heart attack. Then he stormed off – no doubt to report me to Commander Robbins.

There were grins around the room, which I silenced with a glare of my own. Sam came across with the files. "Sorry, Angie. I've had a word with the super at Kilburn and he didn't want to talk to me; seems I've overstepped the mark."

"Did you catch his name?"

He looked at the file. "Yeah. Superintendent Ackerson."

"And what did he say exactly?"

"Well, you know, he was more or less – huffy. Wanted to know why my superior officer hadn't contacted him."

I frowned at the implication. So that was what had upset Glasson. Ackerson had obviously been in touch with the super. It was just as well, because now I could sort it out with Jim and see if he agreed with me.

"That's okay, Sam. Spread the workload round the room – say the instructions have come from me. I want this investigation to begin immediately."

"Okay. Will do."

I picked up another file, determined not to allow Glasson to discourage me. This was about an unpremeditated shooting in Brixton. Two young men, both black, had walked into a bookie, selected a couple of the punters, and shot them through the head.

Some kind of revenge shooting. It was yet another tragic case, but I didn't feel it warranted our attention.

Then my phone rang. It was Jim, asking me – asking, not ordering – if I would go up to his office.

"Now?" I enquired.

"Yes. If you don't mind, Ange."

Superintendent Glasson was sitting in Jim's office, a scowl on his face.

"Ange, the super here has informed me that you evidently went over his head to contact Ackerson in Kilburn, and when he tried to discuss it with you were impertinent. Can you explain?'

"Jim," I replied, "there are two issues here I would like you to deal with. The first is that no one informed me that whenever I want some action on a case then I am duty bound to clear it with Glasson here. If that is the case then you can have my resignation. The second thing is I do not like to be abused or shouted at by my surname so everyone in the room can hear him. That I will not accept.

"Now, do you want me to tender my resignation?"

"Hold on, Ange. I'm not supporting either of you at the moment."

The superintendent leaned on the table, still glowering. "One of her officers going over my head is totally unacceptable. And her disrespect for her immediate boss also needs to be dealt with."

Jim glared back at him and thrust his face forward until he was almost touching Glasson. "No. It doesn't. If you want respect, superintendent, then you have to earn it. My understanding is that the chief inspector demanded that you first give her the respect she is entitled to, which evidently you failed to do.

"And as for contacting another super in a different station, then you have to accept that Ms Crossley's department is not under your control. She has my full authorisation to contact whomsoever she needs to – whether that is a superintendent or even a more senior rank. That is up to her and her department.

"As for the present issue, it seems to me that if your colleague in Kilburn is refusing to speak with one of her officers then she is perfectly entitled to take over the authority and responsibility and organise whatever appropriate forces she feels are necessary to deal with the situation.

"Now, Superintendent Glasson, do I make myself clear?"

He stood there, open-mouthed, unable to say anything. Then he came out with, "Yes, sir; that is very clear," and walked out, a deep blush on his face.

After he had gone, Jim grinned at me and said, "That didn't take too long, did it? Now, what's with the resignation issue?"

I shook my head. I wasn't sure where it had come from but it seemed to me to be symptomatic of the way I was feeling. "I don't know. But ... I have to tell you, Jim, I'm finding these visions very worrying."

"I can understand that, Ange. They worry me too. The question is, how do we stop them – or do we really want to stop them? I'll have to think about your situation, see what I can come up with."

"Sure – but they are so vivid they frighten me."

"I thought you'd had only the one – the story of the bank robbers?"

"That's only correct as far as I told you. But there have been others and I do know it has some connection with Danny O'Brien."

"The kid in Manchester? The one with the deceased twin sister?"

"Yes. And don't ask me to explain it, because I can't. I think I might go up there and talk to him – see if he can throw any light on it."

"Hmm," he said. "I can see what you're thinking – but can't you just ring him?"

"No, Jim. I can't. This has to be face to face."

"So when do you think you might go up there?"

I shrugged my shoulders with the frustration. "I'm not sure. I want to sleep on it and see how I feel then."

"Okay. And your resignation?" He grinned at this, as if I were joking.

"I'm sorry, Jim. But, these visions aside, I don't really feel I fit in here." I felt myself frowning. "I don't like the set-up here, I don't like your change of decision making and I certainly don't like Battersea."

He stood up. "Why don't we both sleep on it, Ange? And talk tomorrow? Is that alright with you?"

I nodded my agreement, and then said, "What about Ackerson? What do I do about him?"

"Okay. Let me have a word with him. Then I'll get him to contact you direct.

"Quite a morning, if you don't mind my saying."

"Well, thanks for your support, Jim," I said. "I doubt I could have carried on working with Glasson without it."

"Oh, I don't think we've heard the last of him. My understanding is he has some heavyweight support from up above; it won't take him too long to contact whoever that might be. I'll keep you informed, but if it is brought to a head then we might be lucky and get rid of him."

"I hope you're right."

"Have you thought about moving from Battersea?"

I shrugged. Actually, it was bloody awful, and I wasn't sure how long I could stick it. "What can I say? I can't afford some of the more expensive flats on this side of the river," I said. "Not what I would call home yet but it's handy for the Yard. Perhaps if I get a rise I might find somewhere else to live.

"How about you? Are you happily married now?"

He grinned. "Yeah. You could say that. Audrey, my wife, is delighted to be back living in London – we have quite a nice house in Islington." There was brief pause, then he added, "Let me think about your domestic situation, Ange. I'll talk to you tomorrow."

"I'm glad for you. I hope it works out as you wanted. I'll speak to you later."

CHAPTER FOUR

The office was quiet when I got back to my desk. Glasson was keeping his head down, but I could still see the flush on his face. I doubted if he would ever be the same again after Jim's admonishment. And neither would it have endeared him to me.

I called Sam and Laura over. "Collect the files from Mark, will you? He will have listed out all the details of the girls. Then try again with the superintendent; I would like his team to go over the ground and interview the victims. I think you'll find him very cooperative."

They grinned. "Do you mean the rapist files or the ones about the murders?"

"Or both?" Laura chimed in.

"The rapist files. You can tell him about the two murdered girls but inform him that we will be looking into that. Then arrange for me to talk to the inspectors dealing with the cases."

I checked the files through to Glasson's desk to see how he would react. He put on his charming face, went through the files with them and nodded his agreement. Would you believe it - He was going to play ball – which might make my life easier.

* * * * * *

I thought about my conversation with Jim and the consequences it could have on my career. What I had said to him was absolutely true: at the present I didn't feel I would be able to fit in here. It wasn't so much the job and the new faces; it wasn't even Glasson, the insufferable prick; I simply didn't feel at home in this environment.

Sure, I remembered all the details when it came to chasing criminals; some of it was interesting – provided I kept away from the sharp end. From time to time I still suffered from severe headaches, no doubt due to the small plate in my skull after the incident in the basement with Connie. But what I believe was influencing my decision most was the dreams. I didn't know how to stop them and I felt as if they were beginning to control my life. I felt I had to go and talk with Danny O'Brien as soon as possible and ask him for help.

When Superintendent Ackerson contacted me he was quite charming, no doubt influenced by Jim's overtures. I had just put the phone down when Sam appeared. "I've just had a Detective Inspector Summerville, from Kilburn, on the phone; he can see us this afternoon, Angie." He looked at his notes. "Laura tells me that the other one, Detective Inspector Harding, at Maida Vale, won't be back until tomorrow. Do you want me to come with you?"

"Yes. You and Laura. What time is the meeting?"

He grinned. "After lunch. Which is due about now, if you're ready."

I stood up. "Yes. I could do with a break. Ask the others if they can join us."

* * * * * *

I wasn't impressed with the canteen – even less so when the others told me I was entitled to dine with the echelon in their private dining room. It was a long bare room, almost stripped of all essentials. There was faded lino on the floor and the walls reminded me of one of those old-fashioned hospital waiting rooms. I didn't relish the prospect of dining here, but, however unfortunate it might be, there was no way I was going to eat upstairs with the higher echelon.

"That isn't for me," I said to myself after a moment, and ordered the fish and chips from a cold plate. "I would much prefer eating with my own bunch than with higher-ups."

We talked during lunch. Actually, it was more a case of me doing the talking, asking them questions about their backgrounds, their families, their children, whilst they were providing the answers.

Of the five of them the only married one was Mark. He had two children, both boys, aged five and two. His wife was a schoolteacher before they were married and Mark had met her following a break-in at the school.

Sam Layton was a 'jack the lad'. I doubted if he would ever get married, he was so attractive to the ladies. Sally Walker had been married, for a while. She didn't seem to want to talk about the split with her husband, so I didn't pursue it. And as for the two DCs, Peter Wadkins and Laura Metalski, they were too young to contemplate marriage. Peter had come from a family of detectives – his father had only recently retired – whilst Laura, who was descended from Polish refugees, was too keen to get on in the force even to think about a relationship.

It was an informative lunch – and very enjoyable, apart from the food. It broke up when Sam asked me if I had ever married. My relationship with Pauline in Manchester wasn't something I would discuss with anybody, so I simply grinned and said: "No."

* * * * * *

I was surprised to learn, when we arrived at Kilburn, that Detective Inspector Summerville was an attractive woman in her early 40s, with auburn hair and pale blue eyes. There was something formidable about her, almost making a statement that she would brook no interference. No doubt she had years of experience behind her, and I certainly wouldn't have liked to cross her.

I shook hands with her and introduced my two colleagues as we went into her office. It was rather cramped, as is the style these days, and we had a job to fit into the tight space.

"You want to talk about Kathleen Fisher, I presume?"

"Yes. I will also want to talk to her family."

"Do you think that's wise?"

Oh, shit, I thought to myself. Here we have another one. What is it about power that makes some people so fucking insufferable?

"I believe I'm the best one to decide if it's wise or not, Detective Inspector Summerville. Now, what can you tell us about Katherine Fisher?"

Her face coloured up – not the first time I'd seen that today. "I'm sorry," she said. "Of course, you're right." She opened a copy of the file and passed me a photograph of the young girl. She had probably been pretty at one time – before her assailant had attacked her with a knife. Now her face was bloated from all the bruising, a knife tear had ripped open one side of her cheek, and some of her teeth were missing. She had obviously suffered terribly in her attempts to resist him.

"She was 19. Spending her first year in college, studying to be a solicitor. Nice family – her father works for the local council. I believe he's some kind of a bookkeeper."

"What can you tell us about her?" Sam asked politely.

"Nothing of any consequence. She was pretty, although you can't tell that from the photograph, intelligent, and had a number of friends. Spent most of her spare time studying rather than playing the teenage game. It is a real tragedy."

"Where was she killed?" I asked.

"We're not sure. We know she got off the tube at Kilburn High Street; after that we have no idea, except her body was discovered the next day in a nearby tip." She trembled at the telling of the story. "We can only assume her attacker must have followed her from the train, then perhaps had a van parked nearby, and grabbed her."

She pointed to a photo of the victim. "These bite marks are the only clues. It may be possible to trace him from these – especially with the new DNA formula."

"Why haven't you announced the murder – publicly, I mean?"

"Well, we have, but only in the local news. We were going to announce it to the nationals when a second girl was murdered. Nearby, in Maida Vale. She was in her early 20s and had similar bite marks on her neck. I believe Forensics are now comparing the tooth marks to check if there is a match."

"Okay," I said, "I can understand that; but why haven't the two case been brought together? We have two separate files on the victims, and it was only because of our own cross-referencing that we were able to tie the two together."

The detective inspector coughed, somewhat embarrassed. "I think it was due to a misunderstanding between the two forces: I thought Inspector Harding from Maida Vale would tie them together, but he thought I would be doing it. I'm so sorry if this has complicated matters."

I shrugged. What the hell – at least we had found the connections.

"When do you expect to hear from Forensics?"

"I'm not sure. They have only had the cases for a few days; I expect it will be some time next week."

I nodded to Sam. "Chase them up, Sam, will you? Tell them we want the results today."

He was already on the phone giving instructions.

"Do you have a copy of the Maida Vale file here?" I asked.

"Yes." She handed me the file with the victim's photos, both before and after her murder. She too had been attacked viciously, either with the murderer's fists or, possibly, with a knife. Her face was a terrible mess.

"Where was her body discovered? Do you know?"

"Only from the reports. She was found in an alleyway, and we understand he must have been disturbed, because it seems he ran away and jumped over a fence into somebody's back garden."

"So who now is handling this, inspector?"

"Well, we thought you were – the Serious Crime Squad. I mean, both files have been passed to you, together with the appropriate details, so we assumed it will now be your responsibility."

I sighed at her presumption. "I can understand you assuming that; however, these decisions have to be made by our commander. It might have helped our cause if you'd waited for the forensics to come back."

"I take your point," she retorted sarcastically, "but the decision wasn't mine to make. You'll have to take it up with our superintendent. I believe you've already spoken with him."

"I will certainly do that. But, in the meantime, I'll leave contacting the parents until we get the results. What other evidence have you uncovered?"

"Well, we've already set-up an incident scene, we've made comprehensive enquires with the train company, including CCTV images, and with locals who we suspected might have been in the area at the time. We've also conducted house-to-house enquires around the district to see if anyone saw or might have heard anything. So far, nothing, other than the Maida Vale case, where he was seen running away."

"Did you check the sex offenders list?"

"Of course. We do that as a matter of routine. I believe the same line of investigation has taken place in Maida Vale under Inspector Harding, and again, I believe, the results are the same. We have nothing except the bite marks. No semen; no skin marks under the girls' fingernails; no fabrics that might identify him." She shrugged. "I'm sorry, chief inspector, but we're at a dead end."

I stood up to go. "We'll leave it at that for now, detective inspector. And thanks for your help – we'll be in touch."

"What do you mean, 'thanks for your help'?" Sam asked as we left. "She was hardly helpful."

"Politeness, Sam; that's all. You don't know when we might need her again." I paused as we got into the car. "Have you got the address of the other girl who was raped – the one with blood on her neck, who we believe might not be connected to these two murders?"

"Sure. She lives in Camden." He checked his watch. "I'm not sure if she'll be home yet – that's if she's back at work. She was pretty devastated, according to the file."

"Let's try her, shall we? But this time you can drop me off; I'll speak to her alone. You two get on back to the Yard. She might be more responsive with a female asking the questions."

He shrugged. "As you wish; you're the boss."

CHAPTER FIVE

Camden was a trendy place, with a long high street filled with boutique-type shops and fashionable restaurants, a busy weekend market that attracted thousand of tourists, and rows and rows of terraced houses that would cost a fortune these days. I found Rachel's flat a couple of streets behind Camden Town tube station. She shared it with a female friend; neither was in, so I decided to take a cup of coffee and go back in a half an hour.

I found a nearby café with outdoor seating, where it was nice to sit out in the winter sunshine. I noticed, unlike the area in which I lived, that there were more Asians living in Camden, so the place was ablaze with colour. The time passed quickly, and when I returned to the flat Rachel Humphries, the girl I wanted to see, was at home. She still appeared distressed as she opened the door, making sure the lock was on the chain. She was also a brunette, with her long hair framing what must have been at one time an attractive face. Now her face was lined, as if she had borne a lot of grief, and one or two tears were still forming in the corners of her dark brown eyes. I felt sympathy for her at her ordeal.

"Yes," she said in a whisper, "what do you want?"

"Miss Humphries," I said, brandishing my warrant card, "do you think I might have a word?"

"If it's about the rape, no, I don't want a word. I've spoken to the local police and told them I wouldn't try to identify him."

She showed me her throat, where I noticed she had a small but visible wound. "Have you seen this? He said he would kill me if I talked. So, no thank you, inspector; I don't want a word with you or anyone else."

"Do you mind if I come in?" I asked. "There is another matter I want to talk to you about. This is something more serious."

"What? More serious than being raped?" she said in astonishment.

"I'm afraid so, yes. We are now talking about murder and we believe that the man who attacked you may be responsible. I'd just like a few words, if you don't mind?"

She hesitated, but then she nodded and opened the latch, having a quick peep outside before closing the door again. It was evident that she was really stressed-out. I followed her into a small lounge — at least, it was bigger than the one in my flat — and settled myself in a room that was cosily warm. I noticed that there was a new carpet on the floor and that the curtains were gleaming out at me, as if they had suddenly appeared from a store. Someone, possibly Rachel, had spent quite a bit of money furnishing the apartment. There were photographs on a small table, some of her family, one of them just of her and her boyfriend. She was smiling as though the future held out a golden promise for her – quite the opposite to how she looked now.

"What is it you want to say?" she asked, defensively.

"We believe you were the last person this man attacked – when was it now? Six weeks ago – would that be right?"

She nodded. "More or less." She touched her throat. "You can see where the knife wound has started to heal – it wasn't so much painful as terribly frightening."

"I can see that, Rachel. It must have been very distressing for you. However, since your attack two girls have been raped and strangled – one in Kilburn and the other in Maida Vale. There were only a couple of weeks between the two deaths."

"And you believe the same man did it? I mean, the man who raped me?"

The thought came into my mind that she seemed quite fond of using the word 'rape', as if it had some strange quality to it.

"That's correct," I said. Only this time he left bite marks on the girls' necks. We're trying now to compare the marks but we do believe it is the same man."

Her lips trembled. "He … he tried to bite me, but I put up my hand to stop him. That's when he used the knife."

I put my arm on her shoulders, and then withdrew it as she gave an involuntary shudder. "What I wanted to say to you, Rachel, is that you are the only one who might identify him. I don't want to say this but perhaps, and I am emphasising only perhaps, had you come forward at the time, we might have stopped the murders. As it is, we have to put some flesh on him to try to stop him from killing again."

"I see," she said, frowning. "But don't you think that, if I described him now, especially after he's killed those other girls, he'd come back and finish me off?"

"I think it's hardly likely he will visit this area again. Less so after the murders."

I didn't tell her that some psychopaths did indeed tend to return to the scene after their attacks.

"Does he know where you live?"

"Yes. He followed me off the train – he must have known that my flatmate wasn't at home. Then he forced his way into the flat, tore my clothes off, and spread me on the bed." She laughed without humour. "He even found the time to put on a condom before he fucked me. And now you expect me to describe him – knowing what I might face?"

"Yes, Rachel, I do. You could help save a number of lives."

She got up from the settee, clearly agitated. "I don't know. I'll have to think about it. Do you have a card where I could ring you?"

I gave her one of my newly minted cards, with the New Scotland Yard address and my mobile number on the back.

"Hmm," she said, a puzzled expression on her face. "New Scotland Yard. I didn't think you operated in this part of the world."

"We do now. We've assembled a new task force to deal with these serious crimes on a national basis."

"Yes," she said, nodding, "I seem to remember reading about it. So let me dwell on it and I might ring you back, chief inspector."

"Thank you, Rachel. But please, don't leave it too long, will you?"

* * * * * *

It had started to rain when I left her flat, but at least I was close to the underground, so I could catch a train to Euston and go from there to Battersea – for another lonely night. I used to quite enjoy the evenings when I was an assistant professor at Warwick University. We all used to gather in the common room and exchange chitchat about the day's events.

Sometimes, one or another of the teachers would bring in some spirits, some vodka or whisky, and we would make an enjoyable night of it. Nowadays I was destined to spend my nights alone, either cooking for myself or dining out at a local burger bar. There were times like this when I felt so lonely that all I wanted to do was cry. I still wondered what the hell I was doing in London. I felt that cloud of depression start to infiltrate my thinking, and I wished I could simply disappear and find myself back in Warwick.

On the train I couldn't help thinking about what might have happened to me had I gone to the FBI as a profiler, working in some dingy office in Quantico? I doubted if I would have been very much happier; I still wouldn't have any friends, even though my father was an American citizen and lived down in Florida. That was about as far as I would be able to travel in the whole of Europe; I could hardly ring him from Washington and say I was coming down for the evening.

I tried to shake off my depression during the train ride, but it didn't work.

When I got back to my flat I had decided that the next day, when I spoke to Jim, I wouldn't hand in my resignation immediately, but I would insist that I went up to Manchester to speak to Danny O'Brien. After that – well, it all depended on what happened whether or not I would end up staying.

CHAPTER SIX

I abandoned my evening meal and went to bed early, with ten milligrams of Temazepam to help me sleep. I had been prescribed the drugs some years back by Dr Simmons, who looked after Connie in the hospital. I mean, I didn't take them regularly, other than when I needed them, but they did work.

I woke up refreshed, or at least better than I had been doing of late. I had a long shower (my bathroom only had a half-bath), shampooed my hair and dressed in jeans and a loose top. I didn't need makeup to talk to Danny – he was still only 14. Or was it 15 now? I collected my purse, my mobile, and a small overnight case, and set off for the Yard.

* * * * * *

It was still only eight in the morning when I arrived and I expected to be the first one there. I was surprised to see both Mark and Sam at their desks, and Sally Walker was on the phone. There was yet another pile of files on my desk.

"What the hell am I expected to do with these?" I asked of no one in particular.

"Have a good night?" Mark asked me, cryptically.

I nodded without commenting. There was nothing really I could say.

"How come you're all in early? I thought we weren't supposed to start until after nine?"

Sam grinned at me. "I don't know where you worked before, boss, but this is the police force. We get here when we have things to do. Sally is contacting Forensics."

I scowled at them. "Is that right? And just what exactly have you got to do that couldn't wait until later?"

I got another grin from Sam. "We were mapping out the rapist's schedule. The places he's attacked and the various dates. It seems to us that, first, it isn't trains he's stepping off but the underground. And if we take the last 12 months the schedule was originally one girl each month. But of late this has stepped up to one per fortnight – especially if we believe the two girls from Kilburn and Maida Vale are his victims."

I didn't return the grin. "And now, as I suspected, he might have turned to murder. And, by the way, I figured out that he was travelling on the underground and not the trains, but thank you for apprising me of that.

"So, if we're right, and his last victim was – what was her name?"

"Glynis," Mark said. "Glynis Stranark."

"Yes, right. Glynis. She was murdered ten days ago, which means…"

"…He could now be closer to another killing," Sam interrupted.

"Do you people know anything about profiling?" I enquired. "Have you had any experience of it?"

"I have," Sally replied, coming off the phone. "We went after a serial killer some 12 months ago, and we used the services of a profiler."

"Was he or she any good?"

"Waste of fucking space," Sally said, emphatically. "She told us everything we didn't need to know and nothing that would help us catch the killer'"

"And did you catch him?"

"Yeah – too right we did. You might have read something about it in the papers."

"Wasn't he the homophobic psychopath? The one who was murdering the homosexuals?"

"Yeah, right. You got it."

"Well, let me tell you that not all profilers are a waste of space," I said indignantly. "Some of us are quite talented, except we do admit that only police work eventually will catch the killer."

"So what is it you do, Angie?" Sally wanted to know.

"I'll have to explain it to you – but not today. How did you get on with Forensics? I really do need to have that comparison."

"Does this come out of your session with Rachel Humphries?" Sam enquired.

"Yes. I didn't get anything from her; she promised she would think about it and maybe give me a ring. If we get confirmation then I'll go back there with the evidence."

"Can't we hold her for obstructing the course of justice?"

I stopped for a moment. It was a good point Mark had made.

"I'm not sure. Check it out, Mark, will you? And Sally, you haven't answered my question about Forensics. Any news yet?"

She checked her watch. "About mid-morning they reckon; they'll come back to me."

"Right."

I turned to the fresh folders on the desk, wondering why they had all managed to be allocated to me. I went across to one of the other senior officers, a detective inspector called Frank Sinclair, and asked him if he knew anything about them.

"Yeah. It was Superintendent Glasson who instructed us that all new files had to be passed on to you first."

"Did he say why?"

"Well, only that you were the intelligence officers and before we acted on them they must first be cleared by your department. It makes sense to me, Angie."

"I agree. Except, given the volume, I don't see how we can give them the scrutiny they might deserve. I think I'd better have a word with the super – when he comes in!"

He chortled. "Would you like me to have a word with him? It might be more diplomatic coming from me."

"Good idea, Frank. Let me know what he says."

After I returned to my desk I opened the first file. Strangely enough, it was from Peter Conway, the superintendent in Greater Manchester, where I had last worked. It had been faxed through. I thought he was joking when I saw that the case was about an arsonist who, arbitrarily, was setting fire to buildings around the Manchester area. It wasn't until I came across the fatalities that I paused for breath. Evidently, whoever the culprit was, he had now turned his attention away from factories and onto domestic premises; the last two fires he had set off had caused the deaths of seven people – three adults and four children. Another tragedy, but I still didn't think it belonged to Serious Crimes.

I took the file across to Mark and handed it to him. "Perhaps you'd better read this," I suggested. "It's a case in Greater Manchester where an arsonist has now begun setting fire to houses with women and children as the occupants."

"Christ, Angie, how the hell are we going to cope with all this lot?" he said, his arms pointing to all the files. "We can't possibly handle them all."

"I know. You're right, Mark. Input them as I suggested and then I guess we'll just have to accept the most serious cases and reject the rest.

"I wonder what the Yard was doing in setting up this new department? I mean, if we're to be a national bureau, like the FBI, then we must have the resources to deal with the multitude of cases."

"You mean it was a good idea in principle but in practice it stinks?"

I smiled. Smart-arse! "I wouldn't exactly describe it in those terms, but, yes, I know what you're saying. Anyway, have a glance through it, Mark, will you, and if you think we might be able to help then give Superintendent Conway a ring and ask him if he wants our assistance or if he's just flying the flag."

"Will do."

My phone rang. It was Jim, asking me if I could go up to see him.

"Here it comes," I thought; "decision day."

CHAPTER SEVEN

Jim met me at the door of his office, giving me one of those knowing smiles, and led me by the arm into his office.

"So, how've you been, Angie? Had a goodnight?"

I sat down opposite him, and noticed that his hair was starting to go demonstrably grey.

"Alright," I said. "But I still want to go up and speak with Danny."

"Thought you might. Have you received the fax file from Peter Conway – about the arsonist?"

"When did he speak to you about it, Jim?"

"Last night. I thought you might want to have a look at it so I asked him to fax it through. Isn't that up your street?"

I wondered what he was getting at – not that it would take much genius in working it out.

"Arsonists are usually cases for profilers, yes. What have you got in mind?"

"Well, I just thought that whilst you are up there you might pop in to see Peter, talk to him about the case. Perhaps see if you can't help him."

This time it was my turn to smile. "You're plotting again, aren't you?"

He looked at me seriously. "I'm just trying to help you, Angie. Now, you can go to Manchester, sort out what you have to with Danny O'Brien, and try to help Peter with this case. That way you can go on expenses. Mind you, I don't want you staying at the Midland Hotel again. Find something a little bit cheaper. We can talk about your resignation again when you get back."

"You're being very kind, Jim. I'm not sure I deserve it."

"Trust me," he said. "It will all work out for the best. Leave Sam Leyton in charge whilst you're away. He can handle it in your absence."

* * * * * *

I told the team I was due to go to Manchester, possibly that morning, and that Sam would be in charge whilst I away. I was tidying my desk when I heard Sally's phone go. It was Forensics.

"The good news is that we have a match – the bite marks are from the same teeth."

"And the bad news?"

"There is no DNA match."

"So, all we have to do is apprehend someone and make them give us a teeth sample," I remarked caustically.

"Hey. Didn't that happen to Ted Bundy? In the States?" Sam asked.

"How can you possibly leave a bite mark on someone's neck and not leave DNA?" Mark wanted to know.

"Look. It doesn't really matter. The chances are our assailant wouldn't have been on the computer – these psychopaths very rarely are. So we would have to apprehend him and I believe, despite what Sally has to say, that a profile of the attacker will help the police.

"Now. As I said yesterday, I'm going back to Rachel Humphries in Camden. Sally, why don't you come with me – maybe two females are better than one."

* * * * * *

This time she was in, along with her friend, a flighty blonde who had the figure of a model and an intellect that didn't rise above her breasts.

"May we come in?" I asked, abandoning any pretence of politeness.

"If you must," she said, leading the way.

"This is Sergeant Walker, also of the Serious Crimes Unit. I was hoping you might have phoned me."

Her bottom lip came out below her top one. "I didn't say I would. I just said I would think about it."

"And are you still thinking about it, Miss Humphries?"

"Yeah. I suppose. Why are you back here?"

"Because, as I explained to you yesterday, the two murders near here are by the same man – quite likely the same man who raped and attacked you. So I want your description of him."

"You can't just come in my home and demand…"

"Yes we can, Miss Humphries," Sally said briskly. "Failure to do so on your behalf might constitute obstruction of the police in the course of justice."

"You can't be serious."

"We are deadly serious," I said. "But for your reticence it was possible we might have apprehended this killer by now. As it is we now have two bodies on our hands – to say nothing of the distress it must be causing the parents."

Sally took out her notebook. "Where would you like to start?"

Rachel Humphries sat down abruptly. Her face had gone significantly paler.

"'I think I need a solicitor."

"If that is who you require we are duty bound to provide you with one. However, in the meantime I will have to arrest you. Will you cuff her, sergeant?"

Her eyes opened wide. "Jesus! I didn't realise this would happen. I'm sorry I even reported it now. Alright, alright," she said hastily as Sally went to handcuff her. "I don't want to be arrested. Let me think for a minute.

"He was of medium height, quite stocky – he had bodybuilder's biceps and the strength to go with them, but his face was pinched..."

"Pinched? How do you mean?" I interrupted.

"You know, sort of thin and angry; his lips were tight as if he were determined."

"Colour of hair?" Sally wanted to know.

"Sort of sandy. Not exactly blond but fair."

"Any distinguishing features? You know – tattoos, similar marks?"

"How do you expect me to remember something like that? I was lying on the sofa, he was ripping my knickers off, and I had a knife to my throat." She shivered at the thought of her ordeal and closed her eyes. "I seem to recall, on his right arm, I thought I saw a tattoo. But I can't be certain; I was very frightened."

"I can imagine. Did you notice the colour of his eyes?"

"Yes. They were very clear."

"And?"

"Olive. Almost like the olives you find in your drink."

"I see. Well, you've been very helpful, Miss Humphries. Have you anything to add? Anything at all that might help us to recognise him?"

She scowled at me as those I were the enemy. "I...I don't think so. But if I were asked if I could recognise him I would have to say 'yes'. I definitely could.

"Thank you," I said. "We'll let ourselves out. Someone will be along later for a statement. Good day, Miss Humphries."

I rang the office and spoke to Sam once we were outside. "Sam, will you arrange for two DCs to go immediately to the home of Miss Humphries and take a statement."

"She's given you a description?"

"Yes. She has. And it could be very helpful. We're on our way back now."

"I'll do it straight away."

When I got back I instructed the team to check with the various tube stations to see if they kept their CCTV camera footage. It could provide a link. I also asked Sally if she and Laura would visit the families of the two girls and see if they couldn't get some background. In addition, I asked Sam to arrange for a photofit artist to visit Rachel and draw up a picture from her description. This could be vital.

CHAPTER EIGHT

By mid-afternoon I was on my way, in a pool car Vauxhall, to Manchester. I wasn't sure whether or not Peter Conway genuinely needed my services – he was a much better cop than I was. It could be that he and Jim had conspired to create a case that would be worth my while travelling to the north for. In any event, I certainly would have paid him a visit, if only for old time's sake.

As usual, the pool car didn't have a radio, other than the one connecting me to the various police stations, so I was unable to entertain myself. Not that I was very much into music, but it might have been nice to listen to a play or something. For a while the hypnotic rhythm of the windscreen wipers kept me occupied.

Then I kept myself amused by thinking of what I would say to Danny. I wondered if he was expecting me. It wouldn't surprise me if he was, having myself had the visions from Katy. Since the last one, the one some time after that with the bank robbers, I had heard from her – if 'heard' was the right word. It would be nice, though, if at some stage I could relax and talk to her, ask her what was it she wanted of me. Or did I have that right? Perhaps she didn't want anything other than to help me in my search for clairvoyance. That, at least, would be better than going to church and praying for God's help, as Edith had suggested.

* * * * * *

The miles slipped past. I bypassed Birmingham by taking the motorway toll road. It was much speedier than the equivalent part of the M6. I also missed Wolverhampton, my old hunting ground. I thought about my Rastafarian friend, Henry, who had helped me on a couple of occasions. I went past the Keele service station, where I had had a dispute with Jim on the previous case. Finally, feeling somewhat weary, I went through on the bypass motorway, through Knutsford, on to Princess Park and down into Manchester. By now it was seven o'clock and I wondered if Peter might still be at the station. I considered phoning him but then I thought to myself, "What the hell? I can go and see him in the morning."

Having been refused permission by Jim to use the Midland – I didn't actually want to stay there anyway, as it had too many sad memories for me – I took myself of to the Grand, just off Piccadilly. It was a five-star hotel nonetheless, but with a few more modern facilities than the Midland had.

They had a room to spare; in fact, they offered me a double as a single. It was an enormous room with a large double bed, no lounge attached, but very comfortable.

After settling down for a few moments, I took out my mobile and rang Danny; it was the first contact we had had since the dreadful traumas of a few months ago.

"Hi, miss," he said. "I was expecting you to ring me. Howya been?"

"Hello, Danny. I thought you might. I've been okay, really. How are things with you?"

"Well, now'ts changed, but where are yer, and when are yer comin' up to see me?"

I laughed. He hadn't changed a bit. "I'm in Manchester, Danny, checking on a local case. I thought I might come up tomorrow – if that's alright?"

"Sure. I ain't at school tomorrow; we've been 'avin' those mock things, so I have a day off."

"So why don't I see you in the morning?"

"Sure."

"Will you let your gran know?"

"I'll tell her, yeah. But you do know I'm now 15?"

"I'd an idea you were. So I guess you don't need supervision. I'll see you tomorrow, Danny."

It didn't surprise me that he was expecting me to call – no different, in fact, from Edith Morrison, who had said the same thing. It was something I was beginning to accept philosophically.

* * * * * *

I stepped outside for a minute, planning on finding a local restaurant, when the downpour hit me. There was an absolute deluge of rain, so I decided I would stay in the hotel and eat there instead. As I was re-entering the lobby a police car drew up, and – surprise, surprise – Peter Conway suddenly appeared. The fact that he was a much better policeman than I was had slipped my mind; it hadn't been difficult for him to find me.

He grinned at me – something that was so alien to him it surprised me.

"Couldn't it have waited until morning?" I suggested.

"How've you been, Angie?" he asked after kissing me on the cheek. "We've missed you around here."

"Really? I can't understand why. And you still haven't answered my question."

"Yeah, well, it was such a miserable night I thought you might like a bit of company for dinner. On me, by the way."

I shook my head. "How did you find me? Or is that a silly question?"

He led me into the hotel and steered me towards the restaurant.

"Table for two," he said to the maitre d'.

"Of course, superintendent." And led us to a table in the corner well away from prying eyes.

"So, you're well known here, Peter. Why doesn't that surprise me?"

"How are you finding London?" he asked, ignoring my rhetoric; it was becoming a habit with him.

I shrugged non-committally. "'S'okay. Nothing to write home about."

"So you're regretting the move, are you?" he asked, frowning.

"I didn't say that. It's just taking a bit longer to settle in than I thought."

We ordered from the fixed menu, and when the waiter had left us I asked, "Why am here, Peter? Is this something you and Jim have cooked up between you?"

He leaned forward and placed his arms on the table. "You're kidding me, aren't you? Whoever this guy is, so far he's caused the deaths of three adults and four children. For God's sake, Angie, we need a profile on this killer. I thought you would have jumped at it."

"Sorry," I muttered, wondering why he always made me feel like shit. "I suppose it's because I don't trust Jim's charitable approach. So what have you got so far, Peter?"

"Not a great deal more than I put in the file. About three months back factories and warehouses started to go up. It was obviously the work of an arsonist because the MO was the same; the fire inspectors confirmed it. This fellow must be some kind of an expert in explosives because each of the fires was started with a controlled device. He wasn't trying to hide himself."

"So it was evidently not a revenge attack," I commented, almost to myself. "But you're an experienced policeman, Peter; surely you can work this out for yourself?"

He shook his head in denial. "No. You're wrong. If it weren't for the recent tragedies, yes, the case would have remained with the local force. But when lives are being lost, and there are very few clues, and we have no idea when this fucking madman is going to stop, then we need help. And that is why you're here, Angie. And that is why it couldn't wait until tomorrow."

He pulled out a file from his briefcase. "Here – read this. It will bring you up to date."

I read the file whilst we were having dinner; I had glanced through it back at the Yard but this had more detail. What I was searching for was a map of the territory. Pyromaniacs tended to behave in certain ways. Generally, they don't live far from their targets, and this did appear to be the case here.

"So most of the fires occurred in or around Wythenshawe?" I stated.

"Yes. Probably he could have walked from fire to fire."

"That's one of the things I'm getting at, Peter. Were you aware that arsonists tend to follow almost specific patterns?"

"Well, I read something about them in the past, but, I'm sorry, no, I can't recall. So, enlighten me, Angie."

I smiled at his attempted humour. "Yes. That is a fact. And invariably they are recidivists, so you might check criminal records. The other feature about them is that they fall into approximately four or five categories.

"There are the revenge types: someone has upset them and they want to get their own back. Then there are the excitement types – the ones who get off, probably sexually, from setting off fires. You should always look for semen in the vicinity."

"Didn't find any," he muttered.

"Did you look?"

When he shook his head I continued. "Then there are those who set fires for profit; they're pretty easy to identify. There are those who wish to conceal a crime. And finally, if you will, there are psychopaths who cannot give a reason for setting off the fires other than they get immense satisfaction from them."

"Very explicit. I didn't realise you were so au fait with these people."

This caused me to smile. "Peter, I've had years of experience in studying criminal psychology. All kinds of psychopaths, deviants of whatever category you might care to describe them, misfits – call them what you will, but I have come across them in my studies. And, as you may remember, I have had some practical experience."

"Sorry. I wasn't trying to teach to you suck the proverbial eggs; it just isn't something we were ever taught in the police force." He looked sufficiently apologetic to persuade me to carry on.

"I can understand that. Otherwise you might start concluding that every criminal is a psychopath or a sociopath! Anyway, back to the subject. First off, as I suggested, check the criminal records; I'm sure you'll find this character will be there somewhere. The other thing you might check is at the scene of the crimes – on many occasions the culprit will stand and watch. See if there aren't any CCTV cameras in the vicinity; if there are, you might catch him that way.

"The other aspect is to ask the firemen. Check if there weren't any kind of innocent bystanders in the area who jumped in to help them. That is a favourite tactic of the pyromaniacs; some of them want to become the local hero."

"I doubt that would happen here, Angie. Not with the tragedies he's caused."

I sighed; I was just too tired to go on. "Look, Peter, we can't really go through this tonight. Why don't we leave it for now and I'll come in and see you tomorrow?"

"In the morning?"

"No. It will be the afternoon. I have someone to see in the morning."

He scowled at me. "Are you suggesting that your talks with young Danny boy are more important than this case?"

I was shocked. It surprised me that Jim must have put him the picture; this was supposed to be a secret. "Yes. I am. Important to me, that is. And you have enough to be working on until I get there. Oh, Peter, the one thing you might bear in mind is that the majority of these arsonists tend to be teenagers or in their early 20s. However, in a case where the arsonist is using controlled devices you will probably have to look for an older man; but if my statistics stack up he will still have a criminal record."

He stood up and gave me a peck on the cheek.

"Thanks for that. Goodnight, Angie. I'll see you tomorrow."

"Thanks for the dinner," I said.

CHAPTER NINE

The following morning, after an enjoyable breakfast at the Grand, I rang the office to check if there had been any overnight developments with the rapist. Sally and Laura were on their way to talk to the parents of both girls, whilst the others were contacting the local tube stations. One of those, the Maida Vale underground, did have some recordings of the night in question, so we might strike lucky. I asked to be kept informed.

I set off into the high ground to visit Hyde, where Danny lived. I knew the directions by heart I had visited there so many times in the past. It was still raining, though more like a drizzle than a torrential downpour, and I remembered the cold of winter I had endured some months ago.

As I travelled through Stockport and started climbing the skies began to darken, almost closing in on me. I shuddered as I recalled the first time I had gone to Hyde, and the oppression it had visited on me. I wished I had a wireless, something to take my mind off the environment.

With the traffic it took me almost an hour to arrive at Danny's house. I knocked a couple of times but there was no answer.

"I know what the little sod is doing!" I thought. "He'll have his I-pod on!"

The front door was open, so I went in. I was right – Danny boy was sitting there, in the same chair I had last seen him occupying, with his earphones on listening to God knows what. I pushed him gently before he realised I was there. When he stood up, he measured himself against me; it was obvious he had grown a couple of inches since I had last seen him.

"Would you have kept me waiting there all morning, Danny?" I asked sarcastically.

"Hi, Angie," he said cheekily. He had always called me 'miss' before. "Sorry about that – I should have been listening out fer you."

"I'm alright, thank you," I said, reminding him of common courtesy.

"But you're not okay, are you?" he said.

I took off my coat and perched on the old settee. "No, Danny. I'm not. Let me ask you a question. What was your sister, Katy, wearing on the day she died?"

"A red dress," he said.

Oh, shit! So it was her, I said to myself.

"And how did you know I was going to speak to you? Let me guess. Katy told you?"

He laughed. "She told me she got in touch with you. Then she said you were comin' up to see me." He spread his arms out. "And here you are." He pointed to his chair. "Sit here, miss. You'll be more comfortable and closer to fire."

I did as he suggested. He was right – it was warmer. Despite the early spring weather it was always cold in this house. Maybe it was because we were so high up.

"Why is your late sister tormenting me?" I asked. "Have you any idea what Katy has done to me?"

"Sure. She told me she visited you after you had seen that old bat in the Midlands. And – as I think I told yer before – you're a 'Sensor'; it were easy for her to come again to yer. Didn't she tell you then about the robbers?"

I nodded. I knew he would be aware of what she was doing. What he didn't know was that she was scaring me. He must have guessed, though, because he said, "Y'haven't to be scared, Angie. She's only trying to help yer."

I sighed. "How is she trying to help me, Danny? How could she possibly know what she is doing to me? Or why? Why does she think I need her help?"

"'Cos we both knew that yer were askin' the question about whether or not you were a clairvoyant."

I was beginning to feel angry. I had come all this way for an explanation, thinking it might be difficult for him, and here he was rhyming off the patter as if it didn't matter. Well it mattered to me.

"Why didn't you telephone me? You could easily have rung and let me know what Katy was trying to do, couldn't you?"

"Yeah. But she asked me not to."

"Did she say why?"

He shrugged, as if to say he really couldn't tell me. So I pushed him a little further.

"She said yer were tryin' to find yer way and only she could help you but I'd to leave yer alone. It did'n make much sense to me, Angie, but I've always trusted her, so I did now."

"I see," I said – which of course was nonsense; I didn't see at all. "Have you asked her what she intends doing now, Danny? Only I do think you should tell her that I am truly scared of how she's affecting me. And if she'll allow it I would like to resign."

"Yeah. But yer can't just walk away from it. She says this is something that once yer've asked for it then yer got it for life."

"Dear God. Does she truly believe that? What if I decide it isn't for me – which is what I was going to ask you to do for me. You know, please could your sister leave me alone?"

"I'll talk to her again, but I don't think yer can do that. We've talked a lot about you, Angie, especially since we had the trouble in the winter. She left yer alone, as yer know. She said it weren't right for her to do owt then. But once yer been to see that woman in Midlands and asked to be helped, then you invited her in. And you have to understand she doesn't mean any harm. She is tryin' to steer yer to becoming a full – what d'yer call it?"

"Psychic?"

"Yeah. You got it. Isn't that what that woman told yer – that you were a psychic but you 'ad to pray?"

"Yes. She did. And I thought she was a nutter. Now I'm not so sure."

"Look, Angie," he said, with a maturity I wasn't expecting, "go along with Katy. She is there to help you. In time you will become adjusted to this phenomenon and then you will accept it is a normal part of your life. And you are lucky; I wish such a blessing had been bestowed upon me."

I sat there gasping at his articulation. It was more the voice of a mature adult than that of a 15-year-old boy.

Where the hell did he learn to speak like that? I thought to myself.

"So what am I supposed to do, Danny?"

Now he reverted to his traditional style.

"Well, yer gotta ride it out. Let Katy do what she has to do – if she thinks yer can't handle it she'll back off. Yer'll have to trust her, like I do."

"You don't give me much choice. If she won't listen to you then I'll have to go along with it. Do you mind if I contact you again?"

"I expect yer to, Angie. And let me know, won't yer, if yer gonna stay in London or we can expect you back at the Uni."

I laughed. "What are you like?" When he stood up I went over and gave him a big hug. "Thanks for listening to me, Danny. I'm not sure it's helped me a great deal but it has cleared my head. I'll contact you whenever…"

CHAPTER TEN

As I left the house I thought, So this, then, is my destiny – my revelation. It was something I had queried ever since I had met Connie all those years ago. Now I had confirmation, proof, that this was a – I hesitated in calling it a blessing, at least not just yet; perhaps in time I might come to regard it as that, but in the meantime it was something of a curse; and a shock. But, according to Danny, I had brought it on myself by asking the question: "Who am I?" Now I was clear, and I would simply have to endure it. But the one thing that did encourage me was what Danny had said: "If Katy feels yer can't handle it she'll back off." I could live with that.

On the way back to Manchester, peering through the windscreen wipers, I spotted an independent electrical shop on the outskirts of Stockport and bought a small radio I could use in the car; at least it would give me something to listen to rather than the sound of my own thoughts. There was also a sandwich shop opposite with one or two tables inside, so I bought a tuna and salad sandwich and a cup of tea and spent some 15 minutes gathering my mental records of pyromaniacs and the categories in which they subdivide. Finally, when my thoughts had become more unambiguous, I set off for the police HQ. By now the rain had stopped and the sun was attempting to expose itself through the clouds.

* * * * * *

Gaining entry to the offices still hadn't changed since I was last there; even my warrant card didn't allow entrance, and it wasn't until Peter Conway had cleared me that I was allowed to enter.

His secretary was waiting for me on the ground floor. She was a cheerful middle-aged woman.

She smiled at me as she commented, "Sorry about the difficulty in getting in. Peter is on the seventh floor, if you'll come with me."

It wasn't exactly the first time I had been there, but I said nothing.

Peter was sitting at the same desk as Jim used to have; it was strange seeing him there, as if he were just borrowing the office.

"Hi, Angie." His tone was friendly, as it had been the night before – quiet unlike him, actually.

"Hello, Peter." I checked my watch. "On time, as I said I would be." I took a seat in front of his desk, but he stood and went over to the conference table.

"We'll be more comfortable here," he announced.

"Is someone going to join us?"

"Well, yes. I thought John – you remember John Watkins, don't you?"

I nodded. He had been a good friend of mine when I was based here.

"Well, John is now an inspector, and I thought it would be beneficial if we both heard what you have to say."

The secretary ushered John in, and the big black man smiled and gave me a warm welcome, with a nice hug that I felt I needed after my session with Danny O'Brien.

"How you doing, John?" I asked. "And congratulations, by the way." He had a peculiar presence about him that I couldn't quite penetrate. I had no idea where it came from, but it upset me. I shook my head, hoping it would go away.

"Hi, Angie. Thanks, and I'm fine. How are you getting along in London?"

"Don't ask," I said, hesitatingly.

"That bad, hey? Are you alright?" John asked.

"Yes," I almost snapped. "I'm fine – thank you."

That must have been the second or third time I had been asked that question in the last couple of days.

"Well, back to the arsonist. I will do my best to try and profile him, but, as I've said before…"

"…It will take solid detective work to apprehend him," John interrupted.

I smiled, glad he'd remembered. "Absolutely. Anyhow, as I was saying to Peter last night, the majority of pyromaniacs are youngsters, some even in their teens, and most of them will have a criminal record, which shouldn't be too difficult to trace. More often than not they will live close to where they started the fires, possibly even walking distance from their homes.

"The records show that in virtually all cases they will not be married, have a deficiency of intellect, and suffer from a great sense of inadequacy. Some of them – and these are the very rarest – they get sexual satisfaction from setting off the fires.

"There, you now have the typical profile," I stated, grinning.

"Wonderful," Peter responded. "So how do we catch him? I mean, you've described the type, Angie, but you haven't put any flesh on him."

"I haven't finished yet. The worst kind of offender is the excitement one, and especially the ones who use automatic incendiary devices. These men will no doubt be approaching their early 30s, will be wise enough not to leave fragments for Forensics, and they are very dangerous. It sounds to me as though you might have one of these in your midst."

I looked again at John, my old friend, and my thoughts seemed to be suspended. I could see him clearly now; he had cancer. It was cancer of the bowel – one of the worst types. I shuddered and wondered how I should tell him. I decided to wait until the moment was right.

"How do you catch him? Well, when was the last fire?"

"Three – no, four days ago," John said.

"And was this also in Wythenshawe?"

"Yes."

"So, I would like to visit the site, if I may?"

"Of course," Peter said. "Do you want to go now? It will be dark shortly."

"That doesn't matter. It was probably dark when he set the house alight."

CHAPTER ELEVEN

I didn't actually remember Wythenshawe; all I knew was it was one of the largest of Manchester's council estates, although I understand that many of the houses had been purchased from the council after Maggie Thatcher come to power. Peter was right; it was beginning to get dark (thank God it wasn't raining), although he found the property without problems. It was a semi-detached house in a narrow cul-de-sac; there would have been no more than 12 houses in the street. The house was cordoned off with yellow tape, designating a crime scene, and the property was just a shell. Most of the upstairs was burnt out; anyone who had been sleeping in the bedrooms would either have been burnt alive or suffocated from the fumes. Downstairs, most of the house remained more or less intact, although the passageway was destroyed, along with part of the staircase and the kitchen.

We went over the house carefully; I covered my nose with my handkerchief from the lingering smell of burning. Downstairs it was possible to identify where the fire had started, as the remnants of a container were protruding from the remains of a cupboard where the stairs used to be. Whoever had set this off was a premeditated killer. He would have broken into the house initially, without leaving evidence, so he could have set up his device. He would also have known that a family lived there. as toys and a carrycot were in what was left of the kitchen.

I shook my head at the evidence of the tragedy. "What did the firemen say?" I asked.

"Well, as we suspected, the fire was started deliberately," Peter said. "Obviously he must have planned it, because the first device to go off was a small gas cylinder that exuded smoke that would have choked the occupants, more especially the children. This was then followed by the explosion of the petrol canister." He pointed around the ruin. "And you can imagine what happened after that."

"Did Forensics find anything?"

"Nothing of any consequence," John said. "There was no sign of a break-in, and the only clues we have were one or two footprints, although they could have belonged to one of the parents."

"Anything on the canister?" I asked. "Fingerprints? Some residue? Anything?"

"No. Nothing we could trace." Peter shook his head. "We're at a dead end. That's why we reported it to the National Crime Unit."

I glanced across the road. There was a small park bordered by a hedge. "Did the firemen say that there was a volunteer helping?"

"No," John answered.

"Has anyone checked the park?"

"Well, no. I mean, why should we?"

"Let's have a look, shall we?" I said, without answering the question.

I borrowed John's torch and wandered over to check behind the hedge – within the park. There were a couple of sheets of literature on the ground. I bent over and picked one of them up with a pair of tweezers; it was a pornographic photo. I thought I spotted something on the ground close by and checked it with my torch. It appeared to me to be dry semen.

"Fucking hell!" Peter exclaimed. "Why didn't we check this out?"

"Probably because you're not too familiar with the tactics of pyromaniacs. As I said in the office, this is one of the excitement arsonists. Someone who gets off from watching the fire burn, and probably watching people, even children, burn to death." I pointed towards the dried semen. "There is your evidence – that and the porno photo."

"Can you help us in apprehending this bastard?" Peter asked.

" I'll have a look at your suspects." Was all I could say.

John collected the samples and placed them in an evidence bag for testing. We were back in the conference room, out of the cold, within the half-hour.

* * * * * *

"So, what have we got? Other than dried semen and a porno photo? It tells us who he is, and with the forensic evidence, you should be able to trace him without difficulty; and now we know more or less where he lives – in the immediate vicinity of the fires. So, now you check your criminal records. What you're looking for is a man, in the early to mid-30s, who lives within a circumference of, say, a mile around the fires. He won't be married, probably lives with his parents and could be employed in a white-collar job. And, very definitely, he will not be an intellectual."

"You make it sound so easy," John said.

"The problem with Forensics is we could be talking about a week to ten days," Peter said. "Before we get the results this guy could have killed scores more people, and children.

"We can't do anything tonight," he went on. "So, can we leave this over until tomorrow?"

"I don't see why not. But do you need me here?"

"Yes, I do. When we catch him I would like you to do the interviewing."

"Okay. Then I'll see you in the morning – what, about nine-thirty? John, would you walk to the car with me?"

"What's this about, Angie?" he asked as we left the building. I watched him lighting a cigarette.

"You don't smoke," I pointed out.

"Hmm. I used to but then I stopped. But lately I've been feeling so shitty I started again. So, come on, Angie: what is it you want?"

"When you say you feel so shitty, what do you mean, John?"

"I don't want to talk about it. It's personal. And you still haven't told me why you wanted to talk to me."

"I think you should go to the doctor's. As soon as possible."

"What the hell is this all about?" he snapped. "Have you spotted something?"

"John, I believe you have cancer. Bowel cancer." I couldn't think of any other way to tell him. It was terminal and it wasn't the time to be sensitive.

He said nothing for a moment; just drew on his cigarette, letting the nicotine go deep into his lungs. Then he said, "I'm not going to ask you how you know; that would be silly of me. The truth is, I've had problems with my bowels of late." He placed his hand over his abdomen. "I've tremendous pain here and I've lost some weight."

"Hasn't your wife spotted it? Surely she must be worried about you?"

"Probably. But I wouldn't listen to her. The last thing I wanted to hear was about the dreaded 'C'. I take it you're certain?"

I nodded, sadly. "Yes. But as you said, John, you don't really want to know how I was able to diagnose it." I squeezed his arm. "John, please go to the doctor's – promise me."

He looked as if he might start crying, so I put my arm around him. "Is it too late?" he asked, simply. "I mean, has it gone too far?"

"That I don't know – believe me. It could well be they will have caught it in time."

I said it but I knew it wasn't true. I could feel the touch of death on him, and part of me was crying inside.

"Thank you, Angie," he said, humbly. "I'll follow your advice. See you in the morning."

Somehow I didn't think so.   "Goodbye, my dear friend," I whispered.

CHAPTER TWELVE

That night I trudged through the rain to the French restaurant in St Anne's Square, where Pauline and I had shared that closeness together. It wasn't that I wanted to be picked up; I just wanted to sample the atmosphere that had brought us together. I also thought it might bring me some closure, I hadn't had it with Connie, she was still in my thoughts every day, and I really hoped I could achieve it with Pauline.

As usual it was a busy place, with the same-sex couples sat at two-seater tables. I felt isolated sitting by myself, and wondered if I should leave. Then I noticed that a single girl on a nearby table was glancing towards me. She had dark hair almost spilling over her shoulders, with brown eyes that seemed to delve inside me – or was that my wishful thinking? She had high cheekbones and an angular face; she was very pretty, and I was surprised to see her here on her own. I smiled at her, and she came across straight away.

"I hope you don't mind," she said, "but I noticed we were both on our own and I wondered if I might join you?"

"Yes. Of course. Did you come on your own?"

"Not really. I was let down. And you?"

I shook my head. "No. Not let down; my partner died and I was just sampling the atmosphere we used to share."

"I'm sorry. That must have been terrible for you. Was…"

"…She," I interjected.

She laughed. "Of course! Was she ill? Or was it an accident?"

"She was ill. I am still in the grieving stage." I decided that that was the better course to take.

She stood up. "Oh. I'm really sorry. I didn't want to intrude – I thought you might like the company."

I waved her to sit down. "Please; don't mind me. I'd be happy to share a table with you. My name is Angela – Angie for short."

She reached across to take my hand. "Hello. I'm Kelly. Do you live in Manchester?"

"No. I live in London. I'm here for a couple of days to sort out a criminal problem."

"You're a policeman?" she said; I could hear the shock in her voice.

"I'm afraid so. Does that put you off?"

She smiled. "No. It was just a surprise. But, then, why should it? I also live in London – well, close by, about 20 miles away, in St Albans. Do you know it?"

"Yes – although I've never been there. I'm told it's a very nice city. What are you doing up here?"

"I'm an illustrator; I design posters for shop displays. I'm having a showcase in Kendals and the purchasing officer is a…well, I thought she was a close friend of mine, but" – she spread her hand round the room – "I think I might have confused her."

I placed my hand over hers and felt the warmth of her blood.

"Don't be disheartened, Kelly. These things happen. Do you have a partner in London?"

"No. I used to have; she worked in Selfridges – that's where I met her. But she's moved overseas now. I think she lives in Spain."

"So you're lonely?"

"I guess. But aren't you, Angie – lonely, I mean?"

"Yes," I admitted. "But I'm not in here to be picked up. It was just the memories…"

"I know," she interrupted. "So why don't we order and just enjoy our dinner together?"

Which we did. The food was quite incredible – the last time I dined here with Paula I could hardly remember tasting the food, I was so obsessed with lust. Now it was different. We shared a bottle of wine together, and afterwards we split the bill.

There were no come-ons, no suggestion of what might be; just a very nice meal with a very nice young lady

As we left the restaurant I gave her my card. "Do you think you might ring me when you get home?"

She gasped when she saw the identification. "Wow! A detective chief inspector. You must really be something."

"Will you ring me, Kelly?"

She handed me her own card. "Of course I will. If that's what you want."

"Like you, Kelly, I'm lonely. I live on my own in London and I don't have any friends there. So of course I want you to ring me."

She leaned across and gave me a sweet kiss on the lips. "You'll be hearing from me, Angie. Goodnight."

"Goodnight, Kelly," I said.

And we went our separate ways.

CHAPTER THIRTEEN

I thought a lot about Kelly that night. There was something rather special about her. It wasn't so much that she reminded me of Pauline; she was quite different. But there was a sweetness and gentleness about her that attracted me to her. I knew we would be seeing each other again. Since Pauline I had questioned whether or nor I might be a lesbian; Pauline assured me I wasn't but, she did say I was probably bisexual. I think Kelly rather confirmed that, because she certainly excited me – and I was so lonely.

I chuckled when it occurred to me that I might be the first lesbian psychic.

* * * * * *

The next morning I arrived early at HQ. I wanted to see how John Watkins was faring.

He wasn't there.

Peter looked at me and scowled as I went into his office. "What did you do to John last night? He telephoned me this morning to tell me he's been admitted to hospital."

"What I told him, Peter, was confidential, between him and me. If he wants to tell you that's up to him. So, how did you get on with checking the criminal database?"

He shook his head. "I've got someone onto it. I'm hoping they might come back to me this morning. Do you want a coffee?"

Anything to change the subject, I thought to myself.

"Yes. I'd like a coffee. So, there weren't any more fires during the night, then?"

"No. Why? Did you expect there to be?"

"It would be common practice for the incidents to become closer together. It's now – what – four or five days since the last one?"

"Five days. So we have to catch this monster before he kills again."

"I've had a thought about this character, Peter, and there's been a slight change of mind."

"Tell me. So what's different about him?"

"Well, considering how he broke into the house, quite surreptitiously, and how he was able to set up the explosives. It would take someone with a degree of intelligence to undertake that."

"So he isn't a man with a low intellect then?"

"No. Sorry about that. It doesn't make any difference to catching him – everything else I profiled about him is accurate. I still believe you'll find he has a criminal record."

"We'll soon see," he commented dryly, as one of the officers came into the office brandishing a printout.

"What have you got, sergeant?" It was one of the, what I would call, young detectives.

"We have two candidates, superintendent. Both in the same area."

He handed the list across to Peter, who nodded with satisfaction.

"Sit down, sergeant," he said. "Angie, this is Simon Hanson. Simon, meet Angie, our profiler."

We shook hands. He was a pleasant enough young fellow. He probably came from university to have made sergeant at his age, I thought – but, then, so did I.

He pointed to the list. "I think this one is the favourite."

A strange expression, it seemed to me. I picked up the list from Simon. The two candidates didn't seem to gel with me. One was a 23-year-old, unemployed, living with his parents about a quarter of a mile away from the fires. He had a record of stolen cars and break-ins. The second one was in his mid-20s, living not too far from the incendiaries, but married with a young son. His pastime was setting fires to bushes – nothing too serious but still a cause for concern.

"These are not right," I announced.

"What?" Peter challenged. I guess he was getting somewhat fed up with me by now. "We've done what you asked: we've selected two possibilities close to the scene, both of whom have criminal records, and the last one has a habit of setting off fires. So why don't they fit?"

"Well, I would watch the one who sets off the bush fires – at some juncture he too may become dangerous. But at this stage neither of them fits the bill. Simon, spread your search outward from the fires. Go to up to a mile. Let's see if that drags our man in."

Peter just snorted. He never did have much time for profilers; in fact, it seemed to annoy him that he had called me in.

"Trust me," was all I said.

He came back again some ten minutes later, with another sheet.

"Try this one," he said.

I looked at the name – and something was triggered inside me.

"This is the one." Jack Mellor. The man was in his early 30s, lived alone – that is, he had no girlfriend – and his criminal record consisted of breaking and entering. He lived about a mile away from the fires.

"How do you know?" Peter asked, his voice now heavy with sarcasm.

"Like I said before, Peter – just trust me. What you need to do now is to organise an arrest. You should only need a couple of patrol cars; I think you'll find he will come quietly."

Peter turned towards Simon. "Get on to it, will you? And when you're ready let me know – I want our profiler here to accompany us."

I turned away to grin. I wouldn't want him to feel I was humiliating him.

I went in the second patrol car with Simon. Peter was ahead of us. Despite the traffic we arrived at Wythenshawe in a short while and parked outside the suspect's house. It was a ground floor flat on the edge of the estate. Someone was in because we could hear the television.

Peter knocked. With a warrant he could, I suppose, have smashed the door in, but this was terribly civilised.

The door opened and a man appeared.

"You're here to arrest me?" he said, sotto voce. Then he held out his hands for the cuffs. Peter read him his rights, cuffed him and led him to the front patrol car.

He turned to me. "Well done, Angie. I'm not sure how you did it but let's say I'm genuinely impressed."

After we had left Forensics entered the house. They reported to us later that it was tantamount to a bomb factory. There were small gas bombs, a number of filters, a dozen or so timers and a substantial amount of petrol. He had enough ingredients to burn down the centre of Manchester.

I returned with them to HQ and asked Peter if he still wanted me to interview the man.

"Yes, I do. I want to know why a man deliberately murders young children, knowing they will be in the house. What is it that motivates him, and why? Can you do that for me?"

"Sure. After you've charged him formally let me know – I'll be in the canteen having lunch."

* * * * * *

Pie and chips: part of my standard diet when I was last in Manchester. God, I could get really fat if I stayed here. I had almost finished when Simon came in.

"They're ready for us, Angie."

"Fine," I said, finishing my meal off.

"So tell me," he said as we were going up in the lift, "how where you able to spot that the first two suspects were not the right ones?"

"One of the mysteries of being a profiler!" I joked. "Actually," I lied, "it was all to do with deduction."

"Deduction? Well, I wish I had it."

* * * * * *

The prisoner, Jack Mellor, was seated in one of the interview rooms. A constable was standing by the door. When I sat down Peter turned on the tape, and stated the date and announced that Superintendent Peter Conway and Detective Chief Inspector Angela Crossley would be conducting the interview.

"You do realise you are entitled to a solicitor?" Peter informed him.

"I don't need a solicitor."

"You do understand that you are charged with murder?" I asked him.

He nodded, and Peter said, "Please say 'yes' or 'no' into the tape."

"Yes. I do," Mellor said.

"Very well. Would you like to begin, chief inspector?"

"The first question I would like you to answer, Mr Mellor, is: how many fires are you claiming to be responsible for?"

He shrugged.

"Will you please answer into the machine," Peter repeated.

"How the fuck do I know? I didn't keep count."

"You must realise there are seven dead in recent times? Three adults and four children. Do you know about these, Mr Mellor?"

"I guess. There were one or two factories I started as – what do you call it? – a trial run."

"So, tell me, why did you deliberately set those fires off, knowing there would be children inside?" My voice was quiet, almost a whisper, as though I was in a state of shock. This seemed to please him, because he said, "Don't you see? That made it all the more exciting. Watching the faces of those attending the fires – the firemen, the police, even the passers-by – seeing the shock and the horror on their faces."

"So killing the children didn't disturb you at all?"

He shrugged again. "I'm not altogether sure why I wanted them dead, but I have to tell you I got an incredible thrill when their bodies were brought out."

I laid a restraining arm on Peter's. I thought he was going to hit the man.

"So you get off on it?"

"Too fucking right I do. I was watching across the road at the last fire, and when I saw the children being brought out – fucking hell! I had to ...well, ejaculate, especially when a couple of the firemen threw up."

"And the parents, Jack? Were they just incidental, or did you also plan to kill them as well?"

He laughed: an almost maniacal giggle. "I could hardly just kill the children and ignore the parents, now, could I?! I mean, don't you think that's a fuckin' daft question?"

"Yes. Of course it is," I said apologetically. "One dies, they all die. Is that it?"

"Now you're getting it."

"Would you be prepared to sign a statement to that effect, Jack? Just so we have your words on record. Admitting to the two fires that caused the seven deaths?"

He stopped for a moment and then nodded. "What the hell! I did it so why should I try to hide it. Will I make the papers?"

"Oh, you're sure to, Jack. You'll become something of a national celebrity."

He grinned, delighted at the news that he was going to become something of a hero. There was nothing more I could say; he had confessed, even gloated about it, and hoped he would make the national papers. He beamed at that, and we ended the interview.

Peter shook my hand, and then gave me a kiss on the cheek as I was preparing to leave.

"One for the profilers – eh? I'll be sending a recommendation to your boss. Bye, Angie."

* * * * * *

I had already checked out of the hotel, hoping I would be able to leave by the afternoon. I was right. This was a very tragic story and I felt a terrible loss for the children. But at least we had caught the bastard. He wouldn't be killing anyone else.

By 4.0 p.m. I was on my way, with the music from my old radio scratching in my ears. Still, better that than thinking about my clairvoyance – and Kelly.

CHAPTER FOURTEEN

I had a clear run home; especially as I used the toll road and bypassed Birmingham, and I arrived at my flat at about seven-thirty. Having had my pie and chips in the police canteen, I thought I would give dinner a miss, so I arranged a small salad and settled with a cup of tea in front of the television. I wondered how the team was getting on in my absence – not that I could do anything about it.

I thought I might have felt a bit depressed coming back to this utilitarian unit, but the possibility of hearing something from Kelly quite excited me. I was really tired after the journey so I took my tea to bed, read a little and then crashed out.

I awoke the next morning with no phone ringing – quite different from my last visit to Manchester. Obviously I wasn't so important now. Also, I had had a dreamless night; perhaps Katy had decided I needed a break from her.

I made myself a leisurely breakfast and sat in front of the television to hear the news.

Oh, shit! There were the bank robbers, on the television, being led away, handcuffed, in police cars.

I'd forgotten that this was a Friday – supposedly the day they might strike. My vision was accurate in almost every detail, except that the manager involved hadn't been shot and was still very much alive. I wondered what Superintendent Mackellar might think about it. I knew that it would piss Glasson off, and secretly I was pleased.

I was still grinning as I made my way into the office. There was no sign of my team; officers who I had not met occupied the desks.

"Anyone know where the intelligence team is?" I enquired of no one in particular.

"You're on the third floor," a sergeant said to me. "You'll have to ask the commander – he arranged it."

"Christ! What a result. I wondered how he managed that?"

The truth was, it had actually emanated from Glasson. He had reported both Jim and me to the deputy assistant commissioner. Jim had indeed confirmed that he didn't wish for any of our team to report directly to Superintendent Glasson, and, after a heated row, I understand that we were moved up to the third floor in a suite of private offices close to where Jim was established.

I popped my head round his door. "Are you pleased about the move?" I asked.

He looked up from his papers. "Not really, no. I had to have a monumental bust-up with the deputy assistant commissioner, which won't help my career, but I was fucked if I was going to give in to that prick Glasson." He waved a hand in a gesture. "So, here you are. I'm sure you'll be more comfortable up here than in that cattle pen downstairs. And you won't have to cross swords with Glasson."

"Sorry about your career, Jim." I shrugged. "I don't think you need worry too much; from what the grapevine says the guy upstairs is a plonker, and I doubt anyone will care too much about what he says."

He laughed. "So, your bank robbers have now been arrested. That's one up to us. It's a pity I had to have someone from your unit making an anonymous telephone call. How did you get on in Manchester? Did it help talking to Danny?"

"Sort of. At least it cleared my head – I now know what is happening to me."

"Are you going to tell me, Ange? Or is it something you want to keep to yourself?"

I forced a smile. "If you don't mind, I'd rather not talk about it."

"And your resignation? Have you withdrawn it?"

"Well, I never really handed it in, did I? At that moment I felt I wasn't going to fit in here. I'm not terribly happy about the flat, either; it's about as comfortable as a dog's kennel. And I wasn't sure I would be able to make some friends. But..."

"Has any of that changed? You do sound as if you've cheered up a bit."

"I'm not sure. Let's wait and see, shall we?"

"And was your trip nostalgic? Did it wake up some old memories? Peter tells me you soon cracked the arsonist problem."

"It wasn't too difficult. I'm sure if it happens again he'll now have the experience to deal with it himself. Well, I'll go and check on my team; see you later, Jim."

* * * * * *

The offices were a joy to behold. Enough space for the six of us, and then some. As I walked in the door the team stood and applauded.

"Hey, hang about, you lot; these offices weren't my idea! It was Jim who made the arrangements."

"We're not applauding you for that, Angie." It was Sam who spoke. "It was your intuitive deduction about the bank robbers." He waved his hands in the air. "We caught the bastards, all thanks to you. And none of us here is going to ask you how your perception works. Even Sally is impressed."

She grinned. "Too right I am! And when you're ready I'd like to hear about profiling; there must be something that I missed before."

I smiled, a little embarrassed. That was all I could do.

"How did you know?" I asked.

"'Cos the commander asked Sam to make the anonymous telephone call," Sally remarked. "We're all very proud of you."

I sat down at what was obviously my desk and asked, of each of them: "What has happened with the rapes and the murders? Have we made any headway?"

"Laura and I met the parents," Sally said. "The report's on your desk."

"It was heartbreaking," Laura added. "They were so distressed."

"Mostly it was the fathers who did the talking – not that there was much to say," Sally went on. "These were simply two young girls who got on the train at the wrong time."

Sam intervened. "We've also checked the CCTV cameras at the stations. The ones at Kilburn are just a blur – you can't make out anything from those. But the Maida Vale cameras give us quite a good outline, although I doubt if we'll be able to identify who we believe might be the suspect."

"Why is that?" I wanted to know.

Sam produced a printout. "This, we think, is the guy."

Whoever it was, he was wearing a hood wrapped around his head and his face. But it did give us some clues. He was of about average build, somewhere in the mid- to late 20s, dressed in some scruffy clothes with a pair of old trainers. His hands were thrust deep inside his pockets.

"How do you know this might be our suspect?" I asked.

"Partly because of the way he was dressed, trying to hide himself away, and partly because he was evidently tracking Glynis Stranark; you'll spot that when you see the film."

"He must have known he was on the camera," I said. "But at least we have some form of identification. We now know we're not chasing a middle-aged man; this fellow is young, and looks quite athletic. What did you get from the photofit?"

"It's also on your desk. Rachel Humphries didn't think it really looked like him; these things seldom do, but I suppose it's a guideline."

I picked up the photofit from my desk. Sam was right: it really wasn't very clear. But it might help us to publicise this character in the papers; it certainly should scare him.

"Have we been able to trace anyone who was on the same train? Someone who might have seen him, perhaps give us a more detailed description?"

"No. I'm afraid not," Sam said. "Also we've had a house-to-house enquiry team out there to ask if any of the tenants saw anything. Nothing. Most of them were in bed."

I shook my head wearily. This was par for the course.

"What about the autopsies?" I asked. "Who attended?"

"I did," Mark said. "At least, the second one; Kathleen Fisher's had already been carried out."

"Anything of any consequence to disclose?"

"Yes. There might be some tracings under her fingernails. I have to emphasise it's only a case of 'might be'. Forensics are now analysing these; they're still not sure whether they are scrapings or whether or not Glynis fell against the wall and gathered some of the debris. They expect to give us a DNA report, whenever. But I wouldn't build up our hopes, Angie."

"Yes, but we are making progress," I said. "So far, the description from the film seems to tie in with what Rachel Humphries told me; it's a pity the artist's drawing isn't terribly clear. Rachel was so positive she would be able to identify the man if she saw him again." I pointed to the picture. "Looking at this I would doubt it. But I still think we can frighten him.

"Okay! Anything else?"

"Well, changing the subject," Sally said, "We have a report on a possible paedophile murder."

"Oh, shit! Not again." This was one of the cases I was dreading, given my past experiences. Again, I began to question what the hell I was doing in this place. And then something reminded me that at one time I had been considering joining the FBI as a profiler – so what did I expect? Surely it was a job that dredged up the scum of humanity? And someone had to deal with them. Perhaps that's why I had been blessed with my psychic vision.

"Where has this come from, Sally?"

"I got a phone call from a Chief Inspector Givens at the Middlesex Division in Wembley; that was before he sent on the file to us. Evidently a little boy, a Phillip Rodgers, aged eight, has been found murdered. His body was hidden in some woods close to Harrow. He'd been strangled and buggered; his body was a terrible mess of bruises. His penis had also been removed and taped inside his mouth."

I watched as Laura turned her head away, trying to hide that she felt sick.

"The inspector says this is the second child who has disappeared within the past month."

"Was this also a boy?"

"Yes; a seven-year-old."

"Have they discovered the body yet?"

"No. He says the boy was removed from his house while his mother was in the rear garden."

"So, he's obviously an opportunist. Did Phillip have semen inside him?"

"I don't know, Angie. We'll have to wait for the autopsy. That's taking place this morning."

I struggled not to let my features drop. These were the most sickening crimes the police would ever have to deal with. "We appear to have yet another sadistic monster in our midst. How long ago since the first boy disappeared?"

Sally checked the file. "Almost four weeks. The police have had the army combing the woods in the immediate area, and a task force of some 50 police officers are also involved in the search. So far, no trace of Robert."

"Right. What I want you to do, Sally, is visit the chief inspector. Take Peter Wadkins here with you, it's time he was initiated, and collect all the details you can from him. Exactly what day and date and time the boys disappeared. Aside from Robert, who we know was alone in the house, what was Phillip doing, where was he? Get everything you can on him that isn't in the file. Then ask if he has checked the sex offenders' register, not just in that area but the file we have here at the Yard. Go through that with him; take any names he will have, for anyone who might be suspicious. Then attend the autopsy with him; I want to know the cause of death.

"And anything else you can think of that I might have missed.

"And, Sam, pull out an incident folder – put it up on the board. I want a list of all the girls who were raped: the dates, the details, the times and the type of rapes – that is, Vaginal or Sodomy. List them in chronological order with the dates first, then the names, then were they were at the time.

"Mark, I have a job for you. I want you to go back over these girls – interview them again. Take the photofit with you and see if any of them can recognise this man. Ask them for any details they may have remembered since their last interview. Let them know that we have a witness now who may trigger their memories, in case they were too frightened before.

"What I am going to do is concentrate on a profile of this character; see what I can come up with."

"Can I watch?" Sam wanted to know.

"Not at present, no. When I've finished I'll take you through it. In the meantime I do not want to be disturbed."

CHAPTER FIFTEEN

Sally Walker and Peter Wadkins set off on the Friday for the Central Middlesex headquarters in Wembley. Sally had already phoned ahead and arranged to meet Chief Inspector Givens at the mortuary. It was a lovely sunny day – one of those uplifting days that come at the end of a long winter.

Peter towered over Sally. Not that he was that tall – probably just over six feet, she thought; it was simply because, even with high heels, she wasn't much over five feet four.

"So, tell me about yourself," she said after they'd been motoring a while. "Do you have any family? Are you married? Children? Or perhaps you have a girlfriend – or even a boyfriend?"

She had come to the conclusion that this young man was extremely taciturn; it was like getting blood from the proverbial stone.

"No. I'm not married. I live with my parents. And, no, I don't have either a girlfriend or a boyfriend."

She raised her eyebrows. "God, Peter, you really stimulate the conversation. How did you get to join the police force? I mean, it isn't exactly a vocation."

"I graduated in criminology – at Bristol University. After that I decided the best career move I could make was the police force."

"How long have you been a policeman?"

"Two years. In patrol cars, and then I was upgraded to detective."

"Not bad after two years. It took me five years before I was accepted as detective. I suppose that's what a degree does for you. And what do you hope to become, Peter – Commissioner?"

"Very funny." He didn't smile, though. "I'd like to have a career that satisfies me. What about you, Sarge? Do you have a boyfriend – or married, perhaps?"

She laughed. 'I have a girlfriend, Peter. We live together. Have you attended an autopsy before?" she asked, changing the subject.

"Well, no, but it doesn't bother me. It's all part of the job."

"Here we are," Sally said as they pulled up in front of the mortuary. Chief Inspector Givens was waiting in his car.

"Follow me," he said without introduction.

"Christ, we have another one who's lugubrious," Sally said aloud, but quietly. "'Follow me' – as if I don't know the inside out of every mortuary building!"

Chief Inspector Givens was of medium build, balding, and with one of those thin, pinched faces that displayed misery rather than a sense of humour. His eyes had a darkness to them, as though he had witnessed all the world had to offer in the way of cruelty.

The medical examiner was waiting for them. The body of Phillip was laid out naked on the table.

"Good morning. I am Dr Sullivan, medical examiner." She was late thirties, mousy hair that was tied back in a bow, and deep blue eyes that were almost circumspect.

She pulled the microphone in front of her mouth, and her assistant, a young man who didn't appear to be much older than Peter, handed her the forensic saw, which she switched on.

The procedure was something Sally had witnessed many times before, so the sewing through the sternum didn't disturb her; neither did the skin being pulled down past the pubic bone. But she did keep an eye on Peter Wadkins when the outer muscle was being cut; despite his bravado she knew that the first time anyone watched this dismantling of a body was bound to be very unsettling. To put it mildly.

He didn't appear to blink an eyelid when Dr Sullivan extracted the internal organs and weighed them, muttering something into the microphone. It was only when she used the forensic saw again to cut through the head bones and peel the skin down over the face that Peter changed colour. Finally, it was when the saw cut through the bones and revealed the brain that he fainted and fell onto the floor.

"Who brought that neophyte in here?" Dr Sullivan demanded to know.

"Sorry," Sally muttered, "I didn't expect this. I'll try to bring him round."

"Well, if you can't you'll have to drag him out of here. I can do without this kind of disturbance."

Sally took the glass on the table and poured some water across Peter's face. He spluttered and then came round, apologising.

"Humph!" was all that Dr Sullivan said as she continued with the autopsy, making appropriate comments as she went along.

The autopsy took around one hour to complete; by this time Peter had left the room.

"Well," she remarked as she tore off her gloves and dumped them in the waste bin, "I don't suppose you need me to tell you what the boy died from? He was strangled, after he was sodomised. His anus is a brutalised mess," she sighed heavily, "there is severe bruising internally and he must have bled profusely. This poor little sod has undergone a savage attack by someone who has no regard whatsoever for a child's sensitivity. The severing of his penis took place post-mortem, so at least he was spared that suffering and indignity."

She turned to DCI Givens. "You have to catch this monster, Kevin. What he has done to Phillip here he will do, and much worse, to the next victim he snatches."

He nodded, and then asked a couple of questions about semen residue that might have been discovered inside his anus.

"There are traces. Obviously he couldn't have used a condom with his buggery. We should have some DNA for you in a few days."

That was very strange, Sally thought. If this character was on the sex offenders' register then he must surely have used a condom, otherwise it would be easy to identify him.

She shook her head as they left the mortuary. Outside, the chief inspector handed a file over to Sally. "This is the update of the details we have on this case. There isn't much more I can say. We've had extensive press and television coverage of this crime; we've dealt with over 400 telephone calls since the first abduction of Robert, most of which were false alarms; we have had house-to-house enquiries, halted passing traffic, for any witnesses who might have seen something – anything." He shrugged. "I don't know what else we could have done."

"What about the sex register? Have you trawled through that for anyone who might be suspicious?"

"Yes. Of course," he snapped, as if Sally were insulting his intelligence. "We did have a couple of candidates but their alibis checked out. We have also been in touch via your central computer, but with no positive results. But if we do have his DNA and he is on the sex register then – bingo! – we will have him. As Dr Sullivan says, 'We have to find this monster' – and we would be grateful for your help in tracing him."

"How was Robert abducted, inspector?"

"Straight from school – during playtime. We don't know how it happened but the man must have had some authority, because Robert went with him willingly. Are you going to help us, Sergeant Walker?"

"I can't confirm that, chief inspector; that will be a matter for our commander. But when I pass on the file I will recommend that we take on the case, in the event the DNA doesn't throw up a suspect. Leave it with me, sir."

* * * * *

It was after midday when they left Wembley. They stopped for a bite to eat at a roadside café – or, at least, Sally did; Peter seemed to have lost his appetite.

Eventually he came out with, "I'm sorry about my…"

"…Fainting, you mean? Sure. But if you don't say anything then neither will I."

"You're very kind, Sally."

"Of course I am. But you owe me one; remember that, young Peter."

CHAPTER SIXTEEN

I took out a folder and began copying the facts we had on the computer.

First off, we were making the assumption that it was the same man who raped the women and then killed the two girls in Kilburn and Maida Vale. Therefore, he was a sadistic offender. Accordingly, I brought into my mind as many details as I could remember about the category of 'sadistic rapist'. I also included elements of the 'power assertive rapist', as sometimes one graduates from one category to the next.

The majority of each type of rapist were probably raised in a single-parent home and physically abused in childhood, by the father, or even by the mother. Rapes would occur with a frequency of approximately 20 to 25 days. There would be multiple assaults, including both anal sex and oral sex.

This was a kind of common denominator between the two. In the case of the sadistic rapist, however, he tended to be in his late 20s, with degree of formal education, and to be a white-collar worker, possibly a professional. Generally, he would have no arrest records and would be difficult to trace. The violence against the victim shown by this category will increase; he tears off their clothes, subjects them to increasing physical torture and, finally, kills them.

This, then, was my memory of the violent rapists. How did our man fit into this profile?

Obviously, I had no idea of his background; on many occasions these men turned out to be married with a family, and the wives would have no suspicion of their husbands' repressed desires – or, indeed, their sociopathy; in any event, they would be able to disguise their inclinations. The wife, however, might possibly have had a hint of his obsessive personality. So I had to assume that he would be married and have a family.

Secondly, I had no idea of his occupation. In the case of the murders he travelled by underground rather than by car, so I took it that he wouldn't be a professional but a white-collar worker, possibly a civil servant.

I also assumed he would have no arrest record; that he would suffer from retarded ejaculation; and that he would indulge in degrading language when attacking the women.

So, how then will our rapist fit into a profile?

1) He will be raised in a single-parent home.
2) His father or his mother will have abused him.
3) He will be in his late 20s.
4) He will be married with a family and have no criminal record.
5) He is a white-collar worker.
6) He has a compulsive personality.
7) He stalks his targets.
8) He attacks women frequently and on an increasing basis.
9) He is a confirmed psychopath.
10)   He has retarded ejaculation.
11)   His compulsion forces him to be neat and tidy in everything he does.
12)   Finally – he kills the women.

And there was our rapist. It was a fairly textbook profile, but if anything else came up I would add to it. I put the summary into the computer, printed it out at font size 16 and pasted it on the board at the side of the names of the women. I still wasn't sure if our man had progressed from being a power assertive rapist to a sadistic rapist. Not that that mattered to any great extent, because we now had him identified, if only in outline.

* * * * * *

It had been a long day; Sam and Mark had gone home, and I needed something to eat. I was also tired from the effort of struggling to recall such a large amount of detail. Sally had left me the folder she had been given by the Wembley chief inspector – she and Peter had also left. I was too tired to read it now, but I was also aware of her recommendation that we should accept the case. I would pass that on to Jim, and let him decide after he had studied the evidence.

I left the office at about seven and went into a nearby Italian for some pasta and a glass of wine. I didn't have any company but I had had an interesting day, albeit a chilling and tragic one.

I got home just after eight; there was a message for me on the answerphone.

It was Kelly, letting me know that she was fulfilling her promise to ring me; she was now at home in St Albans and she would be in town tomorrow for a presentation at Selfridges. She also asked if I could meet her.

I rang her back and told her I was delighted she had rung, and, yes, I should be able to meet up with her on Saturday, and perhaps we should have dinner together. It was very exciting. I arranged to pick her up at the perfume counter in the store at about six in the evening.

* * * * * *

It took me a while to fall asleep; I kept thinking of Kelly, and hoping that this might be the start of something.

In my dreams I had another vision – again with the same clarity as in the dream of the bank robbers. This time I was on an underground train, watching a man who kept gazing furtively at a young and pretty girl on a nearby seat. As she got off so did he; I had the distinct impression he was stalking her. The name on the station's signs said Kensal Green. I followed the man across one or two streets; he had a hood hiding his face and head. When we reached a quieter part of the street he pounced, grabbed the girl, holding his hand across her mouth, and dragged her into a nearby alleyway.

I tried to stop him, but I was helpless. He tore her undergarments off, including her knickers and forced her down on her knees with a knife pointed against her throat.

Oh, Dear Jesus! I thought as he pushed his penis against her mouth.

"Suck it, you fucking bitch!" he snarled.

I started to scream and scream and scream.

I woke up half drowned in a mixture of perspiration and tears. I realised then that what I had seen was a vision of something that would happen in the future – almost the same type of vision that Connie had experienced all those years ago. I got up and peered through the curtain. It was still dark outside and the bedside clock showed that it was about 5.0 a.m. The sun was beginning to appear from the edge of the darkness, and it looked as though it was going to be another fine early spring day.

Normally I would have to get up in about an hour from now, so I decided I might as well rise now and get in early.

There was no one I could share the vision with – but there was something I could do about it.

* * * * * *

I got to the office at about six on the Saturday morning; understandably, I was the first there.

I checked on the board to confirm what had happened to the two murdered girls. Both of them had had their underclothes ripped off. There was no semen in evidence but the bruising suggested there had been anal as well as vaginal sex. These poor girls had been thoroughly violated, and the pattern seemed to stack up with my profile of the offender – exactly as it did with my vision.

I then went through the patterns of the earlier girls, who had been raped, and they were almost identical – except that they were still alive.

I doubted if I would be seeing Mark this morning; I was hoping he would be on the road interviewing the victims. Perhaps nothing would come of it but sometimes memories can play tricks, and a nudge here and there, especially with the murders of the girls, might just prompt some reminders.

Later I gave him a call on his mobile; it was now nine o'clock, so he should have been out and about. He answered on the first ring.

"Hi Angie. What can I do for you?"

"Where are you?"

"I'm in Hampstead. Checking on the second victim. The first one says she has no memory of the assailant and she's still traumatised."

"Are you calling in to the office today, Mark?"

"I can do if you want."

"Yes. Would you? Come in about lunchtime – there's something I want to discuss with you."

"Right. See you later, then."

I was glad that he hadn't asked me what I wanted. It was something I would prefer to discuss with him personally. What I had in mind was to employ Mark as a kind of observer on a train running into Kensal Green at about midnight tonight, to see if the suspect might be travelling on it. Saturday might well be the right time, especially if a girl had been visiting a London nightclub. The vision I had had didn't give a timetable but something told me it was imminent. It was now about two weeks since his last attack and, if my experience was anything to go by, his compulsion would definitely have progressed to the point where he was compelled to kill with increasing regularity. We would see what this weekend might bring.

I looked down at my desk and saw the file that Sally had left. I picked it up with the intention of reading it, but then changed my mind. I would read it later, after I had briefed Mark on what I wanted him to do.

CHAPTER SEVENTEEN

Whilst I was waiting for Mark I popped my head inside Jim's office. The commander's chair was vacant. Evidently our boss had decided he only wanted to work midweek. I guessed his wife would be pleased. There was a folder on his desk marked 'Angela Crossley'. Curiosity tempted me to open it. It contained an internal and confidential memorandum from P. Davis, deputy assistant commissioner to J. Robbins, commander of the National Serious Crimes Unit. "Serious stuff," I thought. Then I started to read it.

"Commander Robbins, following our meeting of today concerning Ms Angela Crossley, you will immediately transfer her department to the third floor of this building and inform her that, as and when required, she is to report directly to Superintendent Glasson, who, as you know, is in charge of day-to-day activities of the Unit. If at any time Ms Crossley refuses to accept a directive from Superintendent Glasson then I will make it my business to suspend her immediately from duty pending a full enquiry from the appropriate body.

To conclude, her disrespect for her superior officer has been noted on her file and will be referred to during the course of any future disciplinary hearings."

It was signed and dated three days ago, after I had set off for Manchester. Jim had elected not to warn me about it – no doubt knowing how I would react. I wondered if the deputy assistant commissioner had taken note of the recent successes our department had achieved. I thought about phoning Jim at home, but then changed my mind when I realised there was little he could do about it. One thing was clear, though: there was no way I was going to report to that dickhead Glasson, and if he tried to impose his will then Jim would certainly have my resignation.

I sighed. I had thought it was going to be a perfect day. I had planned to leave just after midday, soak in a long bath, shampoo my hair, and make myself up slowly and methodically for my date with Kelly. Now, I wasn't sure how; I could simply dismiss this memo, and pretend that nothing had happened, or explode when I saw Jim. Jim had said that Glasson did have some powerful friends, and now he was clearly exploiting his position.

* * * * * *

I wandered back into the office, to see that Mark had arrived back.

"Have any luck with the victims?" I asked.

He grimaced. "Not a lot. The girl in Hampstead did say she could now remember the rapist sported a tattoo on his right forearm. She couldn't be sure but she felt it had something to do with the army."

"Not the SAS?"

He grinned. "Hardly that – though, as you said before, Angie, he is athletic. You wanted to see me?"

"Yes. I do. I didn't want to say this over the phone in case it caused you some distress. What I want from you, Mark, is to travel on the underground tonight, on the route that stops at Kensal Green, say between eleven and one in the morning, and see if you can't identify our psychopath. Travel backwards and forwards – that is, first go to Willesden Junction, if he isn't there at first then go back to London and get the first train back again to Willesden. He may be going each way, hoping he might spot a target.

"If you do see him he will no doubt be eying up a pretty girl travelling on her own. She will get off at Kensal Green and our suspect will follow her. At that point make sure you call for back-up. Wait until he snatches her and drags her into an alley before you apprehend him.

"Is that clear, Mark?"

He frowned at me. "Clear, yes. But it all sounds pretty bloody weird to me, Angie. I mean, how do you know this is going to happen? Especially tonight, and especially at Kensal Green?"

I knew this was coming, but the only answer I could give was the policeman's best friend.

"You don't expect me to disclose my source, do you?"

"What? Well, no, of course not. But it seems strange to me that someone should be so well informed."

"Will you do it?"

He shrugged. "You're the boss. Yeah. Okay, I'll do it. When do you want me to report?"

"If nothing happens tonight – and I have to make clear that it might not be tonight – then you can leave it until Monday. But if anything should happen then call me on my mobile, straight away."

He went away still shaking his head. I took myself off for a light lunch and then for my bath, trying not to let the memo upset me. But I would have to say something to Jim on Monday before Glasson tried to dig his claws into me.

* * * * * *

As it happened I did have a pleasant afternoon, relaxing in a perfumed bath and tarting myself up. I decided, on reflection, not to overdo it, as I was meeting Kelly at one of her places of work. So I dressed in a beige trouser suit, which was fashionable but not over the top; I had on a white blouse, an artificial pearl necklace, my favourite earrings and a touch of my special perfume, which I knew was sensual. I arrived at Selfridges shortly after 6.0 p.m., pleased that we had enjoyed a fine spring day. She was waiting for me beside the perfume counter. The store was just about to close.

She came up to me and gave me a kiss on the cheek. "Lovely to see you, Angie. You're looking very nice."

"You too, Kelly. I've dressed for the occasion – you don't think it's too much, do you?"

She shook her head, smiling. "You look simply perfect."

She took my arm and steered me out of the store. "Shall we start with a drink?"

"That would be nice. But I'm not sure where we can go. I only know the dives around here where the gangsters hang out!"

She giggled. "Leave it to me! I know some nice bars off Regent Street; we could relax there, have a couple of drinks, and then go on to dinner. Have you been to Langhams's, near Piccadilly?"

"I haven't, no. But I've heard of it. But have you got a reservation?"

"Of course. I'm quite well known in this part of town."

* * * * * *

The bar was a lavish cocktail lounge; it was early so there weren't many customers about, but I did notice, again, that they were all same-sex couples. Kelly certainly did know her way around town. We spent around an hour in the lounge and then took a taxi to Langhams's. The place was very busy but they recognised Kelly as a regular customer and seated us in what I believe was a quiet corner; that meant there weren't any other couples within hearing distance. I must confess I was beginning to get a little worried about my companion. She was well into the lesbian scene, and that was not something I wanted to involve myself in.

"How come you're so well known in these places?" I asked as we sat down at the table.

She laughed. "I suppose it's partly because I associate with the pink crowd – afterwards I'll take you to a pub in Soho – and partly because I'm a well-known designer. Why? Does it bother you?"

"Yes, Kelly. It does," I said indignantly. "I thought we were going to have a kind of one-to-one relationship. I didn't realise I'd have to share you with the pink crowd."

She looked at me as though I had shocked her. "There must be some misunderstanding, Angie. Haven't you come out yet?"

"No, I haven't. And there's no likelihood that is going to happen. You have to remember, I am a senior police officer and I really don't think it would go down well if it got about that I was gay.

"Actually, I'm not gay," I went on to insist defensively; "I'd have to say I was more bisexual than a full lesbian."

I got up from the table. "This is all very embarrassing!" was all I could say.

Kelly got up with me. "You can say that again!" she snapped. "You might have said something earlier." She shrugged. "End of a not too beautiful friendship. Bye, Angie."

With that she walked out, leaving me to explain to the headwaiter why we wouldn't be needing the table. I was damned if I was going to eat there on my own. I couldn't afford it, anyway.

I almost crawled my way to Green Park underground, hoping that no one would see me. I felt absolutely devastated. But it was my own fault, for not clearing the air with her from the start. Kelly must have assumed that I had 'come out', but the subject just hadn't come up; I doubted if I could have handled it.

Still – there might be hope for me yet. I might actually find another fella!

* * * * * *

I got a takeaway from a nearby Chinese and dined at home in front of the telly. God, Saturday night was either all about Eve, or another Come Dancing – or something like it. I decided I would have yet another early night. I went to bed feeling despondent, even a little depressed: the one-day I had been looking forward to had ended in disappointment.

CHAPTER EIGHTEEN

I had completely forgotten about Mark Reed. That is, until I was woken up by the telephone.

"Ms Crossley?" a voice asked me.

"Yes. Who is it?"

"This is Inspector Wallace of Kensal Green police station. We found your number in the wallet of a Mark Reed."

"Mark?!" By now I was wide awake. "What has happened? Is he alright?"

There was a pause. Then he said, "He does work for you, doesn't he?"

"Of course he does. Will you please tell me what has happened to him?"

"Well, I'm afraid he's been attacked. He has serious knife wounds to his abdomen and at present he is in Willesden General Hospital undergoing surgery."

I couldn't speak for a moment, too shocked at the news. "Who attacked him, inspector? Was it out of the blue?"

"We have a young woman here who informs us that she was grabbed by a man, a stranger, and dragged into an alleyway off the main road. Your Inspector Reed heard her screams, went to intervene and was stabbed in the stomach. I'm told that the knife wound penetrated his liver; he's in a bad way."

"Oh, fucking hell! Where are you now, inspector?" I was completely stunned.

"I'm at Kensal Green police station. Two of my officers travelled with him to the hospital. Do you know where it is?"

"No. But if I come to the police station can you show me the way?"

"Yes. Of course, chief inspector. I'll await your arrival."

As soon as I put down the phone I called the Yard and ordered a patrol car; five minutes, I was told.

I could not believe this. I had told him specifically to call for back-up as soon as the girl was snatched. And now the poor sod could be at death's door. Christ almighty, what a disaster, for Mark and his family, and for the unit. I prayed that he would be alright.

I grabbed some clothes from the closet, not the same ones I had worn during the day, and went downstairs to await the police car. When it arrived I instructed the two constables to go to Kensal Green police station with sirens flashing. By now it was around one o'clock in the morning; it took us only ten minutes to get there. Inspector Wallace was waiting outside for me so we used the same transport. He gave directions to the constables and we arrived at the hospital a few minutes later.

Mark was still in the operating theatre; there was no news yet on his injuries. I decided to wait and send the constables and the inspector back to the station. I dreaded this, but I had no choice but to ring the commander.

" Who's that?" a voice mumbled irritably.

"Jim – it's Ange here."

"I hope this is fucking important," he snapped.

"Jim. Mark Reed has had an accident..." – a daft use of the word. "He's been stabbed."

"What? Where was this? Where is he?"

"He's in Willesden Hospital undergoing surgery. He was trying to rescue a young woman who was about to be raped when the man stabbed him." I was close to tears. but I managed to swallow them back.

"Oh, shit! Where was this, Ange?" By now he was wide awake.

So I told him. I told him about my vision and how I had instructed Mark to travel on the train to Willesden Junction that night, and as it happened I was proved right.

"You and your fucking visions," he said scathingly. "Why didn't you tell him to call for back-up?"

"But I did. I gave him specific instructions that as soon as he saw the man he was to call for back-up. He ignored me."

"So you say. Where are you now?"

I gasped; I couldn't believe that he doubted me. "I'm at the hospital. Mark is in the operating theatre – they think his liver has been punctured."

"Stay there. I'll be with you as soon as I can."

As I put the phone down I burst into tears, glad that no one could see me. Poor Mark. What the hell was he thinking? And Jim – trying to suggest I hadn't given Mark instructions for back-up. But even if this were true this man was a professional copper – an inspector, no less; he would surely have known what to do in those circumstances. Unless he thought he might become a hero. I dried my eyes with a tissue and took a seat in the waiting room.

Jim arrived about a half an hour later, dressed in his old jeans, a T-shirt and trainers. He would never have passed as a commander at New Scotland Yard.

He scowled at me, obviously angry. " You'd better tell me again what happened."

"There's nothing I can add, Jim. I've told you everything – I had the dream, or the vision, last night. It seemed there was a sense of urgency to it so I decided I would act on it straight away. So I sent Mark on that train last night. I never believed this would happen.'

"Have you seen the doctors yet?" He was still angry; in fact, 'furious' would be a better description.

"No. I'm still waiting. They know I'm here." I turned away trying to hide my tears.

"And the rapist? I take it he escaped?"

"Yes. It was the girl who reported it to the police; that's how they found my phone number."

"Has anyone put out a bulletin for this man?"

"Yes. Inspector Wallace at Kensal Green; but I think it will be too late, he'll have long gone."

Just then a doctor appeared; his coat was bloodstained.

"Are you waiting to hear about Mr Reed?"

I nodded. "Is he going to be alright, doctor?"

"It's too early to tell. His liver was badly damaged; we've tried to repair it but we won't know if we've been successful for another couple of days."

"Can I see him?" I asked.

He shook his head. "No. We've transferred him to Intensive Care. If you leave it for another 24 hours you might be able to see him then. But I have to tell you both, he is in a critical condition. Has his family been informed?"

Jim looked at me, expecting I would confirm that his wife had been notified. When I shook my head his mouth fell open in astonishment. "You're kiddin' me, right?"

"I don't have his home phone number – only his mobile." I hesitated, still in shock. "Inspector Wallace gave me his wallet; I'll check if it's in here." I went to one side to telephone Mrs Reed, and as gently as I could I broke the news to here. I then arranged, through the Yard, for a police car to collect her from her mother's, where she would leave the baby.

"We'll come back again tomorrow, but if there is any news will you please ring me?" He handed over his card with his mobile number on the back to the doctor.

"Yes, commander, I'll do that."

* * * * * *

"Why did you send him on his own?" Jim wanted to know when we were in the car. "Why didn't you give him a colleague?"

I sighed, still heavy with tears. "Because I wasn't sure whether it was a vision or a dream."

"What? You mean, after your vision of the bank robbers? And you still weren't sure?"

"Jim, give me a break, will you? I'm having a hard time of this as it is without you going on and on."

"Sure. But not as bad as Mark Reed."

There was silence after that.

CHAPTER NINETEEN

I got to the office early on the Monday morning and announced the news to the rest of the team. There was a shocked silence. The attack had now made the national newspapers, although no details were listed, other than the name of Mark Reed, detective inspector, of Scotland Yard. No doubt Jim would be pestered now for a press release and any information he could give about the rapist.

Sam asked me, "I don't understand, Angie – what made you send him on his own on that particular train?"

There it is again," I thought: "'on his own'.

"I don't know; it just occurred to me that that was the route the killer had taken before so I guessed he would follow it."

He stared at me, his lips curling over. "That's some presumption," he said sarcasm in his voice.

Sally tried to change the subject, "Is this some kind of a gift you have, Angie?" she wanted to know.

I still had to talk to her about the autopsy and what Chief Inspector Givens had to say. I also wanted to know – at some time – why Jim had instructed her to make the 'anonymous' phone call regarding the bank robbers.

I just shrugged. There wasn't a lot more I could say or wanted to say.

"I'm going down to the hospital shortly," I said. "Sam, will you check with Kensal Green, see if they've had any response to last night' s APB?"

There was a message from downstairs. Superintendent Glasson wanted to see me urgently. No doubt Jim must have told him about last night's incident. I ignored the request and set off for the hospital.

It was a different doctor from last night who I questioned.

"I'm afraid he's still in intensive care,' he informed me. "His wife is with him."

"Can I see him, please?"

"Well, just for a minute, but you won't get anything out of him – we have him on a ventilator."

Before I entered the intensive care unit I saw his wife sitting outside, a handkerchief held over her eyes. I introduced myself and mumbled my apologies, but other than that we didn't speak. Then I saw this man lying in the bed surrounded by tubes and breathing through a ventilator, and it wasn't the man who I used to know. He was so pale and fragile my eyes filled up. I sat at the side of his bed and held his hand.

"Why, Mark? Why didn't you call for back-up? Oh, dear God, what have I done to you?"

A hand took hold of my arm. It was the doctor's. "I think you should leave now, miss. Call again later in the day; we may have some news then."

* * * * * *

It was lunchtime when I got back to the Yard. I decided to miss it; my stomach couldn't face the thought of food. A second note was on my desk, this time from Jim asking me to see Superintendent Glasson. I sighed. I suppose I'd better get it over with.

The black man was at his desk – it was as if he had been waiting for me. He looked at me, a contemptuous smirk on his face. I felt like hitting him.

"Chief Inspector Crossley, I have referred your performance in the matter of Inspector Reed to the deputy assistant commissioner, and on his authority you are hereby suspended from all duties."

He had been reading it out from a sheet in front of him.

"That didn't take long, did it?" He smirked again.

"You can't do this, you arrogant little prick," I snapped at him. "You don't have the authority."

He stood up from the desk. "Come with me," he said.

I had no choice but to follow him. I was literally shaking with anger. We went up the stairs to the third floor, where he knocked on the door of Jim's office.

"Enter," Jim announced.

"Commander, I have given instructions that Chief Inspector Crossley, here, is suspended, and she informs me that I don't have the authority. Perhaps you'd care to enlighten her."

Jim looked at me, almost with pity.

"I'm sorry Ange, but there is nothing I can do."

"Where does he get his authority from, Jim? You told me I reported only to you."

"Well, there was a memo from the deputy assistant commissioner…"

"And you didn't think to refer it to me? Is that it?"

"Well, yes, but be that as it may, I've checked the hospital this morning and Inspector Reed is still in a critical condition, and, at the moment, we have only your word that you gave him back-up instructions at the time. So, under the circumstances, I am obliged to suspend you. I still believe we can work this out, given time. Will you please leave your warrant card with Superintendent Glasson?"

"Dear God! I don't believe this." My hands were now trembling, and I started to feel faint. I genuinely couldn't believe that this was happening to me.

"Do you really think I would send one of my officers out on a stalking trip without asking him to call for back-up?"

Jim looked at me, a solemn and absorbed look on his face. "No. I don't. But, as I have said, with only your word for the back-up instructions – at least for the time being – then, as a matter of course, I am obliged to suspend you."

"And do you really believe that an officer of Mark Reed's standing wouldn't have had the sense, in those circumstances, to call for back-up on his own initiative? Or do you actually believe he's an idiot?" My lips were shaking as well now, and Jim could see I was obviously deeply upset at the action he was taking.

He shrugged, almost in slow motion. "I'm sorry, Ange, but the matter has been taken out of my hands. You are now relieved of your duties."

I took my badge and placed it on his desk. "You're telling me you couldn't protest against that plonker upstairs? You just allowed this to happen?"

"Ange, I tried to tell you last night; what the hell were you doing sending out an officer on his own without support? There should have been two of them there, then this wouldn't have happened."

At this I walked out. I walked out of the building – with an escort I hadn't asked for – and I walked out of my job. As I had said before to Commander Robbins, there was no way I would ever report to that arsehole Glasson. I tried to shrug it off but for the second time that morning I was close to tears.

I felt that Jim had betrayed me; I wasn't even allowed to say goodbye to Sam and the others. And I had never been sacked from a job before. And what really pissed me off was that I now had to leave – up in the air – the cases of the rapist/killer and the paedophile.

So it was goodbye to my flat as well; there was no way I could afford to live there now, and after the debacle last night with Kelly there was no way I wanted to. And I certainly had no intentions of trying to get another job in London. But, at the moment, I didn't know where to go, and I still had the visions to contend with. What would I do if I had a further one about the rapist? I had no idea, but one thing I had to do before I left the city was to go back to Willesden General and see how Mark was getting on.

Fortunately, he was slightly improved; still in a critical condition but nevertheless stable. I felt better about this, and I really hoped he would be back to normal soon.

Leaving the hospital I returned to my flat, and started to pack. The only thing I could think of was that I might be able to return to Warwick University and ask for my old job back. Failing that, I would ask for a teaching job in another part of the country. It did cross my mind to go and stay with my mother in Gloucester, except that her latest boyfriend drove me to distraction.

I set off for Warwick that afternoon after leaving a note for my landlord. Goodbye, London. What was it Kelly had said to me last night: "The end of a not too beautiful friendship"?

I left, tears streaming down my face at the shock I had received.

CHAPTER TWENTY

Having said my muted farewell to London I set off in my old banger towards the Midlands. Before I got onto the M1, however, my mobile went off. It was Jim. I decided to ignore it; there was nothing I wanted to say to him and I certainly didn't want to listen to his excuses. It rang and rang and rang until eventually I turned it off.

I stopped at Watford Gap, just before I turned off onto the M6, and dried my tear-stained face. I had had no lunch and I was feeling hungry. There were a couple of messages from Jim, the last urging me not to be too hasty as this was something he could sort out. Like hell he could! There was a further message from Sam, saying: "What the fuck has happened?" I rang him back.

"Sam, it's Angie. Sorry I wasn't able to say goodbye to you and the others but I really had no choice. I was escorted out of the premises after being suspended from duty."

"Fucking hell, Angie!" He sounded shocked, as if he couldn't believe the news. "What happened? Did you try and shoot that bastard Glasson?"

"No, but he was part of it. Jim Robbins told him about the fracas with Mark, so he went upstairs to his favourite DAC and got me suspended."

"What did the commander say? Surely he must have defended you?"

"I'm afraid not, Sam – just a minute, I'm paying for my meal."

"Where are you?"

"I'm at the Watford Gap service station; I'm on my way back to Warwick University, hoping I might get my old job back."

"You can't just fucking leave," he said, angrily.

"Look, Sam, if Jim Robbins had supported me then I might have felt differently. But he didn't. He more or less told me that to send Mark out on his own was a dereliction of duty. In other words, I was responsible."

"What – for the actions of a detective inspector?" I could almost see him frowning. "I can't believe this. He should have enough nous to have called for back-up without you telling him. I'm going to see the commander and tell him what I think..."

"No, don't do that, Sam! You'll only get yourself into more trouble. Say goodbye to the others for me, won't you?"

I ended the call.

It was late evening when I got to Warwick; I wasn't sure whether to leave it overnight or literally go and knock on the door. "Fuck it," I said to myself; "they can only say 'no'."

Surprisingly, and this cheered me up no end, I was greeted with a ready welcome. The dean grinned at me, and told me that some of the tutors had placed bets on how long I would stay in London!

"Did anyone win?"

"I don't think so, Angie," he remarked, "but we didn't believe you would stay very long at all; but even this has surprised us. Anyway, welcome back. I do have to tell you, though, that your Commander Robbins has been on the phone to me. He says you are refusing to accept his calls, and please will you speak to him?"

The dean was a venerable old gentleman in his mid-60s, with an academic air about him. He was someone you couldn't help but admire and have affection for.

"I'm not surprised he discovered I was here – but I have nothing to say to him."

"Shall I tell him that if he rings again? Which I am sure he will do."

"Yes please, if you don't mind. Is my old job available?"

"Of course it is; we haven't had time yet to publicise it. But if you are agreeable, Angie, I would prefer that you just rest here for a few days – collect your thoughts. If you wish you could deliver one of your lectures to the group approaching graduation; I'm sure they'd be delighted. Oh, and by the way, your old room is still available."

What a lovely old man, I thought. And he was right – I really did need a rest.

"Thank you, dean, that would please me too. And I'm not sorry to have said goodbye to the police force."

"You can tell me all about it tomorrow. I'll get one of the porters to help you with your baggage"

I didn't open my phone; I didn't care who might have tried to contact me. What I needed was another long soak in the bath, followed by a good night's sleep.

* * * * * *

That night I had another vision. It wasn't about anything in particular, except that Katy appeared to me as an apparition, smiling as ever.

"What is it you want from me, Katy?"

"I don't want anything, Angie. I'm here to support you."

"Really? And, you know, there was I thinking it was you who had managed to get me the sack."

"You mean with the vision about the train?"

I nodded. I was too weary to say anything more.

"That was an unusual situation, Angie. It wasn't the fault of either of us that your inspector decided he didn't need to call for back-up. Anyway, don't worry about it; I'm sure it will sort itself out. By the way, I am now your Spirit Guide. Nice, isn't it?"

I looked at her, puzzled. "Aren't you a bit young for that? I thought Spirit Guides were old and ancient."

"I have had many incarnations, Angie; I am far older than you imagine. Now I am with you to guide you through this ephemeral maze. What you will see is what your psychic self imagines. After that it is up to you, except that if you ignore the visions they will never leave you."

"So I have to do something if I'm to get any peace?"

"Yes. But I will help you."

"So what about these visions I have of the rapist and the killer? What am I supposed to do about them?"

"Well, you won't have to worry about him for a while; he has now gone into hiding. But he will return in time, I promise you. There is also the other matter of the paedophile in the south. He will have to be dealt with."

"When? And how? You do realise I'm no longer with the police force?"

She smiled again – something that, at this moment, infuriated me. "That too will be resolved, my dear.

"For the moment you need to rest, Angie. It will come to you in time."

And then the vision disappeared; leaving me with those hypnotic olive eyes of the rapist I had dreamt of before. After that I slept the whole night through.

* * * * * *

The next morning I felt refreshed, more than I had done in days. It was as though the night's sleep had blown the cobwebs of London out of my mind, and that I was home again.

Before I had breakfast and greeted my old colleagues I rang the hospital, to enquire how Mark was getting along. It was good news. He was now off the danger list; still in intensive care, but making good progress. That was a huge relief.

It was nice to receive such a warm welcome from the other tutors; evidently, after the Manchester incidents, which had made the local papers, I was now something of a celebrity, and they all made a point of coming to talk to me. I began to relax.

It didn't take too long before the dean came up to me and said that word had got around that I was no longer with the police force, and Midland TV had contacted him and asked if I would be prepared to do an interview.

"Why would they want to interview me?" I asked, genuinely puzzled.

"Well, they appear to have some information that you were instrumental in capturing an arsonist in Manchester, and they want to know what your secret is."

"But that was simply detective work."

"That may be so, my dear, but they did mention clairvoyance – if that means anything to you."

I tried to laugh. "That's absurd, dean. I've no idea where they got that from. But I'm damned if I'll let them interview me. I hope you said as much."

"I will do. I'll let you finish your breakfast."

It will be a nightmare if the media started chasing me.

I went up to my room and began preparing for my lecture. I still had the case histories of the paedophile and the rapist on my computer. I was tempted to erase them, but then I thought of the message I had had from Katy. Were I to do that the visions might return to haunt me. So I ran through them, wondering how Sally had got on interviewing Inspector Givens; I also thought about the autopsy she was due to attend on the murdered child. These were important issues that should not be left up in the air. I suppose if I were asked how I was feeling at that moment I would have to say I was in a dichotomous situation: part of me wanted me to discharge my responsibilities to that young boy and the murdered girls, whilst the other part of me was intensely angry at the way I had been treated.

Still, there was nothing I could do. It had been taken out of my hands now, regardless of what I might have to say about the subject.

I went back to my lecture, writing and rewriting the text of what I would say. After that I went for a walk around the grounds of this lovely old university.

CHAPTER TWENTY-ONE

The following few days I rang Willesden Hospital each morning to check on Mark; I was pleased that he was slowly recovering and was now out of intensive care and back into a main ward.

I finalised the notes of my lecture, and then decided that I would ring Sally and hear her news about the autopsy of the young boy.

"Angie?" she said, in a shocked voice. "Where are you – are you coming back?"

"Hi, Sally. I'm at Warwick. And, no, I don't see how I can come back after I was sacked."

"That isn't what the commander is saying. He says you were temporarily suspended because of Glasson's interference, supported by only having your word about the back-up instructions; evidently he's now dealing with it."

I let out a heavy sigh, deliberately so that she could hear it over the phone. "Sally, it was the commander who suspended me. He accused me of sending Mark out on his own on the Kensal Green train. I don't really care what he's saying now; as far as I'm concerned he and I are a broken record."

"So, tell me, only because it's been concerning me: what happened during your visit to Wembley? I wasn't able to read your file; I was going to read it on the Sunday, but that didn't happen."

"That's disappointing, Angie," she said, sadness in her voice. "If you'd read it I'm sure you would have come to the same conclusion I did – that this case is so serious we will have to take it. Evidently there was some semen found in the boy's anus and we now have DNA; but whoever it is he doesn't show up on the sex register or in our files.

"But what are we going to do without you? There's no one here who can deal with it."

"I'm really sorry about that, Sally. It certainly wasn't of my choosing. But I'm sure Jim will find you a suitable replacement."

"Shall I send you the file? We could do with your views on it. I've talked to Sam and he agrees."

I thought about it for a moment. It wouldn't do any harm, and I did feel I had a residual responsibility. After all, it was original my case.

"Yes. Why don't you do that, Sally? You know my address?"

"Of course. I'll send it off today – unless, of course, you have a fax."

"Yes, we do have one."

I gave her the number, and was about to say goodbye when she said, "Do you think you might come back, Angie?"

"I don't think so. Not unless that arsehole Glasson goes. Anyway, I'll get back to you on the paedophile case. Bye, Sally."

I read the file with a mixture of horror and dread. Horrors that some unknown perpetrator had savagely attacked the child and treated him to such suffering, and dread that this was one of the cases it was prophesied that I would have to deal with. I wasn't even sure how I was going to deal with it; perhaps I should let the future visions counsel me.

* * * * * *

Two days later, some ten days after my dismissal from the force, I was standing in front of a crowded assembly hall, giving my lecture to the pre-graduation students. Most of the lecture was by the book; something they could have read in many of the manuals. But, from time to time, I changed the slant of what I was saying and interspersed it with my own experience. I centred on the arsonist attack in Manchester and how it was plain deduction, based upon my experience as a profiler, which led me to the pyromaniac and the murderer.

I was asked a question from the hall about the type of deductive reasoning I had adopted. "Surely, if it was as easy as you imply, then why did the Manchester police send for you?"

"You're not working for Midland Television, are you?" I asked, straight-faced.

There was laughter. But the questioner persisted. My answer did not satisfy him.

I continued, "You have asked a very good question, except now you are asking me to disclose my informants. And, as you will learn, in the criminal profilers' handbook that is something you must never do." Not a very good reply, but it was the best I could come up with in a difficult situation.

Finally, I ended on the work I was doing in the rapist/murderer's case and how I had sent Mark Reed alone on the train to Cricklewood that Saturday night, and how he tried to rescue a young girl and received a serious stab wound to his liver; how he had been in intensive care with a life-threatening condition and how, as a result, I had been sacked from the police force because I had sent him on his own.

"But didn't you give him notice of back-up?" a questioner asked.

"Yes, I did. But he chose to ignore it.

"So, ladies and gentlemen, my advice to each of you who might be considering joining the police force as a profiler is – don't! We are individuals who have our own special talents and they cannot be subordinated to the bureaucracy of the police. Stay on your own if you wish to become a profiler, employ your talents when the motivation stimulates you and charge the police a fortune for your skills. Thank you very much, everybody."

As they stood to applaud a loud voice spoke up, so everyone could hear him; I was astonished to see that it was the commander: "What Angela says is not entirely true. There are facts that you might like to hear about."

This was Jim, dressed in his commander's uniform, speaking with the voice of authority!

"First of all, she was not sacked; she was suspended as a matter of course since an officer was injured in her care. She was also subjected to an unfair attack from one of her superiors, a superintendent who has since been replaced. Furthermore, as the officer who was injured is now in a stable condition, and has apologised to Angela for not obeying her instructions to call for back-up (he was attempting to become a hero), we can now reinstate her.

"Let me say something of a personal nature, regardless of what she has just said to you about the police. I encouraged Ange to join us at the National Serious Crimes Unit, because I knew full well precisely what her talents are and how the unit cannot function without her with the same strength and resolve.

"So I urge her to reconsider her position – to come back with me to London. Her team misses her and without her special talents there will be many a perpetrator who will be allowed to escape free.

"Thank you for listening."

Instead of me getting the standing ovation they rose to salute Jim Robbins, and stood on their feet for longer than I might have expected.

After we had left the hall Jim took my hand. "What I had to say in there was sincere, Ange. Your suspension was a matter of course – it would have been the same had you shot someone. And Glasson has been relieved and another chief inspector has taken his place.

"And, fuck me, Ange, we do miss you. So, please, will you come back with me? You can leave your old banger here and come in my car."

I didn't know what to say. Except for 'yes'. Much as I disliked London, the job was beginning to give me some immense satisfaction – and I still had my clairvoyance to contend with.

"Let me get my things, Jim. And thank you, for standing up there, in public, and saying what you did. I'll have to find another flat, but that won't be a tragedy."

"The welfare office can help you there; I think you'll be better off this side of the river."

I agreed.

* * * * * *

Before we could depart the dean came out to see me off. He kissed me on both cheeks, which made me blush; he had never done that before.

"Now, my dear, I'm rather glad that the commander appeared and that you're now going back to London with him. And don't worry; you'll soon get over your dislike of the city.

"What I wanted to say to you, Angela, is I hope you will always think of Warwick as your home; we will be here when you need us and your room will always be available if you just fancy a few days' break."

"Thank you, Dean Foster; you've been very kind and I will always think of you and the other tutors who've made me so welcome."

"Bye, my dear; and take care, won't you?"

"Bye, dean"

CHAPTER TWENTY-TWO

The journey back to London was a kind of transformation for me; as opposed to my old banger, here I was sitting in the back of a luxury limousine with Jim, whilst a uniformed driver was chauffeuring us. Jim handed me back my warrant card without comment.

"If you don't mind my asking, how did you manage to get rid of Glasson?"

"I don't mind you asking at all – as long as you keep it to yourself. I went over the head of the deputy assistant commissioner."

I looked at him with a new light. "What? Direct to the commissioner? Hell, Jim, that must have taken some courage."

He shrugged. "It was either that or else he would have walked all over us. As it was, I think the commissioner agreed with your assessment of his deputy."

"You mean he's a plonker?"

He laughed. "He didn't say so in so many words, but yes."

"So," he said to me after a while, "how are your visions going? Had any of late?"

I nodded. "Are you sure you want me to talk about them here?" I asked, pointing to the driver.

He closed the dividing window. "We'll be alright now – he can't hear."

"Well, yes, I've had one further vision. But it wasn't prophetic like the others were. This was to tell me that I needed to rest for a few days, but then they would start to appear..."

"...And?" he said, enquiringly.

"What was said to me was that if I ignored them they will haunt me for ever. In other words, Jim, I have to take notice of them or I will have nightmares."

"I see. Is there anything I can do to help?"

"Yes, there is. First off, I'm glad to be coming back to the police force; I wasn't sure how I would manage the visions if I were on my own. And, second, you can give me all the support I believe I will need."

"Of course I will. But, Ange, you have to talk to me. Don't keep these secrets to yourself. And, if you wish, this will be our secret if you don't want me to tell any of the others."

"Thank you," I said, as his mobile went off.

"Robbins. Hi, Sam. What can I do for you?"

He turned to me. "Yes. She's here with me in the car. We should be back by mid-afternoon. What? Oh, right. Here she is.

"It's Sam," he said, handing me the phone; "he wants a word with you."

"Hi, Sam. What? Yes, I'm fine, thank you. No, I'll tell you all about it when I get back. What can I do for you?

"I see. When was this? This morning. And where was the body discovered? Ashridge Park? You'll have to tell me where that is, Sam; I have no idea."

I turned to Jim. "They appear to have found the body of Robert Sanford; he's the little boy who disappeared from his school in Wembley about five or six weeks ago."

"Where was he found – Ashridge Park?"

"Yes."

"I know where it is. It's in Berkshire. We can be there in less than an hour."

I went back to the phone. "Sam, we can be there in less than an hour. How was the boy discovered? A deer? A deer kicked over the traces of his grave?" I shook my head. "Look, we'll head there now; before we get to the park I'll give you a ring on the mobile and you can direct us. Yeah. Thanks, Sam."

"You heard that, I take it?" I said. But Jim was already giving instructions to the driver.

"Is this something you've been alerted to?" he asked.

"No, not in so many words – although I was given a warning that it would come up. Other than that I have no knowledge."

We didn't talk for the rest of the journey, until Jim said, "You can ring him now, we're almost there."

We were in a tree-shrouded lane with thick forest either side of us; the trees seemed to be closing in on me they were so dense.

"Tell him we're close to Ashridge golf course – we'll meet him there."

Which I did. Sam told me the body wasn't too far away. He also informed me that he had Sally with him, which I was glad about.

* * * * * *

We left Jim's car at the golf club and travelled in Sam's police vehicle – with three of us in the back. After some ten minutes we drew up alongside a number of police cars, and we were led to where a taped-off area, in dense woods, that was concealed. It was then that something hit me. Out of nowhere I sensed the evil that hovered over the scene.

"Leave me alone," I said to the others. "And, please, ask the police and the forensics team to step aside. I want to observe this for myself."

"What does she mean?" I heard Sally ask. No one answered her, but everyone did step aside.

After a few steps I could see the body protruding from thick undergrowth. Had it not been for the inquisitive deer Robert could have laid there forever. Hesitatingly, I took the few paces I required for the grave site to envelope me. It was like a cloud of evil descending and wrapping itself around me. There was no way I could escape from this pervading cloak of malevolence. There were shapes all around me, figures I couldn't distinguish, but they seemed to be pointing at me, trying to tell me something.

I knelt down and touched the body of Robert, and when I did it was as though he pulsated in front of me. I was sure I could see him move a fraction, as if I had breathed new life into him.

I stayed at the scene for a few moments until I had a sense of consummation with the body, and I was able to discern the terrible sequence of events that had happened here. Then I joined the others.

"Anything?" Jim asked.

"No. Not yet. Except the man who carried this out is a stranger to these shores. He was not born here."

"You mean he's an alien," Sally said.

"Yes. I believe he's from the East, but I could be guessing." I wasn't, of course, but I didn't want to tell them that. "You won't find him on any British sex register either, and if I'm right, and he is from, say, Poland, then I doubt we'll find him there either."

"How do you know this, Angie?" Sam wanted to know. "Did you deduce that from the scene?"

I nodded. "There is nothing other than his residue remaining by now. A lot of the traces of him have disappeared. But he is an older man – probably in his early 50s. And he is pathologically evil. You don't need me to tell you that."

"I'm sorry, Angie, but I don't understand this," Sam said. The expression on Sally's face indicated that she tended to agree with him.

"Do you think you should say something, Ange?" Jim said. "Otherwise they'll think all this is serendipity."

I looked at him, as though he were a stranger. They all were strangers at this moment in my life.

"You're right, of course. I sense things," I announced. "It isn't as if I have visions or anything like that, it's just that – well, I can't explain it; I just sense things. And if it gets out around the squad it will hurt not only me but also the unit." It was as near as I could get without disclosing my true self. At least this might be something they could understand.

"And it will annoy me," Jim added harshly. "I've protected Ange through these personal phenomena, and I do not want anyone, other than the three of us, to share them. Am I clear?"

"Yes, sir," they both agreed.

"Is it okay if we ask questions?" Sally said.

"Of course, Sally. You don't have to be frightened of me."

She smiled. "Oh, I'm more frightened of my dog than I am of you, Angie. It's just that I wanted to ask you if that is what you saw about the rapist – you know, the one on the Willesden underground."

"No. That was simply police deduction. And I have to tell you that this 'sensing' thing of mine won't help us to catch criminals; sometimes, like now, it might steer us in the right direction, but it is still left to us to apprehend them." I looked around at the scene again, and shivered. "See if you can find out when the autopsy is going to be, will you, Sally? I would like to attend."

She went across to the medical examiner and exchanged words with him (this time it was a man).

"Probably tomorrow. About eleven. It will be in Wembley. I've arranged for us both to go – if that's alright?"

"Yes. Perhaps it will give us a better time of death." I looked at Jim. "Shall we go back, commander?"

He nodded. We got into the police car and returned to Jim's car.

* * * * * *

The journey back was mostly silent, other than Jim asking me why I had changed my stance.

"Because I would hate for people to guess that I'm a psychic. Every time a crime occurs they'll be asking me to second-guess the criminal. I couldn't stand that, Jim. Let them believe I have the same kind of idiosyncrasy as Danny O'Brien has."

"Yes. I clearly remember him – and you did seem to have something in common with him. Okay. We'll leave it at that. Where are you going to spend tonight?"

"There's a small hotel close to the Yard; I'll check in there. How long do you think it might take Welfare to find me a flat?"

"I'll put some pressure on them. I should think they'd have something for you to look at tomorrow or the day after. I'll let you know."

CHAPTER TWENTY-THREE

The hotel was quite nice – commercial and a bit dowdy, but reasonable. And it was in walking distance from the Yard. I checked in for a couple of nights, hoping I wouldn't need any longer than that. I had asked Jim if Welfare might find me a flat in Camden; I'd quite liked the look of that area when I went to visit Rachel Humphries.

The next morning Sally and I went to Wembley for the autopsy of Robert Sanford. Chief Inspector Givens was also there, waiting for us. So was Dr Sullivan, the medical examiner. I hadn't met her beforehand, but Sally, who had, told me that she was looking unusually strained, as if she were carrying the weight of Robert's body around on her shoulders. It was not for me to say anything.

It was a shock to see the little boy naked on the table. Parts of his body had started to decompose; his arms were stick-thin, and only one side of his head was still intact. I shuddered at what he must have gone through, but I tried to dismiss such thoughts, as I knew they wouldn't help my job.

Dr Sullivan took us through the autopsy, commenting on her microphone that, aside from the brutalisation of parts of his body, he was a healthy seven-year-old boy.

"As with Phillip, this boy has been buggered; his anus is ravaged, blood clots are still in evidence and there is semen lodged there. Cause of death is strangulation." She pointed to the deep scar marks on the skin from around his neck. "Fortunately," she went on, "for some reason we do not have knowledge of, his penis is untouched."

Again she pointed, this time to his open mouth. "However, if you examine the inside of his mouth you will see that it has been penetrated by the offender's penis, and, furthermore, there is evidential traces of semen deposited there."

Finally, she shook her head. "I really don't know what to say. This is one of the worst brutality cases I have ever dealt with, and I am finding it very hard to keep my composure."

With that she left the room. All of us in that room were shaking our heads, in disgust at what that monster had done to that little boy, and in sadness that such a young life had been snatched away out of innocence.

Outside, Chief Inspector Givens asked me, "Have you decided yet whether or not you will take the case?"

"Yes," I said determinedly, "the commander has instructed us to accept the case, Inspector Givens. We have the file, and I don't suppose there are any more details you have to pass on to us?"

"No," he said, "You have everything. And may I wish you good luck, chief inspector. I'm sure you'll want to contact me very shortly."

"Thank you."

We shook hands and Sally and I left in the patrol car.

On the journey back Sally asked me, "What are we going to do now, boss?"

"I've been thinking about that and my view is that we should contact the Polish Embassy."

"What the hell will we achieve there, Angie?" she asked, aggressively.

"I'm not sure. Except I believe that is where this bastard came from, and not that long ago."

"Okay. But if we contact the embassy aren't they likely to ask which part of Poland he comes from? I mean, does he come from Warsaw, or some other part? How will we know?"

"You'll have to trust me, Sally," I declared, somewhat self-consciously, "but our killer comes from Krakow."

"Fuck me, Angie, what are you like? I don't suppose there's any reason to ask you how you know that – is there?"

"No. Like I said, you have to trust my judgement. When we get back see if you can get hold of the Criminal Department in Krakow; the embassy will have the details. What we want to know is: does Krakow have a sex register? That's the first question we need answering. Second, if they don't have a register then do they have records of any criminal activity, especially..."

"...Yeah – with boys," Sally interrupted. "Okay, I'll get back to you."

* * * * * *

When we got back to the Yard a call had come in from Chief Inspector Givens that another boy had been snatched that afternoon from his school. This was the third possible victim.

Sam had just taken the call.

"I'm sorry," he said.

"What's his name?" I enquired.

"Joshua. Joshua Reynolds. He's eight years of age."

"How was he abducted?"

"I've only got what Givens has told me. Somehow, he was snatched at his school; his mother was waiting for him outside at three, but he wasn't there. The inspector doesn't know if he was taken between leaving the classroom and the gate where his mother was waiting, or before then."

"What does he mean, 'before then'?" I asked impatiently. "Is he suggesting someone took him from his classroom?"

"No. But there was assembly before the end of classes; he could have disappeared from there."

"That sounds more likely. Take Sally with you, Sam, and go and interview the chief inspector again. See what else there is that might help. No doubt he will have the force out searching for the boy?"

"Yes. He said if we wanted to speak to him he would be joining the army search teams, but we can get him on his mobile."

I sat down and thought about it for a few moments. Whoever this man was he must be a master of disguises. Three children disappeared, two of them now dead. Each from different areas of the town, one from his own home and two from their schools. The questions were going round in my head. How did he do it, without being seen? How did he know that Phillip's mother would be in the back garden, long enough for him to have had the nerve to sneak in and grab the child? How was he able to enter the schools, not one but two of them, and brazenly take two of the children away with him? And not be seen by anyone?

I shook my head in frustration, at the invisibility of the man.

"Sam, do you have Givens' mobile number?"

He handed it over.

"Chief inspector," I said after he had answered, "I've just been given news about Joshua's abduction. I realise you're out with the team searching for this man, but what I need to know is: did anyone, anyone either in the school or in the vicinity, see him? Any sign of his vehicle? Surely, someone must have spotted him – I thought it was almost impossible for a stranger to enter a school these days and snatch a youngster. I see, nothing. No one saw him, so the child must have simply vanished? Is that it?

"Well, I'm sorry too, inspector. I'm not blaming you, but I just can't believe that Joshua has vanished into thin air and no one has seen anything. Can you?"

I took the name of the school down and the address in Wembley, with some directions on how to get there.

I put the phone down after a while; the inspector knew nothing other than what he had already told us.

"Does he have anything to say?" Sam asked.

I shook my head. "Nothing. Go and check the school, Sam. Here is the address. Talk to the teachers, anyone who works there; I know the police will have spoken to them but insist, tell them we want to know first-hand. Check in the area; ask around, local shops, businesses — someone must have seen something. I cannot accept that a young boy can be snatched from his school without witnesses."

CHAPTER TWENTY-FOUR

"So, what do you think of our chief inspector?" Sam asked as they drove towards Wembley.

"Dunno," Sally answered. "I mean, it's all a bit weird, don't you think?"

"Sure is. What do you think she means by this 'sensing' thing? Have you ever heard of it? I haven't."

"No. But it might mean she's a kind of…well, psychic, or something like that."

"You mean clairvoyance?"

"I don't know what I mean, Sam. It isn't something I've had anything to do with. How about you? Are you familiar?"

"Is that a joke?"

"What? Oh, I see what you mean: a familiar." She laughed at the double entendre. "No, it wasn't a joke. I just wanted to know if you'd had any dealings with the psychic thing."

"Yeah, I did once. When I was over in Paddington we used a psychic to try and help us trace a serial killer. I was only a constable then. It was weird."

"Did it work? I mean, did you find the killer? Or was it like that profiler we had once – waste of fuckin' space?"

"No. She was quite good. We did find him eventually, and it was largely through her insight. She said she was having visions of the dead people. The chief didn't believe her – it wasn't his idea to bring her in – but she would blow your mind. And then we found him, just as he was about to finish off his next victim. So, if Angie's like that I wouldn't knock it."

"Well, it's certainly weird. She says that this paedophile comes from Krakow – how the hell she knows that, God only knows. I still have to get on to the Polish Embassy when I get back – or, at least, I will in the morning."

"Well, we'd better not let on that we've been having this conversation, or the commander will have our badges back."

"Do we know how to get to the school"

"Yes. St Joseph's. I've given Constable Hesketh a map; can't be far from here."

"Is that a Catholic school?" Sally asked.

"Yes, I believe so. We'll start there, shall we?"

The driver took them into the school's car park and they went into the grim-looking building. As they left Sam asked Frank Hesketh if he would ask around the area (there were some local shops in the vicinity) to see if anyone had heard or seen anything.

The headmistress was severely stressed out. She was a middle-aged woman, with short greying hair and pale green eyes. She looked to Sally as if she would burst into tears at any moment.

"Miss Griffin," Sam said as he introduced himself. "I know you'll have spoken to the local police but we're here from the Yard and we've taken over this case. So, I wonder if you'll be good enough to describe what has happened here – you know, anything, anything at all you can tell us."

"I...I don't know where to start," she said tearfully. "It was just a normal day. We had assembly before the school finished..."

"Was Joshua there?" Sally interrupted.

"I don't know... Er, he must have been, because his teacher didn't say anything. If he'd been missing she would surely have said something."

"So, in your opinion, Miss Griffin, you think he was snatched between the assembly rooms and the gate?"

She frowned between wiping her eyes. "Well, yes, I suppose. But how? There were all these children about; how could someone just appear among them and take Joshua. Wouldn't they have noticed?"

"How old are the children?" Sally enquired.

"Well, up to 11; then they go on to the senior school."

"Did you see anyone suspicious hanging around the school – either this morning or beforehand?"

She sniffed and wiped her eyes. "If there was I didn't notice. But I wasn't on duty in the playground; perhaps we should ask the teacher in charge."

She led them out of her study and along a long corridor to what was presumably the common room. One of the teachers was in the room, a distressed younger woman with tears streaming from her eyes; ordinarily she would have been attractive but now, with the child missing, her face was something of a mess. Sitting in one of the chairs was a second young woman, looking dazed. It was as if a thunderbolt had hit her; she was evidently Joshua's mother.

"Miss Thornton," the headmistress said, "these are two of the policemen from Scotland Yard; they want to talk to you." She then pointed across to the other distraught women. "That's Mrs Fennel, Joshua's mother. I don't think you'll get anything from her today. I've sent for the doctor – I think she should be sedated."

"Thank you," Sam said, at a loss what to say. It was Sally who took up the questioning.

"Miss Thornton, we were asking if you might have seen anyone suspicious hanging around the school – either before today, or possibly this morning?"

The teacher rubbed at her eyes and said nothing for a moment. Then she said, "I didn't notice anyone – but we're on quite a busy road and we don't notice any passers-by."

"Yes, but did you see anyone who wasn't familiar – someone whose face didn't quite fit?"

She shook her head. "No. I didn't notice anyone. I suppose during playtime I always have to watch out for the children. I try to watch over them – it isn't always easy, they run round such a lot."

"We're not blaming you, Miss Thornton," Sally said. "I'm afraid these things do happen – more than we'd like to think. But thank you for helping us."

As they left the common room the woman began crying again.

Frank Hesketh had some better news. A newsagent at the end of the block had seen a dark-coloured van pull away from the school at about the same time as the disappearance of Joshua. He didn't get the number but he thought there was something suspicious about it as the van sped away as if it was being chased. Frank had taken the name and number of the newsagent so that they could keep it on file.

"Anything else we can do here?" Sally asked.

"I don't think so," Sam said. "I believe the patrol police have canvassed the area for eyewitnesses. They obviously missed the fucking newsagents though, didn't they? And we didn't get much out of the school, did we?"

"About what we expected. These people are not private detectives – why should we want more from them?"

"Because sometimes they see things," Sam snapped. "Maybe they spot something unusual out of the corner of their eye, which, under questioning, they remember. You might want to bear that in mind, sergeant."

"Sorry. I didn't mean to be insensitive."

"Let's go back. It's getting late."

CHAPTER TWENTY-FIVE

I left the office quite early that afternoon. First I had to check on a couple of flats the Welfare Department had found for me in Camden. One thing I did learn from Jim was that the department would contribute towards the cost of the flat – something I hadn't been aware of beforehand. The first one I looked at was a bit on the drab side, so I shook my head; the second one, just behind Camden tube station, was more than acceptable. It had two bedrooms, a nice lounge that was comfortably furnished, a neat kitchen and a modern bathroom. I jumped at it, especially as I would be able to walk into the centre with all the shops and the restaurants. Even better, I could move in tomorrow.

That cheered me up no end. I bought The Standard at the station and saw in the advertising columns there was a spiritualist meeting just off the High Street. I had never been to one before and I was curious as to what went on, so I decided to attend.

There were only about 30 or so people in attendance when I got there. Feeling somewhat nervous, not knowing what might happen, I stood at the door. Then a satchel was thrust in front of me and a voice said, "That will be £5, please, but that pays for the raffle."

I paid him the money and went inside. Nothing happened for some five minutes, until a speaker announced, "We will sing a hymn, and afterwards we have Roselyn Shepherd with us to say a few words."

I was puzzled but nevertheless I picked up a hymn sheet on the chair and joined in Amazing Grace – wondering what this had to do with spiritualism. When we had all sat down again an elderly woman, with a deep, blue colour to her eyes, came up to the platform.

"I will move amongst you. If anything comes to me I will address the person concerned but, please, do not ask me any questions. If it is not your turn tonight, don't worry; it will come again."

Ms Shepherd wandered among us and then stopped at a middle-aged man with a sorrowful expression on his face.

"You are in grief," the psychic said, "but Edith says that this will disappear in time. And you must know that she is very happy. What you must do now is to care for your pigeons and get them flying again." The man smiled gratefully.

She went on, stopping next at a woman in the audience. "Your sister, Elaine, misses you too. She says you have to pray now; do not give up your religion just because she was killed in an unfortunate accident. It was not God's fault that she died."

And then she came to me, and stopped.

"You are the blessed one," she pronounced. "One day, in time, you will become a healer and Katy says that she will visit you tonight. It has been a privilege to meet you, Angela."

I sat there gob smacked. Not only had she mentioned Katy, which was entirely accurate, but she had also used my name. How the hell did she know that? And what was that point about me becoming a healer? I could hardly cure a cold, must less cure someone else's illness.

I didn't wait for the raffle – my mind was in too much turmoil. So I left the meeting early. As I stood on the pavement outside, wondering whether I should take a taxi or walk, the psychic came out of the hall.

"I wonder if I might have a word," she said.

"I'm still stunned at what you said to me inside," I replied. "But if you want to say something I won't stop you."

"You must have the same experience as I do, surely? You're a fellow psychic.

"I don't think so; of course I do have visions, but I don't see any of the...well, the departed."

"They speak highly of you in the Other World – what we call home. There is a great deal for you to do in this one, especially in apprehending those who have lost their way. But there is one thing I wanted to say to you, if I'm allowed?"

I nodded. This was becoming more mysterious.

"You might not like this," she said, "but I have been urged to say to you that you must pray. If you wish to develop your gift then you must ask God to guide and help you, otherwise you will be haunted by the visions."

This was something that Katy had said to me in the past, so it rang a bell. I didn't mention Mrs Morrison to her; she had said the same thing.

"I hear what you say, Roselyn, but I have to tell you I am not the least enamoured with religious practices. I haven't been to church for aeons; if I went I'm not sure what I would have to say. In other words, God and I are not on speaking terms."

She smiled at my comment. "God never falls out with people. If you go to church, on your own, if you care to, you will certainly find the right words to say to Him. And He will understand. Anyway, Angela, I have passed on the message I was instructed to give you; if you don't act on it then I don't envy you for the future. Goodnight, my dear."

So, there it was: that was three times three different people had warned me now. I didn't think I could choose to ignore it any more.

I had noticed a church on the way here; it was at the back of the town and quite close by. It wouldn't do any harm for me to go in.

It was closed. I remembered the day when churches were always open; nowadays they were probably too afraid of burglars to have an open invitation. I put it to the back of mind until later, and went and had pasta and a glass of wine.

This would be the last night I would be staying at this hotel, so, relieved, I undressed and had an early night. One of these days I would go truly mad and have a wild late night on the town. One of these days something might happen to me that might make me less lonely than I had been of late.

* * * * * *

As Roselyn had promised I had a visit from Katy that night. The visitations didn't disturb me now, as I was becoming used to them. As usual she smiled at me, and then, to my astonishment, I noticed a presence at the side of my bed. It wasn't a clear image and it didn't frighten me, but I could tell it was an outline of Katy.

"You met Roselyn, then?" she said.

I nodded. I couldn't seem to find the words to say anything. I just looked at her, dumbstruck.

"Don't worry, Angie, you'll soon get used to this; I can't as yet appear to you as an individual but I'm hoping that might change with the passage of time. What did you think about the message? Have you acted on it yet?

"Er…the church, you mean? Well, no…" I was stammering. "I went but it was closed. Did you give her the message, Katy?"

"No. I'm not allowed to do that. It came from a higher authority. Keep it in mind, won't you; it could help you a lot in the future."

"Yes. I will. Can you tell me anything about the paedophile we're hunting?"

"Only what I have already said to you and that he is from Krakow, in Poland. And to say to you that you will have to visit the police there; you need to look at where he lived."

"So the police know him?"

"Yes. But only as a suspect. They have no real evidence; that is something you will have to obtain – and, believe me, Angie, you will in time. Now I must go. Remember to visit the church."

And then the outline vanished. I had the most wonderful sleep for a long time.

* * * * * *

The next morning I packed my belongings, signed for the hotel bill and took a taxi to the flat in Camden. The representative from Welfare was waiting for me with the keys.

"I hope you'll be happy here, chief inspector," she said as she helped me with my luggage.

I thanked her; I didn't know whether to shake her hand or give her a peck on the cheek. Instead I smiled as she left. Today wasn't a very good day; my period was due to start and I was hoping I wouldn't have the usual pain it caused me. I used the bathroom, for the first time, and made myself ready. Then I jumped on a tube and crossed town to the Yard.

I was the last in. Sam and Sally were on the phone whilst Peter and Laura were updating the computers from the files. They all seemed very busy.

"How did you get on?" I asked Sam when he was free.

He shook his head. "Nothing from the school – neither the headmistress nor the duty teacher noticed anything. But we did get something from Frank, the constable. He chatted to a newsagent, close by, and he told him he had seen a black van leaving the scene at some speed. I've put out an APB on the vehicle and we're hoping someone will spot it. We're still waiting evidence from the SOCOS but that will take time. Other than that, we have nothing."

"And the mother? Did she have anything to say?"

"She was too shocked to say anything. I thought we would send Peter back there when she's recovered."

"Good idea. We need her input."

Just then Sally came off the phone. "I've been talking to the embassy, Angie. They've given me the name of a chief inspector in the Krakow police force, together with his number. They tell me he speaks quite good English. Shall I give him a ring – or do you want to do it?"

"No, you do it, Sally. You know what we're after."

I turned to Sam. "Anything on the rapist yet?"

"Peter and Laura have interviewed the last victim…" – he coughed – "well, the last one alive. There wasn't much she could tell us, she says it was too frantic to notice her attacker, but, as Mark has already told us, he was wearing one of those hoods that hide the face. It was the knife she remembers; she says it was about six inches in length, and before he attacked Mark he pointed it at her throat and threatened to kill her. She was frozen in terror as he ripped off her clothes. When Mark arrived he turned and stabbed him twice in the abdomen."

"They did well to get that out of her," I said. "Has anyone been to see Mark?"

"Yes, a few of us have. He's back on the normal ward by now; we're hoping he'll be discharged in a few days."

"How's his wife now?" I asked because she must also have been in a state of shock.

"Okay, but she still wants him to leave the force."

"Can't say I blame her," I remarked. "It must be difficult with a young child and a husband who might be in constant danger."

Sally was still on the phone so I went for a coffee.

So far, I was feeling all right; I hadn't had my normal sense of desperation.

CHAPTER TWENTY-SIX

As I went to the canteen for a coffee I knocked on Jim's door. He opened it himself, as if he were expecting me.

"Hi, Ange. Come in. I heard about you new flat. Welfare tell me it's very nice."

"It's very comfortable, Jim. And thank you. I want Sally Walker and me to go to Krakow."

"Krakow? What – Poland?! Have you been having one of those visions again?"

I nodded. "Yes. And I'm told I have to go there; that's where the killer comes from, and I have to see where he lived and where he worked. There's something there for me to see."

"Okay," he said. "I'm not sure how I'm going to explain this but, yes, make your plans. When do you want to go?"

"This afternoon. There's a flight leaving Heathrow at four o'clock; I've checked and we can be on it."

He frowned at me. "Is it so urgent? Can't it wait until I get clearance? I mean, you are entering someone else's territory."

"No, Jim. This is urgent. That paedophile has snatched another boy, yesterday. We have to catch him. Sally is already on the phone with the Krakow police."

"Right! I've already set up an incident room downstairs; Chief Inspector Ian Blakey is heading it up. He will want to talk to you when he's ready."

"I'll get Sam to liaise with him."

"Okay; then, if Krakow says it's fine, go and get your tickets. Do you have your passport with you?"

"Thank you, yes. Pity you can't come with us."

He laughed. "That would have been nice – but I've got to do so much here. Good luck, Ange."

* * * * * *

Sally was just discussing some issue with Laura when I got back. She looked at me and grinned.

"I think we might have found him," she announced. "His name – or at least the name of the man they suspect – is Kowalski, Edward Kowalski. He's in his early 50s, lives on the edge of the city; lives with his half-sister, and is suspected of murdering two young boys from the school where he worked as a caretaker."

"Good. But do they have a warrant our for him?"

"No. They have no evidence – merely suspicions. After they started to question him, following which they followed him and harassed him, he flew the coop. They didn't realise he might be over here – but they say if he is he will be an illegal alien."

"I don't see why. The Poles no longer need work permits to come to the UK. Have you put out a search for him?"

"Yes. But we have no record of him over here. Laura has been on to passport control at the various airports but, understandably, they have no record."

"I doubt if he'll be using his real name anyway. Have you asked the inspector if we can go over there?"

"Well, no, Angie. They're sending us a photo; they reckon it's an old one and he may not look like that today, but it is something. I mean, why would we want to go there?"

"I want to see where he lived. I don't suppose you know where his sister, or his half-sister, is living now, do you?"

"Yes. I do. She's living with her mother, a pensioner; she has a flat in Warsaw." She looked at me with curiosity. "And you really think we have to go there?"

"Yes, I do. Do you have your passport with you, Sally?"

"I do, yes, but I'll have to make some phone calls – I'm expected somewhere tonight. I'll have to ring the inspector back; I think he'll be amazed when I tell him we want to travel there."

"I doubt it. But I'll make the arrangements anyway," I said.

* * * * * *

The flight from Heathrow took approximately two and a half hours. I had to visit the toilet to change my towel but otherwise I was fine. The only subject we discussed on the plane was the paedophile. Sally wanted to know something about profiling.

"Did you see the notice I put up on the board?" I asked.

"About the rapist? Yes, I did. And it seemed to be a lot more specific than the last profile we were given. But how do you arrive at that analysis? I mean, it was so kinda precise."

"It's simply a matter of training, Sally. Years and years of training and studying. I don't know who you had last time but I doubt if she could have been that experienced. As I have said, many times in the past, we do not always get it right, but it is always helpful to the police, to a greater or lesser extent, if they know who they're looking for."

"Well, I am impressed," she acknowledged.

* * * * * *

We arrived at Krakow at about 8.0 p.m. their time. It was already getting dark but a faint smudge of the sunshine could still be seen on the horizon; it had obviously been a fine spring day.

Sally had spoken earlier to Chief Inspector Kaczynski and he said he would be waiting for us at the airport.

He was as good as his word. This tall man, with an almost military bearing, was waiting for us in his full dress uniform. He smiled when he saw us and politely shook our hands, bowing slightly at the same time.

"I am sorry about the uniform," he said, "but I wanted to be sure you would identify me. How was the trip?"

A sign would have done, I wondered to myself.

"Fine," I said out loud. "And it was on time."

"I hope you do not mind but I have booked you for two nights in the Hotel Francuski; it is in the centre of Krakow and I believe you will be very comfortable there. They do not have any single rooms but I have managed to book two doubles as singles."

"That is very kind of you, inspector…"

"Please, you may call me Gregoria," he interrupted.

"And my name is Angie, and this is Sally."

"Ah. You are the chief inspector?"

"Shall we drop the titles…er, Gregoria; tell us about your suspect."

"Kowalski," he said as he motioned them towards a waiting police car. "Edward Kowalski. Yes, we would like to know where he is."

"So would we," Sally commented dryly.

"Can I suggest we leave the interrogation until the morning," I proposed. "It's quite late and I'm tired; I don't know about you two, but an early night would be welcome."

"Have you eaten?" he asked.

"Yes, on the aircraft. Right now, I need a drink and then to bed."

"So, goodnight, ladies. I shall pick you up after breakfast in the morning."

* * * * * *

The Hotel Francuski was evidently one of the oldest hotels in Krakow, situated almost in the centre of the city and close to the main Market Square. I looked forward to seeing the city, especially the Gothic features at St Mary's Basilica, which I had heard so much about; it was a place I intended to visit whilst we were here, but right now I was exhausted, especially because of my monthlies. I don't think Sally felt the same way because after we had checked into our rooms she had a drink with me at the bar and then went out on the town. She also had a tourist guide with her.

Good luck to you," I thought; just don't turn up tomorrow with a hangover.

The next morning it was another bright spring day with a hint of summer in the air – and Sally didn't have a hangover.

"Where did you get to last night?" I asked with interest.

"I wasn't as tired as you were so I went on one of those tourist tours by night buses. It was fascinating – I didn't realise Krakow was so old."

"It used to be the capital city of Poland many years ago. It's where the previous pope came from. Did you see St Mary's Basilica?"

"Yes. But we didn't get off the bus. I thought I might go inside later, if we have the time."

Gregoria was waiting outside the hotel, standing against a police car. He was dressed in jeans and a T-shirt, "Good morning," he announced – and there was the bow again. "Did you sleep well?"

"Good morning," we chorused. "Yes, thank you."

"That looks better," I commented, looking him up and down. He looked more like a human being than someone in the military.

He grinned. "That's what my wife says! Now, first I thought we should visit the police station, so that I can show you the details of the murdered boys. We have a file on each of the cases, when they disappeared and the clues we discovered." He gave a sigh. "Not much, I'm afraid, but it's all we have.

"And then, later, we'll see the apartment where Kowalski lived. It is now empty. And if there is time today we'll go to the school where he worked as a caretaker – otherwise, it will have to be tomorrow. Is that alright for you?"

"That will be fine," I confirmed. He seemed to have dropped the perfect English he was speaking last night. "I'd also like to have a look at the autopsy reports of the two boys. Do you have those available?"

He nodded. "Yes, but they don't make nice reading."

We climbed into the police car and he gave instructions to the driver. The police station wasn't too far away; it was a low building with just three floors. He told us that after the Russians had withdrawn from Poland the force moved to another, more modern building.

Gregoria's office was on the second floor; it had a large conference table, at which we all sat. A young police officer came in to the room with files. This one was about in his mid-20s, slim and with dark hair. He nodded to us as he was introduced.

"You're a long way from home," he said.

"Are those the autopsy reports?" I enquired, ignoring his remark.

"Yes." He handed the folders to the inspector, who passed them across to us.

The results on both boys were almost identical to those on the two bodies we had found in the UK. Both had been raped, and had ravaged anuses but no semen there. One of the boys, the older of the two, had had his penis cut off and placed in his mouth. They made terrifying reading, as Gregoria had suggested. I shuddered when I thought of what the two children must have gone through at the hands of this monster. I closed my eyes for a moment, trying to blank out the horrors of the photos.

"What do you think?" I was asked.

I couldn't speak; I was still trembling at the savagery. At last I said, "It's the same man. The autopsy reports are almost identical with the two boys in the south of England. They must have suffered terribly. What made you suspect Kowalski?"

Gregoria examined the file. "He had a record of a sexual nature. Nothing that would send him to jail; it was more he was peeping at the boys while they undressing. And he was also the caretaker at the school where the boys attended. It seemed to us he was the obvious suspect."

"But you didn't arrest him?"

He shook his head. "There was no clear evidence, merely circumstantial. No semen, no DNA, no real clues that might identify him. The fingerprints we were able to collect, well, they were part of his job function anyway. But we didn't let him go. We pestered him, questioning him endlessly, followed him, even talked to his half-sister about our suspicions."

"Did she say anything?"

"Nothing of any consequence, although she did manage to express some distaste for Kowalski." He sighed again. "In the end, the only thing we managed to achieve was to chase him out of the country. Now

- 120 -

you tell me he's been murdering young English boys. I don't know what to say; I'm terribly sorry."

"It wasn't your fault, Gregoria," I hastened to add. "He hasn't exactly left us any clues either – except we will have some DNA."

"At least you've got something that will apprehend him."

"Yes. He left sperm in one of the boy's anuses. But we first have to catch him. Do you know how many Poles there are now living in England?" I asked.

He shook his head. "I know there are many of us there – but how many, I don't really know."

"Over 600,000. Most of them are in legitimate employment – they don't have to have work permits any more. But many of them are not registered; evidently they work for themselves or they're doing the odd menial job and work without paying taxes. That is what we have to contend with. Sally here showed me the photo you sent; it helps a little but I'm not convinced we'll be able to find him from that. Do you have a more recent photo?"

"I'm afraid not. We got that from his half-sister."

"Did Sally tell you that another boy has gone missing?"

"Yes. And I think you were right to come here. Now you know that we are chasing the same monster. Shall we look at his apartment? It's in the district of Nowa Huta, quite close to here. It will take us about a half an hour to get there."

"Yes. Let's do that."

Sally was still examining the autopsies and the pictures of the naked boys, and I saw tears in her eyes. "Ugly, aren't they?" I said. All she could do to reply was nod.

Kowalski's flat was in one of the drabbest areas of Nowa Huta. The centre had recently become a rather celebrated part of the city, especially with the tourists. The building we were looking at was one of the remnants of the old Krakow. It was in a run-down apartment block that looked as if it were scheduled for demolition. Most of the building was empty, the tenants having vacated them for a payment from the owner. Kowalski's flat (or technically his half-sister's, we were told by Gregoria) was on the fourth floor. It was a long climb with no lift, and my legs were aching by the time we arrived. The door was open, as if the tenants would be back shortly.

I asked Gregoria and Sally if they minded if I went in my own. It was something I had to do and it was the real reason I had come all this way. They agreed without discussion. I went inside and closed the door behind me, leaving the two of them on the landing.

That was when the smell of evil hit me; it was though it had permeated the walls of the shabby apartment and taken up residence there. I could feel it enveloping me as if it wanted to invade my body, take possession of me and draw me into its embrace. I shuddered but I was determined not to succumb to the threat. There was very little furniture remaining, and I could only assume that his half-sister must have taken it with her when she left. The living room was small but probably large enough for two people. I noticed that there was no central heating; it must have been bitterly cold there in the winter. There was a small electric fire fixed to one wall, but it couldn't have given out much heat.

Next I wandered into the kitchen. Again, it was on the small side, but probably commercial. The sink was empty of dishes, which was a compliment to the occupant. The smell in here was very light, as it was in the lounge. So far it appeared only to have pervaded the hall. It wasn't in the bathroom either.

At least, I thought that until I went into what was obviously Kowalski's bedroom. I was very nearly overpowered by the aroma. I sat down on the floor and leaned against the wall and allowed the malevolent atmosphere to circle around me. I doubted if I would have experienced it if I weren't a psychic. But I was; and I had to try to let it consume me if I were to learn anything in this place. So I welcomed the invasion and then challenged it to reveal its secrets.

"Tell me what you know," I pleaded out loud. "Come, tell me your secrets."

There was silence, but I did notice that the cloying aura seemed to pulsate as if it were hesitating, considering what I had said. Then a whisper inside my head said, "So, you want to know where my master is?"

"Yes. Why has he abandoned you?"

"He has had to flee – but a certain part of me has gone with him," the whisper said. "He is not alone in England; I share part of his life. I am now an integral part of him; we coexist within each other."

"So will you tell me how I can find him?"

There was a muted explosion in my head; I couldn't work out if the entity was laughing at me or it was incandescent with rage at my impertinence. I tried to shake it away; it was like having the worst kind of migraine. Then it subsided and, when all was quiet again, the whisper said, "You may find that as you seek him he will also be seeking you."

Then there was something that I might describe as a snigger.

I was finished here. There was nothing else I could learn from this creature. I left the apartment, leaving the door open, just as I had found it.

CHAPTER TWENTY-SEVEN

"Did you learn anything?" Gregoria inquired.

"Not as much as I hoped to," I replied shakily. The ordeal with the entity had left me drained. I really didn't want to talk about it. I checked my watch, which was still on UK time. Where we were it was now after four – and we hadn't had lunch.

"Is there a café close to here?" I asked.

"Yes. I'm sorry – we haven't had lunch," Gregoria said. "I will take you to a place in the city centre."

"You were in there a long time," Sally commented. "We wondered what you were doing."

"I wanted to see for myself where he lived – not simply the apartment but his bedroom. I had to see how he lived."

"And did it tell you anything?"

"Yes. Not something I can describe here, but it did suggest he was a meticulous man; everything had to be in order, as if he were controlling it.

"But right now, people, I need something to take the taste of that monster out of my mouth; perhaps a coffee and something to eat might help. Are we too late to visit the school?" I asked.

"I'm afraid so. Everyone will have left by now."

"I don't need to see the children or the teachers, Gregoria; I just want to see where this man worked. You said he was a caretaker at the school. Didn't he have some kind of an office?"

"I suppose so. We can go and look. But first we should have something to eat."

* * * * * *

The school wasn't too far from Kowalski's apartment. After a much-needed late lunch, and fortified with strong cups of coffee, the three of us paid a call there. It was a bleak and soulless building, dating back to the communist regime, but Gregoria assured us the children were happy there. It was only on one storey, accommodating some 300 boys and girls.

We were taken to the rear of the building, where a caretaker's hut was based. As with the apartment I went in alone, and the cloying sense of evil assaulted my senses. I needed only a few moments to ascertain that it was the same presence I had felt, not only in his apartment, but also at the hastily dug graveyard of Robert in Ashworth Forest. This was an essence I could not share with anyone, so I decided to say nothing of the ethereal entity I had experienced.

I came out of the hut and announced, "I'm convinced this is the man we are after. Now we will require all the help we can get to catch him."

"Why are you so sure?" Gregoria wanted to know. He was puzzled at my conviction.

I looked at him levelly. "You will have to trust me, Gregoria, but I know it's him; my training and my experience confirm that. This is the same man. Tell me, did he have a passport in his name?"

"That I don't know. I believe that after we joined the European Union we were not too concerned with our examination of passports. I suppose he could have travelled under a different name; in fact, this is more likely, given that he was under investigation."

"I thought that might be the case," I said.

"And the photo you passed on to us hardly does him justice," Sally intervened. "The only thing it tells us is that he is a man in his 50s, with a sallow face and what appear to be dark or black eyes. Evil-looking character, isn't he?"

Gregoria said, "You will keep in touch, won't you? And if there's anything we can do, please let us know. Now, you will be staying the night – yes?"

"I guess. I suppose we've missed the last plane home?"

"I'm afraid so. But there is an aircraft at ten tomorrow morning. I have something to do in the morning but I will arrange for a car to take you to the airport."

When we got back to the hotel I told Sally I wanted to rest.

"Bad week for you, is it?"

I nodded. "I'll be okay – it just makes me feel weary. Perhaps we can have dinner together later?"

"That'll be nice. In the meantime, I'm going to have a long bath."

* * * * * *

Dinner was nothing spectacular; it was probably just as well, as I wasn't feeling too hungry. Sally was disappointed; she had believed that the Polish food would be more like what you were served in Paris or London.

"Shall we go to church?" she asked.

I laughed. "You mean, you want to pray?"

"No – I was thinking of St Mary's. It should still be open and we won't have time in the morning."

"Sure. Why not? I'm told it's worth a visit."

The cathedral was fairly close to the Market Square, and Sally was right: it was still open. People were queuing up at the door.

"Do we have to pay?" Sally wanted to know.

"I don't know – but I don't have any zlotys. Perhaps they take euros."

They did. It cost us €3. I'd thought about coming here to say a few prayers, as Katy had suggested, but it was too crowded and it was hardly the place for a quiet moment. So I gave it a miss. Instead, I viewed with admiration the paintings – some of which had been returned by the Germans after the war – and the sculptures. The altar was decorated in solid gold ornaments; in days past I would have known the Saint names, but now I couldn't remember them. I lit a candle for Pauline, paid a couple of euros and said a hurried prayer. That was all I was able to do.

As I was about to leave I saw a shadowy figure hovering around the candleholders: it was Katy. She was shadowy, insubstantial; she seemed to flicker in and out of the candles. She didn't say anything but she gave me a welcoming smile. It actually cheered me up no end and made my trip to Krakow worthwhile.

It truly was a magnificent cathedral. They had a museum but, after seeing Katy, I decided to give it a miss.

Sally was waiting for me at the door.

"So, what do you think?" I asked her.

She gave me one of her philosophical shrugs. "It's okay. But if you've seen one cathedral then I guess you've seen them all. Do you want to go back or are you up for a night on the town?"

"No. If you don't mind, Sally, I'm a bit whacked. But you help yourself; I'll see you in the morning."

The next morning Sally did have a hangover.

"Late night?" I suggested.

"Hell, yes. This is some town – you should have come. Mind you, you have to watch out for those bloody trams; they'll kill you if you're not careful." She didn't go into any detail about her outing; I wondered if she had found some lesbian bars in the town, but didn't say anything.

I hadn't even noticed any trams. "What, and wake up like you do? No thanks, Sally. Are you ready to leave?"

In the police car on the way to the airport Sally said to me, "Do you mind if I ask you something?"

"Go ahead."

"Well, you don't seem to have any happiness in your life, do you? I mean, there is no joy about you; it's as if your whole life is spent concentrating on catching killers."

I was a bit startled at this insight. "You think I'm miserable all the time. Is that it?"

"Yeah. Well, I don't see any sense of humour about you. You smile but you never laugh; it's as if you're haunted by your visions; they're like a dark cloud hanging over you, stopping you from living a normal life." She shrugged. "I'm sorry to have say this to you, Angie, but it isn't just my perception; the others have started to talk about it."

It wasn't easy for me to respond to this. "You may be right, Sally. But what do you suggest I do about it?"

"I don't know exactly, except you should try to live a little. Enjoy those aspects of everyone's life that give meaning to existence." She placed an arm on my shoulder and said, "Try coming out for a drink with the gang; I'll teach you some dirty jokes, try to make you laugh."

I was quiet for a moment. There was something in what she had said; most of my life did seem to be based around these visions. Now Sally was almost echoing what I had heard in the past: the same thing, except that she was saying that, in a way, I was hiding from life.

I gripped her hand, sighing, and said, "Thank you, Sally, for bringing this home to me. I believe you're all correct, I do seem to be hiding from reality, and, if you will help me, I promise I'll try to change."

What an eventful trip! I thought to myself, as we departed on the plane for Heathrow.

CHAPTER TWENTY-EIGHT

We arrived back at the Yard mid-afternoon, after an unexceptional flight from Krakow. There was a message waiting for me from Chief Inspector Givens from Wembley.

I rang him immediately, hoping that Joshua might have been found. He had been found – or, at least, his body was: the army had discovered it in some woods just out of town. The autopsy would be tomorrow. I put the receiver down, sadly. That poor, poor boy. The prompting from Sally about my joyless existence went completely out of the window.

"Are you alright?" Sam wanted to know.

"No. They've found Joshua, the boy who was missing from Wembley; he's dead, Sam." I shook my head, wondering if there were anything I could have done to prevent it; probably not.

"Jesus!" was all he said. He went across to inform Sally and the others. There was a note of depression amongst us all that day. We had been to Poland, searched this monster's flat and the school where he worked, and I had become quite familiar with the two missing boys from Krakow; I had felt their fear and terror. I wasn't sure what else we could do to catch Kowalski; all I know is that I shared the frustration we were all feeling.

I went along to see if Jim was in. I suppose I was in need of reassurance.

"What's the problem, Ange?" he asked when he saw my face. "Didn't Krakow go well?"

"It went very well, Jim. At least I confirmed that this man Edward Kowalski is the man we're after. The autopsies of the two murdered Polish boys were almost identical with the MO of the boys from Wembley. It isn't that; it's just that I've been informed that the body of Joshua, the last one he snatched, has been found in some woods close to Wembley."

Jim shook his head in commiseration. "That's very sad. But it was only what we expected – it was hardly likely he would have let the boy go."

"I know. But it doesn't help discovering that what you thought might happen…well, and then it does. I find it very depressing."

He looked at me levelly, his eyes seeking something within me. "You're not in danger of taking this personally are you? It upsets us all, believe me, but the worst thing you can do is take it all personally. It wasn't your fault Joshua was abducted, and it isn't your fault that he's dead. It is your responsibility, Angie, to catch this bastard, and anything I can do to help you can rely on." He got up and poured out two cups of coffee. "Come on, tell me about Krakow. It will take your mind off Joshua."

So I did. I told him about the presence of evil that had invaded me in Kowalski's flat and how the presence had exchanged mocking comments with me.

"It's what it said, Jim, that frightens me."

"Why? Why should some ghostly entity frighten a psychic?"

"Because I suspect the killer is protected by an ephemeral evil, and that whatever I try to do in apprehending him it will be difficult, if not impossible, to penetrate that veil. It's that that frightens me, Jim; that he will almost be invisible."

He leaned forward in his chair. "Let me say something, Angie; I think it might help you. I believe you're becoming somewhat obsessed by these visions you've been having. I've said this to you before, but I'll repeat it again: if you're not careful you'll be waiting for the visions to appear before you do anything as a policewoman. Put them to one side, stop relying on them and do what I think you do best: that is, penetrate the criminal mind. Profile this man, try to analyse him, put him into one of your categories so we can each of us see what it is that makes him tick.

"In other words, Angie, become a Criminalist."

I knew he had a point, and it was strange that his advice came hard on the heels of what Sally had been saying. It was true I was waiting for Katy to appear to me and give me some guidance – in other words, help me to apprehend this monster. But that wasn't why I had gone to Krakow; that was of my own volition, to see if what I had discovered at Robert's grave site I would find in Poland. And I was right.

"Do you agree with me, Angie?" he was asking.

"Yes. But only up to a point. There is something in me that is waiting for a vision to appear, and maybe it's stopping me from fulfilling all my duties. But I have been employing my talents in other directions…"

"Yes, I realise that's why you went to Poland," he interjected. "But, nevertheless, there is some substance in what I'm saying. Think about it, Angie, and see if I'm right. Go to the autopsy tomorrow of Joshua, but in the meantime give some thought to profiling this monster who is carrying out the violations.

"What was it you used to say: 'Profiling is only a tool to help the police find their man, but it will be hard-won police work that catches him'? We still need the profile, which, along with a faded photo, might well help us to catch him."

I nodded, and left the room without finishing my coffee. I would have to consider his words of wisdom.

* * * * * *

At my desk I began to sort out in my mind an outline profile of the killer – and that would be the word I would use, 'killer'. We were dealing here with a situation that was almost identical to that I had experienced with Connie, all those years ago. Our killer was a mysoped, a sadistic paedophile who put into practice his desire for sexual gratification and destructive violence.

I referred to one of my teaching manuals, Profiling Violent Crimes, by Ronald and Stephen Holmes, and I hope they won't mind my quoting their text.

Typically, this aggressive offender chooses child victims who are strangers to him. He may stalk the victim [as I believe he did with Robert, the first victim in the UK] rather than use any form of seduction.

This type of paedophile has no love of children in the traditional sense. He is interested only in causing harm and death to a vulnerable child, having fulfilled himself sexually, over whom he feels great superiority. The mysoped inflicts fatal physical harm on the victim and then, in many cases, brutalises the body; where boys are the victims then often the penis will be cut off and inserted into the child's mouth.

The crimes against young boys are premeditated and often ritualised.

One example of a sadistic offender is Westley Dodd, who was executed for his crimes in Washington State. This man murdered three young boys, including a five-year old child. His last victim, Lee Isely, he took from a public park, and sexually abused him over a period of several hours that resulted in death. Dodd then placed the body in a cupboard and went to work; when he returned he retrieved and committed anal sex and other forms of necrophilia sexual abuse before disposing of the body. Attempting to abduct a fourth young boy at a neighbourhood theatre finally apprehended him.

I remember the case of Dodd quite clearly, as this was one we had studied at Warwick.

So, to sum up the classic sadistic offender, we can list the profile as follows.

1) Harmful to the child?		Yes
2) Aggressive personality?	Yes	
3) Antisocial personality?	Yes	
4) Child sexual preference?		Yes
5) Child a stranger?		Yes
6) Does intercourse occur?		Yes
7) Abduction of the child?	Yes	
8) Intends fatal violence?	Yes	
9) Large number of child victims?	Yes	
10) Uses computer bulletin boards?		Yes

The sadistic child molester will invariably be geographically transient, although, so far, that did not appear to be the case with the Wembley killer. But we did know that he had a van, though what we didn't know yet was whether or not he had committed offences in other parts of the country.

What we knew was that our man was in his early 50s; was Polish by descent (we should check if he could speak English or not); had thin features with high cheekbones, and his teeth seemed to be well stained, suggesting that he was a smoker; he was not well educated and therefore would have only a menial job, or he could be self-employed, possibly as a gardener or a maintenance worker; he would live alone, probably in a bed-sit with very few amenities, possibly even in his van, and have no social friends or even colleagues; he would not drink, for fear of betraying his indulgences; and he would probably spend his free time reconnoitring schools either in the area where he lived or on a wider geographical basis. It was possible that he might have use of an Internet service, maybe through an Internet café, although, if I was right, and he did have a limited intellect, then this was unlikely.

It was early evening by the time I had finished the profile. I had already put it into the computer, so I printed out a number of copies and distributed them to all the officers in the Serious Crime Division, including Jim Robbins. I hoped he would be pleased with my efforts.

The last thing I did was to phone Chief Inspector Givens on his mobile and arrange for Sally and me to attend the autopsy tomorrow, and to ask him to wait for us to arrive at the mortuary. I also left a note for Sally to let her know that I would pick her up in the morning.

CHAPTER TWENTY-NINE

It was raining again when I left the building, and I didn't want to face another restaurant. As my difficult time of the month was coming to an end and I was still feeling freaked out, I decided I would merely have a salad for dinner and then simply crash out. It had been an exhausting couple of days, and I was shattered both physically and mentally. I didn't even put on the telly, which, on reflection, I was rather glad about. The headlines, which I saw in the morning papers, were all about Joshua's body and the maniac who was carrying out these barbaric attacks. My name was also mentioned as the senior officer conducting the enquiry, including my photograph. Commander Robbins had already given a statement to confirm that he had every confidence in his officers and was hoping that a result would be forthcoming shortly.

A typical Robbins quote, I thought to myself.

I had had a further thought during my sleep, and that was that we should place patrol officers in each of the schools in the Wembley area. Inevitably, this would require that a great deal of our resources be employed, but what I wanted to do, aside from protecting the children of Wembley, was to force the killer to go further afield; make him have to use his van.

I put the idea to Jim that morning, before we set off for the autopsy.

"Let me think about it, Angie," he responded. "By the way, I liked your profile, especially quoting that bastard, Dodd. I'm sure it will make an impression on everyone here. Why don't you circulate it to the Wembley force? It might sharpen their perspective."

"Good idea. But you'll let me know about policing the schools, won't you? We'll have to move quickly on it."

"I'll get in touch with you after the autopsy."

I ran-off some more copies of the profile to take with me and give to Inspector Givens. Sally really didn't want to attend another autopsy, but I 'twisted her arm'. It wasn't something I wanted to go to on my own.

When we arrived a very depressed chief inspector was waiting for us outside the mortuary. His head was down and he looked as if he was bearing this tragedy entirely on his own shoulders.

I squeezed his arm in reassurance. "Is it going to be Dr Sullivan?" I asked him.

His glance was one of appreciation. "No. She refuses to dissect another dead child. I can't say I blame her. How are you getting on with the enquires?"

I gave him copies of the profile and asked him to distribute them around the force. I also informed him about my idea of policing the schools to prevent any further abduction.

"That's going to take a hell of a lot of resources," he exclaimed; "I'm not sure we have the manpower."

"If the commander approves the idea then it won't come out of your budget – Scotland Yard will stand the bill. Shall we go in?"

I noticed Sally hadn't said a word throughout this exchange. I got the impression that she was already beginning to feel sick. Understandable, I thought; I was going to have to hang on to my own stomach.

We were introduced to a Dr Malcolm Jones – probably a Welshman, I thought, not that that would make any difference. I was right; when he shook our hands and greeted us he betrayed a slight but definite Welsh accent.

His shook his head, almost in sorrow. "Very sad day," he commented, gazing at Joshua's naked body on the slab. His penis was still in his mouth.

"Shall we begin?" he asked, pulling the microphone closer to his mouth.

Before he could start, Sally muttered, "I can't take any more of this, Angie. You'll have to excuse me."

I couldn't stop her – she was already on her way out, throwing up on the floor.

"I'll get someone to clean that up," Dr Jones said. "Has she been to any of these before?"

"Yes. This will be her third one."

He shook his head. "I don't think anyone will blame her; no one is going to blame Dr Sullivan either – she can't take any more."

Then he began cutting, whilst his assistant cleaned up after Sally.

There was nothing one could say about the autopsy. I could see the strangulation marks on the boy's throat, just as I could see the brutal damage to his anus. There was also semen inside Joshua's rectum, which would give us some of this bastard's DNA.

It was the remorseless dissection of the child that disturbed me; it wasn't that I felt sick, it was more that I was engulfed by the sadness of it all. I asked myself the question, "How could anyone do this to a child for sexual gratification?"

Dr Jones promised us the report as we shook hands and left the mortuary.

Sally was standing by the car, smoking a cigarette. Her face was still pale, as though she had seen a ghost, though she was more composed now.

"Sorry about that," she apologised. "I just couldn't take another one. You should have brought someone else, Angie."

I put my arm around her shoulders. "Don't worry about it, Sally. You weren't on your own." Then my mobile went off. It was Jim.

"Okay. I've got approval for policing the schools; the commissioner thought it was a good idea and should give encouragement to the parents. Is Chief Inspector Givens with you? Put him on, will you."

Clearly, he was giving the inspector the okay to go ahead with the scheme and to confirm that Scotland Yard would be paying. The inspector was relieved that something positive had come out of the tragedy. I left him to make the arrangements as Sally and I set off back to the office.

"Are you going to give me away?" she asked contritely.

I laughed at her phraseology. "Of course I'm not. I'm surprised at your asking. I just hope I don't have to attend another one myself."

"I've read your profile," she said, changing the subject. "I mean, it's very analytical and…well…descriptive. But, fucking hell, Angie, did that man in the States really savage those children as you describe?"

"It's a true case, Sally. Dodd was executed in Washington State. And I've tried to make it as descriptive as I could so people will take notice."

"They'll do that alright."

"Probably. But you will remember, won't you, that it isn't profiling that catches criminals? It is hard-working police methods. All we try to do is give them an outline of the person who might be responsible."

"Christ, Angie. How many times have I heard that before?"

* * * * * *

Back in the office I called in to speak to Chief Inspector Ian Blakey. He was a thickset guy, probably not much older than I was, with brown eyes and dark hair, which had a slight curl edging over his left brow; he was also quite fit looking. I discussed the profile with him and the outcome of the autopsy on Joshua. Ian suggested we have a meeting of the two teams, which I agreed to.

At lunchtime I went out of the office and caught a cab; there was a small church I had noticed at the top of Marylebone High Street that I wanted to visit. It had been impossible to follow Katy's suggestion to pray whilst we were in Krakow, but I hadn't forgotten it.

The church was called St Anthony's, and it was open. There were only a couple of people in the pews; I went to the front and knelt in front of the altar. I wasn't sure what I was going to say. I had forgotten most of the prayers I used to recite, but then that was possibly just as well, since whoever it was I was praying to would surely only want to hear words straight from my heart. Which is what He got.

I thanked Him for the blessing of being a psychic and prayed with all my heart that He would guide me through all the traumas that would inevitably come with it. I asked Him to help me to accept those instances when only good would come from my blessing and reject those that might cause harm to others. I promised Him that I would now always pray for His guidance and intervention.

I wasn't sure how much good would come from my prayer, but I had acceded to Katy's wish that I would ask God for help. I did admit, though, that the brief session gave me an awful lot of encouragement. I felt uplifted as I left the church.

* * * * * *

That afternoon I called the team together and we went downstairs to meet up with Ian Blakey. I let him address the meeting, at which there were some 40 officers of all ranks – most of whom I hadn't met.

He introduced the five of us to the floor and gave a mention to Mark Reed, who was still in hospital. He also very kindly offered me, as a temporary replacement, a Sergeant Phil Collins, who came and shook hands with me. He seemed a very nice guy – for a policeman: small, quite slim, with fair hair and blue eyes and a quick smile, which I liked. I thanked Ian and said I would be grateful for any help.

He took out the profile of the paedophile. "I think you've all read this," he announced. "It is very informative and gives us a clear idea of who we're chasing. This man, if you need me to tell you, is an evil monster who dedicates his existence to the brutalisation and murder of young boys. So far, we know of three children he has killed in the UK, but Angie and Sally have just come back from Krakow, where they discovered that the killer has also barbarically savaged and murdered two young children over there.

"We know him as Edward Kowalski, and, as you will have read in the profile, he is in his early 50s and lives alone. He also has a dark van that we need to be on the lookout for, especially now that Angie has got the commander's agreement to place constables in all the schools in Wembley. That is likely to force him to travel further afield. Let the police forces in the Home Counties know what they'll be up against and give them his description. Inform them that it is highly unlikely he will be assuming his real name but, given that he is no academic, they should look for names with perhaps the same initials. He may try to get a job in one of the schools, which is what he did in Krakow. And bear in mind that in this country he is not on the criminal sex register.

"Five little boys, officers; that's how many we know of that he has killed. Some of you will have children the same age; I want each of you to defend the boys at risk out there in the same way you would do if they were your own children. Now, Angie and her team will be around if you want to ask them any questions. You don't need my permission; you'll find them on the third floor, and they'll do everything in their power to catch this bastard.

"Thank you all – but if you have any questions now, fire away."

There were no questions – at least, not at that stage. The whole assembly looked as if they had been stunned; their faces, each and every one of them, registered a look of shock. I was rather pleased that my profile had had that effect; it was certainly meant to motivate them.

CHAPTER THIRTY

I had some tidying up to do, so it was quite late when I left the office. I'd only had a quick lunch, so I decided to gorge myself in one of the many restaurants in Camden. I chose a Chinese, had a glass of beer and decided to start with prawns in sweet and sour, followed by sizzling beef in black bean sauce. I was still waiting for the first course to arrive when Rachel Humphries walked in. She spotted me and came over. She was dressed in a tailored suit – rather conservatively I thought, as though she was still hiding from the world.

"I didn't know you lived in this part of the world," she said.

"Yes. Round the corner. I moved after seeing your flat. It's a nice part of the world – especially after Battersea."

"Are you alone?"

I groaned. I really didn't want any company tonight. But what could I do?

"Yes. Quite alone."

"Do you mind if I join you."

I pulled a chair out and she sat down. "How is your rapist pursuit getting on?"

"I think he's gone quiet, for the moment. After his attack on one of our officers he's faded into the background. But I expect he'll be back when he thinks it's quietened down."

"From what I remember of him – which, by the way, has not faded away – he'll definitely be back. This man is an out-and-out rapist; and now he's become a killer. He'll wait until he thinks it's safe – mark my words. What have you ordered?"

I told her, and she followed suit. "Do you often come here?" I asked, hoping she might say 'yes' so I could give it a miss in the future.

"No. Well, maybe once a month or so. I like Chinese but only now and again.

"So, Detective Crossley, what are your plans for when the rapist does appear?"

I smiled, grimly. This was becoming an ordeal, and for a moment I was sorry I'd decided to move into her area.

"I can't discuss that with you, Rachel. You should know that by now."

"Oh, yes. I'm sorry. I suppose I was just trying to make conversation. Now I'm embarrassed."

"Don't be. It happens all the time." Then I felt ashamed. This was a young girl who had been viciously attacked by a rapist who then became a killer; she could have become the first victim had she not been able to defend herself.

"Do you have a boyfriend, Rachel?" I asked, genuinely interested.

She shrugged. "I did have. But after the rape I couldn't stand anyone near me – I still can't. Whenever we tried to have sex I became frightened that it might happen again."

"So he left you?"

"Yes. He put up with me for as long as he could but when I refused counselling he gave me the push." Her mouth was trying to force a smile and I was the one who felt embarrassed now. This young lady deserved some pity.

"Have you thought again about counselling? I mean, just for you, not for anyone else?"

The food arrived before she could answer; suddenly I wasn't very hungry any more. With the advent of the paedophile and my trip to Poland I had allowed the rapist to slip to the back of my mind. Perhaps it was also because he really had faded from the scene. I nibbled at the food and thought seriously about Rachel Humphries, suffering so long after the event, and with no helping hand to guide her through the trauma.

"You haven't answered me," I said between mouthfuls.

"I've thought about it, but I wouldn't know where to go."

I was astonished. "You mean, the police haven't offered it to you?"

"No. Not so far."

"Would you like me to arrange it for you?"

"Well, if you wouldn't mind. It might help me."

"I could organise it so you don't have to take time off work."

There was a pause before she said, "I'm not working at the moment." She rubbed her face with her hand. "I...I haven't felt like it. All those people staring at me as if I were somehow spoiled."

I took hold of her hand. "Rachel, why didn't you say something, to me at least?"

"You can say that now," she said stridently, "but the last time we met you threatened to arrest me for withholding information. You would have been the last one I would go to for help."

Sweet Jesus! I wondered to myself. What have I done to this poor girl?

"I can only apologise for that, but it was one of those things. We were not just chasing a rapist – he has now become a murderer. Do you think we can put that behind us and start again? Please let me help you, Rachel."

She thought about the offer as she chewed some of her food. Then she said, "Can I let you know? I mean, you have sprung this on me. Don't misunderstand me; I am grateful, inspector, but I need to think about it."

"Well, you can call me Angie, for starters. And do think about it. I'm sure it can really pull you through this crisis in your life. And it won't cost you anything. Tell me, have you applied for compensation from the Criminal Injuries Board?"

"No. I don't know how to go about that, either."

"You'd better leave this with me, Rachel. In the kindest possible way you need sorting out. I'll get started on it tomorrow. How about your flatmate? Is she supportive?"

She shook her head. "She's left me. She was afraid the rapist might return and she could get caught. I've put another ad in the local paper to share, but right now her room is vacant."

"There isn't much I can say," I uttered, regretfully. "Except to leave it with me – I promise I will get someone to contact you tomorrow."

When they brought the bill I took it from the waiter. "How much is half?" Rachel asked.

"Nothing. Have this one on the police force. Come on, I'll walk you home."

She didn't live too far away. It crossed my mind how easy it would be to drag some unsuspecting girl off the dark street and push her into an alley.

"I saw you sitting there – in the restaurant, I mean. And I wanted to talk to you; that's why I came in. I hope you don't mind."

"I'm glad you did. You've brought two things to my attention tonight: one is your situation, and I really will be glad to help; and two, the rapist. I had allowed him to slip into the background, possibly because we have another urgent case on our hands."

"You're talking about the abductions, aren't you?" she exclaimed.

I nodded. "Yes. We have another monster out there who's been torturing and murdering children – young innocent boys. I've had to concentrate on that for a couple of weeks, but I will not forget the rapist; thank you, Rachel, for bringing it back to my attention."

She laughed. "I'm sorry about this, but you do sound formal when you have to. And you're not at all like that when I get to know you."

As we arrived at her door she said, "Thank you for listening to me – and for the dinner. Do you think we might see each other again?"

"Yes," I said. "I would like that." I gave her my card with my mobile number on it. "If you ever want to chat, Rachel, you can contact me on the mobile. I'm only around the corner – perhaps we can have dinner again? A different restaurant, though, next time."

"Goodnight, Angie. I'm so glad I was able to spend the evening with you."

"Goodnight, Rachel."

CHAPTER THIRTY-ONE

I went to sleep that night – still on my own – thinking of Rachel Humphries and how we had let her down. In fact, it was inexcusable that we had allowed her to suffer as she had and done nothing to help her. I made a note to follow it up the next morning. I was dozing, I suppose, thinking about one thing or another, when Katy suddenly appeared – or at least it was the same image I had seen before. I say 'suddenly', but that's something of a misnomer, because that's how she usually appeared.

"Hi, Katy," I mumbled, not quite sure if I were awake or asleep. "Why don't you visit me when I'm awake?"

"Perhaps one day I will," she said. "As it is, you only allow me in when your subconscious is at rest. One day you will learn to control it; however, here I am and we have things to talk about."

"We do? What things?"

She smiled. "Well, I think your friend, Sally, was right. You should try to live a little and not keeping thinking all the time about criminals." Before I could say anything, she went on, "I was pleased that you tried to contact me in St Mary's in Krakow; everyone was glad that you went into the church here in London and said the prayers I was hoping you would."

"Yes. Well, I did as you suggested. I just hope it works."

"And tonight you thought of Rachel?"

"Did you send Rachel Humphries to see me?"

"No. Not exactly. But we sent her past the restaurant where you were dining, and when she saw you she thought it would be a good idea to talk to you. I'm glad we did. Look after her, won't you? She needs help.

"The other matter I want to discuss is the paedophile. I'm sorry if you feel I have led you astray but I wanted to warn you that a cloak of evil hides this man. It is almost impossible to penetrate. Therefore, we do not know where he lives or what he might plan next. Angie, please, you will have to pray for God's guidance; no one else can help you."

I sat up in the bed and glanced towards the clock; it was 2.30. "How do I know that God will help me find him? I don't have a special relationship with Him."

"He will give you an insight. He will help you at least to see what the killer plans next; I'm afraid I can't do that."

"Okay, Katy. I will do that, I promise. And I will also look after Rachel. Have you any news about the rapist? We haven't heard from him in quite a while."

"Not yet. But he hasn't gone away. But be careful, Angie; the paedophile, when you find him, he will know. In the meantime, my dear, try to enjoy life."

Then she vanished as quickly as she had appeared.

I slept soundly after that.

* * * * *

I awoke to the sound of birds singing. It was late spring, almost early summer, and they welcomed in the day as I did. I opened the curtains and looked out onto a blue sky, with the sunshine streaming in through the windows. A few clouds were gently nudging each other, but far, far away. A much better day than I had experienced in Manchester. I went on the tube to the office with a spring in my step.

The first thing I did was to contact Welfare and inform them of my discussion with Rachel Humphries of the night before. They promised they would help immediately with counselling and would also contact the Criminal Injuries Board for some financial assistance. I felt better after this, and rang Rachel to let her know what I had done. She tried to thank me but I wouldn't let her; at least the day had started better.

There were two detectives from the basement waiting to see me; again, I couldn't remember their names.

"I wanted ask you, chief..."

"Angie," I interrupted.

"Sorry. Yes, Angie. I wanted to ask you about the uniforms you have placed in the schools in Wembley?"

"Yes, what about them?"

"Well, do you think if they dressed in plain clothes, rather than uniforms, the paedophile might not be aware they're policemen and he still might try to have a go at abducting one of the children; especially if they aren't seen?"

I thought about this; it was a good idea, and perhaps one I should have thought of.

"What's your name?" I asked.

"Andy – Andy Murray...er...Angie."

"A good old Scottish name – and the same as the tennis player! Well, I think you're idea is a good one; perhaps it's something I should have thought of myself. I'll have a word with the commander and see if we can't implement it. Thank you, Andy, a hell of a good contribution."

I got on the phone, but unfortunately Jim was out; I left a note on his answerphone and mentioned Andy Murray's suggestion.

"What is your name?" I asked the second officer.

"Paul – Paul Sanford. I was wondering if we should put out an APB on the black van. Usually vans these days tend to be white in colour, so it shouldn't be too difficult to spot a black one."

"Good call, officer, but we've already done that." I shrugged. "But keep thinking; you never know what might come up."

As he walked away I turned to Sam. "Anything else come in, Sam?"

He handed me another folder. "Yes. This came in this morning. I'm not sure what we can do about it, though."

It was an account of a gun-shooting rampage in Moss Side, Manchester. So far, in the last four weeks, five young people had been killed by gunshot injuries. I remembered, when I travelled up there with Jim and we passed through that area, Jim had described it as the gun capital of the north.

"Send it back downstairs. Let them deal with it or pass it on to the Gun Crime Unit. That's one location we do not wish to become involved in. Right – by the way, where is Laura? Is she sick?"

"I gave her permission to take the morning off; she's looking for accommodation."

"Really! I thought she lived at home with her parents."

Sam grinned. "You know what parents are like – especially for a young and attractive copper."

"Okay. Let's look at what we've got. Here" – I pointed to the board – "we have a rapist who has gone into obscurity; this will not last. I believe he's waiting until the pressure comes off him, we decide to go away, and then he will attack again. By now, I imagine his lust must be consuming him; what will make him worse is he has lost control over the scenario. That will upset him terribly. So, what can we do to force him out of his hideaway? Any suggestions?"

It was Phil Collins who spoke first. "How do we know he isn't still travelling the trains expecting to see one or two policemen?"

"We don't know that, Phil, because we only have an outline description. We can hardly arrest every single bloke who happens to be travelling on the tube late at night, can we?" I gave him one of my equable looks, not wishing to discourage him.

"Not if we only see him the once, no, of course we can't. But what will we do if we spot someone who is on the same train night after night. Surely, isn't that someone we might like to talk to?"

I sighed. These young policemen. "And which train do you suggest we put men on, Phil? He could be on any underground travelling to any station."

His face tightened. Obviously I had put him under some pressure. "You may be right, Angie, but since he's already had a failure on the Willesden Junction line why shouldn't he travel on that same train? It's also part of his territory – Maida Vale, Kilburn and then Kensal Green."

"It makes sense to me," Sam said, nodding his head. "He could also be reconnoitring that line to see if he spots the police."

I thought about it for a moment. Maybe their suggestion wasn't such a bad idea. "And as of now he won't – because we are strangely conspicuous by our absence. So, instead of travelling on the tube, what if we leave a couple of the plain clothes at Kensal Green station – concealed, I might add – and see if our suspect gets off following a young lady?"

"And then what will we do?" Sam asked, a note of cynicism in his voice.

I scowled at him fiercely. "What the hell do you think you do? You tail him. See where he goes. He might just be an innocent civilian going home and not following the woman off the underground. If he happens to be our suspect and he hasn't spotted us, then he will make a move against her. That's when we catch him."

Sam blushed at my remark, and then he said, "I like that. At least we'll be doing something, rather than just sitting on our arses doing nothing."

"Do you all agree?" I enquired, not really caring if they did or didn't; I was just being diplomatic.

They all nodded. "Right. Sam, will you get on to Maida Vale and Kilburn forces and set it up? Mind you, I think we should restrict it to a Friday and a Saturday night, between 10.0 p.m. and 1.0 a.m. See if they have anyone spare. And from now on, Sam, I want you to head up this case, and take Phil and Peter in your team. Sally, Laura and I will head up the paedophile unit.

"Now, let me say something about the latter case. We have a profile of the type of man we're looking for: we have his approximate age; an outline of his appearance; the kind of dwelling he will reside in. And he will be a loner who has committed these brutal crimes against young boys, possibly over many years. The only factual information we have is that he has killed two boys in Poland and three in this country.

"The question we each have to ask ourselves is: How do we catch him before he abducts another child? Or is that asking the impossible?"

"Did you get any feedback from the commander about changing police protection units into plain clothes?" Sally wanted to know.

"Not yet. But on reflection I think it might be too late. We've already had the units in place for almost 24 hours, and if the paedophile is watching the schools in the Wembley area then he will already have spotted the uniforms. To change them now would a dead giveaway." I shook my head. "Better, I think, to leave them as they are."

"Yes, but if you believe that that would push him further afield, then where precisely do you think he might go?" It was Laura asking the question, I was pleased to note.

"Good question, Laura. My opinion is that he will push outward towards the next counties. So what we do is contact the schools in the Hertfordshire area – that is, those effectively bordering on the two counties – and alert them to the possibility that a sadistic killer could be operating in their area."

"What? And do nothing else?" Sally asked.

"What do you want us to do, Sally?" I snapped at her. "We can't patrol all the schools in the UK. But what we can do, having alerted the schools we think might become a target, is organise the parents – that is, before schools starts, during the playtime, during the lunch periods and when the schools close for the day. If we can get them to oversee the children as watchdogs then, hopefully, it will restrict his access to the children. Do you go along with that?"

"I guess so," Sally answered.

Laura simply nodded, apart from adding, "Ask them to look out for a black van."

"Okay, let's get on to it. We'll carve up the schools between us from the computer; I'll take the first half-dozen, Sally the next, and Laura, you can bring up the rear."

That's how we spent the rest of the morning, and by lunch, after having a hasty ham sandwich, I was free to visit the church I was last in a couple of days ago.

It was virtually empty, which suited me; probably because it was a sunny day outside. I went to the front of the church and knelt before the altar. I was still stuck for the words to come out, so I prayed in my own inimitable style. I asked God if he would either give me the vision to pierce the protecting veil the paedophile had incorporated around him, or at least enhance my intuitive senses so I could discern what he might be planning next. The words tumbled out, some of them in a disorganised way, but I felt that God would know what help I was imploring him for.

I stayed for a while, after lighting a candle for the dead boys, and prayed that they might have peace. I was just about to leave when a voice said, "You have been here a long time; have your prayers been answered?"

It was a priest who had asked the question. I didn't really know what to say at first; it was a kind of innocuous question that didn't actually require an answer.

I nodded. "Good day, father; yes I hope so. But I suppose I'll have to wait and see."

His smile washed over me and I felt a sense of peace. "This is the second time this week you've been here. I hope you don't mind my saying, but I sense your urgency. Is there anything I can do to help?"

I smiled at the suggestion. "Not unless you have prayers that might help a novice psychic."

He frowned for a moment. I couldn't help it but I looked into the depth of his eyes. "Yes. I might be able to help you. Come," he said, kneeling at the altar; "let us pray together."

This was so bizarre; I didn't know what to do. He knelt beside me, closed his hands together and bowed his head. Then he began reciting words in – well, I guess it must have been Latin, because I didn't understand them. The meaning did become clear to me, however. He was asking God to relieve me of my burden by granting me the blessing of insight so that I might see the evil attached to my position. He went on like this for quite a few minutes. When he had finished he stood and took my hands in his. Again, I felt his eyes probing me, searching for my goodness, and I fell into their depths, wishing I could stay there forever.

"God will certainly bless you now, Angela Crossley," he said. "He has laid His hands upon you. Go in peace."

With that his eyes began to fade away in front of me as he departed from the church, leaving me in a state of shock and bewilderment. I didn't have to ask how he knew my name – I just knew. I also knew that my prayers would now be answered. As an afterthought, out loud, I thanked the priest for what he had done for me. He half turned at the door, smiled and raised his hand in a farewell gesture.

When I left the church my mood was lighter and I felt inspired; I couldn't remember when I had last felt this sense of serenity.

CHAPTER THIRTY-TWO

After returning to the office I learned that Laura was still having some difficulty in securing a flat. She was – what? – 22 years of age, very personable, and I thought she might partner Rachel Humphries very well.

I asked her where had she been looking. "Anywhere, really, Angie. Somewhere I might be able to afford."

"Do you remember Rachel Humphries, the girl who lives in Camden?"

"You mean, the one who was raped?"

I nodded. "Yes. Well, she's looking for a flatmate. She has quite a nice two-bedroom place just off the High Street. If you're interested, I could give her a ring?"

"Would you?" she said excitedly. "I think that would suit me down to the ground."

Rachel was indeed very interested, so I gave Laura her address and told her to get round there straight away, as someone else was coming to view it that evening.

I then talked with Sally about the call-outs to the schools.

"They all favour the idea," she confirmed, "except it has put the fear of God into one or two of them. One headmaster was contemplating closing the school down until he's been caught. I dissuaded him."

"How many schools have we covered?"

"About 18 in all. All of them bordering the Hertfordshire border area. Downstairs are getting feedback from the Wembley schools where the uniforms are in place; nothing yet to report. And no signs either of a black van."

A thought came to me then. "Sally, you live in or around town, don't you?"

"Yes. In Paddington. Not too far from Edgware Road. Why do you ask?"

"I was wondering if you know the church at the top of Marylebone High Street, St Anthony's I think it's called."

She looked at me, a half-smile on her lips. "Yeah. I've been to a couple of services there – you know, like Christmas carols and that. Why do you ask?"

"Do you know if it's a Catholic church?"

She shook her head. "No, it's Anglican. I used to know the vicar there; he had a break-in when I was in Burglary. Nice guy. Nice wife too. Why, are you interested in becoming a parishioner?" The hidden smile was still there.

I grinned at the suggestion. "I wouldn't think so. Someone mentioned it to me and I thought it was Catholic. Never mind, it's not that important."

The man I had seen at lunchtime was definitely a Catholic priest. My heart beat more strongly when I thought of him. He obviously knew my name because he was there to hear my prayers to God. This was becoming a wonderful world to live in, I thought. Perhaps Sally might tell me one of her dirty jokes!

* * * * * *

That night I had a further vision, as though it was the answer to my prayers. It reminded me very much of the visions that had haunted Connie, my old psychic, except that I was not terribly disturbed by the apparition.

I saw a school; an almost brand new building close to a town that I saw was Harpenden in Hertfordshire, quite some way from the Wembley district. A man, evidently an old man, was planting some flowers in the grounds; he was still there when the children came out to play. He spotted a small boy – he looked to be about eight or nine years of age – and he summoned him to help him plant the flowers. No one seemed to be paying the old man any attention, as though he had always been there and was part of the fixtures.

When the boy came over to him the old man took him by the hand and led him outside the playground. He opened the back of his old van – this was not black but dirty white – and dragged the boy inside, smothering his face with what appeared to be a chloroform cloth. Then, rapidly, the van drove off, and no one in the school would be any the wiser until well after playtime had ended.

I wasn't able to follow the van, but I had been given a vision, a rehearsal of what this paedophile was planning to do. That was how the children disappeared and none of the teachers noticed that anything was amiss; as far as they were concerned the old man almost literally didn't exist.

I woke up and witnessed this strange apparition standing by my bed; it was Katy.

She smiled at me, almost angelically. "Your prayers have helped you penetrate this evil cloak he has wrapped around him. Now you know how he abducts the children; trust me, Angie, he too will know that your powers have spotted him."

"Do you think he will threaten me?"

"I'm sure he will – when he finds out who you are and the gift you possess. You have become a danger to him. You must be careful in the future, Angie."

"How will he know who I am, Katy?"

"Because he has similar powers to yours, though in essence they are not so strong. But he will find you; he might not know where you live but from his prescience he will discover where you work and he will plan accordingly. I will watch out for you, my dear. Please be careful, won't you?"

"Thank you, Katy. And thank you for helping me with my prayers."

She smiled. "Did you like my priest?"

"I thought it was you. But tell me something. If I want to speak to you at any time, what do I have to do?"

"Now you are asking the right questions. All you have to do from now on is speak: I will answer."

So now I had a problem, rather like Connie had had when she was pursuing the paedophile. I just prayed he wouldn't catch me; otherwise I too might become a victim.

CHAPTER THIRTY-THREE

I had an undisturbed and restful sleep after Katy's visit. Physically I was back to normal again – feeling relieved that another of my monthlies was over. I stopped at a local coffee shop, sitting outside in the sunshine for a full breakfast and strong coffee.

The effects of Katy's warning had registered with me but I wasn't too concerned; aside from my Spirit Guide's protection I had a whole army of police officers to shelter behind.

As I went into the Scotland Yard building and made my way to the lift I felt a tugging at my elbow. I looked around, thinking it might be someone I knew who wanted my attention. There was nobody there. It alarmed me. Then I felt that I was being pulled towards the stairs that led down into the basement, where Chief Inspector Ian Blakey had his unit; I had no control over the pressure. Now it began to frighten me. I had no idea what it was. I tried to resist but the pressure increased, and I was led, almost inexorably, towards the stairs.

Ian was at his desk on the telephone; he looked up at me and waved me towards a seat. I couldn't move. I seemed to be gripped by the sudden drop in temperature. All around my body there was an icy flow, making me shiver and look for its source.

I looked around the room to see if I could identify what had drawn me to this place.

Most of the officers seemed to be well balanced and functioning as expected, given the stress they were all under, but one of them, a young guy who I hadn't met, was on a course of antidepressants, and so far they were not working. It was not my call to say anything to him or to report him to Ian Blakey. Another officer, a girl, I saw was pregnant; she wasn't aware of it yet but I felt she would be devastated when she discovered it.

The feeling of fear still hadn't left me, and neither had the sharp drop in temperature; there was some manifestation of evil that had brought me to this place. Then I noticed a dark cloud, almost black in colour, settling over the head of a young Asian guy. It was his aura I was seeing. It had a malign presence that, when I looked, thrust itself at me as if in retaliation. It was as though my probing of his mind had unleashed a fury of resistance at myself.

He still hadn't raised his head; he sat at his desk inputting whatever it was into the computer. But he knew I was here, there was no doubt about that.

As Ian finished his telephone call I asked him if he would call the officer over so I could be introduced to him.

"You want to meet Ajas?" he said, puzzled at the question. "He hasn't been with us long – only a couple days, actually. I have great faith in him." He called the officer over.

"Ajas, Chief Inspector Crossley wanted to meet you. Angie, this is Ajas Sahib; I recruited him from the Murder Squad."

I was still trembling when I shook hands with him, and if I needed any confirmation then this was it. This man was the essence of malevolence; it was extremely difficult to look him in the eyes but I forced myself to do so. I shuddered as he returned my gaze, as if he too understood that I was probing his mind. Then I realised what it was that Katy had tried to tell me, that as I was interrogating evil so evil might create a backlash and interrogate me; I had grabbed the tail of the tiger. The look he gave me tended to confirm this.

I nodded and mumbled that I was pleased to meet him and hoped Chief Inspector Blakey was right in his assessment. The man raised his head, no doubt so that he could look into my eyes; it was a malicious and penetrating stare, as if he knew what was happening. The exchange left me shivering; it troubled me deep in my soul.

"Did you want something, Angie?" Ian asked me when Ajas had returned to his desk.

I was desperately trying to get my feelings under control again. Eventually I muttered, struggling to get my words out after my encounter, "Yes. Do you know Harpenden – I believe its in north Hertfordshire?"

He looked at me, baffled. "Yes. I live quite near there, in Luton. Why do you ask?"

"I'm not sure but I've had a premonition. I believe one of the schools there will be selected by the paedophile for his next victim."

He grinned when he heard this. "Jim was telling me the other day not to ignore your intuitions; I didn't believe it might happen to me. What is it you want us to do about it, Angie?"

"I…I don't know yet," I stammered, trying to shake off the sense of ferocity that Ajas had unleashed upon me; Ian had no idea what had just happened. "It might be too early," I went on, "but at some time in the near future I want the schools in that area supervised by plain clothes police. Not today – I'll have to let you know when I think it's appropriate. Is that okay with you, Ian?"

"Of course." He rose from his chair and followed me out of the office and into a quiet corner. "Are you going to tell me why you wanted to meet Ajas? Is there something about him I should know?" I was surprised at his insight.

"I don't want to talk about it; let me have a word with Jim Robbins first, then we can discuss it."

"You get curiouser and curiouser," he mumbled irritably.

I left him, suitably annoyed, and went up to the third floor, trying to still my trembling nerves, and decided I would visit the toilet. I went into one of the closets and talked to Katy.

"Did you lead me down there?" I asked of her.

"No, Angie. I didn't," she replied. "Now you have begun your role as a Seer you must expect these things to happen; you are drawn instinctively to evil, and that is what occurred today. But remember my warning about communicating with evil."

I wasn't happy with her response but nevertheless, as I was running out of time; I left the toilet and knocked on Jim's door.

"Hi, Ange. What can I do for you?" He looked at me, blankly at first, and then added, "Not another vision? Please don't tell me, you've had another vision." At least he was half- smiling.

"Not in the sense you mean, no. However, when I came into the building this morning I was drawn by some force, which I had never experienced before, to go down into the basement. I wasn't sure what it was until I spotted an Asian police officer. Jim, there was a black cloud surrounding his forehead; an aura of evil, and I know what I'm talking about."

He frowned. "Go on."

"I asked Ian if I could meet him. He was very puzzled as to why I would want this, but he did call the man over. That was when I realised who he was."

"You wouldn't like to get to the point, would you?" he said cryptically. "I have a very busy morning."

"Sorry. I have to tell you, commander, that this man is a senior terrorist. He heads up a group of four of them; they share a flat in the East End of London. They also have a separate warehouse, where they assemble bomb-making equipment. The mission this man has committed to is to blow himself up, together with the others, in a spectacular suicide explosion in a very public place where there will be hundreds, if not thousands, of people. They already have the equipment prepared, seemingly the venue has been selected, and now they're waiting for the instruction to come from Afghanistan. When and where it will happen I'm not sure; what I am sure of, though, is that I have been warned, and I suspect that Ajas – the man involved – already knows that I have psyched him."

"Fucking hell, Ange!" he gasped. "I don't suppose you have any proof of this?"

"None you could take to court. But what does occur to me, Jim, is that if you were to contact MI5 and explain the position I'm sure they'd be very interested."

"Really?" he muttered sarcastically. "And how do you suggest I'm going to explain the situation?"

I shrugged. "I don't know. But you have to take this seriously. If you don't and thousands die we'll never be able to live with it."

He waved a hand at me. "Okay, okay, you've made your point – at least to me. I'll have to give it some thought as to how I contact MI5."

"Why not give them that anonymous telephone call? The one we implemented with bank robbers. Do you think they might act on that?"

"I doubt it. It will just go into the folder, especially as we're talking about a police officer. Did you disclose all this to Ian Blakey?"

"No. He asked me. But I said I wanted to discuss it first with you."

"Well, we'd better bring him up," he said reaching for the phone.

Ian came into the office without knocking. "I was waiting for your call," he said. He glared at me. "Just what the hell is going on, Angie? I've had to try to calm that young officer down – I believe you've put the fear of God into him."

I didn't respond that he had put the fear of God in me.

"Sit down, Ian," Jim ordered. "And listen to what Ange has to say. It will blow your mind!"

I took him through my assessment of Ajas and what he had projected to me – namely that he was one of the country's leading terrorists who, previously, had practised at the North Finchley Mosque. Prior to that he had spent part of his late teens training in Pakistan and Afghanistan, where his cousins were involved in an Al Qaeda group. He had been a sleeper in this country since he was 20.

I then went on to tell him what Ajas was planning, along with three others of his group; I confirmed that I wasn't able to identify the venue or when it might happen, but happen it most definitely would.

" Angie, what kind of a game is this you're playing?" Ian scowled at me. "And all of this you were able to uncover with just a simple handshake? Who the hell are you, chief inspector? You're not someone I've ever met before."

I shrugged. "I have to tell you I am still processing the information; it appears to be coming through spasmodically."

"Ian," Jim said, "I think you should be told that Ange is one of these special people who senses things; she sees things that very few people would ever notice, and you have to believe me that this is true because I have actually witnessed the phenomenon before."

Ian simply laughed – it was as though it was the only thing left for him to do. ""

"You're winding me up, right?"

"No, I am not," Jim assured him. "And what I have disclosed to you must always be held in confidence…"

"You don't seriously think anyone would believe me, do you?" he interrupted. He turned and looked at me. "Is this the same kind of intuition you mentioned earlier about the paedophile?"

All I could do was to nod.

"Blood hell, this is some morning; I had a feeling this wouldn't be a day that would go smoothly. So, commander, you accept that what Angie here has told is accurate, so what do you propose to do about it?"

"Good question. We were hoping that you might come up with something."

He laughed – a little hysterically, I thought. "You're not suggesting we go to MI5 with this story, are you? We'd be laughed out of the building. Fucking hell, Jim, can you imagine us saying we have this detective chief inspector here at the Yard who 'senses things', and she informs us that one of our police officers – a man, by the way, who I regard as very promising – is actually a terrorist who is planning to blow himself up in a public place? She either won't or can't tell us where it will be or when it will happen, but she assures us that it most certainly will take place. Is that what you have in mind?"

"Don't be so fucking obtuse, Ian. I'm trying to have a serious discussion about this. I don't know yet what I'll say to MI5, but they do have to be put in the picture."

"Follow him," I announced peremptorily. "Tonight, follow him from the office and see where he leads you to."

"What? To west Hampstead?" Ian growled. "And then what?"

"He won't be going to West Hampstead; he will be going to the flat in the East End of London. He knows now he will have to communicate with his masters in Afghanistan to let them know he may have been uncovered. He'll also have to be careful because, like yourself,

Ian, he realises they won't be too impressed if he discloses that a 'Sensor' has unearthed him."

Ian shook his head. "I don't know what to say, Jim, except that if I can disprove this outrageous theory then I don't mind going on a wild goose chase." He thought about it for a moment before he pointed at me. "You are going to come with me," he said. "He finishes at about six, so I think you and I should leave here before he does and trail him; I just hope he doesn't discover us."

"Right," Jim added; "we'll leave it at that for now, but I suggest you each have a change of clothes, something dark so you won't stand out. Hopefully it might start raining, so Ange can wear a rain hat.

"If he does go to the East End flat then ring me as soon as you have something."

Ian nodded, but there was a look of despondency on his face as he left the office.

"Good luck," Jim called after us. "I hope it goes well."

CHAPTER THIRTY-FOUR

Sam was waiting for me when I went into the office.

"You do know today is Friday?"

"So? Does it mean anything?"

"Well, you asked me to get in touch with the Maida Vale and the Kilburn forces to stand watch at Kensal Green tube station."

I clasped my hand to my forehead. "So I did! Have you made arrangements for the observation to take place tonight?"

"No. That's what I'm trying to say, Angie. The forces at both Maida Vale and Kilburn won't agree to take part in the scheme because they say that the territory is not in their jurisdiction."

I was tempted to swear. Sometimes the force was peopled by a bunch of arseholes. "Okay. Then take Phil with you tonight and stand watch yourselves. If you should spot someone, anyone, who might be suspicious, then do as I instructed. In other words, Sam, unless he attacks a girl, you leave him alone and simply follow him. Understood?"

"Are we on overtime?" he queried politely.

I gave him a look that told him to fuck off without actually saying it.

"Okay, okay, we'll do it. Two nights, you said – right?"

I nodded. "Tonight and tomorrow. I'm not really expecting anything to happen, but – well, we'll wait and see, shall we?"

"I'll take my iPod with me," Sam said sardonically.

"Don't take your eyes of the passengers; if you see a young girl, on her own, and she appears to be scrutinised by a man, then do as I said."

Then I turned to Sally. "What have we got on today?"

"Well, we don't appear to be getting the same number of files that we were."

I shrugged. "That's because the system has changed. They're all going first to Ian Blakey's department; he will assess them and only send up to us those he thinks that should be of interest to us."

"Right. That will save us some time. The other thing Laura and I were planning was to contact the Herts force to see if they've had any reaction from their supervision of the schools. Nothing has come in so far."

"I've already discussed that with Ian Blakey. Let's check further afield. Spread the circle out towards Hemel Hempstead, St Albans and, in particular, Harpenden. I'm not looking for police supervision yet but I do need to identify how many schools we'll be talking about."

" Angie, that's a hell of a lot of schools. Are you sure we need to cover that many? I mean, why don't I start with St Albans first, see how many there are there and then work outwards?"

I thought about the suggestion for a moment, and then decided I would go for broke. "No, forget that, Sally. Just concentrate on Harpenden – and let Ian Blakey know what we're doing. It should help him."

She looked at me in puzzlement. "Harpenden? What's so special about there? Not another vision, is it?"

I sighed. Here we go again.

"You know the expression 'You'll just have to trust me'? Well, that's what I want from you."

She came over to my desk and leaned over, as if to whisper in my ear. "Tell me, Angie, in absolute confidence; are you a clairvoyant?"

I grinned at her. "Which part of 'fuck off' don't you understand?"

She joined in the laughter. I had made a point, albeit not very convincingly.

"You coming for a drink this evening? A few of us are meeting at the Old Crown after work."

"Sure. Why not?"

She nodded, still unsure how far she should go with her theory but wondering how to put it into practice.

It didn't take Sally too long to sort out the schools in Harpenden; there were seven in all, in the junior classes. She took them over to Angie and said, "Now what?"

I looked at them and decided that it shouldn't take too long to inspect them all. I checked my watch; it was around 12.30. "How long do you think it might take us to get to Harpenden?"

Sally shrugged. "I don't know; isn't it somewhere near Luton?"

"Yeah. I guess so. What – about 45 minutes?"

"Let's say an hour, to be on the safe side. Why? Do you want to go there now?"

"I want to get a perspective."

She looked at me, still puzzled. "Are you sure you're not...oh, forget it. Shall we go now – have a bite to eat on the way?"

It actually took a little more than an hour; we got lost somewhere off the M1 and finished up near to a zoo. I asked directions and eventually we found the right road. Harpenden was a pretty little town, edging close to the countryside; I imagine the residents would argue it wasn't so much a little town but a bustling one on the north Hertfordshire borders. It wasn't that easy to find the schools, either; they were all down side roads, and for most of them we had to ask directions. It was the fourth one that decided me: it was an almost brand new school in a low-rise building – that is, it had one storey. Sally and I went into the headmistress's office and introduced ourselves.

Miss Harkins, a late middle-aged lady with her hair tied back in a bun, was mystified as to why we were there until I mentioned that we were from the Serious Crime Squad at New Scotland Yard.

"Good God; you don't think…?" She left the question unfinished.

"We don't think anything, yet," I answered. "You do know, of course, about the paedophile who has snatched some children from the schools in Middlesex?"

"Well, yes, of course I do. Hasn't everyone heard about him? Do you think he might strike here next?"

"We're covering the area around here, Miss Harkins," Sally intervened; "just checking what facilities each schools has. It isn't that we're worrying too much about him coming here specifically, but we're trying to be careful."

"You're not very convincing. What kind of facilities do you expect a school like this to have? Armed guards?"

"Sorry," I said. "We're trying to be careful because we believe this monster might be pushed out of the Middlesex area and into Hertfordshire. What we would like to do is familiarise you with his tactics so you might be prepared in case he does show up here."

"Now you're trying to frighten me."

"We know. Worrying, isn't it?" Sally said sharply. "But if we hadn't turned up here, if we'd said nothing, and this monster did appear, wouldn't you have had cause to criticise us?"

She looked at me as though I were a naughty young schoolgirl; I had to turn away to keep from laughing. "You're probably right," she said eventually, but I do hope you're going to be wrong about him turning up at this school. So, what do I do?"

"You look out for a gardener: someone who magically appears out of nowhere and offers to plant some flowers for you. He will be a middle-aged man and he will speak in a foreign accent. And if you're not careful you might not even notice him."

Miss Harkins looked suitably shocked. "How do you know all this? Is this what he's done before?"

I ignored the question. "You have been briefed, Miss Harkins. We now expect you to be alert to the possibilities; advise the rest of your staff to be on the lookout. And bear in mind, headmistress, that this is a daily routine. Are you clear?"

"Yes. Very clear, chief inspector. I will inform everyone here of your visit."

As we left the school Sally asked me, "I did ask you earlier if you'd had a vision about this school, Angie. But you didn't answer me."

"Why do you ask that now?"

"Because you were...well, you were so specific. Not about him being foreign, we know that to be true, but about him planting flowers, and possibly remaining undetected. Isn't that what you were warning the headmistress about?"

"It's just an intuition, Sally. Something I learned to accept some years back – and act upon. Come on, let's get back; I have things to do."

"So, that's the only school we're going to talk to? Is that it?" she asked, frustratingly.

"Yes. You've got it. And please don't ask me your usual unanswerable questions."

We got back to London just as it started to rain. I hoped it wouldn't be the end of our glorious sunshine but it might help me with that evening's work.

CHAPTER THIRTY-FIVE

I left the office just after four o'clock and went home to change, having given my apologies to the rest of the team about not joining them for a drink.

Dark suit, black shoes, a black rain hat and a dark umbrella. I met Ian in the coffee shop outside Westminster station. He too was dressed in a dark suit. He nodded at me as though I was something he wished he had never come across. I cringed at the look on his face; we headed back to stand, deep inside a bus shelter and without speaking, outside Scotland Yard.

We were there for almost a half an hour before the figure of Ajas emerged. He didn't seem too concerned at the rain; he wasn't even carrying an umbrella.

Cautiously we followed him, waited at Westminster tube station and then checked in at the end of the carriageway where he was seated.

"This is the way he would usually travel home," Ian said to me in a whisper. It was almost like 'I told you so'.

"Wait," I whispered back.

Ajas got off at the Embankment, looked around him as if to check he wasn't being followed then jumped on a District Line train. We stepped surreptitiously behind him, but at a distance, trying to hide ourselves in one of the corners. Stop by stop, as people disembarked, we decided, through whispering, that we should separate. I got off that carriageway and went into the one behind, standing as close as I could to the door. We crossed under the river, but there was still no sign of Ajas alighting. Finally, we arrived at Stepney Green, and I saw him get off the tube; Ian was some way behind him but he was still in contact.

This was strange territory to me; I don't believe I had ever been in the East End before. I caught up with him and said, "Is this the way he usually goes home, Ian?"

"Fuck you," he said, but this time he was grinning.

And then we were lost. Ajas led us through a whole range of side streets with terraced houses, no doubt converted into flats. It was Ian who was making a note of the names of the streets. Eventually, Ajas disappeared into one of the many three-storied terraced houses. We checked but we couldn't determine which of the flats he had gone into.

"Shit!" I pronounced.

"Don't worry, Angie; the address is all we need. I don't pretend to understand how you did it but you were right. This man is not who I thought he was. Come on; let's get outta here. I have to ring Jim."

God! I was tempted again to say "I told you so", but I didn't. It wasn't necessary.

I pre-empted him and rang Jim myself.

"Where are you?" he asked.

"Some place called Stepney Green; it's in the East End."

"So, you were right."

"You surely didn't expect me to be wrong, did you?!" I laid on the sarcasm a bit. "Anyway, Ian has the address of the building that we believe he has gone into; I'll pass him over."

Ian dictated the address of the flats where Ajas had disappeared. Then he paused and asked me a question: "Do we want an armed response here?"

I took the phone off him and said, "No. He has a warehouse somewhere where he has been building his bombs; I don't know where it is but I think we have to find it. Remember, this guy is one of the leading terrorists in the country, and no doubt he will have passed on the information to his colleagues."

"So what do you want to do, Ange?"

"I want this area under surveillance, Jim – 24 hours a day. But it has to be kept completely hidden from the terrorists; one hint they have been discovered and we could have a shootout."

"Then I believe the best thing I can do is liaise with MI5 immediately. I will inform them we have had Ajas under our own surveillance for some time, but before we could report him we had to have some evidence. Now we've got that."

"So what should we do in the meantime? Stay here?"

"Yes. You and Ian. I will get backup to you as soon as possible. Keep the phone open; I wouldn't want anyone to hear the chimes."

It was now seven in the evening. I reported to Ian what Jim had said, and he asked, "What do we do if Ajas comes out?"

"I suggest you follow him; I'll stay here and watch the flat."

It took only 20 minutes for a senior member of MI5 to turn up and introduce himself. He was a rather good-looking man, probably in his late 30s, with fair hair and a blue chin; it looked as though he hadn't shaved that day. I liked his deep blue eyes and his slim build. I didn't like his dress code, though; he had on a scruffy pair of torn jeans, flip-flops, and a T-shirt with a patchy anorak over it. But he certainly looked as though he could handle himself in a tricky situation.

"Hi," he said, brandishing his warrant card, "I'm Steve Jenson." Then he looked at us and frowned. "'Aren't you a bit OTT?" he said as he eyed us up and down.

"We're not used to the spying game," I answered, indignantly.

"Tell me, what you've you got?"

"Didn't Commander Robbins put you in the picture?" Ian wanted to know.

"He did, yes – but only up to a point. I believe your suspect is in some kind of conference in a flat over there with possibly three other suspects. Is that right?"

"'Yes," Ian confirmed.

"Are you on your own?" I enquired.

"No. There's a whole tribe of us here; you won't see them but they are in the picture.

"So, tell me, what made you suspicious about this officer? I mean, how did he betray himself and prompt you to follow him?"

"Oh, shit!" I thought to myself. It was a question I was hoping wouldn't be asked. Now what did we do?

Ian jumped in quickly, before I could think. "We had a report that he was visiting a north London mosque that is known to be frequented by people who have terrorist links. It is not the place for a senior police detective to be involved with. So we followed him, when the time was right."

"Really?" He sounded cynical. "That's very commendable. But how did you know that there were others in the flat?"

"We watched them go in," he said, disarmingly.

"Very astute. Right, if you don't mind, we'll take over now." He pointed towards me. "There is another question I have to ask you, Inspector Crossley, and that is: how do you know that your man has a warehouse filled with explosives? I'm asking these questions because I do need to know where the information has come from. So...?" he went on, when I didn't respond. "Do you have an answer or is it just guesswork?"

I took him to one side, thinking that I might try to explain, when his right hand moved ever so slightly; I saw these shadowy figures moving into doorways and shop windows. Then a tramp suddenly appeared on a doorstep trying to roll his own cigarette, and an old, badly dressed woman was pushing a battered pram, with all her worldly belongings, along the footpath.

"Sorry," he said abruptly, "I have to go; there's been some movement. Give me your card, will you? I'll have to ring you later."

Instinctively, I handed it over; it had my mobile number on the back. Ian and I walked away, and I was left wondering just what I had dragged myself into. Whoever this guy was he was very persuasive, it was almost as if he had conjured my card out of my purse. If he were to ring me later I wasn't exactly sure what I would say to him; secretly, though, I was hoping he would ring, he was getting me horny.

"We handled that well," Ian was saying.

"Do you think so? And what I am going to say to him if he does ring and asks me about the warehouse? What do you suggest I say?"

"Don't know. But if your story ain't right then we'll all be in trouble."

"Then would you like to think about it, Ian? It was me he asked the question of, so he must have some inkling."

"Ask Jim," he said as we were boarding the tube; "he might have said something."

So I tried my mobile. There was no signal, however; I would have to wait.

CHAPTER THIRTY-SIX

I left Ian at Westminster, changed tubes and got to Camden at around 8.30 – it was still early but I was too exhausted to join the others. It was Friday night and I was feeling lonely and with nowhere to go. I was also feeling very distressed at the overpowering sense of evil that was still clinging to me. I thought of going to the theatre but it was too late for that; it was too early to go to a club, though, and, besides, I was feeling too weary for a late night. I didn't know why but I always seemed to be overtired these days; perhaps the visions were wearing me out. I decided to have a Chinese takeaway and a bottle of wine; maybe there would be something watchable on TV, although I doubted it.

I settled down with the plonk, hardly touched my dinner and thought about all the traumas I had suffered in recent weeks.

"Stop feeling sorry for yourself," a voice said.

I laughed. In the past I would have been shocked but now I knew it was Katy; she made me smile.

"Yeah, you're right. So what am I supposed to do about it?"

"Well, you can talk to me if you like. Or you can get yourself a boyfriend."

"Yeah, sure. Good call. What I'd like to know is, why do I keep attracting evil? Why can't I see something good in people? Why is this…this…abomination plaguing my life?" I shrugged. "And why am I so fucking tired?"

"Because you are the instrument who has been chosen in our fight against this malevolence; as it manifests itself in those who are disposed to this mephitic disease so we must choose those who have the most powerful resistance. Does that make sense to you, Angie?"

"Does it hell, if you'll pardon the expression! I think I know what you mean, but then I would ask the question: Who is the chooser? And why me?"

"Because you were born that way. You had your first introduction to the spiritual aspect in your relationship with Connie in the west Midlands. That was only a precursor. Thereafter, you had a more open exposure to it in Manchester, with my brother Danny and myself. Now, you are on the verge of becoming a true matriarch of spirituality.

"As of this moment you are having difficulties in dealing with the phenomena, but trust me, Angie, it will get easier. Do as I suggested to you before: go to your church and pray. Pray for guidance and pray for help in dealing with this transition; it will come, believe me. And your weariness will I ease, I promise you."

I felt better after this. Katy had cleared my confusion; I was reassured and I knew it would come right.

"How is Danny getting along?" I asked after her words had duly penetrated me. "Has he had any more problems with his kidneys?"

"Yes, he might lose one of them – he's feeling the strain. But he's trying to play football again and he doesn't go up to the moors as much as he did. He still asks after you, Angie."

"Give him my love, won't you."

"Yes. He'll be glad of that. By the way, have you thought about the answer you have to give that detective?"

I sighed. "I have thought about it, but I've still got no idea what I'm going to say. Have you any thoughts?"

"You shouldn't be asking me. I am supposed to give you spiritual guidance, not answers to questions. You do know he will be coming round, don't you?"

"What? Coming round here? He doesn't know my address."

"He does now – and please don't ask me how he got it, because I can't answer that either."

"Oh, shit! When is he coming? Not tonight, surely?"

"He'll be here soon. So you'd better put on your thinking cap and come up with some ideas."

I had forgotten I was supposed to ring Jim to ask him if he had said anything to Steve Jenson. I rang him on my mobile; his was switched off. Then I thought about what Katy had just said. "Why don't I tell him the truth?"

"Do you think he'll believe you?"

"I've no idea, but I know from experience that if you're in trouble then the best thing you can do is tell the truth. I might try that."

"It's up to you, Angie. I'd better hide – he'll be here in a minute."

Just then the doorbell rang, and my heart gave a jump.

* * * * * *

He hadn't changed his attire; so much for him trying to impress me.

"Come in," I said. "How did you find my address? It wasn't on the card."

"It wasn't difficult. I came early because I thought you might be going out on a Friday night. I believe you know why I'm here."

I shrugged philosophically. "No. I have no plans for tonight. And, yes, I know why you're here. You want the answer to your question."

"I want the truth, inspector. Not some half-baked story that might stack up with the authorities at Scotland Yard."

"You can call me Angie, if you like. Would you like a glass of wine – or are you still on duty?"

That seemed to throw him a bit, as though he had forgotten his manners.

"Right. Yes. And you can call me Steve; and I will have that glass of wine – it's been a long day.

"So, Angie, are you going to explain the inexplicable?"

"The only thing I can do is tell the truth. Have you heard of spiritualism – you know, clairvoyance?"

He grinned. It was rather a nice smile, I thought. "You're not going to pull that one on me, are you?"

I sighed, deeply. This was no use. Whatever I said he wouldn't believe me.

"It isn't something I'm pulling," I said irritably. "There are things that I am able to see and others cannot. I was able to see who that monster was in the basement and I was able to sense what it was he was planning. Now, that might not make any sense to you…er, Steve, but for me it has become part of my life."

"So you see spirits, then?" he asked, sarcasm in his voice. "Dead ones?"

I glared at him. "No. I don't. I just sense things. How else do you think I knew about Ajas? Do you think he might have thought that this senior detective was interested in joining his group and blowing up half of London?"

"Alright, alright – you've made a point. So that business your colleague was mentioning about this guy worshipping at some mosque was just a come-on?"

"He had to tell you something – well, something that was credible."

"Yeah. We knew that couldn't be true; we've had that mosque under surveillance for some time. And you still think that this story you're now weaving is believable?"

I shrugged again. "I suppose not. And it isn't something I can explain; these things just happen and I can only tell you it how it is. By the way," I enquired, desperately trying to change the subject, "how did you get on at his flat? You haven't mentioned that yet."

He looked at me intently, suggesting that he knew exactly what I was up to. Then he said, "You were right. He is a terrorist. And there is a group of four of them living in that flat. What we don't have yet is the site of the warehouse with the explosions. That's really why I'm here. To ask if you might have some knowledge."

"I don't. I explained that to the commander. If it comes to me you'll be the first to know. So, what is MI5 going to do about Ajas? Are you going to arrest him?"

His lip curled up at the suggestion. "Are we hell!" he said scathingly. "We're keeping him under surveillance – 24/7. It will be interesting to see if he comes into the office in the morning.

"So," he went on, "you're not going out on a Friday night?"

Now he was trying to change the subject; not that I minded, as he was a very handsome man and he still made me feel horny; I'd have to watch myself or I might get carried away.

I showed him my watch. "You do realise it's after ten?"

"So? Don't they have some nice pubs in this area? They don't close on a Friday, you know, until after midnight."

"If you're sure?" I said.

"Yeah. Come on. And you can tell me all about your clairvoyance thing. I'll be fascinated."

"Are you being sarcastic?"

"No…no… Really, I'm not. I've never met anyone before with this talent, and I'll be really interested in hearing about it."

* * * * * *

The pub we went to was the Golden Bear – it sounded like Jack Nicklaus, the golfer. It was on the High Street and it was extremely busy, not so much with youngsters, more with people about my age. Steve squeezed himself to the bar and I found a quietish corner where we could talk. He was having a pint of lager; I was having a whisky and lemonade.

"Cheers," he announced. We clicked glasses and then he asked me, "So, how did this miraculous 'sensing' of yours materialise?"

He wasn't grinning.

"Does your wife think you're working late?" I asked him, innocently.

"Listen, chief inspector, if you're trying to 'sense' me then you're making a mistake. I am divorced; have been for about three years. And I have a little girl – she's four now. How about you? Are you married – divorced or whatever?"

I shook my head. "Never had time; I was always studying."

"Really? Where was this?"

"Warwick Uni. I studied criminology."

"So you have a degree then?"

"Yes. A PhD, if you must know."

He swore. "Hell! What the hell are you doing in the police? I mean, I thought you'd be lecturing or writing books or something."

"How about you?" I asked, ignoring his question. "How did you get into...well, you know what I mean."

"I was recruited straight from Oxford. I was studying politics and economics."

"Clever bastards, aren't we? Have you got a girlfriend?"

"I did have, but she got fed up with having to put up with the unsocial hours. Not many people can. We split a couple of months ago. So, can we get back to the question I asked: about your 'sensing'? You still haven't answered me."

"There isn't much to tell. I suppose it began when I was a young PC in Birmingham. I met a young teenager who was a psychic; she was having visions of a paedophile who was murdering young children – girls. I stayed with her after she was hospitalised..."

"Hospitalised?" he interjected. "With what?"

"She suffered a breakdown. Her visions had a tremendous psychological effect on her. She was in a psychiatric hospital for over four years. I became a detective sergeant and I guess I was her – well, her mentor. If you don't mind, Steve, I won't go into the details; it's far too painful.

"After that, Jim Robbins asked me if I would go to Manchester and help solve a case of a serial murderer; someone was abducting girls, after they had had terminations, and then crucifying them."

"You don't half meet some monsters, don't you?"

"Yeah. Probably as many as you do."

"Did you do a profile?"

"Yes, I did, actually. But how we caught him was more to do with my...shall we call it my 'sensing'.

"I went back to Warwick – where I became an assistant professor – when Jim turned up to tell me he had been appointed as commander for the National Serious Crimes Unit. He talked me into joining him as a chief inspector. And here I am, still 'sensing'."

"That is some fucking story, Angie. I can't compete with that."

I laughed. These mysterious spies. "I'm sure you have but I doubt you're going to tell me about it."

"Another drink?" he asked.

"Let me. It's my shout." I wriggled past him and went to the bar. I ordered a repeat and brought them back; he was talking on his mobile.

"Important?" I queried as soon as he put the phone down.

"Yes," he said taking the drink from me. "Interestingly our young Ajas has just reported to his local mosque; this is the first time he's ever visited that place. We know there are one or two suspected terrorists involved there so it should be interesting. Don't worry, we have a 24-hour watch on him; he can't get away."

"Why can't he just go to, say, Heathrow, and catch the first flight out of there?"

He smiled. "You don't give us much credit, do you, Angie? Don't you think we haven't alerted all airports, docks, buses, anything that can move him out of the country – even the private airfields? He won't be able to travel without our knowing about it."

I pointed to his mobile. "So why do they keep contacting you on something so trivial?"

"Let me get the drinks in," he said; "they'll be closing shortly."

Mind you, it was a silly question when I thought about; if Steve was the senior in charge of this case then he had to be kept informed.

"Tell me," I said when he returned from the bar, "does this man Ajas have any connections to any other cell, that you might know of?"

"You know what the spies say, don't you? 'If I answer that question I'll have to kill you.'"

"Yeah, sure. But I have to ask; have you come across him before now?"

He shook his head. "No, to be honest. If we'd had any kind of suspicions he wouldn't have been allowed to work in the force. And we certainly didn't know he was such a senior figure; nor did we know he was a sleeper. Sometimes we do get it wrong, and we're grateful to you, Angie. Shall we go?"

Go where? I wondered.

"Are you going to walk me back to my flat?" I enquired, in my most innocent voice.

"Yes. And then I'm planning to stay the night with you – that's if you don't mind."

So here it was: the kind of situation I thought would never happen.

"If that's what you want, Steve. I hope you don't mind my asking, but why would you want to do that – spend the night with me?"

We were outside the pub by now; it had stopped raining, and I waited for his answer. He leaned across and gave me a kiss on the lips, nothing sensuous, but seriously inviting.

"You're a very attractive woman, Angie, and I fancy the hell out of you. Does that answer your question?"

I smiled and returned his kiss. "The nicest answer you could have given."

He put his arm around my shoulders and I leaned against him. We didn't say anything, we just held each other tightly until we reached the flat, and then I locked the door, took off my coat, and helped him to undress as he was unbuttoning my blouse.

It was a wonderful night of lovemaking. He was gentle, almost as though he hadn't done it before, and I eased his penis into my vagina with a soft moan. We stayed that way for what seemed to be hours; after that he wrapped his arms around me and hugged me tightly. It was as if he had lost something in the past and he was trying to resurrect it. I didn't mind; it had been so long since I had been with a man I had almost forgotten what a delight it was. I purred against him and forgot about my visions.

I fell asleep, and later I woke up suddenly and looked at the clock. It was five o'clock in the morning, and Steve had disappeared. I sighed, thinking the same as every other woman would do in those circumstances: that he had exploited me and left in case there might be some commitment. And then I saw the note. "Angie. Had my beeper on and called out on an emergency – nothing to do with your guy. Here's my card – if you don't ring me I'll ring you. What a wonderful night. Steve. PS – Your secret is safe with me!"

I lay back in the bed and gave a sigh. It was just after five and today was Saturday; I didn't have to decide yet whether or not I wanted to go into the office.

I went back to sleep, and didn't wake up again until after seven.

I was having my breakfast, tea and toast, when my mobile went off. It was Sam.

"Anything to report?" I asked, munching the toast.

"Yeah; I could do with a slice of that toast. Nothing on the tube last night – we stayed until after one at Kensal Green. I suppose you want us to do it again tonight?"

"That's what I said, Sam. Tonight and for the next few weeks, if necessary; but I will arrange for some help to relieve you."

"Great. Are you coming in today?"

"I wasn't planning on it. Why?"

"There's a message here from a Chief Inspector Givens – from Wembley. He wants you to contact him."

"Did he say why? I mean, is it important?" Now I was becoming irritated. Didn't they realise today was Saturday and we're all entitled to a day off?

Then I sighed. "Okay, Sam, I'll come in. Is Sally there?"

"She's just come in."

"Will you ask her to telephone Chief Inspector Givens and see what he wants. I guess it'll be important."

CHAPTER THIRTY-SEVEN

Sally had her coat on when I arrived at the Yard.

"What does he want?" I enquired, looking at her topcoat. "It must be important."

"They've identified a suspect in Wembley," she said, excitement in her voice. "Apparently he's a loner, as you described, and he's also Polish."

"Really? How old is he?"

"I don't know – they didn't say."

I took my own coat off, picked up the telephone and rang Chief Inspector Givens.

"I believe you have a suspect?" I said. "Yes. Sally has given me the details; I just want to know how old this Polish man is. About 50. Does he speak English? A little. Where did you find him? I see. Are bringing him in for questioning? You are. Well, if you don't mind my saying so, I'd have an interpreter available. We'll be there shortly."

"Let's go," I said sharply. I didn't need this on a Saturday morning; I knew damned well this would not be our suspect; ours would be carefully hidden away. But I had to go through the motions.

We hardly spoke during the journey; to put it in the vernacular, I was pissed off at having to do this on a Saturday morning. Eventually it was Sally who spoke first.

"Er, how did you get on yesterday? Weren't you following someone home?"

"It isn't something I can talk about, Sally."

"Why? Is it a personal matter between you, the commander and MI5?"

I laughed. I could always rely on Sally to raise my spirits.

"So you do know something, then?" I declared.

"Not really, no. I just knew that Jim Robbins had put in a secure call to MI5. What it was about I've no idea."

"Better it stays that way. Right, here we are."

We had arrived at Wembley police station. I parked in a no-parking space and we went inside to talk to Chief Inspector Givens.

"Here," a burly sergeant at the desk said curtly, "you can't leave yer car there."

I flashed my warrant and said, "So give me a ticket. And then you can call Chief Inspector Givens."

He coloured up and got on the phone. He then pointed down a corridor. "You'll find him along there, Chief Inspector, second door on the right."

I thanked him. The chief inspector was in his office, along with a woman, who I took to be an interpreter, and another policeman, who was introduced to us as Sergeant Driscoll. The woman's name I couldn't remember.

"Hah. Angie," the chief inspector announced, after the introductions. "We have the man in a custody cell. I thought I'd wait for you to arrive before we questioned him."

"Has he said anything?"

He shook his head. "Not a word; but, then, the interpreter here hasn't spoken to him yet. Shall we go?"

We followed him out of the office, and into an interview room that was so small that Sally and the other sergeant had to stand. A policeman brought in the suspect. I gave him one look and decided that this was, as I had expected, a complete waste of time. This was not our man – but I could hardly disclose that to Givens. This man was greying and looked sallow, with a thin face as if he were ill. And I thought he was a lot more than 50 years of age.

The interpreter asked the man his name and he mumbled some reply that, again, I didn't understand.

"Do you want to begin?" the chief inspector asked me.

"Sure. Ask Mr..."

"Zalenski."

"Right. Ask Mr Zalenski why he was breaking into the school."

The interpreter translated but the man had already understood. "Because I have no money and nowhere to live. I thought that with school closed for weekend would be somewhere to stay. Worked as carpenter until became ill; then had to give up work. Won't take money off government."

"Very commendable. Ask him how long he has lived in the UK."

There was an exchange of language and finally the interpreter said, "He doesn't remember. He says it was a long time ago, but I can't get anything more from him."

"Ask him why does he like little boys?"

"Jesus!" she gasped. "You want me to ask him that?"

I nodded. "And when he denies it, which he surely will, ask him then why does he rape and then murder them?"

I watched his face turn colour, first red and then white, after she had asked him the second question. His eyes bulged, then he put his head in his hands and shook violently from side to side, moaning incoherently.

The interpreter turned to me and shook her head. "Well, you can see what the questions have done to him."

"Yes. But has he given you an answer?"

"Only to say he was in the hospital with pneumonia when the news of the first boy was announced."

She then gave me the name of the hospital, which I handed over to Sally. "Check it out, Sally. Also get a description from the ward; if they're not able to give one we'll have to take Mr Zalenski to the hospital for an identification check. I think we should turn him over to Social Services, don't you, inspector?"

He let out a sigh and then nodded. "Yeah, I think you're right. I'll let the crime of breaking and entering go." He pointed a finger at him, and said, "You, Mr Whatever Your Name Is, will have to register with Social Services; they will find you somewhere to live and something to eat..." He looked towards me. "I don't think he's eaten for God knows how long. Sorry about this, chief inspector, but I thought for a moment we had a candidate."

"Don't stop looking," I replied. I asked Sally, "Any luck with the hospital?"

"Yes. A Mr Zalenski was hospitalised for about ten days during the period in question; his description stacks up."

"Okay. We'll be on our way. Sorry about all this, Mr Zalenski, but we are looking for a very dangerous man and we have to check out everyone who arouses our suspicions."

As we were leaving he grunted, as the interpreter translated the information.

* * * * * *

In the car on the way back Sally said to me, "You knew he wouldn't be our man, didn't you?"

"Of course. But I didn't want to let the chief inspector down; he needs all the encouragement he can get at the present."

"I agree with you, Angie, but I felt sorry for that poor man. He looked to me as if he hadn't eaten a decent meal for ages, and he looked so poorly."

I snorted; it was a Saturday morning and we weren't in Social Services. "So, we did him a favour. Now Social Services will look after him: he'll have some money in his pocket, a place to stay and food in his stomach." I laughed. "He should be thanking us."

There was nothing happening back at the office; no new files had appeared. I went downstairs to see if Ian Blakey was in. He was – he was in a confab with one of his detectives.

"Angie, I'm glad you're back – I was looking for you earlier." He handed me a file. "I think you'll agree this belongs with your department."

I groaned. Not another one! "What is it, Ian? Serial killer? Rapist? Child abductor? Or is it one of those crimes that fall out of the classification?"

He gave a smile; a little bit forced, I thought. "Read it, and then come back to me. You'll be here all day, won't you?"

"I wasn't planning on it but someone seems to have made up my mind. I'll get back to you later."

I opened the file, alone in the office; everyone else had cleared off, and I didn't blame them. And, when I thought about it, what the hell was I going to do on my own on a Saturday afternoon?

It was a serial killer I was reading about. Old hat, I knew, but this was a character who was murdering prostitutes in the Midlands. He wasn't simply murdering them but, rather like the Yorkshire Ripper, he was carving them into pieces, disfiguring them with a sharp-bladed knife and hacking out their eyes. I saw the photos of the corpses and shuddered; whoever was doing this was yet another monster. The vulvas of the women had been savaged so much it was impossible to make out what remained. Their throats had been hacked away, and I found myself looking at deep wounds that carried on into the back of the vertebrae; one woman had had her spine almost cut in two.

"Oh, dear God!" I thought. "Not another one."

My eyes filled with tears as I looked at the photos. I would never understand how any human being could do this to another, regardless of what she did for a living.

"Oh, Katy, what am I to do with this savagery?"

"You will deal with it, Angie. In exactly the same way you are dealing with the others"

"But I don't seem to be making any progress. We've hardly moved a step since the first case."

"You will, trust me. You have all the basics in place, and things will begin to happen."

I can continue to guide you, Angie; and I will do so."

I was devastated by this latest tragedy to be dropped in my lap. I didn't know where to begin in solving these crimes in the Midlands. Why hadn't they been reported earlier? Probably because the police there believed they could apprehend the criminal, I thought. Isn't that why they ended up on my desk – because the local force had had no luck in finding the culprit? And isn't that why we were here – to shine a torch into the darkness and discover who it was who was hiding?

I placed the file to one side. I would leave it for now, consider it fully over the weekend and perhaps plan to go to Birmingham on Monday. With Sally. "Should I warn her?" I asked myself. Probably not; best to let her have a peaceful weekend. I rang down to Ian and informed him that we would look into the case but that I wouldn't act on it until Monday.

"Good luck, Angie," he said. "But remember, won't you, if you do need any help then we're here for you."

"I'll let you know, Ian. And, thanks."

CHAPTER THIRTY-EIGHT

I swallowed my disappointment at not having heard from Steve, and decided I would travel that night on the tube to Kensal Green, where Sam and Phil would be keeping a watch.

I gave the drink a miss that night, watched the proverbially bad television for a bit and then travelled from Edgware Road down to Kensal Green. It was 10.30; possibly a bit early for the rapist, but I did need to settle my nerves. At each stop I changed carriages; it was eerily quiet. There were very few passengers on at that time of night: a couple of young girls, possibly coming home from the cinema; a rather tired-looking businessman, working unusually late on a Saturday night; and two teenage black guys, strutting out as if they were hunting girls but not presenting any danger. I read the evening's paper and tried to look unconcerned at my surroundings.

I got off at Kensal Green and approached Sam and his partner.

"What are you doing here, Angie? Checking up on us, are you?"

It wasn't even funny. With a straight face I said, "If I had to check up on you two then you wouldn't have the job in the first place. No, I had nothing to do so I thought I would travel on what might be the same tube as the rapist and see if I can't spot something."

"Are you going back to Edgware?" Phil asked me.

"Yeah. For just as long as you two are around. So, if you see some guy following me then you'll know who he is – so for Christ's sake don't lose me."

Three times I travelled on that tube, and each time it got busier and busier; it was good to let the officers know that I too was putting in a hard night. On the fourth journey I spotted him; I couldn't help it, as he was casting gloating eyes at me, ignoring two separate and attractive girls. He was slim with a shaved head and looked vaguely like the photofit Rachel Humphries had sketched out with our artist. It was his eyes that I was drawn to; they were a pale shade of olive green, almost exactly as Rachel had described. I lifted the paper to cover my face; I wouldn't want him to see that I was watching him.

I got off at Kensal Green and looked for Sam and Phil, but I couldn't spot them. "Shit," I thought; "I hope they haven't disappeared." I walked out of the station and headed off up the road to nowhere; I had an uncomfortable feeling that this character was following me but I daren't look behind me.

The road became quiet, with hardly any pedestrians about. Just as I came to an unlit section of the road someone suddenly grabbed me from behind, a hand around my throat. I tried to scream but he was squeezing my windpipe. I was dragged forcibly into a nearby alleyway and I felt my jeans being pulled down. I tried to scream but then a knife was forced into my throat, and I felt a trickle of blood easing down my neck. I was absolutely terrified, and there was no help from the officers; I was completely alone with this monster and I watched in horror as he pulled my knickers down to my ankles. He was grunting, inane mutterings that I couldn't decipher. His knife was pressed ever more firmly against my throat, and the blood became even more profuse.

I moaned, "Oh no, please no, don't do this to me." He thrust his penis into my hand, expecting me to slide it inside my vagina.

"Fucking bitch! You know you're going to love this. Come on, put it in your cunt!"

Suddenly, I had a flash of inspiration. I pulled him towards me to open him up, and then I kneed him in the testicles, not once but again and again, until he doubled up in agony on the floor. As he was going down, though, he forced the knife he was holding into my neck, causing the blood to spurt out and soak onto my blouse. I thought I was going to faint.

At that moment Sam and Phil came charging into the alleyway, astonishment on their faces. Sam knelt down and handcuffed the suspect, whilst Phil held up my torn jeans, out of decency. I couldn't speak for a few minutes; I was overcome with shock at this outrage. My hands were shaking and my whole body trembled with distress.

Eventually I dressed myself and said in a furious but wheezy tone, "Where the fuck where you two?"

"Sorry, Angie, but we were following another character from off the earlier train. We genuinely thought it was our suspect."

Phil put a handkerchief to my throat to stem the blood. "We'll have to get you to a hospital. Someone's gotta look at that."

"How the hell did you know where to find me?" I croaked.

"Because when we got back to the station a train pulled in which we knew was yours, but you weren't on it. It was Phil who guessed you must have arrived whilst we were following this guy and you were the one being followed. Angie, I am so sorry. If you hadn't had the foresight to knee him…fucking hell! You might have been dead by now."

He dragged the rapist to his feet. I noticed, with my weird sense of humour, his penis was still dangling – a spent force, I thought. Phil delivered him a caution, charging him with attempted rape and attempted murder. The man said nothing; I doubted if he could breathe. I had a close look at his face at last, and noticed that it bore little resemblance to the drawing we had got from Rachel Humphries, although I was too shocked to make a meaningful comparison.

Outside the alleyway a police car was waiting, with two uniforms standing at the side of the vehicle.

"'Take him in," Sam said. "He's been charged with rape and attempted murder; I'm sure they'll be other charges in due course. Tell your inspector I'll be with him shortly to fill out the forms.

"Oh, and ask him his name, will you? I haven't had the chance yet. And call an ambulance straight away; our chief inspector needs attention."

I was still shaking, imagining what might have happened if I hadn't acted so promptly. That bastard would have fucked me and then murdered me. I was partly embarrassed that Sam and Phil had seen me naked, but that was part of the job and we had caught our killer. I did notice, however, that Sam was the one who was surreptitiously glancing at my pubes.

The hospital, the same one that Mark had been in, wanted me to stay the night, but I refused. A nursing sister bathed my throat and placed padding on it. "You might require stitches in the morning, and you have lost quite a bit of blood. I still believe you should stay the night; you are in shock and the doctor wants to give you a sedative."

She was right; I was feeling very shaky. I nodded and lay back on the bed. A doctor arrived and gave me an injection, which made me drowsy. The next thing I knew it was morning and I had a monumental headache. I asked the nurse for some pills and was given some Panadol. Then I tried to get up but my legs weren't working; a restraining hand was placed on my shoulder and a soothing voice said, "You've had a terrible shock and we think you should stay here for another day."

I couldn't argue. My throat was throbbing and I felt absolutely exhausted. I was in a side room now; they must have moved me when I was asleep. I closed my eyes and sank into myself. When I came to a doctor was examining my throat. "I'm going to have to put a few stitches in here," he announced. "I've given you a local anaesthetic so you won't feel a thing."

He was right; I felt nothing. Then he bandaged my neck and eased me down in the bed.

"Rest for a while. You should be feeling better by this time tomorrow."

I tried to speak but my voice was still croaky. Then I told myself, what the hell? It's Sunday today; I'll be fine tomorrow. I drifted off again, wondering if Steve might have phoned me.

I woke up later that afternoon to see him standing at the side of my bed; I thought I was hallucinating.

"Took your time getting here, didn't you?" I croaked. I reached out and touched his hand. "My God," I squealed, "you're real! I'm not dreaming."

"Jim Robbins rang me and told me about your experience the other night…"

"You mean last night?" I interrupted.

"No. Today is Monday, Angie. You've been here for two nights. That was some shock you went through; at the moment I don't think anyone is talking to your two officers. And Jim said he'll be along later."

He sat at the side of the bed and held my hand. It was very comforting.

"Thank you for coming, Steve; I really appreciate it. I can't tell you how distressing it was. I can imagine now how those other rape victims felt. It was a disgusting violation."

"I rang you on Saturday but your mobile was turned off. Then yesterday I heard about the rapist, but they wouldn't let me see you. I am so sorry, Angie; I can't imagine what you must have gone through." He touched the padding on my throat, gently. "If I'd been there I'd have killed the bastard. As it is he's appeared before the magistrates and been remanded in custody. I hope he gets life."

We talked for a little while, and then the nurse came in and said I should sleep. It was nice to have someone to look after me; it reminded me of when I was young and I had a caring mother – before she started to have her flings with other men. Willingly I drifted off again.

I dreamt of Katy. It was almost like one of my visions, but I really didn't want to talk to her. I mean, she really ought to have warned me.

When I woke up, Jim was there. He shook his head at me. "I can't have a go at you this time, can I? You're the one who put her life at risk, although I should ask you why you didn't wait for the officers to appear."

"I thought they were right behind me, Jim.' I noticed I was speaking better. "I had no idea they were following another suspect."

"Like I said, Ange, I'm not going to criticise you; but, fucking hell, he would have killed you if you hadn't acted so propitiously."

I smiled. "Still good with the words, Jim, aren't you? What does it mean?"

"It means you acted advantageously. In other words, Ange, if you hadn't kneed him in the balls I doubt you would have been around today."

He stood back and looked me over. "It reminds me of the time I came to see you in Birmingham hospital; you were almost at risk of death then. I'm not sure I'll be able to forgive those two – they should have known better. One of them should have stayed behind at the station."

"Then they still would have been in trouble, Jim; you would've crucified them for acting individually."

Reluctantly he nodded. "I guess you're right. Anyway, Ange, I don't want to see you at the Yard for a couple of weeks. Go home and rest."

"Who is this guy?"

"Frank Bartley; would you believe he's an inspector on the underground? He has a wife and two kids; they're in shock now they've been told the news."

"That would explain why he always attacked from the tube; he'd be able to travel free and no one would know where he was. I expect I'll have to give evidence."

"You will, unless he pleads guilty."

"I would love to have had a crack at interrogating him."

"Don't even think about it; you're a victim not a policewoman. He's on remand – I guess he'll be there for the next six months or so."

"Good. Jim, I've had a new case passed on to me by Ian; this is a vicious serial killer murdering prostitutes in Wolverhampton. I promised him I would go up on…well, yesterday."

"I know. I've sent Sam and Sally up there. No doubt they'll get in touch with you when they get back."

He walked towards the door. "Meanwhile –go home and rest, heroine. I'll ring you later in the week. Bye, Ange."

"Bye, Jim; thanks for coming."

CHAPTER THIRTY-NINE

They discharged me the next morning. I was still feeling wobbly but Phil was there with a car to take me home. I grimaced as I climbed into the front seat.

"Thanks, Phil. How did you know they were letting me out?"

"I rang them. And since I was partly responsible for your injuries the least I can do is to take you home."

He helped me up to my flat and offered to make me some coffee.

"Thanks, but I'd rather rest." I waved him away and went to sit on the bed.

Katy's image appeared; she was smiling, as if nothing had happened to me other night.

"You're a great Spirit Guide," I proclaimed, irritation in my voice.

"I know you've had a bad time of it, Angie, but you didn't ask for my help, did you?"

"What? You mean, I have to ask for help even when I have a knife at my throat?"

"Not in as many words, no. But you have to bear in mind that when you're awake it is difficult to penetrate your subconscious – even when you are terrified. To put it simply, you are out of sync."

I grunted. "I didn't ask you to appear now –so why did you?"

"Really? Then you should question your subconscious; you were already talking to me, asking me why I hadn't helped you. Think about it, my dear."

There was that expression again – 'my dear'. Fucking hell, she was younger than me.

She grinned this time – not simply a smile but a grin spreading all over her face.

"What are you grinning at, Katy?"

"Your blasphemy. You forget I'm able to read your mind when I have to. And you might think I'm younger than you, Angie, but I have lived so many lives I must be over 1,000 years older than you are. So, can I suggest you forget the Katy who was Danny's twin sister, and try to think of me as an ancient, wise prophet."

"I'll try. But how will you be able to help the next time I have an experience like the other night?"

"I have told you once already. You have to pray. So, instead of having that soak in the bath you planned, visit the church on Marylebone High Street. Will you do that for me?"

I did as she suggested, except that this time there was no priest in the church. I went to the altar and prayed; I poured out everything I was feeling and asked God to help me. I asked him also to help me contact Katy when I needed to, either consciously or subconsciously. I don't think I have ever prayed so much in all my life – and I really meant it. When I left the church I couldn't help grinning. Here I was, about to become something of a devout Christian, when for most of my life I couldn't even be bothered to attend church even at Christmas.

When I got home I went to bed, forgetting that I needed a bath. When I woke up I was feeling a lot better, and decided I'd have some lunch today. It seemed to be ages since I'd had anything to eat and I was starving. I managed a cup of coffee and a poached egg on toast and then decided I would now have that soak in a long bath – sort of ease my troubles away. Just then my mobile went off. God, wasn't I allowed to have any peace?

"Angela Crossley. Oh, Sally. Yes, thanks, but I'm okay now. I was just about to soak in a hot bath. I hear you and Sam have been to Birmingham? What have you found?"

I listened to her horrifying story of butchered prostitutes who were almost unrecognisable: organs torn out, vulvas slashed and throats cut with a sharp-bladed knife. It wasn't a story I wanted to hear at the moment, especially after my own experiences. I was tempted to tell her that she was being insensitive when she broke down on the telephone and began to cry.

"Where are you?" I asked. "You're at home? Right, do you know where I live?" She didn't, so I gave her my address and told her to get herself across here. That was the bath gone – now I would have to be the proverbial Aunt Sally!

I hadn't thought too much about the Birmingham case, which was understandable, given that I had just had a knife wound stitched and bandaged. But I did remember the crime scene photos; they were horrifying. It was if someone had had an uncontrollable rage against prostitutes and attacked them with a frenzy that was literally psychopathic. Whoever it was he was a maniac; he was not someone we could ever regard as sane.

When the doorbell rang I was tuned into the case, having refreshed my memory.

It was a tear-stained Sally standing there.

"Come in," I gestured, giving her a hug. She leaned on my shoulder for quite a while, shuddering. I already had the coffee pot on so I led her into the kitchen, poured her a cup and sat down beside her. I didn't speak for some minutes; she was obviously distressed and I allowed her to try and recover her composure in her own time.

Then I said, "What is it that has so upset you, Sally? Was it the photos?"

"No." She shook her head. "It was the nightmare. I had this vivid picture that this man was attacking me with a knife; I was the prostitute and he bludgeoned me again and again whilst I was still alive. Angie, you can't imagine what it was like."

Then an image flashed in front of me about Sally. She had been a prostitute, and in Birmingham, where the murders had occurred; that's why she was so terrified. I put my arm around her and hugged her again.

"Shh," I whispered. "It was only a dream. It won't recur, I promise you."

"Yes, but you don't realise…"

"I do realise, Sally," I interrupted. "I know what you were, but that was a long time ago; it's in the past and you should put it behind you."

She looked at me, with tears still streaming down her face. "You know? How…how could you know? No one knows, Angie. How did you find out? Have you been spying on me?"

Sometimes my gift was capable of backfiring on me; this was one of those times.

"No, Sally. I haven't been spying on you. I've told you before, I sense things. They just come to me without any warning. This was one of those times."

She sniffed. "I knew you were a fucking clairvoyant. Do you want me to talk about it?"

"Only if it helps you." I ignored her remark about clairvoyance; it was something I would have to get used to.

"I was young – very young. I ran away from home when I was 15. I met up with some bad people in Birmingham, couldn't get a job – I was too young. So they put me on the game…"

"What, at 15?" I interrupted again, astonished at the news.

"Yeah. Well, like I said, they were bad people, and it was the only way I could earn a living. I hated it. I hated it then and I hate it now."

"Where did you originally come from, Sally?"

"From Bristol. We were a very poor family and my father used to beat me and sexually assault me. So I ran away. Haven't seen any of them since then."

"Good God, Sally. I had no idea you had been so brutalised. It's not surprising you were never attracted to men."

She smiled faintly. "I never questioned my sexual side, Angie. What I do know is that since I was a prostitute...what I mean is that, since I gave it up I have never been with a man. Nor do I ever want to." Then she grinned. "How do you know about my lesbianism? Was it Laura who told you?"

I shook my head. "I just knew. Another of those inspirations. So, the police obviously never picked you up?"

"No. They were too careful for that. I never went on the streets – not even when I was old enough. It was a kind of brothel, a massage parlour, where I used to give blow jobs at first, then the real thing." She shuddered. "Then one of the girls on the street was murdered. The MO was almost identical with these girls we're looking at."

"When was this?"

"Oh, I don't know. About ten years ago now." She shuddered. "It was horrible. To see her all mutilated, her body slashed to ribbons."

"And I suppose they never found anyone?"

"No. I'm not surprised I have nightmares now. Did you see the photos of those poor girls?"

I nodded. "Yes, I did. And you needn't worry about your secret, Sally; it's very safe with me. So, what if anything did you learn in Wolverhampton?"

"Well, Sam and I spoke to a senior inspector – can't remember his name offhand; he was very helpful. They've been looking for this character for almost a year. Five girls he's brutalised, savagely..."

"I know; I saw the pictures. I also read the autopsy reports."

"Yeah, well the last one was nearly a month ago and they're afraid he'll strike again. The commander informed us this would definitely be our case; I hope you don't mind him sending us to the Midlands."

I gazed at her - she seemed to have recovered. "I don't mind. In fact, you and Sam can have this case, if you like?"

She shook her head. "I wouldn't think so. We were told to go up there on your behalf and see what we could gather."

I thought about it for a while. Perhaps the maniac who had murdered one of Sally's friends all those years ago was just starting his career. Maybe he'd been in prison and was released at the same time these latest killings began.

"Has anyone checked the records – for criminals released?"

She went to get another cup of coffee. "I wouldn't think so. How could they tie them together?"

"No. Of course not. But we can. Why don't you get on to Ian and ask him to trace all releases in the west Midlands area, say up to a year ago. Let's see if we can make a contact. Tell him I've asked him to do it, so he'll have a good idea what it might be connected to."

"Right. Shall I do it now?"

"Are you sure you're up to going back to the office?"

She nodded.

"Do it, then. But go down and see Inspector Blakey – you'll find him more cooperative."

"I'll let you know what he says. When do you think you might be back, Angie?"

"Dunno. The commander says I'm to take the rest of the week off; I'll go out of my mind if I do. Do you fancy lunch, Sally? I'm starving; I haven't eaten for a couple of days. On me!" I pronounced.

"Hell, yes. What do you fancy?"

"I'll tell you what I fancy: a chateaubriand. A great big fillet steak. There's a good French restaurant on Charlotte Street. Shall we go there?"

* * * * * *

I remembered the restaurant, having been there with Jim just before I started at the Yard. It wasn't cheap but the food was excellent. We sat down and ordered. I had bottled water and Sally ordered a glass of house wine. We then ordered the steak.

"How is Laura getting on at Rachel Humphries' – she did move in, didn't she?"

"She loves it; they both do. It's very convenient for Laura and it helps Rachel, not being on her own. She's still suffering, you know."

"I gathered she might; I'm still suffering and I wasn't raped." My hands began to shake as I mentioned this. It was the thought of the knife in my throat and the blood soaking into my blouse.

"Are you alright, Angie? You look shaken, as though you've seen a ghost."

"I'm okay – it's the after-effects. It would shake anybody up. Ah, here's our lunch."

We didn't talk after that; we both enjoyed the food. As the waiter was clearing our plates away, Sally asked, "How did you know I was a lesbian, Angie? You haven't explained."

Here we go again! Another difficult question. More and more I had to deal with these issues.

"I'm not too sure," I admitted. "I guess it just came to me. One of those 'sensing' things."

"Can I ask you something – something very personal?"

"Oh hell; here it comes," I thought, trying to prepare my answer. "Sure. Why not."

"I just wanted to know if you might fancy me."

"Fucking hell, Sally; where did that come from?"

She shrugged, not in the least bit embarrassed. "I thought…well, we do know each other; you know, those of the same disposition."

"And you thought I might be a lesbian?"

"No – well, not completely. But I still think you might fancy me – you know, a bisexual? Are you?"

I tried to look shocked; I wasn't sure it worked. " You don't hang about, do you? And I'm surprised you think I might fancy you; I mean, I haven't made any suggestions to you or any approaches, have I?"

She grinned as if she knew – all about Paula and all about Kelly. "You don't have to," she said. "We just know. It doesn't matter to me. Angie. But if you do fancy me I would like to know. I need to know how to deal with it – I do have a girlfriend, you know."

"And I have a boyfriend," I said stiffly. "And, Sally, if I did fancy you then you would know it by now. So, shall we change the subject?"

"I hope you don't mind my asking you?"

"Of course not. But I would hate you to mention this conversation to the others."

"You don't have to worry," she said, after I'd paid the bill and she left me on the street. I was still metaphorically shaking my head. The truth is, I did fancy her, just a little, but the advent of Steve had kind of changed my direction. Still, it was interesting if nothing else. I tucked it away in the back of my mind for future reference.

CHAPTER FORTY

It was now Wednesday and I was bored to tears, as I had thought I would be. I was also feeling lonely and down in the dumps. The shock of being violated by that bastard still hadn't worn off. I'd heard from Steve again, who regrettably was committed on a different case, but he promised me we would have dinner later in the week. "Perhaps it'll be tonight," I thought to myself. I considered Sally's overtures to me – but only on the basis of my loneliness. I would have to try to resist the temptation.

I decided I would ignore Jim's suggestion and go into the office at lunchtime to see if I could help. I was greeted with a host of smiles, as if I'd been away for years. Sam came over to speak to me and I said, holding out a hand, "Don't say anything, Sam. I'd rather we forgot the other night's incident.

"Anything happening?" I asked of anyone.

Sally gave me her depressed expression. "You're not supposed to be here; you said you were taking the rest of the week off."

"Yeah, tell me about it. I am so fed up staying in that flat on my own…"

"…You thought you'd come in and give us all a hard time!" Phil interrupted.

"You haven't answered my question," I insisted.

"They've found another body in Wolverhampton," Sally replied.

"Same MO?" I asked, trying to keep the weariness out of my voice.

She nodded. "Brutally savaged. Throat cut, intestines pulled out and vagina mutilated. There was hardly anything left to identify." She checked her notes. "She was 22, three previous convictions. Evidently not terribly attractive, so she had to work hard to persuade customers to have sex with her." She sighed deeply. "This is the sixth prostitute he has butchered. Angie, we have to stop him."

"You're preaching to the converted."

"Have you spoken to the inspector in charge of the case?" I enquired.

"Yes. He rang me this morning. He's a DI Sutton, from Wolverhampton New Street; I don't think he wants this case passed over to us."

"So give it back to them. It's not our call."

"I tried to – but the commander has overruled him."

"You spoke to the commander?" I demanded.

She looked at me hesitantly. "Well, yes. We didn't think you were going to come in; you said you might be off all the week."

I nodded my apology. "And what about Ian Blakey? Did you speak to him yesterday?"

She waved a sheet towards me. "Yes. Here's the list. Most of the prisoners are from Winsom Green. In the last 12 months almost 300 prisoners were released; many of them are on parole."

I looked at the list. "What we need to do is delete the short-term prisoners – in other words, those serving less than a five-year sentence. We're looking for someone who originally was sentenced to, say, about ten years or upwards. What I mean is, we're seeking a prisoner who was let out a year ago either on parole or because his sentence was up. Is that clear?"

"I think so. Do you want us to get on to it?"

"Yes. Why not? Here," I said, stretching out my hand, "give me some names." I felt the weariness might leave me if I got on with something productive.

I scanned through the list and started scratching out the names of those who I thought wouldn't qualify. Out of the 100 or so names I was left with four who might fit the bill. Two of these I eventually dismissed as being too old; I doubted if anyone in his 60s would have the strength to attempt the savage slaughter of young prostitutes.

That left me with two names: a Jack McCloud and an Arthur Mortimer, the latter originally a priest who had served the full ten years of his sentence. Interestingly, he was found guilty of rape and sodomy, and since he had never admitted his guilt he was never considered for parole. He was worth considering, although he would now be on the sex register. The first man, this McCloud, was a murderer released on parole after serving ten years of his life sentence. He had killed a prostitute in the Wolverhampton district; I read his MO, and it appeared that there might be a link with the current murders. I placed him at the top of the list. Both men were in their mid- to late 30s.

"What have you got, Sally?" I asked her.

She shrugged. "Nothing of any consequence. There is one character here who might qualify, but I'm not sure." She passed on the name to me, a David Tenet, released after serving ten years of a life sentence for murdering his wife. I couldn't really find any correlation between his case and the present murders.

"I agree; I'm not sure either. What about you guys – have you found anything?"

Sam shook his head; Phil had just finished his list and joined the 'no candidates club'. Laura insisted she had two possibilities; one was on the maybe list whilst the other could be a prime suspect. Peter just shook his head at me.

The first one, a Duncan Williams, was a 45-year-old who had murdered a male prostitute; I might give him a second thought but not too seriously. Her second possibility, an Angus Connelly, was a 38-year-old; originally he had been sentenced to a seven-year stretch for the manslaughter of his girlfriend, which was extended by a further three years after he was found guilty of GBH for attacking one of the sex offenders in the protected wing of the prison. He was not granted an early release.

Laura was right. This man definitely needs to be added to our suspect list.

We gathered around the conference table. "Let's look at what we've got," I said. "We have four or five names who could fit the bill." I listed them out on the board. "I believe they should all be investigated, and they all live in the west Midlands area."

"You mean, they used to," Sally commented. "We don't where they live now – I'm talking of those who completed their sentences. The ones on parole we should know about because they have to report to their parole officer."

"Let's see; how many are there who completed their sentence? We have three men here who I would place high on the suspect list.

"One: Jack McCloud. Murdered a prostitute in the Wolverhampton district. Let out on parole after serving ten years of his life sentence.

"Two: Arthur Mortimer, the ex-priest who served his full sentence of ten years. Guilty of the rape and sodomy of a young boy. Never admitted his guilt.

"Three: Angus Connelly, a 38-year-old, seemingly a very violent man who beat up and killed his girlfriend and was given a seven-year sentence for manslaughter, then served a further three-year stretch for beating up a prisoner on the secure wing. No parole.

"So, gang, let's examine these three, shall we? As Sally says, there is only one man, Jack McCloud, and we know where he lives because he should be on the sex register. The other two we have to investigate."

"Can I say something?" Phil interjected. When I nodded he went on to ask, "How do we know these three men might be involved in the murders of the six prostitutes? I mean, it seems we've plucked them out of thin air. I can't make any sense out of it and I'm supposed to be a good copper."

"That's because your experience is different from mine," I tried to explain. "I remember that when I worked as a young WPC in Steelhouse Lane, about 11 years ago, there was a prostitute murdered in the Wolverhampton district. I checked into it and discovered the MO was almost identical with these latest murders. No one was caught. Since there were no subsequent murders, until recently it seemed to me that whoever did it could well have been sentenced to a long term in prison – that is, either a life sentence or a ten-year stretch without parole. Serial killers, who murder gratuitously, do not ever give up; there is no such thing as a retirement plan or a pension fund. So, that could mean he is either dead, which is unlikely as we have the same MO, or he spent time in prison.

"So that is who we're looking for."

"You have a bloody good memory, Angie," Phil said dryly.

"That's why I'm a chief inspector, Phil, and you have a long way to go." I saw Sally give me an ominous look, as if to say "Stop beating up the subordinates".

I handed out the forms I had written down the names on and announced, 'So, Sally, you go for number one, Sam, you're number two, and Phil, you're number three. Use Laura and Peter to help you.

"I want you to investigate each of the men: find out where they're living now, assuming that's possible, or at least the last address we have for them; are they working and, if so, where? What have they been doing since they were released? But be careful with the ones who have served their sentence; we have no claims on them, at least not for the time being. Have the local police been keeping an eye out for them, and if so what if anything have they uncovered?

"Find out everything you can: partners, children, telephone numbers, social contacts, debts and social habits. This is going to take some time, but my intuition tells me it will be worth it. So, let's get to it."

* * * * * *

It was late afternoon and I was feeling incredibly exhausted; the time spent in the office hadn't helped as I thought it might. I desperately needed a sleep. I hadn't forgotten what Katy had to say to me, that my weariness would ease. Before I left, Andy, one of the officers from the basement, came up with a folder. I hadn't bothered to speak with Ian

Blakey; I was too damned tired, and if anything had happened with Ajas he would have told me – or Jim would have.

"Not another one?" I queried as I saw the file, frustration written all over my face.

He grinned. "I'm afraid so, Angie. I think you might like this one."

"So tell me about it – I'm damned if I'm going to guess."

"Well, I have to tell you that your rapist is still around."

"What?!" I almost shouted. "What do you mean? We caught him last week."

"You caught someone who was trying to kill you in Kensal Green, but it wasn't our man. I've also checked the photofit with the mug shot we have of your assailant and they don't match."

I looked at him, puzzled. "So who did we catch, Andy?"

"Probably you caught the killer, the murderer of the two girls in Kilburn and Maida Vale. However, our rapist is not yet a killer. He raped a young girl in an alleyway close to Primrose Hill – same MO as the previous eight he's raped, except this one he's beaten the shit out of." He handed me a photo of a young girl whose face was badly disfigured. One of her eyes was closed, her nose was badly broken and she had a wide gash down one side of her cheek.

"Fuck me!" was all I could say.

Andy grinned sardonically. "Thought you'd like it, Angie."

"Shit!" Why the hell hadn't Katy told me? "Where is the victim?" I asked.

He scratched his head. "You're not thinking of going there now, are you?"

I shrugged. "Why not? I was going home for a sleep, but – well, who cares."

"She's at home with her parents. They let her out of hospital this morning, but she has to go back for surgery when the swelling dies down."

He gave me the address; it was a place overlooking the park. I called for Sally, as she was the best bet to go with me. I also placed a small scarf around my throat so my bandaging wouldn't protrude.

"Did we make a mistake?" Sally asked on the way to the car pool.

"In one sense we did. We assumed that the murderer of the Kilburn and Maida Vale girls was the same one we have been chasing for the last month."

"And he isn't?"

"No, Sally. He very definitely isn't. The original rapist has just raped another girl, this time near to Primrose Hill, and I'm informed his MO is the same as all the others."

"Shit!"

"That's what I said." I passed over the address to her. "That's where we're going now, to her parents to interview the girl."

"When did it happen?"

"Last night, I'm told. She called the police, who referred it to the Crime Squad. She's also been to the hospital, which has confirmed it is rape. Now she's under sedation at her parents' house; I don't really expect they'll want us to talk to her, but..."

"...You want to know if she saw anything?"

"Yes. Did you pass the name you were given on to someone else?"

"Of course. I gave it to Laura."

"Do you think that was wise, Sally?"

She laughed. "We have to give her a chance, Angie. She has been with the force now for quite a few years."

"As a detective?"

"Well, not really... But she's dead keen, and I know we can trust her with this little job. And thank you for not letting on about my past."

I shrugged. "I told you I wouldn't. Is this the street?" I asked, uncertain.

She went down it and then turned a half-circle to stop outside one of these upmarket houses with an enviable view of the park. I rang the bell, and the door was opened after a moment or two by a relatively young woman with bouffant hair and a smart tailored suit.

"Oh," was all she said. "The police? Come in, won't you."

I introduced us. The woman said she was Anthea Goldring, and she led us into a spacious lounge, where the young victim was lying on a settee. Her face was a wreck – it looked decidedly worse than on the photos. She looked to be in a kind of daze.

"She isn't really fit enough to talk to you," Mrs Goldring announced.

"Yes. We appreciate that, ma'am, but there is only one question I need to ask her for now."

"Did she see her attacker? Is that what you mean?"

I nodded. What else could I say?

Mrs Goldring went over to her daughter and asked, "How are you feeling Sandra?"

The girl lifted her head and gazed across at us. She looked younger than her 19 years, with long fair hair, high cheekbones – at least, on the side that hadn't been slashed with a knife – and a troubled look in the eye she could see from.

"I'm okay," she said, as if even giving that low-key response disturbed her.

"Sandra, I want to ask you one question, if you don't mind," I said in a soft voice.

"Uh-huh."

"Did you see your attacker? Or even partly see him?"

"I saw the knife. And I saw a tattoo on his right forearm. It was a snake and it had some words on it, but I couldn't make them out. I was terrified; I still am."

"Okay, Sandra. That will do for now, but Sally here will come round tomorrow, if that's all right, to talk to you some more. Please try to think about the attack; you may remember something that will help us catch this man."

She nodded, and Mrs Goldring let us out of the house.

"Not a lot of use to us, was it?" Sally declared as we climbed into the car.

I ignored her. It was a beautiful day. One of the things I had noticed about the weather in this part of the world was that the sun was mostly shining and we didn't see all that rain they have in the north. I undid the top button of my blouse to let in some air, and I noticed that Sally treated herself to a sneaky peek at my bosom. I really would have to watch that one.

"I don't suppose we could have expected anything more – the poor girl is still in shock. I know how she feels."

I asked Sally to drop me in Camden, I was still feeling weary and I badly wanted to put my head down for the night.

For a horrible moment I thought she was going to ask me out for dinner; fortunately, she didn't. She squeezed my arm and suggested I have an early night. I really couldn't remember when I last felt so tired. Of course I'd forgotten about my hospitalisation in the west Midlands all those years ago.

I staggered into my flat and headed straight for the kitchen. A cup of coffee and a small salad, half an hour in front of the telly, and then bed. I was rather hoping that Steve might ring me.

He didn't.

CHAPTER FORTY-ONE

I had no visions that night; just a restful, relaxing sleep. I woke up feeling a little refreshed and fit again for work. I came out of the bathroom, and then I saw Katy. At least, I thought it was Katy, sitting at the side of my bed. I recognised her from her mannerisms, but facially she looked older and a hell of a lot wiser.

"Is this better?" she asked.

I looked at her doubtfully. "Why have you changed your appearance?"

"Because you always thought I was some kind of a youngster, and I thought you should see the real me."

"Humph. Well, you certainly do look older and wiser, but I'm not sure I prefer the change. Did my prayers help?" I added.

"Yes. They did, Angie. That is why I'm now able to come through to you when you need something. But you must keep praying; not each day, but try to go to church at least once a week – you have a long way to go yet."

"Thank you. I will. So, why are you here? Is there something you want to tell me?"

"Yes. You asked yesterday why I hadn't told you about the rapist. This is something you're going to have to learn, Angie; we can guide you but we cannot implement anything for you. You will make mistakes – imagine if your life was free of mistakes? How boring that would be for you. So, the rapist, you had to find out for yourself – as you did when that man attacked you.

"Also, I am here for a different reason this morning. I want you to be careful; I cannot tell you why but you are entering a very dangerous phase of your life. Someone is trying to kill you. So, be warned, Angie; I am not able to protect you other than issue this warning."

Then she disappeared, leaving my bonhomie seriously deflated.

" Someone is trying to kill me," I thought to myself. Who? And why? I didn't know anyone who seriously who might want to harm me. Did I? Then I thought about Ajas, the alleged terrorist; could he have drawn some conclusions?

I picked up the phone and rang through to Ian Blakey.

"Ian – hi; it's Angie Crossley here. I just wanted to check if Ajas was in this morning. He isn't. Oh, I see. When did you last see him – I mean, has he given any reason for his absence?" I listened in silence as he told me that Ajas had been missing since last week. He hadn't wanted to tell me, he admitted, as I was trying to recover from the attack on my person. A very police summary: an 'attack on my person'. No, there was no reason given for his disappearance.

Oh, shit! I thought. Was this what Katy was warning me about? I should have had a gun, but it was probably just as well I hadn't since I wouldn't have known how to use it.

"I will have to be very careful today," I tried to reassure myself as I put on my coat. I closed the front door, had a surreptitious look around me, discovered there was no one there and headed for the tube at Camden.

Suddenly a car screeched to a halt almost in front of me, and before I had time to act a man jumped out of the passenger seat, grabbed me by the neck and hauled me into the back of the car. All I could think of at the time was my throat: he was hurting my throat. Before I could look at him, or the other passengers in the car, a blindfold was wrapped hastily around my eyes and I could see nothing. I tried to speak but a guttural voice snapped, "Shut the fuck up."

I tried to still my fears. They weren't quite as bad as I felt they might be, since I had already had Katy's warning. "Was this it?" I asked aloud. There was no reply.

Would they kill me quickly, or was it to be one of those horrible, painful deaths that would remind me I had crossed the line? I kept silent, waiting for one of them to make an announcement; but they too said nothing.

I don't know how long we were travelling; I would guess for about an hour. I heard the sound of running water – a river, I thought. But which bloody river? Then we pulled up, the blindfold was removed and I saw Ajas in the front passenger seat. He scowled at me and pulled a gun from inside his jacket.

"Get out," he ordered.

I had no choice, since the other passenger dragged me out. I saw there were four of them; this must be the gang I had foreseen. Pity there was no sign of Ian or Jim Robbins. Held up by a grip on my arm, I was led fearfully towards what appeared to be a factory.

"Making weapons here, Ajas, are we? Bombs to blast us all to kingdom come?"

"Shut up, bitch. Your intuition has cost us too much already. Now we have to go into hiding. But you are going to pay for your interference, and afterwards we're going to leave your body on the steps of MI5 holding a photo of the bomb factory. Bring her in," he told my escort.

Now I was shaking. My hands were trembling and I seriously felt as if I were going to throw up. I had just received a sentence of death and the shock of it was coursing through me. I tried to resist, but next a gun was held to my head. As we were about to enter the factory a shot rang out, and I saw Ajas slump to the ground. Part of his head had disappeared. A second, a third and finally a fourth shot boomed around me, and I saw bodies falling to the ground. It was as if I had entered a military firing range, and I was terrified that missile fragments might catch me. I fell against the wall as my escort was hurled to the ground, a bullet hole in the back of his chest. Then I realised they were all dead, and I saw Steve, a smoking gun in his hand, walking towards me.

"Are you alright, Angie? They didn't hurt you, did they?"

I couldn't speak for a minute or two; I was too stunned at the sight of bodies all around me. Yet again I was in a state of shock. I turned away and vomited on the ground, over the feet of one of the dead.

"What have you done?" I was finally able to say. "They're all dead. You must have planned this."

He nodded, as if it were the most natural part of his job. "Just as well. And, yes, we did plan it. We suspected they would come for you after we raided their flat and they had scarpered. I'm glad we were right; otherwise, you'd be dead by now."

I glared at him, struggling to find my voice. "So why didn't you stop them when they caught me outside the tube station?" I was trembling and I couldn't stop my hands from shaking.

"Because then we wouldn't have known where this factory was." He pointed towards the building. "As it is, we've got them all, there'll be no problems with a trial and, most important of all, we've discovered the bomb-making factory." He grinned like the proverbial Cheshire cat.

"You bastard!" I hissed at him. I really felt like hitting him, he was so fucking arrogant. "You used me, didn't you? We had a glorious night of sex together just so you could exploit me." I spread my arms out to the bodies on the ground. "Doesn't this mean anything to you? You are responsible for their deaths; doesn't that trouble your tiny little conscience?"

"Come on, Angie," he retorted, holding my arm. "We have to get out of here; the others," he said, gesturing to his companions, "they'll clear up after we've gone."

He led me to his car and helped me into the front passenger seat.

"If you don't want me to, and I'll understand if you don't, then we won't speak on the journey back. But please, Angie, don't ask me any questions, because I won't be able to answer them. In fact, I shouldn't have told you what we were doing...' He shrugged. "I guess it was just the adrenalin."

He turned the radio on so as to silence me with the music. He was right: we didn't speak, not even when he dropped me off at the Yard. I took it from this morning's encounter that I wouldn't be seeing him again.

CHAPTER FORTY-TWO

I virtually staggered into Jim's office. His secretary was with him and he was about to ask me to come back later when saw my face. It was the secretary who was asked to leave.

"You look as if you've seen a ghost," he remarked, with real concern.

I was still in a state of shock. "I've just seen four men killed," I replied. "Shot, by that bastard Steve and his cohorts."

"What?" he shouted. "Shot – killed? You mean Steve Jenson – of MI5?"

"The very one."

He shook his head, trying to come to terms with what I'd just told him. "You'd better tell me about it, Ange. Then I'll draw my own conclusions."

So I did. I omitted to tell him about the warning I'd received this morning, but picked up from where I got abducted from outside Camden tube station. Then the blindfolded car journey, followed by a sighting of Ajas, the former police detective, and finally the shooting.

"Four single shots, Jim. Four men dead." I shuddered at the telling of the story. It was one of the most horrifying scenes I had ever witnessed. I put my hand to my throat after I noticed it was throbbing again.

"They must have planned it. Somehow they knew he would try to get at you and they wanted to know where the factory was."

I bit back the sentence I'd been thinking of saying about how astute he was; it was fucking self-evident.

He paused before continuing. "You're absolutely certain it was Steve Jenson?"

" 'Course I'm certain." That was also another fucking stupid question.

"I'll get on to someone at Thames House – make sure this is reported." Then he looked fixedly at me. "What worries me, Ange, is what to do about you. I got you into this position, into these dangers, and the more time you spend at this job the more uneasy I get."

I laughed, but humourlessly. "Are you trying to get rid of me, Jim?"

"No. I'm trying to think of something that might lessen the risk. Think about the past couple of weeks: you unearthed this terrorist, whose flat was raided and who then decided to kill you; you had one of your visions about the Maida Vale murderer, you travelled alone on the train and in the end you were the one who was almost murdered. What next, Ange? Do I allow these situations to take place, or do I arrange for a chaperone to follow you wherever you go? I'm still making up my mind."

"Yes, but neither of those incidents were my fault."

"I'm not saying they were. But I have to bear in mind that you see things others will never see – like the Ajas situation. You realised he was a terrorist and I believe he knew that. That would be one reason he fled from the safe house. What will you see next? Who next will want to take your life?"

He stood up and let out a long sigh. "I'm going to have to think about this, Ange; somehow try to keep you away from the sharp end. Are you going home now?"

"No. I thought I'd go back to my desk – take my mind off it."

"Okay. I'll get back to you. But if anything else happens, any intuitive visions, then please let me know. That is an order, Ange."

I nodded. What else could I say? I left his office thinking about all the things he had said to me over the years. The dressing down he'd given me in the west Midlands over Connie; the caution he'd exercised in Greater Manchester when he warned me to keep out of the front line; and now, I was still giving him a bad time with my scaremongering adventures. But then, he was the one who wanted me to join the Yard as a profiler and as head of the Intelligence Department. What else could I do but stay in the firing line? And I had to assume I would always have my Spirit Guide to watch over me. Perhaps what I should have done this morning was to stay in bed – not leave the flat at all.

But surely that would be cowardly; wouldn't I be running away from some unknown danger? And yet, I thought of all the dangers I had encountered since I took the job on: the taste of evil in Poland with the paedophile – touching the very essence of malevolence that shielded him; being sexually assaulted, almost raped and murdered by that killer at Kensal Green; and now, being abducted under a sentence of death, by a group of terrorists and witnessing their murder by the so-called good guys. Did I really want this as part of my life? Surely there must be a better and safer way to live my life?

Between leaving Jim's office and my own, I asked Katy what I should have done. "And please, Katy, don't tell me that you can only guide me, not influence me."

"I would have done exactly what you did, Angie. Knowing there is danger about doesn't lessen its impact. I told you what lay ahead so you could be cautious, and you did precisely that. Now you may have to face the consequences, and I don't simply mean your boss's reaction; I'm talking about the MI5 response. They will want to know how you first became aware of the information. When you tell them, as you surely will have to, that you are a clairvoyant, then – what is it you grown-ups say? – the shit will hit the fan."

"Very droll," I said dryly. "Is that the best you can do? I don't regard that as much of a help."

"It's the best as I can do at the moment. But you will let me know what they say, won't you?"

"Do you really think I'll have to?" I sort of clicked off and went into the office, although my mind was still troubled by my experiences this morning. I'd barely been away for 24 hours and yet my desk was covered in files.

"Fuck" I shouted. "Where the hell did these come from?"

Sam shrugged. "From downstairs. There's no one there to clear them; Ian Blakey has had to leave the office."

"Couldn't they wait until he came back?" I was getting tired of this; we were now becoming a dumping ground. I picked up the new folders and handed them over to Sam. "Take them back, and tell those silly sods down there this is not a waste tip. They'll have to wait until their boss gets back. You know, Sam," I added, "this system is simply not working." I spread my arms around the office. "Look at us: there are six of us here, two of whom have hardly graduated, and we're having to deal with some of the most major crimes this country has ever witnessed. In the basement, there are – what? – 30 or so people, and all they have to do is read the files, update the computer and pass on to us those cases they're unable to handle."

"So what do you suggest, Angie?"

I shook my head. "I'm not sure. Maybe the whole system is not designed to work. One thing I do know is that we are understaffed. To cope with what we're having to do I would suggest we have at least as many people as they have downstairs. I also believe there are not enough ranking officers – I mean, we have only you and me in this department, and the same applies downstairs. It's crazy."

"Perhaps we should have a session with the commander – the four of us, I'm talking about," Sam said. "See what he thinks about your conclusion. I do agree with you, though; we need more staff, considerably more staff, and probably a couple more inspectors. 'Shall I set it up when Ian Blakey gets back?"

"Yeah. Why not? We have to sort this out once and for all, otherwise we'll be disappearing up our own arseholes."

Sam grinned. "A nice choice of words," he commented. "I'll see if Ian is back when I return the folders. I'll pass on your message as well!"

Before Sam returned the phone rang; it was a message from the commander asking to see me. "Good thought," I decided. Perhaps I should try and clear the air whilst I had the opportunity. Only it didn't work like that.

"Get your coat," Jim said as soon as I entered the room. "We have an appointment at Thames House."

"Oh, shit. Do you know what they want?"

"Course I do. It's as I expected: they want know how you came up with the idea that Ajas was a terrorist, especially since he had slipped under their radar. You informed them he had been a sleeper for – what? – four or five years. And they had absolutely no idea who he was or what he was doing. I'm sorry, Angie, but there is more than a hint you might be arrested, especially after this morning's disaster."

"You make it sound as though abducting me and sentencing me to death was all my idea." I was still feeling the shock from the killing field of today, and now to be told I might be arrested... "Well, fuck them; I don't care what they do."

We were seated in the back of the car with the window closed between the driver and the two of us, so he couldn't hear what we were saying.

"I wouldn't suggest you take that approach with them, Angie," Jim warned. "These people have powers we only dream about. If they indicate you could be arrested then I wouldn't give them any encouragement."

"Who are we going to see?" I asked, a distinctive tremor in my voice.

"A Sir Charles Masterson, director of the Operating Board. This board is responsible for the direction of the day-to-day business of the service."

"You mean, he makes the decisions?"

"Well, him and his subordinates do, yes. But we aren't just meeting him; there will be two other decision makers with him. I imagine they will be the ones asking the questions. Look, Angie, try to let me do the talking; I'm not sure exactly what I can say but I will try to steer clear of the clairvoyant issue. If they get hold of that then I doubt they will ever let you go."

"What? You mean, they'll arrest me?" I asked, shocked.

"Not necessarily. Frankly, I don't think they'll believe you. Would you in their position?"

"What if I can prove it?"

Jim shook his head. "And how are you going to do that, Angie?"

"I don't know. I'm getting a message that if I want to then I will be able to prove it."

"Fine; but unless you can demonstrate it incontrovertibly then I doubt they'll believe you."

"I wish you'd use English occasionally, Jim. Look, leave it with me; if the opportunity comes up and I get the nod, then I will use it."

"Well, I hope you get the chance because we're here."

The driver stopped outside Thames House, and we alighted.

CHAPTER FORTY-THREE

Thames House, at the corner of Millbank and Horseferry Road, had a prominent position just south of the Houses of Parliament and overlooking Lambert Bridge. It was an unimposing building, dating back to the early 1930s, and belied its position as the headquarters of the national security services.

Angie hesitated a step before entering the building, wondering if she would be allowed to leave after what Jim had suggested to her.

"Did you know that this area was devastated by a flooding of the Thames in 1928?" Jim commented, probably trying to take Angie's mind of what might lie ahead.

"No. I didn't. Does it make any difference?"

"Well, 14 people died in the incident. I thought you might like to know that."

I squeezed his arm. "Thanks for that, Jim. But don't worry about me; I'll be okay."

The security checks were very thorough, and included a virtual body search and an investigation of my handbag, and, once we had been given passes with 'visitor' stamped across them, two escorts led us into the lift and up to the third floor.

We stopped at a secretary's office and were told to wait. After five minutes or so we then entered into a spacious office; three people were seated at a table positioned in the centre of the room. It was an elegant room with a large antique desk and chairs, a padded three-seater settee, plush chairs scattered over the office and curtains I would be proud to have in my flat. My feet treaded softly on the fitted carpet. This was an office the like of which I had never seen before.

The secretary introduced us, first, to Sir Charles Masterson, the director, and then to Jonathan Sinclair, his assistant, and finally to a Sean O'Donnell; we weren't informed at to what his function in the organisation was.

We sat at the conference table – no refreshments were offered to us – and Jim introduced me to the group.

"Ah, yes, Miss Crossley," Sir Charles began; "you are here, as I believe you now understand, to explain to us how you were able to identify the terrorist in your midst, when all the efforts of this organisation failed to reveal him. Um, can you explain, please?"

His tone was of the old school, no doubt Eton and then probably Oxford or even Cambridge; it was cultured compared to my accent, which was noticeably from the west Midlands. The impression it imparted was that he was considerably superior to those he chose to address, and he would brook no argument.

"I'm waiting Miss Crossley," he repeated, no doubt aware that he was trying to subjugate me. It was Jim who spoke before I did.

"Perhaps it's better if I tell the story," he began. "You see..."

"Pardon me, commander." It was O'Donnell interrupting; he evidently had far more authority than we had assumed. "We would prefer Miss Crossley to speak for herself."

"I'm not sure where to begin," I stated. Then there was silence, as if the trilogy were waiting for me to betray myself.

"Go on," Sir Charles insisted. "We're waiting."

"Are you a Muslim?" Sinclair was asking.

"Pardon?"

"Were you the girlfriend of this Ajas character?"

I saw where this was leading, and I was having none of it. "Don't be ridiculous," I almost snapped at him.

"Then please will you explain how you came to identify him?" It was Sir Charles again.

There was nothing else I could do except tell the truth. "I identified him, Sir Charles, because I sensed the atmosphere around him. Then I read him and I had visions of his intentions; they were clear to me and very sinister."

"I see." He folded his arms on the table. "Does this make you some kind of a medium?" he asked. It was a simple question, with no ulterior motive behind it.

"I am a clairvoyant," I admitted. "If people like Ajas, who have an evil intent, present themselves to me, then, more often than not, I sense them and subsequently read them. I also read people when I receive messages."

Jim was frowning, and I saw that O'Donnell was smiling as if I were hatching red herrings to confuse people. He had an arrogant expression on his grinning face.

"Let me give you an example," I suggested as I looked at O'Donnell. "You like to believe you are a perfect specimen; you exercise three times a week; you cycle once a week with your wife and the children, mostly through the park; every morning, at 6.0 a.m. you swim 20 lengths in the baths here at Thames House…"

"Oh, for Christ's sake, that's just guessing," he intervened sarcastically.

"Is it? Then let me tell you something that isn't guessing, Mr O'Donnell. By this time tomorrow you will be dead."

"What?" he gasped, looking around the table as if to confirm that they did indeed have a madwoman here in front of them.

"I would like to apologise but I'm afraid you don't inspire me. So, allow me to continue. You are suffering from a disease called Cardiomyopathy; a widening of the heart that weakens the muscles, and after lunch tomorrow your heart will contract and stop. You will be dead, Mr O'Donnell, just as your father before you died the same way when he was only 42 years of age."

I watched the colour drain from his face, especially after I referred to his father.

"But…but…how can you know this?"

"Because you allowed me to read you."

"Is there anything I can do?" he asked solicitously.

"Yes, sir. Go home to your family and pray. It is your time."

"What the hell is going on here?" Sinclair demanded. "We invite you to Thames House for an enquiry into the terrorist situation and you have turned it into some kind of a séance. And how can you possibly tell what might happen to Sean here – look at him- he's as fit as a fiddle."

"Ask him," I said. "Ask him about his father."

Sean nodded. "It's true, I'm afraid. The only person I've spoken to about this, other than my mother, is my wife. Miss Crossley couldn't possibly have known."

"Despite the omens of death," Sir Charles adjoined, "we still have not had a satisfactory explanation from Miss Crossley about her relationship with the terrorist. Miss Crossley, I must now insist."

"You obviously haven't listened to what I have just said; I am a clairvoyant. I see things that other people do not. I read people, as I did with Mr O'Donnell. Let me read you, Sir Charles. You are expecting that very shortly you will be granted a life peerage; that, I'm afraid, will not happen. Within the next few weeks you will be retired from your position as director and put out to grass. Should you threaten resistance then your extravagant pension arrangements will be nullified." I paused for a second; a message was coming through. "Ah, yes. You have already had warning of this development, which relates to the 7/7 bombings in London; you are trying to decide if you should protest. My advice to you, Sir Charles, is not to; you will forfeit your pension if you do, and you will fail in any event."

"I think we should suspend this enquiry, for the time being," Sir Charles was saying, a furious grimace on his face. "However, Miss Crossley, let me assure you that we shall pursue this matter as we have not yet determined the outcome. I will now refer it to a higher office for their recommendations."

We got up and I leaned across the table to shake hands with Sean O'Donnell. "Truly, Sean, I am so terribly sorry. Please go home – your wife will comfort you."

* * * * * *

As we left Thames House Jim said to me, "Fuck me, Ange, don't ever read me, will you? I'd rather just die as a matter of course without someone forecasting it so definitely." His face was the colour of chalk, as if someone had just walked over his grave.

"I was really sorry about that, but at first he was so fucking arrogant I didn't try to placate him. Now I feel really upset for having done that to him; it was grossly insensitive."

"And was it true?"

I nodded. "Yes. And so was the reading of Sir Charles. There isn't a cat in hell's chance of him receiving a peerage; he's going to be lucky to save his pension."

"Yes, I checked his face when you were analysing him; did you see the colour fade from his cheeks?"

"No. I was receiving a further message. Do you think we've heard the last of this thing, Jim?"

"I'm not sure. If O'Donnell dies tomorrow – and I believe you – then I doubt you'll have heard the last of it. Let's wait and see, shall we? But you and I still need to have that talk about your protection.'

"What, you mean I require escorts?"

He sighed; it always seemed these days that I was the one who frustrated him.

"You have to have some fucking supervision, Ange. I can't allow you to carry on as you have been doing; the next time you could be killed."

"Yes. I'm aware of that, Jim. One of those bullets this morning might have missed their target and hit me.'

"And, equally, the rapist in Kensal Green might have pushed harder with his knife and penetrated your throat just a little more, and – I don't need to say anything more. Look, Ange, why don't we call it a day; go home, have some supper, sleep on what I'm trying to say to you, and we'll discuss it tomorrow. Agreed?"

I couldn't disagree. "Sure, and I do accept that you might well be right, except that when my time comes I too will be forewarned, just as Sean was today."

He stopped, as we were about to step into the car, and held my arm. "You're not suggesting that if we do nothing and some tragedy happens then that will be the will of whoever it is you pray to these days?"

"No. I'm not saying that." I shrugged. "I suppose I'm a bit confused, Jim; I don't really know what I'm saying. Please, leave it with me; we'll talk again tomorrow. By the way," I added, "we have to have a session on the structure of the unit; at present we're snowed under with cases."

"Yeah. I've also thought about that – tomorrow, when Ian is back we'll get together.'

The car dropped me off in Camden High Street. I was starving, having missed my lunch, and I certainly didn't want to cook tonight. So I found a fairly quiet Italian restaurant on the High Street and ordered soup of the day, followed by a large bowl of spaghetti bolognaise and a glass of red house wine. I was becoming comfortable in dining alone. When the thought occurred to me, and provided the restaurant was quiet, I could share some of my thoughts with Kate. After the soup was served, I asked her, in my head, what she thought of today's development.

"You did well, Angie, but beware of the enemies you are making. That Sir Charles will not leave this alone. If he's able to tie you to the terrorist that will be a feather in his cap; he's hoping that you might inadvertently save him."

"I thought of that, but what, if anything, can I do about it?"

"To be truthful – very little. But I hardly think his allegation that you are a converted Muslim and that you are the girlfriend of Ajas and that you and he had a falling out, is likely to gain much support. Your claim as a clairvoyant will be validated tomorrow after we take possession of Sean O'Donnell's soul. I can't see Sir Charles arguing his way out of that, but be careful; he might have other plans to take care of you."

"Do you believe he might do me some harm?"

"In the event, yes. That is why you must tread cautiously. I also agree with Jim Robbins about you needing protection. Look at the cases your trying to handle at present: a rapist here in your own backyard: a paedophile butchering and murdering young boys: a serial killer in the west Midlands: and anything else that might come up. You require some protection, my dear. I'll leave you now; your spaghetti has arrived."

CHAPTER FORTY-FOUR

I slept right through until the phone woke me. It was Ian Blakey, and I could tell from his tone he was about to complain.

"You've dumped a pile of files back on us."

I yawned. It was still early for me. I looked out of the window, and saw that, surprisingly, it was raining.

"I did," I agreed.

"Yes, but why? What are we supposed to do with them?"

"Well, first of all your staff could read the fucking things instead of using us as a dumping ground."

"They didn't read them?"

"No, Ian, they didn't read them. In your absence they just piled them upstairs, hoping we would do their work for them. And that's another thing I want to take up with you: my opinion is that the structure of the whole of this unit is wrong. I've mentioned it to Jim Robbins and he's suggested we have a meeting about it this morning. So, if you'd held your horses, you wouldn't have had to wake me up as you have done."

"Oh. Sorry about that, Angie. I was led to believe you were the one pulling a fast one. I'll wait until you get in."

A rather interesting conversation, it seemed to me.

I had a shower, tidied up my hair and dressed slowly with blouse and jeans (the typical dress code these days), small studs in my ears and no make-up, and I was ready for breakfast. My breakfast tended to be somewhat boring: a bowl of cereal and a cup of coffee. One day, I promised myself, I would sit down and eat a hearty English breakfast. For the time being, though, I was in a hurry, so I gulped down what I had to and set off for the tube. There were no mysterious strangers waiting for me this morning, although, to be truthful, I did glance around me.

I got into the office at my usual time, ignored the pleadings from Ian and went into my office to see if anything had been uncovered for the released prisoners.

Sally was in touch with the Wolverhampton police, who gave her the address of Jack McCloud. He had been released after serving ten years of his life sentence; his address was confirmed, as he was on parole and it had to be checked by his parole officer. He was also on the sex register and had to report to the police each week. So far, Sally said, he was unemployed, drawing social security, and the council paid for his tiny bed-sit. Sally was informed that it was highly unlikely he could be the serial killer, since he wasn't mobile, didn't have the money to make him transient, and whatever money he did have was spent on booze.

"I still don't dismiss him," Sally acknowledged. "I would like to go to Wolverhampton and interview him myself."

"Go ahead," I agreed. "But don't go on your own; take Laura with you. How about your enquires, Sam? Any luck in tracing the ex-priest?'"

"Not so far, no. But that doesn't really mean anything – he could be salted away in some monastery. I'm still checking through the churches register, and I have contacted the police where he is supposed to check in each week, but there is no sign of him. He is on the missing list, although there is no warrant out for his arrest."

"Keep searching, although I doubt if he is high on our suspect list. Phil, were you able to discover Connelly's address, or any details?"

"Nothing. The police in Birmingham checked into his last known address but there are other occupants living there now. There is no record of him either living or working in the Birmingham area, but neither are there any warrants out for him. He too has disappeared."

"Do you still think we're on the right track here, Angie?" Sam asked, frowning at me.

"You'll have to rely on my intuitions, Sam," I shot back at him. "I'm of the view that McCloud is our favourite; he's the one who has a previous for killing a prostitute, and despite what the police have to say they've largely ignored him in their hunt for a serial killer. Sally," I went on as I turned to her, "I think I'll come with you to Wolverhampton; I know the area better than you do."

Fortunately, she didn't say anything about her past misdemeanours; for a second I'd actually overlooked them. "Sure," was all she said. "I thought we'd go up this afternoon, if that's okay with you?"

"Fine. Now, if you'll excuse me, I have a meeting with the commander."

* * * * * *

Ian Blakey was waiting in Jim's office when I opened the door; so were two other gentlemen.

"Angie, these are two representatives from Thames House: Pearson and Entwistle," he said as he nodded in their direction. "They would like you to go with them."

"I'm Pearson," the black man said.

"And I'm…"

"Yes, I figured that one out," Jim snapped.

"Am I under arrest?" I responded, half jokingly, when one of them, Pearson, approached me with a pair of handcuffs.

"We would like you to come with us, Miss Crossley."

" Is that necessary?" Jim exploded, pointing to the handcuffs. "You're dealing here with a senior detective chief inspector, and unless you have a warrant you will not place those things on her." I thought he was going to hit the man, which might have been silly, because the MI5 man was extremely fit and probably knew how to handle himself.

Ian stepped in front of me, blocking the man off. "If you need to talk to Miss Crossley then you'll have to take me with you; I will be her safeguard."

Entwistle pulled a paper from his pocket. "I have a warrant here, commander,'" he said, handing it over to Jim. As Jim was reading it he said to Ian, "Go with her, Ian; make sure they don't discredit her; and take the names of anyone who's in charge of the arresting procedure."

It read: "A Warrant for the arrest of Angela Crossley for consorting with a known terrorist and endangering the security of this country and its citizens."

"Fucking hell!" I gasped, mouth wide open. Before I could close it the cuffs were on me and I was being led away. "Where are we going to?" I asked.

"Paddington Green police station," Pearson answered, "where you will be held in custody until you appear before a magistrates' court in the morning."

"But you have no evidence I even knew this man."

"Not for us to say, ma'am. We're just here to arrest you."

This was a hell of a shock to my system, especially after what I'd been through in the last 24 hours. Paddington Green was a depressing building, as I expected it would be. The interior decor was no different; I noticed its walls had a fading lime green paint on them, as though this was a hospital in terminal decline.

Ian squeezed my arm. "Don't worry, Angie; we'll soon have you out of here."

A sergeant at the desk filled in the paperwork, and, as he wanted me to empty my purse, Ian intervened.

"I'll look after that," he said

"And who are you?" the sergeant asked in a surly voice.

"I am Detective Chief Inspector Ian Blakey of New Scotland Yard," Ian said, producing his warrant card. "And this" – he pointed to me – "is Detective Chief Inspector Angela Crossley, also of New Scotland Yard. Now, if you don't mind, sergeant, we would like some respect around here."

"Yes, sir. Sorry about that, sir." He filled in whatever forms were needed, and then I was led into a custody cell and the door was locked behind me, leaving me to contemplate what might happen.

"Did you know this would happen, Kate?" I enquired.

"Not specifically, but I wouldn't worry; you won't be here too long."

"Really? How do you work that out? I'm told I have to stay here until the morning, when I'm due to appear in front of the magistrates. You don't think they're going to release me, do you?"

"I wouldn't expect so. But…well, let's wait and see."

Katy left me then, so I dozed for a while. It was bloody uncomfortable, as well as degrading, being locked away in a cell. I noticed that my hands were shaking again, and I asked myself how many times that had happened to me in the last few weeks. I awoke when one of the policemen brought in my lunch; it was awful but I needed to have something to eat, so I ate it without tasting it. I was also reminded that about now it was time for Sean O'Donnell to pass away; I wondered if he might visit me in the future. It wouldn't have been so bad if I had had a book to read.

Then the door opened and a man came in. He was middle-aged, a little puffy around the face and balding. His eyes, though, a deep, penetrating almost turquoise blue, had a sharpness about them that reassured me.

"Hello, Miss Crossley. I've been appointed by New Scotland Yard to represent you." He handed me a card stating he was a solicitor, named Aubrey Marsden.

"I never ever thought I would require a solicitor. I haven't done anything."

"Yes. So the commander has told me. I have already applied to the courts for a writ to release you, on the grounds that this is a vexatious charge and reflects very badly on the security services. It will be heard this afternoon, so I will leave you for now and hope to be back shortly with your release form."

With that he left me to my daydreaming.

CHAPTER FORTY-FIVE

This whole matter was bizarre, it occurred to me. I now understood what Kate was referring to when she asked me to watch out for my enemies. Without doubt this was the work of that bloody Sir Charles, seeking revenge.

Time passed; I was growing weary of this of this confinement. Then the door opened and Ian was standing there. "Come on, Angie. We're out of here."

"Was it the solicitor who arranged the release?"

"No. It was the head of MI5. She heard what had happened. She received a report from Sir Charles about his interview with you yesterday; she also had a report from the commander. She realised this was a vendetta, and since Sean O'Donnell died suddenly today, apparently as you forecast he would, she has since removed Sir Charles from his position and cancelled all charges against you."

"So, Masterson is out on his ear and I'm free to go."

"Yes; but there is a caveat. Dame Elizabeth Horsfall wishes to talk to you. There's a car waiting for you outside."

"Bloody hell! What have I done to deserve that?"

Ian shrugged. "I guess its something to do with your being a clairvoyant."

"Are you coming with me, Ian?"

"Not bloody likely. That's a place I wouldn't go near with the proverbial bargepole."

* * * * * *

So here I was again, in the holy of holies, except that this time I was given an escorted tour. Both Entwistle and Pearson were there to meet me and I was whistled through the security checks, into a lift that needed a key to operate it and into one of the largest and plushest offices I had ever seen. At Scotland Yard our offices, including Jim's, were functional; they had the mandatory conference table, a desk that could have come out of MFI, and the number of chairs the would be needed in the event of a conference. 'Utility' would be the word I would use to describe them. But this – it was like something out of a five-star hotel. Carpets that could have come from the East covered the floor, and I sank into them as I walked towards Dame Elizabeth's office; the doors were mahogany, and the furniture must either have been designed especially for the purpose or been purchased from Harrods. I was overwhelmed by the grandeur, and the office of the head of MI5 wasn't in any way different, other than the antique desk where she sat, or the conference table that I would have loved to put into auction.

I was so taken aback by the splendour I hardly noticed that Jim Robbins was seated at the side of her desk. I really shouldn't have been surprised; I was quite sure this meeting was largely a result of his initiative. Seated at the conference table was a man I hadn't seen before; he was middle-aged with a head of greying hair. There was something rather sinister about him: not a man ever to be crossed.

She rose from her desk to greet me, her hand outstretched.

"Miss Crossley – Angela, isn't it? I am so very glad to meet you, and I am so terribly sorry about the confusion this morning."

I didn't think there had been any confusion about it, but I kept my thoughts to myself.

"Good afternoon, ma'am," I responded. "I'm sure that had nothing to do with you."

"Are you feeling alright?" she asked me, concern in her voice.

"Thank you, yes."

"Let me introduce you to Sir Leonard Hinckley. Sir Leonard is the deputy director general of MI5; he's the one with most of the responsibility. Now, I'm sure you would like some coffee – or perhaps something stronger?"

"Coffee would be fine, ma'am…"

"You can call me Elizabeth," she intervened. She rang a bell on her desk, and moments later her secretary arrived with a tray of coffee, which she placed on a large mat on the conference table.

"Come," she pointed, "let's sit here, shall we? I hope you don't mind my asking to see you, Angela, but there are one or two questions we would like some answers to. Is that alright with you?"

I nodded, pretty sure what was coming. The coffee was superb – probably also from Harrods, I thought.

"What is it you want to ask me, er, Elizabeth?"

"I've been describing to Elizabeth what happened yesterday at the meeting with Sir Charles and the others," Jim explained. "Well, especially about your reading of Sean O'Donnell and Sir Charles. It seems you were right on both occasions, and she wanted to hear from you how you managed the forecast."

"I see." Actually, I was bloody furious. Jim had no right to advertise me as an employable clairvoyant. It was not part of my job. "Well," I began; "Sir Charles wanted me to inform him how I was able to identify the terrorist when he obviously had slipped under your radar. The only thing I could tell him was the truth: that I sensed things other people missed.

"Sean O'Donnell was quite deprecating with his criticism of my skills; he forced me almost to 'read' him. That was when I realised he was dying with Cardiomyopathy, and his time was just after lunch today."

"That is quite some miracle," Sir Leonard cut in. "Do you mind explaining just how you accomplish this phenomenon?"

"It's really difficult to explain," I remarked. I mean, how the hell do I go about explaining my relationship with my Spirit Guide? "I'm not like the other psychics that you hear about – I don't see the dead or spirits from the supernatural. I simply have the ability to read people, and sometimes situations."

"What? You read their minds?" Sir Leonard was asking.

"No. No. It's nothing like that." I shrugged. "I suppose that, if someone has something important that either has happened to them or is likely to happen to them, then – well, I look into their eyes and I am able to read them. I can't explain it other than that."

"Is this something you can do regularly, or is it only when you're under pressure?"

"I don't know, Sir Leonard; I've never tried to analyse the phenomenon."

"I see. Could you give me one of your readings now – at this table?"

"I suppose I could, but you'll have to let me finish – no interrupting."

He smiled, one of those sinister smiles that made me feel uneasy. I studied him, especially his eyes, and I asked Katy if she could help me. Then I continued, "You are trying to get over bowel cancer; you have had serious surgery and you were recommended for a course of chemotherapy; at present you're in remission. This has never been made public, because MI5 is afraid it might signify a weakness in the organisation."

I watched his eyes narrow as he listened to what I had to say.

"Dear God!" I heard Elizabeth whisper. It was if she couldn't believe what she was hearing.

"Tell me," he continued on a slightly different track, "am I likely to overcome this disease?"

I gazed at him again; unsure whether or not I should tell him the truth.

"Don't be afraid, Angela," Elizabeth said soothingly.

"No, sir, you are not; this disease will kill you within the next five months." I looked at him again and added, "But you already know this, Sir Leonard. That is why you rejected the chemotherapy."

He turned to Dame Horsfall. "You were right. She is quite something."

"Do you think we can use her?" he was asked.

He nodded. "I'm sure of it. And because of the situation we find ourselves in I think it's very important we do take her on board."

"Would you mind letting me into the secret?" I asked, nonchalantly.

"Yes. Of course." Dame Elizabeth smiled at me sweetly. "As I'm sure you're aware, after the 7/7 bombings in London our institution came under heavy fire from the government; a number of heads rolled, including that of my predecessor, and now we are duty bound to tighten up our resources.

"Sir Leonard and I have given some thought as to how you were able to identify the terrorist. I have read the report from Sir Charles and, although he was derogatory in his comments, we dismissed them as petty. Our principal concern, after 7 July, is to single out suspect terrorists of whatever category and place them under the closest of supervision. We are also duty bound now to inform the local police of the suspects. We need someone who can empathise with these characters, someone who can immediately be aware of whom she is talking to – exactly as you did with Shahid. In other words, Angela, with your talents you can make a significant contribution to the safety of this country."

"Is this so you can murder them, as you did yesterday with the four men?"

She blanched in front of me. I had obviously hit a nerve.

"You do realise what those men intended to do to you, don't you? You were a prisoner, Angela, not a hostage. From my information they were going to show you the bomb factory, let you know the weapons they had available, and then photograph the factory with you in the frame, after which they were going to kill you and dump your body on the steps of Thames House. Then we would have notification of both the factory and what would happen to those who they felt were working for us. Were you aware of any of this?"

"I'm not sure; it was all very confusing. There was a lot of shouting and swearing and I did have a gun to my forehead. But these men were…just shot in front of me. Each one had a head shot … well, one of them was shot in the back, but there was no warning." I shivered at the telling of it.

"It was just as well for you they were killed immediately. And, no, that is not our specific objective, to kill people. But, when the security of the country is at risk, we will have no hesitation in gunning them down.

"What we want from you, Angela is for you to become our secret weapon in the fight against the bombers. We don't expect you to target them for assassination but, rather, to sense out those who we would regard as dangerous – exactly as you did with Shahid. We want you to remain hidden, even from our own operatives, to be called upon whenever the occasion arises; to ask you to interview suspects whenever and wherever the needs originate. Will you do that for us, my dear?"

I was flabbergasted. I couldn't have imagined that anyone would flatter me like this. And of course I would help. I just wondered what she meant by 'whenever and wherever'. But having heard from Dame Elizabeth and listened to her explanation there was nothing else I had to think about.

"I will gladly help," I announced. "How will you let me know when I'm required?"

"Well, you do have a number of other cases to deal with first; we would like those concluded initially. After that we think your job function will have to be reorganised. We will liaise with Commander Robbins as to when you are required." She stood up from the table. "And. Angela, the thanks of the country go with you."

She shook my hand warmly, and the next thing I knew Entwistle and Pearson led us out of the building.

"Quite the hero, aren't you?" Jim said encouragingly, as we got into the car.

"You might think so, commander, but it wasn't intended. I never thought for a second it would come to this."

"I did. That's what I meant when I said the other day that you won't have heard the last of your uncovering Shahid."

"I forgot to ask her why there was no publicity attached to the shooting."

He laughed. "You don't think for a second she'd have admitted a cover-up, do you? Sometimes we have to go along with these people and accept that what they're doing is in the interests of the country.

"I know," he said when I started to protest, "sometimes they do get it wrong; but we'll have to live with that."

When we arrived back at the Yard Jim said, "Go and say hello to your group and then come back inside; we have to have a word about reorganisation and other things. I'll call Ian."

CHAPTER FORTY-SIX

I was quite elated when I got back to the office; a day that had started with me down in the dumps, heading towards despair, had now climbed to the pinnacle of satisfaction. I would have to be careful not to be smug.

"So, did you miss me?" I enquired of the gathering.

"What the hell happened, Angie?" Sam asked, and others in the group echoed his question

"I was arrested by Her Majesty's secret police."

"You mean, MI5?" Sally wanted to know.

"That's right. And I was thrown into prison – in Paddington Green." I shuddered. "Try to avoid that if you can – the food there's bloody awful."

Nobody laughed.

"I don't understand," Sam pushed it further. "Why would they want to arrest you? I mean, what the hell did you do?"

I sighed. Here we go again.

"Let's just say I spotted a terrorist, or at least an alleged terrorist, and it was reported to MI5. They then argued that this guy might have been my boyfriend, and we'd had a falling out and that was why I reported him.

"Some old bastard there, a Sir Charles something or other, put the boot in, and I finished up in prison. So, there you have it; but it's okay now, I'm cleared, and hopefully that will be the end of it."

"It's not the end of it with me," Sally argued indignantly. "How the hell did you spot this terrorist? More clairvoyant antics?"

"Leave it, Sally," I snapped. "I'm off for a meeting. I'll catch you later. Oh, and, Sally, remember we're off to the west Midlands tomorrow."

I stopped at the door. "Sam, have you and Laura circulated the update on the rapist?"

He nodded. "Nothing on the Polish paedophile, though."

"Are the police monitoring the school in Harpenden?" I asked Sally.

"Yes. They're reporting in daily; so far not a thing. Are you sure you're right on this one, Angie?"

"I'll see you tomorrow." I deliberately ducked the question. She would have to wait and see.

* * * * * *

They were waiting for me in Jim's office. Ian was already looking impatient.

"Do you want me to start?" I asked them.

"No. We're not here to discuss the organisation, Ange; that can wait for the time being. What I want to talk about is the procedures we can introduce that will enable you to be protected; we really cannot carry on the way we are doing.

"Do you remember when you were in Manchester and I had to warn the group that under no circumstances were you to be allowed into the front line on your own?"

"I remember," I grunted. "But if you want that to happen here then you should never have offered me the job; this is a front-line position I'm in, Jim, and nothing can alter that."

"Possibly not, but we can reduce the risk, if only a little."

"And how do you propose that can happen?"

"Well, the first thing I want to do is reinforce the senior officers we have in this unit. So far, Ange, we have not been able to replace the loss of Mark, and in Ian's department we still have only one senior inspector. So, what I'm suggesting is that in Ian's group we increase the number by a further two senior officers, and in your unit we also increase the inspectors with a further two enlistments; I do have people in mind. With that in place I am suggesting that whenever you go out into the field you have at least one senior officer to accompany you. This can either be one of the inspectors or you can take Sally Walker with you; in any case, Ange, that is what I am ordering. I will not allow our officers to be attacked in the street with knives or guns without there being an extra policeman to assist them. Oh, and by the way," he added, "you might not know this but John Watkins, the inspector in Manchester, died yesterday from bowel cancer. Were you aware of that, Ange?"

I bit my lip and tried to hide a tear. Of course I knew it – but I didn't wish to let Jim know that I was fully in the picture. So I shook my head and muttered, "That's a damned shame; he was a very nice man."

"Now, any questions?" Jim went on.

I was a bit stunned by all this. I genuinely thought we were going to discuss the reorganisation. So much for my insight.

"A question I would like to raise is – and I do agree with your increasing the staff we have at present – the times I've been attacked either came about because of some confusion..."

"That's exactly what I'm talking about," he interrupted. "Had you had a second officer with you then you wouldn't have been knifed."

"Hey, hang about, Jim; I don't think that's fair. If I d had a second officer with me on the tube then the murderer would have avoided attacking me and would've got away."

"Not necessarily. Your back-up could have sat on a seat away from you in the carriageway and followed you out when he did."

"Okay. I concede that. But I doubt if he or she would have been able to stop me from getting kidnapped and almost shot at yesterday; that would have been impossible."

"Not if you'd had an officer with you; it's twice as difficult to imprison two rather than one."

I sighed. How many times had I been involved in this kind of argument with Jim?

So? Are you thinking about it?" He was almost imploring.

"No, I'm not. Had there been two of us, as you suggest, then MI5 would not have found the bomb-making factory, the terrorists would still be alive and they would have waited for their opportunity to grab me and kill me." I looked at him innocently. "Don't you think?"

"Okay; you have a point, in that circumstance. But I believe that's different from the usual run-of-the-mill scenario I'm talking about. In those instances you do not – and this applies to all officers under my command – go onto the scene without an escort, someone who can dive in should you get into trouble. Is that clear?"

"Perfectly," Ian said, unequivocally.

"I don't know, Jim; I'll have to think about it. It's all very well you talking about escorts but not so easy when you have the small numbers in my unit. Give me a half a dozen more officers; then I'll go along with you."

"And I'll have to think about that too. Let's talk again tomorrow, shall we? See what I can come up with."

"You were a bit forthcoming," Ian said, accusatorially, as we left the office.

"It isn't your fucking skin he's talking about; it's mine. And I'm certainly not going to delegate officers every time we get into some sort of trouble when I've hardly got enough staff to cope with as it is. So, lay off, Ian. You look after your department and I'll take care of mine. I'll see you tomorrow."

* * * * * *

I went to church that evening; I hadn't forgotten the plea that Kate had given me. There was a service on when I went into the church, so I sat at the back; I would hate anyone thinking I was there to join in whatever it was that was going on.

It was difficult for me to pray in the midst of a choir belting out All Things Bright and Beautiful, however much I wanted to creep into a quiet corner and plead my case. So I prayed in my head, repeating the words over and over again, almost like a mantra. In the end I had to smile; I was praying to the music of All Things Bright and Beautiful! I came out of the church nourished in my commitment to the spiritual.

That night I ate a salad with some ham I'd bought from a local store, and I tried very hard not to think of my intense loneliness. If I weren't careful, I told myself, it would turn very easily into depression, and that was the last thing I wanted. I remembered the times, those years ago, when I visited Paul, my friend the psychiatrist, for therapy sessions. Together with the antidepressants he subscribed, they helped me considerably, but I was warned that the bouts of depression might one day return.

It was a terrible position to be in: surrounded by intense activity in my job and yet alone in my private life. I had tried to shrug it off as if it were of no concern, but I still couldn't avoid the reality that, outside work, I had no friends, no relationships, not a single soul I could talk to. No arms to wrap around me, to hold me; no chest for me to rest my head upon, no man to tell me not to worry. No one except the darkness of the night.

I went to bed, rejecting the comfort of a drink, and feeling decidedly low; I didn't even want to talk to Katy.

The next morning, after a restless night's sleep, I tried to concentrate my mind on the coming day's events. Sally was due to arrive shortly and we would set off for Wolverhampton to check into the suspected serial killer. But there was something intervening in my mind that I felt we had to do before that, but I was damned if I could remember what it was. Perhaps it would come to me along the way.

I barely exchanged a greeting with Sally; I was still feeling somewhat down. Even the sunshine didn't cheer me up.

"Had a bad night?" she enquired politely.

"Humph." I couldn't think of anything to say.

"You know the way – to Wolverhampton?"

This time I grunted at her. "What do you think?"

We headed off up the Finchley Road, turned left down towards Hendon and left past Brent Cross, and then on to the M1. Traffic, at this time of the day, was quite light, and we quickly moved on, past the Watford turn-off, then on to Hemel Hempstead. I spotted the A5 exit to Whipsnade, and almost unknowingly I headed down it.

"Hey – where we going?" Sally said.

"Don't know… I'm following my instincts."

"Well, it ain't the fucking way to Wolverhampton, that's for sure."

It was blind intuition that took me on the road to Luton; I know we passed a golf course, came to a junction, where I headed left, and finally came to a roundabout, where traffic was whizzing past me at a rate of knots.

"Now where?" Sally asked me sarcastically. "Or have you found a short cut to Wolverhampton?"

I waited, ignoring the sound of horns blaring behind me.

" Angie," Sally shouted. "We can't stay here holding up the traffic."

I opened the window and waved on the cars behind me. Sally got out of the car and behaved like a policewoman with her arm signals. Just then I saw a black van screaming round the roundabout. I dragged Sally into the car and, leaving a long skid mark on the road, began to follow the van.

"Do you know what you're doing?" she asked me, almost in a state of hysteria.

I said nothing.

I could see the van in the distance, heading towards God knew where. Then it cut left past another golf club – I noticed a sign saying it was Harpenden Common Golf Club – and disappeared into the woods. Slowly, I followed it, probably for a couple of miles, until I saw it parked amongst the foliage, virtually hidden from view.

"Now what?" she said.

"Come with me, but stay behind me," I instructed her.

We wound our way through the woods, finding it difficult to see, until we heard a child's cry, which we followed dutifully. It took some time to scramble our way through the branches, still following the sound of the child, until we came to a clearing. And there was our monster, bending over a young boy who was prostrate across a fallen log, with his trousers down by his ankles, and the paedophile's erect penis beginning to penetrate the child's anus.

I screamed. Not loud enough, because it didn't stop him. So I screamed again, shouting, "You bastard, leave the boy alone." Sally was also screaming, louder even than I was. I watched the man – middle-aged, as we thought, with a thin skeleton-type face – pull back from the boy and gaze at us with puzzlement; he never believed he could be spotted this far from the road. His penis was still in full view, and still erect, as though we were nothing more than a minor interruption.

I leapt towards him, not at all sure what I was going to do; I just had to stop him from brutalising the child, who was now crying for his mummy.

Then the man ran off, towards the trees but away from where we knew his van was parked. Sally and I nursed the boy for a second before I said, "Look after him; I'm going to try and catch the bastard."

I followed him. At first it was a clear run through the trees and I was convinced I could catch him; I was a lot younger than he was. But then the branches from the surrounding trees started to unfurl towards me. It was a strange phenomenon: one moment they were hanging there, as branches are supposed to be, giving me a clear run at the assailant; the next minute they had become serendipitous, taking on a life of their own. They paused for a second as if they were examining me, then they twisted and turned, and before I knew it they were wrapping themselves around me in a violent gesture. They went for my eyes, seeking to gouge them out of the sockets and tear the skin from my face; I fought in every way possible, but it wasn't until I asked Katy to help me that the trees relented and eased back into their natural position.

It was as though they knew who I was and they were protecting that monster; or perhaps it was he who had summoned them. By now my face was covered in scratches and I was bleeding quite heavily. I staggered back to where I believed Sally was with the boy; when she saw me she let out a stifled scream.

"Angie, what the hell's happened? Did he attack you?" She took out some tissues from her purse and dabbed my face.

"I…I'm not sure," I stammered. "It was as though the trees had a life of their own."

"You mean, they attacked you?" she asked, horrified.

"More or less." I felt better with the blood wiped away. "How is the boy?" I asked, glancing at the trauma-stricken child. He gazed back at me tearfully, not sure what had happened to him.

"This is Ben. He's seven and he's been a very brave boy. We're going to take him back to his mummy now." As we went back towards our car Sally muttered under her breath, "What became of that bastard? Did he escape?"

I nodded and pointed towards the vacant spot where his van had been parked. "But don't ask me how, because I really don't know. I'm not even sure how he got back to his van and then disappear."

Sally was already on her mobile to Chief Inspector Givens. He was at the Harpenden school from which Ben had been abducted.

"Tell him we're on our way," I instructed her. "And ask him to get Forensics up here, they might find some meaningful traces of him."

CHAPTER FORTY-SEVEN

There was pandemonium at the school when we arrived. A circle of police cars surrounded the entrance and we could see a number of patrol officers questioning the passers-by. Other officers were knocking on doors in the immediate vicinity. I went over to Chief Inspector Givens; he looked absolutely distraught.

"I'm sorry," was all he could say. "I have no idea how it happened. We had a police presence here at the time but they saw nothing…" His eyes went upwards towards the heavens, as if seeking an answer. "No one saw anything. Whoever this Polish guy is he seems to come and go whenever he pleases without anyone seeing him; I had two officers in the playground watching over the children and Ben simply disappeared.

"How…how did you find him, chief inspector?" he asked, frustration – or was it desperation? – in his voice. "I mean, Ben was only reported missing an hour ago. I was about to organise search teams, and I've already set up roadblocks, and now you suddenly appear with the boy. What are you, a magician?"

"I was in the area, chief inspector, when I saw a black van screaming past me on the road. I realised immediately who it might be so we followed it into the woods past a golf club. We heard Ben crying; the rest you know about."

"So, he escaped – if you don't mind my stating the obvious."

I smiled and took another tissue from Miss Thornton, the headmistress, to wipe away the blood from my face. "Not at all. We were so concerned in comforting Ben that we allowed him to get away; when I tried to follow him I couldn't get through the branches." I pointed to my face. "You can see what happened."

"Have you sent Forensics up there?"

"Of course. They're already on their way but I'm not sure what you expect them to find."

"We have to have all the ground covered – you never know, he might have inadvertently left some evidence."

"Thank God you were around," Miss Thornton acknowledged, her arm around young Ben.

"Miss Thornton, please, let the medics examine Ben. He…he might have been interfered with. Will you do that?"

"Yes. Of course," she grimaced. "I know what you mean."

"Does his mother know?" Sally asked.

"No. Not yet. We haven't had time to notify her." She led the boy away and added, "I'd better get on to it straight away. And, thank you," she said; "thank you so much. I don't know what we would have done without you."

After she had left, Chief Inspector Givens asked me if I thought the paedophile might return.

I shook my head. "No. Not at this school. But he will strike again. When, or where, I have no idea. At least, not for the moment, but I will give it some thought. For the time being I believe he will lie low, having narrowly escaped being arrested. So you can withdraw your police presence, chief inspector.

"We have to be going now, but I will keep in touch. And when you talk to the parents let them know that we were extremely lucky in finding Ben; it might have been a very different story."

He nodded and shook my hand with a grateful gesture.

* * * * * *

On the road – that is, back on the M1 – Sally was quiet for a while. I said nothing; I was too preoccupied with the savage performance of the trees. Something had set them off, and that something must have been the malevolent presence; he evidently had powers a lot stronger than I was able to summon. Had it not been for Katy, however, I could well have been strangled in those woods.

"Are you going to tell me?" I heard a trembling voice demanding. I turned quickly to look at her; her face was a mixture of confusion, puzzlement and some anger, as if I had led her along a strange, mysterious path.

"I want to know who you are, Angie. I've had to question some of your decisions in some of the cases we've had to handle, but all you've given me is this intuitive insight you have.

"These past few months I've witnessed some esoteric happenings that appear out of nowhere, and whenever I question you about them all I ever get is that it's your intuition. That's what you tried to tell me this morning. Well, that isn't good enough. I want to know why we went off the road this morning, who it was that summoned you to come to that spot and who it was that told you a boy was being abducted. And who was it that informed you that Harpenden would be the paedophile's next choice for a victim?

"And, whilst we're on it, I want to know what your secret is. Are you a clairvoyant? A psychic? A medium? Or whatever the fuck you want to call it.

"For God's sake, Angie, I can't work like this, not knowing what you're likely to come up with next. So, come on, detective chief inspector; tell me what inspires you, what is your motivator?"

"Not now," I grunted. "I'm driving."

"So pull over. Go on, pull over. Now," she demanded.

I ran onto the hard shoulder and stopped. Sally got out of the car, walked round the front and gestured for me to change places.

"Right. Now I am the one who's driving, so you can sit there quietly and talk. I'm all ears."

She was right; she couldn't possibly work like this. It was too frustrating for anyone to suffer. So I told her my story. Beginning with Connie all those years ago, how we became friends and how it ended with tragedy. I then went on to explain what had happened to me in Manchester, how I had met a 'Sensor', a young boy who had visions and could read people, and how he told me that I was similar to him and his late sister. I then divulged that it was his late sister, Katy, who was now my Spirit Guide, and after I'd said this, I half turned to see if she was laughing. She wasn't. Not even a dead 14-year-old could faze her.

I went on and on and on, describing the psychic I had been to see in Stourport who had informed me that I too was a medium and that I should pray, and how I had ignored her advice, thinking she was a religious crackpot. And how, eventually, Katy had appeared to me in my subconscious, and confirmed what I was already suspecting: that I too was a 'Sensor' and I too would have visions of things to come.

And how, since then, I had seen many sightings connected with my job: the bank robbers, almost as a foretaste of what was to come; the arsonist in Manchester; the killer from Maida Vale; the terrorist; the Polish paedophile; and so on – the list was becoming endless and I had to stop somewhere.

After I had finished we were approaching 'spaghetti junction', outside Birmingham, and we were on our way to junction 10 of the M6 to Wolverhampton. There was silence between us until we left the motorway; no doubt Sally was thinking of everything I had told her.

Eventually she said, "I'm not at all shocked. Part of what you've told me I'd already guessed; the rest – well, it confirms what I had already suspected. So," she continued, "you don't actually see dead people – you know, the spirits – other than your own Spirit Guide?"

"No, I believe they're the ones who are known as mediums. If you were to ask me to liaise with one of your past relatives, I couldn't do it."

"And this morning? Did you have a vision then?"

"No, I didn't, as a matter of fact. It was a bit like last week, when something drew me to the basement and I spotted the terrorist; it was more like a powerful urge to do – Christ, Sally – something. God only knows but I had to follow this urge. And that is the truth. I don't know why I left the motorway when we did. I told you it was my intuition, and largely it was, except that it was the same urge that forced me to go into the basement the other day."

"So you had no idea what we were going to find?"

"No. None. Not until I saw the black van, and I knew then it was that that was compelling me. Just as well, don't you think? It saved that little boy's life."

"It's a fascinating story, Angie," Sally proclaimed, "and I'm really grateful that you've explained it all to me. But do you know why? Why you've told me all this, I mean? I know I hit on you quite a bit but I didn't realise you'd go all the way."

I rubbed my eyes to wipe away a tear. Bringing back some of the memories were a trauma too many. "Yes, I do," I said eventually. "Partly because of what you'd said about not being able to work like this, and partly because I have no one else to talk to." The very thought forced the small tear to roll down my cheek; it didn't concern me that Sally saw it. "I lead a very lonely life, Sally. I have no friends, no one to share my thoughts with, no one, other than my Spirit Guide, to tell me when I'm going wrong." I shrugged. "I suppose that's the real reason why I told you. And," I added, "Because I trust you."

"Have you told anyone else? Other than me?"

"Yes. Jim Robbins has a good idea, but he doesn't know everything. He realises I have visions but he doesn't know about my Spirit Guide – about Katy."

"And is he happy with it?"

"More or less. I know he's afraid that I might come to rely on these visions and let it affect my police work. What he isn't happy about, either, is that sometimes I put myself in danger. He wants me to have a – well, a chaperone."

She leaned over and squeezed my arm. "I'm really grateful you've confided in me, Angie. You're sure it isn't because you fancy me?" She laughed as if it were a joke. "But if you genuinely do want a chaperone, perhaps I could help?"

"And how could you do that? I would like you to share part of my life, Sally, but I'm looking for a good friend, not a lover; if it's the latter that attracts you then we'd better keep our distance from each other." I was annoyed at her suggestion. "I'm not even sure your offer of a chaperone would be acceptable to the commander."

I wiped away the tear, hoping she might sympathise. She did.

"I'm sorry Angie. It was my idea of a joke – a tasteless joke. But, in any event, thank you so much for trusting me," she said sincerely. "And I too would like to become your friend."

CHAPTER FORTY-EIGHT

We came off the M6 and headed towards Wolverhampton. Sally asked me, "You do know where we're going?"

"Well, yes. We're going to Wolverhampton New Street police station; we're meeting Detective Inspector Sutton, in charge of the southern sector, and Superintendent Bagshawe from New Street will be there."

"I don't think that's where Sam and I went the last time we were here; I'm sure it was All Saints."

"It was probably was; originally that was the district handling the murders. Except that now the case has been taken over by New Street and the superintendent is the SCO."

"And do they know that we're intending to take over the case?" Sally asked inquisitively.

"No. The commander hasn't told them yet. I'm still not sure that we should; we have enough on our plates as it is."

"So, remind me again," Sally said; "these serious cases now have to be referred to the National Serious Crimes Unit in London, and it us that decides whether or not we should take them on? Is that right, Angie?"

"Yes. More or less. But, generally speaking, it's Jim who makes the overall decision – turn left here, Sally; we go round the bypass until it takes us into the centre... Anyway, on this occasion he's left it up to us; probably because we have so much on."

"I see. And how do you feel about it?"

"I'm not sure. Neither am I sure that this Central Crime Division is going to work; we might have the specialised talents there but we certainly don't have the resources they have in the districts."

She frowned at me. "Yeah, but I thought we were going to be able to use whatever resources were available in the outposts."

"In theory, yes. But it seems to me that unless we're petitioned to take on a specific case by the local force then the allocation of resources tend to become restricted." I shrugged. "I don't suppose I should be saying this."

"Have you told the commander how you feel?"

"Yes, I have. And I've told him that for us to be functional then we need a hell of a lot more manpower. Look, there it is on the left."

We arrived at New Street to be greeted by a crowd of what must have been reporters; there were also a couple of TV crews directing their cameras at whoever entered the building.

We parked outside the building but before we were allowed to enter a volley of questions were fired at us. It was one of those 'No comment' cases. Superintendent Bagshawe and Detective Inspector Sutton were waiting in one of the offices.

The police officers were both serious men. Detective Inspector Sutton was thin, with narrow shoulders and slim hips and a gaunt hawk-like face, and his grey eyes seemed to be analysing us all the time. He was around his mid-30s, and a rather forbidding figure. Superintendent Bagshawe was the opposite in build; he was quite bulky, with a heavy-featured face and a scar down one side of it, as though someone had knifed him; his eyes, though, did have something of a twinkle about them.

He introduced himself to me and informed us that DI Sutton was leading the enquiry; the inspector shook my hand somewhat curtly and then led us into the briefing room, where there were a good dozen or so officers assembled.

"These are the officers from New Scotland Yard, the National Serious Crimes Unit," Sutton announced.

"Detective Chief Inspector Angela Crossley and Detective Sergeant Sally Walker. Some of you may have met Sergeant Walker before."

We acknowledged the assembly and let him continue. "The officers are here to help us in the pursuit of the serial killer. They have read the files with all of our evidence, and I'm hoping they may add something we've missed. So, they'll come amongst you and discuss details of the case; if you have anything you wish to say, please feel free.

"One of their suspects, which they have discussed with me, is Jack McCloud. Some of you may remember McCloud; some 11 years or so ago he murdered a prostitute. There was no absolute evidence as to why he brutalised this woman, other than possibly he could be a psychopath. My own view is that McCloud doesn't have the wherewithal to commit such a crime at present: he has no transport; he is currently out of a job; he lacks any kind of financial aid; and he also dresses virtually as a hobo. He is also on the sex register and reports to his parole officer. At present he is living in a down-and-out bed and breakfast, just off the town centre, which is paid for by social services. If he puts one foot wrong he'll be back inside, and he knows it. The disadvantage we have in these cases is that Forensics have not been able to come up with determining evidence: There are fibres, but they could belong to anyone: the are no fingerprints, only faint smudges, and there is no DNA. So whoever is responsible has sufficient knowledge of criminal investigation to disguise their crimes.

"I have expressed my opinions to Inspector Crossley; needless to say, she disagrees, which is one of the reasons she is here. Please give her all the help you can. I'll be in my office if you need anything."

Wonderful, I whispered to myself. He couldn't have made our case any more difficult.

I took one half of the assembly whilst Sally took the other. The first person I spoke to was a detective sergeant, ageing a little, with a heavy and sarcastic droop to his mouth.

"Hi, I'm Bill Gardner. So you disagree with the guv, then?" he said with a slight sneer.

I ignored him. "Have you canvassed the red-light district?" I asked.

"Yes, ma'am." His mouth seemed to turn up at the question.

"Don't 'ma'am' me," I snapped; "I'm not an aristocrat. Now, when you spoke to the other prostitutes did you ask them if they recognised McCloud?"

"Well, no. We were informed he wasn't a suspect."

My mouth fell open at his response. "You're telling me you didn't have a photo of him to see if anyone recognised him?"

He shook his head. "Why should we? We canvassed the street walkers to see if there was anyone suspicious they could single out; we were informed McCloud was someone you lot had dreamed up in your cosy London offices."

At this I stood and addressed the room.

"Can I have your attention, please?" I shouted. When it quietened I announced, "The one thing Detective Inspector Sutton did not inform you of is that we were asked to look at this case by the Birmingham Central Office; it has not yet been decided if we should accept the case or not. That will be a matter for Commander Robbins, who heads up the unit in London. So, for the time being we are here merely as advisers. However, when we put forward a suggestion we would prefer that you listen and accept our suggestions. If you either refuse or you dislike our recommendations, then let me know, please, and we will leave now and discuss the matter with your central control.

"Is that clear?"

There were one or two nods from around the room, so I continued. "Now, coming back to Jack McCloud, the reason we selected him was principally because he murdered a prostitute some 11 years ago, evidently without motive, and since that time, and until his release from Winsom Green about a year ago, no other prostitutes were murdered in this area.

I have listened to what Detective Inspector Sutton has to say about this suspect, and he may well have a point. However, regardless of McCloud's present-day circumstances, he has to be eliminated from this case, and therefore he will receive as much attention as any other suspect. The other clue we have about McCloud is that the MO of the recently murdered women is more or less the same as the woman he killed 11 years ago. I am of the opinion that this is something that seems to have been overlooked.

"So, I want his photo, his recent photo, circulated amongst the prostitutes in the red-light district in All Saints, and I want them to be asked if any of them might recognise him from approaches they may have received in the past few months. I want this to happen tonight; I will clear it with Birmingham, so please assume you are all on overtime. Now, are there any questions?"

There was silence throughout the room, as though they had just received a shock. Sally came across to me and said, "That was a bit harsh, don't you think?"

"I do not," I said sharply. "These bloody people have been sitting on their arses going through the motions whilst women out there are being murdered. And the obvious suspect is overlooked because he doesn't have a fucking car. And the press are having a field day. Do you think it's me or them, Sally?"

She cringed visibly. "'Sorry, I was out of order. Do you want me to carry on talking to them?"

I looked at my watch. It was after five. "No," I said. "We'll have an early supper and then we'll join them on the night duty; I reckon we'll have more luck with the prostitutes than they will. Come on, Sally; let's find a café."

CHAPTER FORTY-NINE

We found a greasy spoon close to the police station. I wanted something more substantial but Sally fancied one of those all-day breakfasts. So I clenched my teeth and went for it. Actually, it was rather nice, and I certainly enjoyed the mug of hot tea.

"Where are we planning to spend the night?" Sally asked between mouthfuls.

"Well, we ain't going back to London tonight." I pulled out my mobile and went through enquires. "I think we'll try to get some rooms at the Britannia Hotel."

"Yeah. Where's that, then?"

"It's in Lichfield Street, right in the town centre."

"I managed to book two twin rooms, let as singles, and told them we'd be there shortly."

"Jesus! Can we afford that expense?"

I smiled. "We're not paying, Sally. This one's on Birmingham Central. Come on, we'll check in first and then go scout out the area; see where the hookers are hanging out."

"Are you sure we want to spend the night in separate rooms?"

I looked at her quizzically. "I'm not sure what you mean."

She shrugged and gave me smile. "Well, I just wanted to know if you fancied me enough – you know, now we have the opportunity."

"What makes you say that, Sally?"

"I thought I should let you know that I know about Kelly. We were an item some while back..."

"And she told you about me, did she?"

"Well, yes. I hope you don't mind my bringing it up – only I do fancy the pants off you."

"I hope she told you that I haven't come out, and neither do I intend to."

"So that was simply a need to have a friend?"

"If you like. And, since you asked, Sally, there is no way I am going to sleep with you, and I'd rather you didn't bring it up again. Understood?"

"Sure. Only I felt I should tell you..."

We parked the car and checked in. The rooms we were offered had a pleasant atmosphere, with a large double bed, coffee-making facilities and en-suite bathrooms. I left my overnight bag on the bed, had a rinse and went downstairs to join up with Sally.

"Very nice hotel," she said.

"I'm glad we're not paying for it. Do you want a drink?"

"I'd love one, but I'd better not; we are working. Have you decided what to do about taking on the case, Angie?"

I let out a long sigh. "I'm still undecided, but if we were to leave it to these characters I'm afraid we'd still be watching out for more bodies to appear."

"Do we know where the last body was discovered?"

"Yeah. The same place as all the others: East Park. Whoever murdered them must have lured them, possibly in a car, strangled them and then carried them off to East Park for butchering."

She frowned at me. It was becoming a habit with her, although I didn't say anything. "Okay, you may be right, but what I don't understand is that, it might have been dark but, even so, how did he escape detection? Not just from transporting the bodies from his car, but carving them up like a dead carcass? Surely there were people in the vicinity, lovers or people like that, someone must have spotted him?"

"It's a good point, Sally. Perhaps I'm mistaken; perhaps he encouraged them to go into the park with him, then he strangled them, possibly in the shelter of the trees."

"You've not had any…visions or anything about this, have you?" Her eyes had rolled over; obviously this didn't sit well with her.

I smiled. If only life were so easy. "If Katy wanted to tell me anything she would have done so by now; I can only assume I have to work this one out for myself. What was it I said to you some while ago about profilers?"

"Yeah. I remember. You're not going through that one again, are you? Well, you've got us this far, so, if you don't mind, I'll leave it to you to take us the rest of the way."

I checked my watch. It was approaching nine o'clock and it was starting to get dark this late spring evening although the clocks had gone forward some time ago. "Come on. The night hawkers should be out by now. Let's go talk to them."

All Saints was an area I knew fairly well in my early police days. The street inhabited by hookers was Raby Street, very close to the hospital; other streets close by were also frequented, but we started on Raby Street. There were at least five or even six prostitutes hawking their trade; as yet I hadn't noticed a single policeman. Two of the hookers were obviously intent on buying drugs from a local dealer.

"Do we arrest him?" Sally asked with a grin.

"Like hell we do. Aside from being out of our jurisdiction these prostitutes, from what I can gather, are mostly into drugs. We read about it all the time."

"Look at this, Sally; not a uniform in sight. And I haven't got a picture of McCloud with me."

"I have," she said, pulling a copy out of her purse. "It's not as you wanted, an up-to-date one, but someone might recognise him."

I checked it over. It was as good as we were going to get. "Good girl. At least we have something to go on."

The first two prostitutes we questioned hardly glanced at the picture. I had to insist that the second one check it over, which she did.

"No. I don't recognise him. But if you wait around a bit Beatrice will be on duty, and if anyone knows him it'll be her."

"And who is Beatrice?" I asked.

"She's like a kind of pimp; she looks after some of the people on the streets – better than having a man."

"How will I recognise her?"

She laughed. "Oh, you'll know her alright; she's over 50 and weighs in at about 20 stone."

I returned the smile and turned to Sally. "Let's go and have a coffee – we'll give her another hour."

There was a canteen in the hospital that we used for our refreshments.

"Do you fancy our chances?" she asked me.

"Dunno. But, like I said, we have to eliminate him…"

"Yeah – from our enquiries," she interrupted. "That wasn't what I was talking about. I was wondering if someone might recognise him." She shrugged. "Just to be positive."

"Sorry about that," I admitted. "Yes, I hope you're right, Sally. With six people from this area murdered, and if it his is territory, then he definitely will be recognised. Let's talk to Beatrice, shall we?"

She was exactly as she had been described: a huge middle-aged lady, who I certainly wouldn't fancy taking on. The first prostitute I had spoken to had now disappeared but that didn't prevent Beatrice from approaching us.

"Carol told me you were asking after someone," she said in a nondescript voice. "Lemme look at the photo."

I handed it over and she examined it carefully. "It's kinda old but, yeah; I think I can make him out. 'Cept the guy we know has a moustache and wears glasses. If this is the same fella he's been around here a helluva lot; I chased him off one of my girls not long back. Why do you want him? Is he one of the suspects?"

"Yes. He's one of the suspects. We just want to talk to him."

She whistled through her teeth. "Fuck me. You think it could be this guy?"

"We don't know," Sally said. "When was the last time you saw him?"

"Couple o' weeks ago. Nasty piece of work, he is. He don't try to pick up the girls, just follows 'em."

"Did you see him go off with one of...these women?"

"Hookers, you mean? No. Not with any of my girls, he didn't. But that don't mean he didn't go off with any of the others. Leave it a bit later and this place gets crowded; you can ask 'em then. Do you know him?"

I nodded. "Yes. We know him alright. Did you see him with a car?"

"Not round here I didn't. But that doesn't mean he don't have one. I hope you catch him – if only to get rid of those bastards." She gestured towards a film crew set up at the beginning of the street. "Fuck knows what they're expecting to achieve."

I looked around; there still wasn't a police presence in the vicinity, but they must have sent out a warning for the TV crew to be here. "Thanks for your help," I said. "Come on, Sally; let's go get the troops."

"Now what do we do?" she asked after leaving All Saints.

"We'll go back to New Street; see if there's anyone there who can help us."

"And if there isn't?"

I shrugged – what the hell? "Dunno. Maybe you and I can visit this B&B where he's staying – have a chat with him there."

New Street police station turned out to be almost deserted: merely the night staff, but not a soul from CID.

"So much for their help," I commented. "We'd better go and check over the B&B."

* * * * * *

The B&B was in a run-down part of town and blended in well with the surroundings. It was on four storeys, badly in need of paint, and the windows needed replacing. It was council-owned, and run and occupied mostly by down and outs and those on probation who were transitory.

I asked the receptionist, a dowdy middle-aged woman, if McCloud was in; she pointed upstairs and said abruptly, "He's on probation; he's not allowed out after ten."

That was a shock. If he was our killer then how the hell was he able to leave the hotel without anyone seeing him?

"What would happen if he tried to leave, say, after ten o'clock?" I asked her.

"Then I'd refer it to his probation officer and he'd be back inside."

"So, to your knowledge he's never tried it?"

She rolled her eyes as if she were talking to a dummy. "What would be the point? He might get past reception but your lot would be waiting for him when he got back. Unless, of course, he tried to do a runner."

"Does anyone visit him here?" It was Sally asking the question.

"Just one man. He comes quite regularly – stays for a couple of hours."

"Do you know his name?"

Her eyes rolled over again. "Now, how the hell would I know that? He doesn't have to sign in, you know."

"I see. Do you mind if we go and speak to McCloud?"

She sighed heavily. "'Sup to you. Room 22, fourth floor."

"There are never any fucking lifts in these places," Sally complained as we trudged up the stairs. I was too busy catching my breath to respond. We knocked on the door of room 22 and waited.

"A minute," someone said harshly. The door opened and there was McCloud, dressed in a baggy pair of shorts and a sleeveless vest. There was a distinct smell oozing from him, and as we stepped inside the room I noticed a half-empty bottle of Scotch on a bedside table. Other than the bed, the bedside table and a battered wicker chair with an old television on top, there was no other furniture in the room. His clothes, such as they were, were hanging across a piece of string tied up in one corner of the shabby room. I shivered at the thought of having to live there, but then I'd never murdered anyone either. I flashed my warrant card at him. "Detective Chief Superintendent Crossley." I pointed to Sally. "This is Detective Sergeant Walker. We would like to talk to you, Mr McCloud."

"Yeah? What about? I ain't done nothin'." I glanced at his eyes, trying to read him, but he quickly dropped his gaze, almost as if he knew what was happening to him.

"We're not suggesting you have done anything," Sally said sharply. "We just want to talk to you."

He picked up the whisky bottle and poured himself a large shot. "Go ahead, then. I'm all ears."

"We are enquiring into the murders of six prostitutes in or around this area during the last 12 months," I stated. I showed him the list of the victims and the dates they were murdered. "Have a look at these, will you? Look closely at the dates. We would like to know whereabouts you were on the dates in question."

"That's a silly fucking question," he sneered. "Where the hell do you think I was? I can't get outta here after ten, and that's since I were released from the nick, nearly a year ago now. So you'd better look somewhere else for your killer cos it weren't me."

We knew this, of course, but I just wanted to check him over and to try to read him. I almost forced him to meet my gaze when I suggested that there might be other ways he could leave the premises.

"What, you mean jump from the fourth floor window? Or, I could have gone down a few floors and then escaped down a fucking drainpipe?" He seemed to find this hilarious as he guffawed at the prospect.

I still couldn't read him.

This might be the man we were looking for; I couldn't tell.

"Thanks for your time, Mr McCloud. We'll be in touch." He was still sniggering as we left the room.

"Well, that was helpful," Sally announced. "Do you mind telling me why we went to see him when we knew he couldn't leave the premises?"

I smiled at her innocence. "I wanted to have a look at him, see if he had a moustache. I also wanted to read him."

"As in clairvoyant?" she asked slyly.

"Yes. But it wasn't possible. Did you notice how he kept his gaze averted?"

"Not really. Most of the criminals I've met do that."

"Yeah, well, it stopped me from reading him, so he might be the killer. On the other hand, he might not be."

"So you found nothing?"

I nodded, still thinking about his gaze as we got into the car.

"So what are we going to do now, Angie?"

"We're going back to the hotel for a good night's sleep. In the morning I want to call into Birmingham Central and report this bloody stupid lot of Wolverhampton cops and see if we can't get something moving."

"You still haven't answered how he managed to get out of the B&B without anyone noticing."

"Because he had help," I suggested. "I guess that's where the moustache came from. I believe he has an accomplice."

Back at the Britannia we got the keys for our rooms and took the lift.

"Wait a minute; you're saying someone came to see him at the hotel, wearing glasses and sporting a moustache, and then they changed over?"

I clicked the room lock. "It's possible, Sally. I think it was someone he met in prison, maybe someone he'd helped who owed him a huge favour. All he had to do then was to place a false moustache over his lip, wear some clear glasses and then leave wearing the same coat his pal had on when he arrived. No one would actually notice any difference. Quite clever, really, when you think about it; he would have a watertight alibi."

Sally shook her head and her mouth fell open. Then she said, "A remarkable deduction, Mr Holmes, but, as you said, all we have to do now is to prove it. And don't you think the receptionist might be suspicious when he returned? And this would be after he'd murdered a prostitute and then butchered her – eviscerated her, I believe. Don't you think he might be covered in blood, Angie?"

"I'll see you in the morning, Sally. Goodnight." Sometimes her insight was penetrating, and I couldn't deal with it tonight.

That night I had a confused kind of vision. It was rather like walking through a snowstorm. I saw Katy, or I thought I saw her, but she became someone else. Then a voice sounded an alarm in my mind: "You're taking the wrong path; you'll never get out of the storm if you take this path."

I didn't know what it meant – that is, if it meant anything. So I put it down to one of my less encouraging dreams. Afterwards I lay awake for some time trying to unravel the message. Then Sally's comments came back to me. It would be true; after McCloud had murdered and butchered a prostitute surely he would be covered in blood. My thoughts were convoluted until I remembered the dream – the wrong path. What did it mean? But what if McCloud, having escaped the confinements of the B&B, stayed out all night – I mean, all night. Then he would be able to abduct a prostitute the same evening and be joined by his partner the following morning. But then what?

It was gone four in the morning before I drifted off to sleep, still baffled.

CHAPTER FIFTY

The next morning we had finished breakfast and I was checking us out when Sally asked me, "Any news from the home front?"

"Yes. We've had a report of gun crimes in Nottingham. Phil and Peter have gone over there. I won't know what happened until we get back."

"So, are we going to Birmingham Central from here?"

"No. First of all we're going to Winsom Green prison."

"Really? What do you hope to find there?" She was shrugging her shoulders again, as if I'd lost her.

"I want to talk to the governor, to ask him what, if anything, he knows about McCloud's time in prison. I want to know if he befriended anyone in particular, whether he had any suspicions as to his behaviour – you know the kind of thing."

"Well, obviously you do, Angie. You know, I quite like working with you; I feel as if I'm learning something every day."

"Are you being sarcastic?"

"No. Not at all. I'm being serious."

"Come on. We have a long day in front of us."

* * * * * *

Winsom Green still had the same effect it had on me the last time I went there, when I visited Henry, not that long ago. I understood the governor had changed and a Mr Barraclough was now in command. I shivered as we stood at the entrance waiting for the security guards to admit us. We went through the same undignified search routine; at least this time it was a woman examining our belongings and us. Finally we were led into the governor's offices, invited to sit and offered coffee, which Sally gratefully accepted.

"How can I help you, chief inspector?" He was quite young, I thought, especially for someone in that position. Not that I would have fancied him, with his bald head and glasses perched perilously on the end of his nose. I guessed someone must have told him that that would make him look more intellectual; probably his wife.

"We're enquiring about Jack McCloud, governor. He was released from here, on probation, about a year ago. He now lives in a bed and breakfast unit in Wolverhampton."

"I see. And what is it you want know about him? You have to bear in mind I've only been here a few months, so I didn't know him personally."

"What about the chief warden? Do you think he might know something?"

"I imagine so. It might help if you were to talk to him. Shall I send for him?"

"Yes please, governor. Do you mind if we talk to him in here or do you want us to move?"

He smiled; quite a gracious smile, I thought. "No, please stay here; you'll be more comfortable."

The chief warden was a middle-aged man, pretty bulky, with a serious expression on his face, as if he was constantly facing the worries of the world.

"You wanted to see me, governor?"

"Yes, Owen; at least, these two detectives do. I'll just sit here and listen, if I may." He then introduced us all and ordered more coffee.

"We want to talk to you about Jack McCloud. You may remember he was released from here about a year ago; he served 11 years for murdering a prostitute in Wolverhampton."

"Yes, I'm aware of him. What is it you want to know?"

"Well, basically, his behaviour throughout his stay," Sally enquired. "Was he friendly with anyone, someone he was pretty close to?"

"Not to my knowledge. He was a pretty lonely kind of a guy — hardly spoke to anyone."

This was very disappointing, and certainly didn't stack up with my own conclusions. I saw Sally looking at me questioningly.

"So, he had no friends, that you know of, er, Owen?"

"No. The only person he was close to was his cellmate."

"'Really?" I said, hope rising in my voice. "And who would that be?"

"A Birmingham guy, a real nasty piece of work. Name of Arthur Scanlon."

This was someone I'd never heard of, but when I thought about it McCloud would have had to be placed on the secure wing, so his cellmate must also be on the sex register.

"How close was 'close'?" Sally asked.

"Well, they weren't exactly buddies, but I know they used to eat together. And, of course, they had one thing in common."

"What – you mean violent tendencies?" I said.

"Not just that. They both killed a prostitute, only Scanlon got away with a manslaughter charge, insisting she was his girlfriend." He shrugged. "Even so, they placed him on the sex offenders' list for the five years after his release because he admitted to having raped her under duress – so he said."

Oh, hell! I wondered to myself. Have we been on the wrong track?

"How did you know she wasn't his girlfriend?"

He grinned. "Oh, these things get around. It wasn't long before he was bragging about how he he'd got away with it."

"So," Sally exclaimed, " they must have been very close. They weren't homosexuals, were they?"

He shrugged. "I'm pretty sure they were – but, then, anything is possible in Winsom Green. I mean, they didn't actually go around holding hands, but I do know one of the wardens did find them in bed together."

"Do you have a recent photo of Scanlon?" I asked.

He pointed to the governor. "There's one in the file," he said.

I examined the photo. It was more or less similar to the guy described by Beatrice, but unlike McCloud. Moustache, glasses, slim. Not entirely different from McCloud, but different enough.

"Thank you," I muttered, disheartened by what I saw.

"Do you mind my asking why you want this information? Have they done something wrong? Something we should know about?"

"We're investigating the murders of six prostitutes in the west Midlands area. Initially we suspected McCloud; now I'm not so sure."

"You think now it could be Scanlon?"

"I'm not sure; Scanlon didn't figure into the equation until now. They're both violent men and, as you say, Owen, they both murdered prostitutes. I don't suppose you know where Scanlon is living now, do you?"

He shook his head. "Not a clue. You'll have to ask the local police – he reports to them, I believe once a month. They will know. I do know he was released shortly after McCloud; who knows, perhaps they stayed together. That's about all I can tell you, officers."

We shook hands, and with the governor, and left the prison, quite happy to say goodbye.

"Now what?" Sally asked me. "Off to Birmingham, are we?"

"I'm not sure."

I was thinking about the vision I had had last night, and the warning I'd been given that I was on the wrong track. Perhaps I should now change tracks and see where that took me.

"Let's get some lunch. I want to have a talk with you."

We found a nice bistro close to the Bull Ring; it was one I'd used in the past.

"What do want to talk to me about?" Sally asked.

"Last night I had a vision…"

"You mean, like a spiritual happening?" she interrupted, grinning.

"This is serious," I muttered, irritated at her reaction. "Anyway, I was being warned that somehow I was in the wrong lane and I would never get out of the snowstorm if I didn't change direction."

"You were in a snowstorm? In May?" she gasped.

"This was not one of your average dreams – you can still dream of snowstorms even in summer. Will you please allow me to finish?"

"Sorry."

"Well, after the dream, I thought about what you had said, about there being blood etc.; I was tossing and turning well into the night. And now, after our visit to Winsom Green, it seems someone was telling me that maybe I'd got the wrong man."

"And you now think this Scanlon could be the somebody else?"

"Sure – why not? They shared a cell together; they were homosexuals; both possibly psychopaths; then surely it could have been one or the other? And Scanlon isn't on parole, so he isn't under supervision, aside from checking-in to the local police relating to the sex register. So why shouldn't he visit McCloud in his hotel for a sexual encounter; perhaps they had exchanged vital details of their murders whilst they were in prison."

Sally frowned at me. "It's all a bit far-fetched, Angie. I don't really know anything about psychopaths or how they function, but I do remember they are invariably control freaks; they're also stimulated by an uncontrollable desire. Surely you know this better than I do?"

"Yes, I do. And part of the stimulation can be through a sexual experience. Look, instead of going back to Birmingham I think we should go back to the B&B and ask the receptionist there if she can recognise this photo I got from the governor."

"And what about the blood on his clothes? Have you given any thought to that?"

"Sort of. It could well be that, if they're in this together, then an interchange of personalities could help them to carry it off."

"Could you repeat that, Angie. You're in danger of losing me."

"Just bear with me, will you?"

* * * * * *

We were lucky. It was the same receptionist still on duty from last night. I produced the photograph and handed it to her. "Have you seen this man before?"

She looked at it, almost reflectively. "Yes. I have. He's the one I told you about last night; comes here probably once or sometimes twice a week. He's a friend of McCloud in number 22."

"How long does he stay?" Sally asked.

"Dunno, really. I'd guess about a couple of hours."

Shit! So there it was. Had we been looking at the wrong man? Or was this some kind of a conspiracy? It left me thinking what the vision had intended.

We left the hotel and Sally repeated what I had said to her some time back. "Now all we have to do is prove it. So, are you going to explain?"

"Yes. Perhaps these two are in it together. Scanlon visits McCloud, they have a sexual interchange as normal – for them, that is – and then he leaves. The following morning, having prearranged it, McCloud leaves the B&B and meets up with Scanlon wherever he might be hiding the prostitute he has abducted the previous night. Together, they strip off then murder the poor girl, carving her up slowly, and in pieces, so she knows she's going to die, and then, between them, they dispose of the body. When McCloud arrives back at the B&B, later in the day, his clothes are clean and he has a watertight alibi and they don't leave anything for the SOCOS to unravel."

And I had missed the obvious – that Connelly, who I'd thought of as the primary suspect, couldn't possibly have shared a cell with McCloud because he wasn't on the sex offenders' register.

"How does that grab you, Sally?"

She puckered her lips, as though she were thinking about my conclusions. Then she said, "It seems okay, about the blood, but where the hell can they hide away a hooker, then disembowel her in the process of murdering her?"

"I don't know. Perhaps they use an old abattoir; somewhere they won't be disturbed. It shouldn't be too difficult if the police follow Scanlon, what, a couple of times a week."

"But it could be weeks now before they indulge in their compulsions again; it's probably more difficult for them now we've been to see McCloud."

"Yeah. You may be right."

"So, what do we tell Birmingham?"

I shrugged. I wasn't too sure. "Well, they'll still need to keep an eye on Scanlon. I doubt those two'll be able to control their urges for too long. But I'll have to think about it."

"Well, you'd better think about it before we get to Birmingham."

CHAPTER FIFTY-ONE

I phoned ahead and let Chief Superintendent Sanderson know that we were on our way. He was the DCS over Superintendent Bagshawe. What he hadn't told me was that reporters and a whole host of television cameras were besieging the premises. I don't know why but I was surprised at the public attention this case had received. A couple of the TV interviewers recognised me from Manchester.

"Are you profiling this case, DCI Crossley?"

"No comment" was all I could think of saying.

The chief superintendent was equally surprised that we wanted to see him; he was even more surprised when I told him what had happened at New Cross.

"You're telling me they were indifferent?" he asked, astonishment in his voice.

He wasn't very much older than Jim Robbins, probably about his mid-40s, but he was thicker around the waist and I noticed that his nose was a little shiny; possibly a drinker, I thought.

"Yes. They thought we were on a wild goose chase," I commented. "When I mentioned Jack McCloud to them Detective Inspector Sutton informed them that he was discounting our suspect. As it happened, he was partly right, but it did lead us to another new suspect, an Arthur Scanlon."

Then I went on to report what we had been told at Winsom prison, and in particular what the chief warden had told us, especially about the two prisoners being homosexuals. I then showed him the photo of Scanlon and informed him that the receptionist at the B&B where McCloud was staying had identified him, as someone who called on McCloud once or twice a week.

"These are both violent men, chief superintendent. Scanlon evidently got away with murder; he convinced the jury that the prostitute he murdered was his girlfriend and they'd had an acrimonious split."

"So you're now saying that it's Scanlon who could the killer?"

"No, sir. What I'm saying is that they are in this together. And if CID at New Street had bothered to follow our instructions and talked to the prostitutes in Rabin Street they would have discovered more or less what we did, and followed their detective noses to Winson Green."

"What did Bagshawe have to say about this?"

"Nothing. He disappeared into his office and left it to DI Sutton."

He shook his head, bemused at the story. "So, they're still not up to date with the details?" he asked me.

"No, sir. And I have no intention of updating them; if you wish to do that, chief superintendent, that's up to you. As far as Scotland Yard is concerned I will inform the commander we have gone as far as we can with the case; the next few weeks will be up to you, but you'll let the commander know what materialises, won't you, sir? What you have to do now, if you don't mind my saying it, is mobilise your forces and check into both Scanlon and McCloud."

"And how would you suggest we do that, chief inspector?" There was an edge of sarcasm in his voice.

It was Sally who interrupted; you could always rely on her to cut across any sarcasm.

"You'll have to put a tail on Scanlon – sir. Watch him; follow him home after he visits McCloud. It shouldn't be too long before they plan another abduction, but this time you'll be ahead of him. It's very sad and I feel sorry for the poor girl who'll be snatched, but at least you'll be able to save her life."

I winced at the tone in her voice, but she wasn't going to retract.

"And is that how you would go about it, chief inspector?" Sanderson asked.

All I could do was to nod my head in agreement. What Sally had said didn't need amplifying.

There was the inevitable silence after her outburst. Then the superintendent virtually apologised. "No. I'm sorry about that – just wasn't thinking too clearly. Right, chief inspector, the ball's in our court now."

"Yes, sir. We'll leave it with you and head back to London; we have a child killer to catch."

* * * * * *

"I wouldn't like to get on the wrong side of your tongue," I said to Sally as we set off for London.

"It was his own bloody stupid fault; he didn't have to speak to you like that."

"No, you were right to respond the way you did; it's the cutting edge of your tongue that got to me."

"Do you think they'll catch him – Scanlon, I mean?"

"I don't see why not. They don't have a lot to do, but they might have to be patient."

I got on the phone to speak to Sam.

"What's happened in Nottingham?" I asked him. "What? I can't hear you. I'll have to get back to you later. Signal's bad," I stated.

"Probably your battery is down. Do you want to try him on mine?" She handed me her phone. I tried again, and this time I got a clear line.

"Sam, I'm using Sally's mobile. I just wanted to ask how they're getting on in Nottingham. What? Tell me again, will you? Inspector Greenridge? When did he join us? I see. They're still there? Okay, I'll see you tomorrow."

"'What was that all about?"

"Sam – telling me we now have another inspector, an Inspector Greenridge. I think that's how you pronounce his name. Anyway, he went off to Nottingham with Phil and Peter; no news yet."

"Who organised the inspector? Was it the commander?"

"Yes. He said he was going to strengthen us by two inspectors." I plugged my mobile into the car cigarette lighter. "This should help."

"'How do you feel about that?" Sally asked.

"As long as he's competent then I don't mind. We're badly under strength as it is. Now we can turn our attention to the Polish paedophile."

"And the rapist. I feel we've been away for ages."

"Well, nothing will have changed," I remarked.

I closed my eyes and dozed, and didn't wake up until we were turning into Camden High Street.

"You must have been tired," Sally commented.

"Yeah, sorry about that. Drop me off, Sally, will you? And I'll see you tomorrow."

The office could wait. What I needed now was a shower and then something to eat. At least we had helped to redirect another of the crimes, but why Birmingham couldn't have done what we did was beyond me. There was no mysterious involvement in this case, just simple hard police work. Or perhaps I was becoming an out-and-out professional – though I did have to remind myself of the vision I had had the previous night. It still might come back to haunt me, depending on the chief superintendent's follow-up.

I checked my watch and was surprised to see that it had already gone nine o'clock; I still hadn't had my shower. I sat down on the bed, trying to make up my mind what I should do: was I hungry or did I need a shower more?

I lay down on the bed. I didn't feel particularly hungry; maybe I was feeling the strain of the past couple of days.

CHAPTER FIFTY-TWO

The next thing I knew the sun was shining through the opened curtains. I opened my eyes slowly and realised I was still dressed; I hadn't had either my shower or a meal. I struggled out of bed and again checked my watch: it was seven in the morning. I had slept for more than nine hours, and I was still hungry. I also had a blinding headache; I felt that it was the plate in my skull pressing on my brain, it happened from to time. I took a couple of Tramedol, strong painkillers that I kept in case these headaches came over me. I made my way into the shower, stripped off and almost poured myself into the hot water. I stayed there for quite a while, had a shampoo and let the stresses of Wolverhampton wash away from me. It was the telephone that alerted me as to where I was at that moment. I wrapped a gown around myself, almost fell over the rug in the bedroom in my haste and grabbed the phone before it rang off.

"Crossley," I mumbled irritably.

"Angie, it's Sam here. Sorry to ring you so early but I've just had a report from Nottingham."

I sat down on the bed, still feeling exhausted. "You'd better explain."

"Well, yesterday Inspector Greenridge, along with Phil and Peter, and three of the officers from downstairs, went off to Nottingham. We had been invited to examine the components behind a wave of shootings in Nottingham city centre."

"Yes. So you told me. But why were we needed – couldn't the local force handle something like that? And why so many of us? It sounds like a fucking gang war."

"Yes, well, it was the commander who sorted out the numbers. And, yes, it is a gang war. Evidently there are two or three groups of black people – drug dealers, we were told – fighting it out amongst each other. So far this week three people are dead and countless others have been injured"

I sighed. My eyes were heavy from exhaustion. "Yeah, okay, Sam. That does concern us. So why are you ringing me at this time of the morning? Has something happened I should know about?"

There was a hesitation. Then he said, "I don't really know how to say this to you, Angie, but Peter Wadkins was shot last night."

"What? Oh, Jesus Christ; not another one. How is he?"

"He's dead. The commander wants us all to assemble in the conference room at eight this morning."

I couldn't speak for a moment. I leaned back as if I were riveted to the headboard. This terrible news had really shaken me. "How did it happen, Sam?"

"He was in the wrong place at the wrong time."

"That's a fucking cliché. I asked you what happened."

"Sorry. I'm still shook up at the news. Apparently, he followed one of the gang members who was trying to get away from the police. The guy spotted him and he shot him. One shot – in the chest. He was dead on arrival at the hospital."

"Did they catch the gunman?"

"No. But I believe they have CCTV images; they're hoping they will show him. Fuck me, Angie; I don't know what to say."

"Don't say anything, Sam. I'll be in shortly."

* * * * * *

I was about to leave the flat, trying to compose myself, when I noticed an envelope on the doormat; someone must have pushed it through the letterbox. I opened it, somewhat curious as to why they didn't simply knock. It was one of those cut-out messages from old newspapers, in some kind of foreign language; it read:

WIEM GDZIE MIESZKASZ. BEDZIESZ MOIM NASTEPNYM CELEM.

I bit my lip. What the hell was all this about? It looked like Polish, but I couldn't be sure. I read and reread the note on my journey on the tube to try and establish who might be behind it. "Is it another terrorist?" I questioned. "The rapist? Or might it be the paedophile?" This was the only remaining possibility.

I debated as to whether or not I should keep quiet about it, but decided I wouldn't. If I didn't inform Jim about it and something were to happen to me, he would never forgive himself. It was 7:50 when I arrived at my office, to meet with stunned associates.

"I'm sorry," was all I could think of to say to them. "This is a terrible, terrible tragedy. Peter was so young and he had his whole life to look forward to. Needless to say, we will catch the bastard who did this to him, but that won't take away the pain. We are all suffering and I share that with you. But we have a meeting with the commander now, so can we try to place our grief on the margins for the moment and concentrate on what we have to do?

By the way, does anyone here understand Polish? Well, I think it could be Polish."

I handed the note to Sam; he puzzled over it for a moment and then announced, "I haven't got a clue."

"If it's Polish I can translate it," Laura said, blinking back the tears. "My father is Polish."

I gave her the note and she said immediately, "It's a threatening letter; it says: "I know where you live. You will be my next victim.""

I shook my head, realising I didn't need a translator to tell me the significance of this. It could have come only from the paedophile.

I was still shaking my head as I followed them into the conference room, where an apparently stunned Jim, and a sad-looking Ian Blakey, were seated.

"Good morning, everyone," Jim said, his voice shaking. "I trust you all are aware of the sad news we were met with this morning. My prayers and my commiserations go out to Peter and his family, and I know you will all join me in that."

Most of us there nodded. There was a feeling of shock reverberating amongst us; nobody said a word.

"I don't want to go over the situation in Nottingham last night, except to say that the police were out in force on the basis of a tip-off that these gang members were planning to have a showdown in an exchange of gunfire that would determine who would survive and who would lead the cocaine war in that city. Many of the gang were arrested but some escaped; three policemen were shot, other than Peter Wadkins, one of whom is dead. Four of the gang were also killed; seven were arrested."

"How many of these dealers were involved?" Sam said.

"We think about 30 or so. This is the kind of open violence that has been brought to this country from overseas. We cannot, and we will not, tolerate it." He pointed with his finger. "A number of the gangs are still out there, and unless we stop them this kind of episode will escalate. That is why you're here this morning. Not only to pay tribute to Peter Wadkins but also to inform you that this new crime unit has not surrendered, nor will it.

"Therefore, I want to organise a team to go to Nottingham, upwards of 12 people at any one time, and take on the gangsters on their home turf. Only those of you who have had training in firearms will go, and you will have as back-up a team of armed response police." He banged his fist on the table. "We are not seeking revenge so I must warn each of you to dismiss this from your mind, otherwise you will put yourselves and everyone else in jeopardy. But you will be mindful of what has happened to our colleague; be prepared, pay attention to the needs of each other. And, before you go, our assistant commissioner will brief you on what is required.

"At the present time we have two officers on duty in Nottingham; one is our new inspector, Alan Greenridge, who has joined us from the Murder Squad, and Phil, a detective sergeant. A further inspector from the basement will join them and he will recruit the remaining members of the unit. The exceptions to the rule will be Ian Blakey and Angela Crossley.

"Now, does anyone have anything to say before we break up?"

"Was Peter Wadkins armed, sir?"

It was Sally, asking the awkward question again.

"No. He was not. Nor were any of the other members of our team. As I have said, that will change from tonight."

At that the meeting broke up, but I stayed behind with Jim and Ian.

"This incident in Nottingham is a dreadful tragedy," Jim declared. "We should have been more prepared than we were."

"How did it come about, Jim?" I asked.

He sighed. "We had a report from Nottingham Central that armed gangs were organising themselves for a turf war in the city centre. Three drug gangs would likely be involved – up to 15 members in each. Evidently there had been a declaration of war, because two of the gangs were trying to intrude on what the prime suspects regarded as their territory. You may recall that in recent months Nottingham has become one of the murder capitals of the country. Well, on this occasion we were asked to oversee the operation – this came down to me from the assistant commissioner. And in truth it was a major crime that was being planned, so it fell under our jurisdiction." He shook his head again. "We underestimated the element of violence that would ensue – or, at least, I did. So in some respects it is my fault that Peter Wadkins was killed."

I intervened at this point. "Come on, Jim. That could have happened to anyone – just as it did for me with the rapist. I wouldn't be so hard on yourself, if I were you. Neither would I overreact."

"Do you think that's what I'm doing?"

"Possibly. How many of these gangsters are still on the loose?"

"Dunno. Could be at least half of them. Why do you ask?"

"I wanted to determine the extent of the risk our officers would have to face. On the basis you have outlined I would say that, no, you are not overreacting. Half of those bastards is a hell of a lot, but if you keep a clear head we can beat them."

"I agree," Ian confirmed. "It is not your fault that Peter strayed from the group, nor is it your fault he was killed. What I would like to know, Jim, is: how are we going to apprehend these bastards? I mean, we can't summon them out into the open having declared war on them, can we?"

"I don't know. I should think that's unlikely. But what we do have is a list of addresses of some of the leaders. What I'm planning is that we hit them simultaneously with our group, backed up by an armed response team. If there is an exchange of gunfire I want everyone there to be protected with Kevlar waistcoats; essentially, I want these bastards cleared off the streets for ever, and if that means some of them are fatalities then so be it.

"Ian, will you now go ahead and organise your team? Firearms will be issued at four o'clock and we should plan to leave here at five. I have liaised with the Nottingham senior detectives; they will brief you on the plans, and effectively we will hit them at six-tomorrow morning. Have either of you any questions? No. Then let's get organised. Ange, before you leave, there's something I wanted to say to you."

"Yeah. There's a little matter I want to mention to you – but you first."

He leaned forward in his chair, eyeing me up carefully. "I've had an Inspector Greening on the phone, from Wembley. He tells me you rescued a young boy in Harpenden."

There was nothing I could say.

"Was this one of your visions?"

I nodded.

He sighed. "Have you seen yourself – the scratches on your face? You look as if a bramble bush attacked you; Ange, you're looking more and more like a ghost. Haven't you noticed how pale you are? I keep saying this, but I'm not sure how long we can carry on like this."

"If I hadn't reacted the way I did that little boy would be dead by now," I said indignantly. "And I'm sorry if my appearance upsets you, but how would you feel if you'd tried to claw your way through destructive trees trying to choke me to death, chasing a murderous paedophile?"

He stood up shaking his head as though he didn't understand what I was saying to him. "I'm not criticising you; I'm simply concerned at the way you dive into situations without fear of the consequences." He looked over at me frowning. "I'm going to have to do something about it, if only to protect you from the inevitable. Now, you have something for me?" he asked.

I allowed the silence to linger before I spoke. I knew that what he was saying made sense, but I could hardly take a back seat when I was the one having the visions. Could I?

CHAPTER FIFTY-THREE

Then I said, "This arrived on my doorstep this morning. I thought you should be aware of it."

He also puzzled over the note. "What does it say, Ange?"

I told him that Laura had translated it and informed him what it said.

"This is exactly the kind of thing I was talking about. Could this be your paedophile?"

"I don't think there's any doubt it is. He knows we're on to him and he's warning me to stay away."

"You know, since this unit was formed I've lost two officers: one left the force because he was seriously injured, the second, as you both know, because he is dead. I do not want to lose another one. So, whether you agree or not, we will have to arrange protection for you."

"And how are you going to do that, Jim? An armed escort on my doorstep?"

He scowled at me. "Can't you at least take this seriously?" he asked, pointing at the note. "Someone is threatening to kill you – and I don't believe this is an idle threat. So, yes, we do have to take it on board. And how we arrange your protection is a matter we can decide between ourselves. For instance, you have a two-bedroom flat, don't you?"

I nodded. "I mean, how the hell can I take this seriously when I'm trying to come to terms with Peter Wadkins, one of my officers, being killed?"

"So why don't we think about someone in the force who might be prepared to share with you? That way you'll have all-day and all-night protection."

"You couldn't find a man who I might fancy, could you? Sorry, Jim, that was uncalled for. I know what you mean – the only person who springs to mind is Sally Walker. But I don't know whether that will appeal to her."

"Then why don't I ask her? That way it will be more credible."

"Okay. But let me ask her first; at least I can prepare the way."

He shrugged his shoulders. "Right, have a word and tell her I want to see her in my office – sometime this morning. And, Ange, try to see one of our doctors, will you?"

Sally was hesitant at first, although she did admit that she had finished with her latest girlfriend, so she was free to move. It was only when I assured her it would just be for a short time that she agreed. I had the feeling that if she couldn't have it away with me then she wanted to have the freedom to circulate. I didn't say that to her, of course.

She came out of Jim's office and informed me she would move in with me that night. I was extremely grateful; in fact, I was almost tempted to give her a hug. I resisted.

"So, what do we do about the paedophile?" she asked.

"At the present, nothing. But I intend to cogitate on it; hopefully I might have a suggestion later. I'll let you know. We also have to worry about the rapist. His timetable, if it goes according to plan, is possibly shortening. How is the young Goldsmith girl?"

"I'm going to see her after I leave here. Do you think the rapist might attack someone in your area?"

"It's possible. This is the area he seems to be haunting; we can hardly police every street in Camden, can we?"

Her shoulders dropped in a philosophical shrug. "Can't we notify females of a certain age not to travel alone? Or maybe we can have a word with Rachel."

"Rachel Humphries?"

"Why not? Isn't she the one who said this guy threatened to come back and kill her?"

"So what are you suggesting?" I asked, horror in my voice. "That we set her up – tempt the guy to return to her flat?"

Her mouth screwed up, as if she realised she'd just dropped a clanger. "It was simply a thought." She hesitated and then said, "You know the problem with spontaneous rapists: that if we don't catch them in the act, or else we get forensic and DNA, then they're almost impossible to apprehend."

I thought about it for a moment. She was probably right. But setting up Rachel was simply not acceptable. All the same...

"Do you know if Laura has circulated this guy's description, as far as we're able, and posted it up in the bars and local clubs?"

"I know she has. But I meant an additional warning that this man, who has attacked Rachel Humphries in Camden, is still on the loose and could strike again any time."

"I'll talk to Rachel about it – and I'll have to involve Laura; she lives with her now, so they both might be threatened if he does return."

"If you like." She checked her watch. "Right now I'm off to Primrose Hill to interview the Goldsmiths again. I want to know if their daughter has remembered anything worthwhile. Then I'll have to pack a few things."

"Right. See you later."

I spent the morning going through the files. I noticed that the number sent up to us from downstairs was diminishing rapidly; there were only two folders on my desk now.

I asked Sam if he had he seen them and he replied that, yes, he had, and these were the only two that I might want to see. He was right. The first folder contained details of a parole prisoner who was on the sex offenders' list. He had disappeared without checking in at his local police station, and, suspiciously, there were now two children, girls, one seven and the other eight, who were missing from the Coventry district. A search was under way through local parks, and the military had been called in. There was also an APB out, including photographs, of the missing prisoner. There was nothing we could do at present but the Coventry police force were duty bound to draw it to our attention. I prayed to God that nothing had happened to the two little girls, though I doubted whether He would intervene. I updated my computer records and put the case on hold.

The second incident that Sam had brought to my attention was a drug-related shooting, or series of shootings, in Blackpool. When I was young this was the fairy story dream of my childhood, to go to Blackpool and spend all my money on the pleasure beach; my mother refused to allow me to go on the big dipper, but with hindsight they probably wouldn't have allowed me anyway because of my size.

The case involved two shootings of youngsters, both in their teens. I knew from past cases we had looked at that Blackpool was becoming the drug capital of the north but, so far, no deaths had involved shootings. A comment on the file suggested that the drug war in this part of the country was in danger of escalating almost to the point of being out of control – rather as in Nottingham – and the Lancashire police force was earnestly requesting our assistance. My own view was that if it were allowed to go unattended we could possibly be facing a situation similar to that of the east Midlands. I decided I would speak to the superintendent in charge of the case before making a decision. I checked the file; it was a Superintendent Calloway, based essentially in Preston but having to spend most of his time in the Blackpool area. I was put through almost immediately.

"Superintendent, this is DCI Crossley of New Scotland Yard, National Serious Crimes Unit. I've been going through the file you sent to us, about the shootings. Can you give me some more information?"

"Well, I can update you, inspector. Since I sent the file to you we have had another shooting. The first two I mentioned were a couple of young dealers; this latest one was a drug supplier."

"So, are we talking about a territorial issue?"

I could almost see his shoulders shrugging in response.

"I don't know. It's possible, I suppose. The real problem is that the drug situation in Blackpool has expanded exponentially in the past few months, so it's difficult to tell who the newcomers are and who the residents are – if you know what I mean. We appear to be heading for a crisis unless it's tackled head-on. And the problem we face is that we don't have the resources to tackle the predicament; that's why I sent you the file, inspector."

"Yes, I can see that, Superintendent Calloway. But I have to say that, right at this moment, we ourselves are overstretched; we have a similar situation in Nottingham, where a gang war has broken out and a number of people have been killed, including one of our own officers. So, if you can be patient for now we will get to the problem when things here have settled down. Can you do that for me?"

I heard him sigh. "I guess so, just as long as it doesn't take too long, but if the violence should increase then I'll have to call upon your division for immediate action. Are we clear about that?"

"Of course. Keep in touch, won't you?"

"You're damned right I will."

He slammed the phone down in a show of temper. I could see his point of view, but what I had said to him was valid: we didn't have the resources to spare at present. I decided I would go back into Jim's office and raise the subject again. I took the file with me.

"Not another problem?" he asked sharply, frowning at me as though I were some kind of an alien.

"Yes," I said determinedly. "It's the same problem I mentioned earlier: resources." I handed the file over to him. "This is a case Lancashire police force want us to handle; it concerns shootings in Blackpool. Apparently, three men are dead, drug dealers, but we don't have the manpower to handle it."

"What have you told them?"

"Exactly that – we don't have the manpower. I spoke to Superintendent Calloway and had to ask him to be patient. He wasn't best pleased."

Jim said nothing. I assumed he was thinking about the situation, but then I saw that he still hadn't opened the file.

"I had a chat about the resource problem with the assistant commissioner; he said he would think about it and come back to me. From my own point of view, Ange, I think we have the division split up incorrectly..."

"How do you mean?" I interjected.

He waved the ubiquitous arm at me, more or less telling me to let him finish. "We have something like 35 officers in the two units – 30 or so downstairs and more or less six on this floor. It seems to me that your unit is over-employed whilst those in the basement are under-employed. Would you agree with that?"

I nodded. "I know what you're going to suggest, Jim, and I'm not sure I'm going to like it."

"Let me finish," he suggested. "If we were to merge the two units, have one DCI in control, then, other than profiling, the allocation of duties could be delegated accordingly. What do you think?"

"What I do know is that you and Ian Blakey have been thinking about this for some time; it hasn't just suddenly appeared on its own, now, has it?"

His lips pursed, as if he'd just been found out. "Not independently, no. However, I've had a call from MI5 asking me how you're getting on with closing off your current cases; they want you, Ange. In fact, it seems to me they may well be considering you for a permanent transfer. How would you feel about that?"

"Er, astonished" was all I could stammer. "I thought they were only interested in my 'sensing' abilities. What you're saying seems to go much further than that."

"Not necessarily. They have obviously thought about your talents, and if anyone can give them an edge in these terrorist times then they're going to grab it. That is one reason I think a reorganisation does make sense." He shrugged again. "I don't know what the hell we can do without you, but if you do transfer over then maybe you can give us a hand on a kind of lease-lend basis. And there will be office space available on the fourth floor in a few weeks, so we could all integrate up there."

"When do I have to get back to them?"

"MI5? This week. I think they'll want to see you and discuss what arrangements they're after."

"I'm not letting go of the paedophile case."

He nodded. "I've already made that clear to them."

"I see." I let out a huge sigh. "So, tell me, Jim, who will be the senior inspector? Or, if I'm on the transfer list, then I don't suppose it matters."

He regarded me with his straight face. "Ian Blakey," he announced. "It's a logical choice, Ange. He's been with the force for a number of years, he's come through the mill, whereas you haven't, and he's had experience in controlling quite a large number of men..."

"...Whereas I haven't," I said, irritably.

"No. You haven't," he said, looking me straight in the eye now. "And I still have to consider what it is that MI5 really want of you."

"So, it's decided, then, is it? I mean, it isn't something I need to think about, as you originally suggested. So when do you make the announcement?"

He didn't hesitate for a second; neither did he blush, which was common when he was dealing with a difficult situation. "I wanted to clear it with you first. And then give you a chance to discuss it with your people, and maybe even MI5." He stood up. "This doesn't mean you're about to be downgraded, Ange. On the contrary, it might even be a promotion for you.

"And, anyway, you get on well with Ian Blakey, don't you? Before you do transfer you can share the duties between yourselves."

"If you say so. Just as long as I recognise that he's in charge. Give me a couple of days so I can talk, at least to Sam. I don't suppose the new inspector will have any comment on it."

I left his office feeling somewhat distraught. Regardless of what Jim had to say it was nevertheless true that I had been demoted. It was a bit like the time I had resigned earlier in the year and Jim had had to come to Warwick. Only this was not a resignation issue. A lot of what he had to say was true: the dichotomy needed to be dealt with, and I couldn't disagree with the fact that Ian Blakey really was the senior out of the two of us. And at least it would ease the burden on my shoulders.

Sam was philosophical about it; after years in the force he was used to change, and in effect it might give him the chance of a promotion. I would talk to the others later, and since Sally was moving in with me later this evening I could discuss it with her then.

I went home during lunch. I really needed to give the flat a thorough clean before Sally arrived; I would hate it if she thought I was untidy. Fortunately, there were no other notes for me on the mat. Perhaps the paedophile considered that the one warning would be sufficient. I had thought about him since the threatening note arrived, wondering what really was on his mind. I suspected that he must have panicked after the incident in the woods at Harpenden; it must have been a terrible shock for him to discover that a force that had similar components to his own had exposed him. Now he was also concerned as to how it was that I knew what he was about to do.

I put myself in his place.

Here I was, having buggered and murdered three children, and got away with it, suddenly detected after abducting another young boy from a school that was miles away from the previous incidents. How was that possible? How could anyone know what I had in mind, considering that I had chosen a school in Harpenden that was remote and where I knew I would be hidden from view? And then this somebody had a clear perception of what I had in mind and acted specifically to apprehend me – and very nearly achieved it.

Was it magic? Did she – and I now know it was a 'she' after she chased me through the woods – consort with the spirits? Possibly in the way that I did? It was a thought I would have to dwell on, but first I needed to trace where she lived. So, discreetly, I followed her back to the school when she returned the boy, and found out she was a Detective Chief Inspector Angela Crossley from New Scotland Yard. It was easy after that to follow her and find out her address. It was easier still to leave the note on her mat. Now I would have to wait and see what she might do in relation to me.

"Am I correct, Katy?" I asked. I was in the kitchen, eating a ham salad and drinking my early morning breakfast tea.

"Well, more or less," she replied almost straight away. "This guy is pretty intent on getting rid of you; you have become the scourge that is interrupting his murderous routine. Somehow he realises he will not be able to continue with his butchery of little boys until you are removed. So, in that regard his plans have been laid open. But please don't ask me how he intends to carry out your removal; as I said to you once before, I cannot penetrate his protective shielding."

"So, I'm on my own – is that it?"

"I'm afraid so; but isn't that also true of any detective? He has let you know that he is threatening you with your very life; your duty now is not so much to prevent him carrying out his threats but to apprehend him and stop him from murdering some other young boy."

"Okay. And thanks, Katy. And I agree with you that I doubt he'll try anything with young boys whilst I'm still around."

"I wouldn't think so. But be careful, Angie. You interrupted his last venture so he still has lust for a boy, and he will try to get rid of you sooner rather than later."

"I'll be on my guard."

* * * * * *

The thought came to me a little later that I would attend church. There was a Catholic church I had noticed just off the High Street, so rather than traipse all the way up to Marylebone High Street I thought I would try my local church.

It was closed; a sign of the times.

I'd already given the flat a kind of spring clean; I was hoping Sally wouldn't notice the dust I might have hidden. I returned to the office, but only after having checked that I wasn't being followed on the way to the tube. I checked by dodging into doorways to make sure that no one was after me before I went down the underground steps. I wasn't at all clear if that was what detectives did these days; it was just something I'd seen on television shows. Frankly, it made me look like an idiot.

CHAPTER FIFTY-FOUR

That same night two detectives were parked in an unmarked police car opposite the B&B on the outskirts of Wolverhampton, waiting for Arthur Scanlon to emerge. DI Sutton had been alerted by the desk receptionist that Scanlon had appeared that night to visit McCloud. He had been upstairs now for the best part of two hours.

"What do you think they're doing up there, Sarge?" Fletcher enquired of his colleague.

"Do you really need to ask?" Cummings answered.

"Well, I know the DI said they were homos, but it never occurred to me they would be – well, you know…"

"…Having it off in his room?"

"Yeah. Unless, of course, they're planning the next murder."

Sergeant Cummings let out a sigh. "You're surely not believing that fucking tripe from the Yardies, are you, that these two are in league committing the murders?"

"So you believe Sutton, then, Sarge, that this is a wild goose chase?"

"Look, all I know is that those two from the Yard have found us a couple of gays – and that ain't illegal any more."

Sergeant Eric Cummings was on the slim side, with a few greying hairs nudging out of his fringes. He was in his late 40s and looked it, with a permanent frown etched on his brow as though he'd seen everything there was to see in his many years in the police force. He was only a few years away from his retirement, and right now he was bored.

DC Warren Fletcher, on the other hand, was a young man with all the eagerness of a newly recruited detective. He was a bit on the heavy side, and should have taken notice of his mother's advice to go to the gym, but he was comfortable with his size. He also should have been wearing glasses – his eyesight wasn't what it should be – but he doubted if he would have got promoted wearing glasses. The problem was that, when he looked at you with his grey eyes, he appeared myopic; he'd thought about wearing contact lenses, but at the moment he hadn't got the time to visit the optician. He was, unlike Cummings, very patient, waiting for Armageddon to happen.

"So why are we here, Sarge, if neither you nor the DI believe these two might be the culprits?"

"'Culprits'? Where the fuck did you get that word from?"

"Oh. Isn't that what we call them?"

"No, arsehole. They might be 'alleged criminals' or even 'villains', but not 'culprits'. And the reason we're here is because Sutton was ordered by a chief superintendent from Birmingham to check these two out. So, that's what we're doing; and don't knock it, Fletcher, cos we're on overtime."

"Right, Sarge. How long have we been here?"

Cummings checked his watch. "Coming up for two hours. We wait here until Scanlon comes out, then we follow him to his home."

"What does your wife think of these late nights?"

Cummings turned to him from the passenger seat and glared at him. "Wife?! What wife? She left me about ten years ago. Found another fucking lover."

"Any children, Sarge?"

"Leave it off, will you?" Cummings scowled. "My private life is my own affair.

"Look – here he comes." Scanlon emerged from the B&B, and the detectives followed him to a side street where he had parked his car. They kept some distance behind him, on the ring road towards Stourbridge, until he turned off and parked behind a pub on the main road.

"Where the hell's he going?" Cummings wanted to know.

"He's going in the pub – isn't he?"

"No he's not. It's closed. He's going into the flats." He pointed towards a nearby building. "Leave the car here, Fletcher; let's see where he lives."

Almost at the side of the pub was a block of council house flats; it was difficult to make them out. There was no washing hanging from the balconies, but Cummings could tell they were council-owned; they had that appearance about them. Then they lost Scanlon.

"Where the hell has he gone?" the sergeant muttered.

Fletcher took off his coat and undid his tie, making himself appear untidy. "Hold this, Sarge. I'll see if I can find him."

He came out of the building a few minutes later and said, "I think it's 4B; at least, that's the only one with a light on."

"Right. Let's call it a night. I doubt he'll be looking for hookers at this time of the night; in fact, I doubt he'll be looking for hookers full stop."

When they reported to Sutton the next morning he just grunted. "Waste of police time and resources."

"How long do we have to do this, inspector?" Cummings asked.

The detective inspector gazed at him ominously. "As long as the chief superintendent instructs us to," he snapped. "I'll give him a ring this morning and let him have the results."

He came back to him later in the day and said, "We wait for a further two contacts from the receptionist that Scanlon has turned up again, then we see what happens." He shrugged. "If, as I believe, we're flogging a dead horse, then we delete these two characters from our suspect list. Agreed?"

Cummings nodded. "You don't fancy searching his flat, then?"

"What the hell for? We have no evidence – nothing that can possibly relate to the murders. I can hardly ask for a warrant simply on the grounds of some tart's wishes from the Yard, now, can I?"

"I guess not."

So they waited for the next telephone call. In the meantime, DI Sutton held a briefing on how far they had progressed the case.

CHAPTER FIFTY-FIVE

Sally and I arrived at the flat in the early evening. There were no further messages from the paedophile. I showed her to her bedroom and took her round the rest of the flat.

"What do you think?" I asked her.

"'S'okay. Mind you, I prefer your bedroom."

"Well, if you don't like it I could arrange for someone else to move in with me." Her comments annoyed me. I know it wasn't exactly luxurious, but it was clean and comfortable. Besides, I certainly didn't want for anyone to stay with me who disliked the place.

She chuckled. "I was joking, Angie. I think it's very nice, and at least I'll have some company."

"As long as you're sure."

She placed a hand on my shoulder. "I like it – believe me. Now, let me unpack, and then we'll go out for some dinner."

"Good idea. I'll have a shower first and change."

It was quite uncomfortable trying to ease Sally into sharing with me; I knew she fancied me, but God forbid I should allow anything like that to happen to our relationship. And I really did want to have a friend apart from Katy.

An hour later we were ready to go out.

"Where shall we go?" Sally asked.

"There's a very good Chinese in the High Street. However, I don't believe we should go there together."

She gave me a startled look. "Why not? You're not afraid to be seen out with me, are you?"

"Now you're being silly. What I don't want is, if the paedophile is following me, to let him know I have a chaperone. So, I will leave the flat first, and then you follow behind me until we arrive at the restaurant."

She shook her head. "You mean we then have to sit apart at the restaurant?"

"No. I will go in first; you follow, sort of surprised to see me, then we sit together as friends. We pay separately for the meal and afterwards I leave before you, with you some way behind me. Are we clear on that, Sally?"

She grinned. A bit OTT isn't? So you're using yourself as bait – is that it?"

"If you like." I gazed at her intently. "Look, we know this guy is going to try to kill me; that's why you're here. I cannot, nor will I, try to hide from him. If he wants to have a go then we should be prepared for him."

"Right," she said, dubiously. "Have you got a weapon?"

"I have a mace gun. If he gets that in his eyes he won't be so keen to attack me."

"Okay. I'm with you, Angie. I'll watch you from the window; if I see it's clear I'll follow and keep a safe distance away. And don't worry, I too have a spray; it's just a bit stronger than yours."

I left the apartment whilst it was still light; I didn't look behind me. I was going out for something to eat, unconcerned whether I was being followed. After all, this was the Camden High Street; who could touch me in this crowded place? I'd tended to overlook the fact that not too many days ago I was high jacked from here by the terrorists.

I felt, rather than saw, Sally some way behind me; I didn't need to observe her, although it was clear that there was no one following her or me. In some regards I was disappointed, but it was still early yet; anything might happen. I went into the restaurant, and took a seat close to the window where anyone could see me. I took up the menu and ordered a drink before Sally arrived. She greeted me like a long-lost friend and sat at my table.

"Anything?" she whispered.

I shook my head. "No, and you don't have to whisper; I doubt if anyone can hear us outside the restaurant. What happened with the Goldsmiths? Where they able to tell you anything?"

"Not really. Their daughter's still traumatised and her face is still a mess; even if she weren't I doubt if she'd be able to describe her attacker." She shook her head. "I'm not sure what we can do, Angie, other than do as you're doing and that's become a potential victim – you know, walk the streets late at night, hoping he might come after one of us."

I thought about this for a while; it wasn't such bad idea. In fact, it was in a way similar to the adventure I had had on the underground. "The problem with that is he could attack anywhere. Oh, I know he's struck here in Camden, but he's also attacked girls from the surrounding area."

"Couldn't you sort of have...you know...one of your visions?"

"I wish it were that simple. They're not something I can summon up just when I feel like it."

"So how do they happen, then? I mean, are you always asleep? Or do they occur during the day – like they did that time in Harpenden? Or do you have to pray?"

"Where did you get that idea from?"

"Dunno. Guess I read it somewhere – in a book, maybe. I remember it might have been a film I saw some years back, about a psychic. All I do know is that this girl, whenever she wanted…you know…a vision, she used to go to church and pray for guidance." She gazed at me, her brow furrowing.

"What?" I asked.

"Bloody hell, Angie, it's like walkin' on eggshells discussing this with you. I mean, you don't give much away, do you?"

I returned her gaze. She was entitled to an explanation as to how this worked for me. "I'm sorry about that, Sally. It isn't as if I mean to be obstructive – it's simply that explaining a phenomenon like this is – well, it's fucking difficult." I shrugged my shoulders, more in a gesture of futility.

"You could at least try. If we're to become friends then we have to start trusting each other. You remember when I told you about my past – about my being forced into prostitution? Well, I didn't hold anything back then, even though I wasn't sure I could altogether trust you with a secret like that. But I let it out; I think it was because I'd had no one to talk to in the past. Couldn't you do the same?"

The food arrived before I could reply. We ate in silence for some time before Sally pressed me on it again.

"So? Are you going to tell me? Or do you intend to keep it a secret from your new-found friend?" Her voice was casual but there was a hint of disdain there. "You know, a secret shared etc…"

"Yeah. A secret shared is a secret doubled," I intercepted.

Sally was quiet after that. After giving her insistence a great deal of thought, I began to tell her, amplifying what I had begun to tell her in the car during the journey to the Midlands, starting at the very beginning when I had first met Connie all those years ago.

"I felt then," I said to her, "that I had some kind of affinity with the psychic, although I never explored it." Then I went on to describe the visions that Connie had experienced of the dead children, and the horrifying finale in the basement of the paedophile's home. "I witnessed Connie experiencing these experiences, some of the more terrible ones, that caused her so much despair, and I vowed then I would keep a safe distance from the phenomenon.

"It wasn't until I went up to Manchester as acting DCI that I was forced to meet it head-on; that was some five years after the Connie disaster, when Jim Robbins needed me because a teenager had asked that I should be the one he would communicate with."

"You mean, some teenager, who you'd never met, asked to see you in the north?" Sally asked, astonishment in her voice.

I smiled. "Spooky, wasn't it? But that's how it happened. This boy claimed, to Jim, that he and his deceased twin sister had what he called 'sensing' abilities. Evidently he had witnessed the burial of a young girl on the moors, and he specifically asked to see me."

"But why? I mean, why on earth would he ask to see you – a stranger he'd never met?"

I shook my head. "When I met him he told me it was his deceased sister, Katy, who had asked him to invite me to Manchester. The only thing that convinced me in all this was that he asked Jim if he would bring the woman to see him, the one whose friend was sick in the hospital. It was because of that that I made up my mind."

"He was talking about your friend, Connie? You didn't tell me she was in hospital."

"It is a penal prison – but, please, Sally, don't ask me any more about it; it's far too painful to comment on."

She shrugged, accepting my admonishment. "Sure. So what happened when you met him in Manchester?"

"I saw him on his own at first. Then he held my hand, asked me to close my eyes, and then he led me on a spiritual plane on the same path he had tracked – on the previous Sunday. I was actually with him on the moors, watching the killer burying the body in a newly dug grave. Then it started to snow, but because of Danny O'Brien's vision I could see exactly what the killer was doing. He had had to force the body into the ground and then he started to pray…"

She looked at me in astonishment. "What a fucking experience! How did you cope?"

I shivered at the memory of it. "I was stunned. For a while I couldn't speak. And, after a bit, Danny said to me (we were alone in the room at the time): 'You saw what I did, miss, cos you're like me – you're a "Sensor". It's wot me sister says as well.'"

"Did you ask him to explain?" Sally asked, her interest at its peak.

"No. I did not. I was frightened to death. But, however scared I was, nevertheless I became involved in a variety of esoteric incidents – either created by Danny or perhaps through his sister. That went on almost for ever; it seemed they just wouldn't leave me alone."

Sally's hand came across the table and clutched my hand. "Poor you. What happened after that? I mean, how did you finally become a clairvoyant?"

"I went to visit a psychic I knew in the Midlands. She said she had been expecting me, because she had realised all those years earlier when I first met her that I had the gift. She then wanted me to go to church with her. So I ran like hell."

"Fuck, I think that's what I would have done. But the visions must have reappeared for you to have got involved."

"You're right. Some weeks later I began to hear voices. It was Katy, Danny's deceased sister. And, surprisingly, I wasn't scared any more."

"Was she the one who urged you to go to that church in Marylebone High Street?"

I laughed. "You must have guessed. And, yes, she did. And since then I have regular visits from Katy; she has become my kind of Spirit Guide. She is the inspiration in the whole of my life – not just as a policewoman."

I let out a long sigh as if I had purged myself; I felt a sense of relief at having discussed it with someone. "And there, you now have the entire story. How I became a psychic, how it began, some of the stress I went through and, finally, the peace it has given me. And that's where I am today. But, as I said to you earlier, Sally, this is not something I can control or cause to happen, even if I wanted to. I do have an ongoing relationship with Katy and she helps whenever I'm in trouble. But sometimes she too has her powers limited. For instance, I've talked with her about the paedophile, but she can't penetrate his protective shield of evil."

"But was she the one who led you off the motorway that day – when we followed the van into the woods?"

"Yes. But that was all she was able to achieve. The rest was up to me."

"And now?" She gazed out of the window as if looking for someone. "Is this up to you?"

I pushed my plate away and asked the waiter for two coffees. "I'm afraid so," I ventured after a while. "Katy might be able to give me a warning – though even that isn't so certain with this guy. Other than that, I'm on my own."

Sally smiled, thoughtfully, and reached out and held my hand. "You're not, you know. I'm here now. We're in this together. And if he finds you then he'll find both of us."

I squeezed her hand back. "Thank you. Now I think we should leave. I'll go first, as before, and then you follow."

"Okay. Are we going to the pub?"

Well, I didn't have that in mind but it was far too early to go back to the flat. "There's quite a nice one on the High Street – the Escourt. I think it's Irish."

CHAPTER FIFTY-SIX

For a Wednesday night the pub was absolutely heaving; there wasn't a quiet corner to be found anywhere.

"Do you think this was a good idea?" Sally asked after I'd brought the drinks. We were packed tightly into a corner with bodies all around us – many of them speaking with Irish accents.

"Not really. But I don't know anywhere else."

"Well, there's a private club I know – just off Lower Regent Street. It's not far from here."

I hesitated. "It's not one of those gay bars, is it?"

Sally laughed. "You do have a bee in your bonnet about that, don't you? No, it isn't one of those clubs. It's a normal club where you don't have to be a member, and it's not too expensive. It should be reasonably quiet there."

I relaxed. Thank God for that. "Okay," I said, though still hesitantly; I wasn't entirely sure I could trust her.

She squeezed my arm again. "Angie – we don't have to go there. Not if you don't want to. I'm guessing it could be a bit less noisy than this place. But if you don't mind the noise, and these Irish accents, I don't mind staying here."

"There're a couple of pubs up the road from here," I suggested. "They might be quieter than this place."

She sighed. "Sure. If that's what you want." She pointed a finger at me. "But next time we're out I'll show you the club – let you see it for yourself."

I said nothing, glad of an excuse for not having to go into the West End. The first pub we tried, about a couple of hundred yards from where we had been, was no different: still the Irish accents, thick with smoke and heaving bodies, and a fight to get to the bar.

"We'll try the other one," I said.

Sally nodded but gave me a look as if I was an idiot. This time we were lucky. The pub was almost deserted. I went to the bar, ordered a couple of drinks and retreated to the corner where Sally was sitting.

"This is quite pleasant," she admitted. "So, now I've got you to myself, you can tell me about MI5. What is it they want from you?"

"How do you know they want anything?" I pleaded, but without conviction. Obviously the grapevine had been working, so there was no point in lying about it. "Sorry," I said. "You seem to know something about it; do you mind my asking how the gossip got to Intelligence?"

She shrugged. "It's no big deal; someone heard the commander talking about it with Chief Inspector Blakey. It wasn't all that clear but the impression was that MI5 want you to join them."

"You mean, someone was eavesdropping?" I snapped.

"Probably. But I wouldn't worry about that, Angie; it happens all the time. So, are you going to tell me? Or is it a fucking secret?"

I laughed. "You have such a way with words. And there isn't a lot to tell. Jim informed me that MI5 had approached him with a view for me to transfer across to them." I shrugged. "What as? Well, I don't know. I suppose I'll have to discuss it with them…"

"Oh, come on, Angie," she interjected. "You must have some idea what it is they want from you. I mean, after that imprisonment you suffered at their hands – to say nothing of the shootings by your boyfriend and his partners – surely they can't simply approach you without disclosing your…what do they call it now? Well, your terms of reference should sum it up. So, come on, my dear, look upon me as your favourite parish priest: confess to me. Does it have something to do with your clairvoyance?"

"Christ, Sally, you're like a dog shaking a bone." I let out a long sigh and leaned my forearms on the table. "They haven't said anything to me, but, yes, I assume it is about my – well, my insight. They more or less forced me into telling one of the senior directors he was about to die the following day.2

She gasped. "Bloody hell! And did he?"

I nodded. "Sadly, yes. There were also a couple of other things that happened. I think what they're after is my penetrative judgement of terrorists. I look at them and something tells me what their plans are. You can call it clairvoyance, if you like." I shrugged. "I don't necessarily have a word for it."

She swallowed her drink and got up to go to the bar. "Same again?"

"Sure."

When she returned she asked me, "Do you think you might go – to MI5, I mean?"

"I dunno. I'm beginning to quite like it here at the Yard. I still have to finish off with the paedophile – and we have so much variety. It'll also be easier when Jim has rearranged the unit…"

"What d'you mean? Rearranged?"

I sighed. My big mouth and me. "I shouldn't have said anything but Jim wants us to integrate with downstairs. All of us to move up to the fourth floor and DCI Blakey will be heading it up."

She took a long drink and considered the impact of what I had just told her.

"I'm not sure I like that – especially if we're going to lose you to the other side."

"Oh, I don't know. I think you'll like the DCI – he's very personable. And, anyway, Sally, I haven't made up my mind yet about MI5. I'm not even sure I'll fit in, especially after – what did you call him? – 'my boyfriend' nearly had me shot."

"You know," Sally said, as she cupped her chin in her hands, "you've told me all about your psychic powers and how they came about, but, in all the time I've known you, you have never said anything about your family. I mean, do you have any brothers or sisters? What does your father do? You know the kind of thing. Do you want to tell me about it?"

I shrugged. 'There isn't a lot I can say. My father is an American – he's retired now and living in Florida; at one time he was a lawyer in New York, but I have never met him – apparently he left us when I was a child.

'Why didn't your mother go to America?'

'She tried. We all did. But she couldn't stand the place, so we split up. My mother and me came back to live in the Midlands, my father stayed behind to live his own life.'

'So do you see your father at all now?'

'No. Not really. He did contact me a couple of years ago, hoping we might become reconciled.' I shrugged. 'I don't know if he was serious – perhaps one day I might find out.'

'And your mother?'

"Bloody nosy, aren't you?"

She laughed. "Not really. I'm just interested."

"Well, my mother now lives near to Worcester. I see her regularly, but – well, she still has a penchant for the opposite sex. In fact, she can drive you to distraction with her boyfriends. Have you heard enough?"

"I thought it was really interesting – you know, to see behind the Angie we normally see. So, coming back to the paedophile, when do you think he might strike at you? Or have you put that to the back of your mind?"

"I'm not sure. As I said before, it isn't something I can ask Katy to help with. I have to do this on my own – or at least with your help, Sally."

She frowned. "Perhaps the note was simply an empty gesture, something to threaten you with."

"I doubt that Jim thinks that," I almost snorted. "He's taking it very seriously – and so is MI5."

She gave me a measured look. "You don't have to bite my head off, Angie. I was only thinking out loud. So, we keep our eyes open, see if there's any way we can spot him."

"Except we don't really know what he looks like. I mean, I saw him for an instant in the forest but I doubt I could recognise him. What about you, Sally. You saw him – can you recognise him?"

"Probably better than you can. I got a good look at him. You want another drink?"

"I don't think so. I've got to be alert."

She emptied her glass and rose from the table. "Right. An early night, then. It'll do me good."

She followed me from the pub, and I saw nothing. No one stalking me; no one hiding in doorways; no one pretending to be someone he wasn't. I was quite disappointed, actually, I had thought for a moment he would slip up and start attacking me.

"Another adventurous evening," Sally stated as she arrived at the flat behind me. "You don't think he'll try to get in here, do you?"

"I don't see how he can; not with the door double-locked and bolted. Anyway, if you don't mind, Sally, I'm off to bed. You know where the TV is, don't you? Goodnight."

I was woken early the following morning with a report from Sam about the raid in Nottingham. It had gone exactly as planned. At six that morning, only an hour ago, a squad of CID and police officers, simultaneously raided addresses on the fringes of the city centre. There were scuffles and one or two of the drug members were injured, but there was no gunfire, no shootings, and 15 arrests had been made, with warrants out for the four missing members. It was a hell of an accomplishment, all the more so because no resistance was offered when the gangs saw that the police were armed.

I woke Sally up with the news.

A couple of days later we had the funeral of Peter Wadkins. It was a sombre affair, and a police cortege led the coffin to the crematorium. A number of the females, and one or two males, were in tears. It was such a waste of a young life. The district commissioner of New Scotland Yard read the eulogy. Jim Robbins, dressed in his full uniform, followed by expressing our sorrow.

It was a very sad day for all of us, especially Peter's parents, who tried to console each other.

We left trying desperately to comfort those who were so distressed.

CHAPTER FIFTY-SEVEN

A few days after the funeral DS Cummings and DC Fletcher were positioned in their car outside the B&B in Wolverhampton, waiting for Arthur Scanlon to emerge.

"If this bastard goes back to his flat again then we're giving this up," Cummings growled. "I think Sutton was right: this is a fuckin' waste of time."

"Well, it will be the third time we've had to do it," Fletcher agreed. "Pity, though, about the overtime."

"You'll have to earn it somewhere else. How long have we been here?"

Fletcher checked his watch. "Not too long actually, Sarge. Only about half an hour. How long are we giving him?"

"That's a stupid question, Fletcher. We stay here until he comes out – and then we follow him."

"Sorry. I wasn't thinking."

"That's your trouble, isn't it? You never think… Hang about – he's coming out. Keep your head down."

They both ducked behind the dashboard. "Which way is he going, Sarge? Back to his flat?"

"Dunno. He's getting into his car; we'll soon know if we follow him."

They trailed Scanlon about 50 yards behind him. For a while it looked as though he was returning to his flat but shortly after leaving the B&B he took a quick turn to the right.

"This isn't the way to his flat," Fletcher announced.

"No. Too fuckin' right it ain't. I think he's heading towards Raby Street."

"Sweet Jesus! I hope this isn't it."

"We'll soon know," Cummings said as he steered the car a little closer. "Get on the radio," he instructed Fletcher. "Tell them he's entering hooker territory." He braked suddenly as Scanlon moved into an alleyway just before Raby Street. "Keep down," he hissed at Fletcher.

"How do we know that isn't a through road?"

"Because I've been here before; that's a cul-de-sac. When he gets out give him a few minutes before we follow him. We know where he's going; I want to see what he does."

Scanlon emerged a few seconds later, looked around for a moment and then proceeded towards Raby Street. They followed at a distance. When they turned the corner there were something like a half a dozen prostitutes plying their trade. It was around eleven thirty at night, so it was becoming quite busy. One or two cars were also in the street with customers dealing drugs. Scanlon was chatting with a young slim girl with dark hair; as far as Cummings could see from this distance she appeared to be a little shy, almost as though this was her first time on the game. It took only a few seconds for Scanlon to agree her terms; then they linked arms and he led her back towards his car in the alleyway.

"This should be interesting," Cummings said as he dragged Fletcher into a doorway. They allowed Scanlon to disappear, then followed him to where they had parked their car. They climbed inside but didn't close the doors in case the sound might disturb Scanlon. It seemed to be an age before his car came out of the alley. On the face of it there was only Scanlon in the driving seat; the rest of the car appeared empty.

"What the hell!" Fletcher said.

"He's obviously put her under – probably chloroform. So this is how he gets away with it."

"Where do you think he's going now, Sarge?"

"If I knew that, my intellectual friend, then we wouldn't be following him, would we? What about back-up?"

"They've been informed at headquarters; they said to let them know if we need their help."

"Okay. Let's see where he takes us – but keep in touch with CID; let them know where we're at."

Fletcher spent some time on the radio, announcing where they were. They left this part of the town and went around the bypass and then on to the Bilston Road.

"Tell HQ he's now heading towards Ettingshall," Cummings instructed. "Tell them I think we should have CID back-up."

"Right, Sarge," Fletcher said, repeating the instructions on his radio. "They want to know where we are now."

"Scanlon seems to be heading towards the old steel works; tell them we've followed him down the Bilston Road and we're now approaching Powell's run-down tyre factory."

They passed the old works for a few hundred yards and then Scanlon turned left and passed between two old buildings.

"Fletcher, tell them he's going into one of the old steel mills. We'll have to wait here, otherwise we'll be spotted."

Cummings hit the brakes and took the radio from his partner. "Are you sending back-up?" he enquired. "What? Right. Okay, we'll wait here. But don't come in with lights and sirens – we have to see what he's up to."

Ten minutes elapsed before two cars silently pulled up behind Cummings. In one of them was Inspector Sutton.

"So, it looks as though the smart-arse from the Yard was right," he muttered to no one in particular. Cummings stayed quiet. They had done what they were commissioned to do, so there was no need to say anything more, except to ask, "Can we come in with you, inspector?"

"I suppose you'd better. It is your case, after all. Do we know which building he's gone into?"

Cummings pointed to the second one on the right. "In there – but I haven't seen any lights, sir."

There were six CID officers now in attendance: three DCs, two sergeants and Inspector Sutton. They pulled torches from their cars and headed towards the buildings. One of the doors was slightly opened, and through it they saw glimpses of low-level illuminations, enough for someone to light up the surroundings.

"Follow me," Sutton said; "let's take the bastard."

They stormed in, and the first thing they saw was the young prostitute lying on what appeared to be an old mattress. She was naked and both her wrists and her legs were bound to wooden posts positioned at the side of the bed. Her legs were spread wide apart and her mouth was gagged. She looked at them, through groggy eyes filled with fear; her body was shaking as if she were in shock. Cummings noticed the injection marks down her arms. She also had the same in marks in her toes, evidently a hard user.

Scanlon was standing to one side of her, slowly undressing. He hardly noticed their arrival he was so occupied with his objectives.

Nearby were the tools of his trade: surgeon's saw, scalpels, scales for weighing body parts, and plastic bins, no doubt to collect parts of the torso after they had butchered her. There was also a surgeon's table for dissecting. When he saw the officers he grinned, as though he had been a naughty boy caught smoking behind the bogs.

"It took you long enough," he remarked casually, pulling up his trousers. "It's a pity, because this was going to become my sixth victim; I was really looking forward to raping her and carving her up. Why do you want to save her, anyway? Look at her; she's just a pathetic waster living her life on drugs." He bent down and gestured with his finger towards her feet. "Have you seen this? There's hardly a vein left."

Sutton said nothing but he pointed towards Cummings, who snapped the handcuffs on Scanlon and then gave him the appropriate warning.

"How did you liaise with McCloud?" Sutton wanted to know. "Was he due to come here in the morning, so you could savage this young woman between you?"

Scanlon smiled. "If you want to catch McCloud, inspector, you'll have to do it on your own. I ain't helping you."

"Call the SOCOs," Sutton ordered. "I'm sure they'll find enough evidence here of McCloud's presence. So we don't need your help, Scanlon. But don't be under any illusions; once we have enough evidence we're going to tell your friend that it was you who betrayed him."

Scanlon made a move towards the inspector, even with handcuffs on. "Fucking bastard. He'll never believe you."

"Watch me, moron."

Fletcher had untied the girl, who was still sleepy from the dope, and helped her to dress, trying not to be too intrusive.

Then they led Scanlon away.

It was on the way back to HQ that Fletcher asked Cummings, "How do you think McCloud could have got here when he didn't have a vehicle?"

"No, but he had enough money for the metro. If you look you'll notice it stops almost opposite this building. And East Park is only a few yards from here, where they dumped the bodies."

"Do you think Sutton will acknowledge the input from that bird, Crossley?"

Cummings grunted. "He won't have any fuckin' choice, will he? If he don't tell her you can bet your life someone will."

* * * * * *

The following morning the telephone rang. It was the chief superintendent calling me from Birmingham, giving me the news of Scanlon's arrest. The details were quite horrific and I shuddered at the prospect the young girl would have faced had we not intervened.

"What about McCloud, superintendent?" I asked.

"Forensics are just tying up the evidence; it places him clearly at the scene of the crimes. He'll be arrested this morning. I wanted to say how grateful we all are for your input, DCI Crossley. Without it young women could have died. Thank you so much.'

'It's part of my job, Superintendent, but thank you so much for the call."

I replaced the receiver with a satisfied grunt. I was relieved it had worked out as I thought it might, but what pleased me more was that it was exacting police work that had led to the arrest; fortuitously, Katy had not counselled me.

CHAPTER FIFTY-EIGHT

Days passed, and slowly we tried to recover from Peter's demise. Jim had announced the reorganisation, and we had all moved up to the fourth floor. There were, at first, the grumblings and complaints, especially from my department, as to whom they were now reporting to, but I explained that as far as they were concerned nothing had changed. They would still be reporting to me; the only difference was that now I would be reporting to DCI Ian Blakey instead of directly to Jim. Also, I had to warn them that it was possible I might be transferred to MI5; nothing was certain yet, and in any event I had to clear up the paedophile matter. The question of Blackpool and the gun crimes came up; Ian sent off Sam and Laura to handle it.

With regard to the paedophile, we had heard nothing from the outlying police forces; neither had he been in contact directly with me. I was wondering if perhaps we hadn't wasted our time by having Sally staying with me. It had worked out fine from my point of view, but I knew she wanted to play the field in the West End gay clubs. It was coming up to the weekend, so I had decided to release her from her commitment – in other words, let her go free to do whatever she wanted.

At first she protested but it was a bit perfunctory, and in the end she gave me a grateful smile and tidied herself up – and by that I mean dressing in the latest lesbian outfits: skin-tight leather trousers, a see-through blouse that exposed her nipples, and flat shoes that denied her height. She wore a small pair of diamond earrings, mascara that highlighted her eyes, and a touch of perfume that was enticing.

"You look gorgeous," I commented when she appeared from her bedroom.

She grinned at me. "Fancy me, then, do you?"

I grinned with her. "I know you might be available, Sally, but unfortunately not with me. Now, behave yourself, and if you're not expected back tonight that's okay; you've got your own key anyway, so you won't disturb me."

"What are you going to do, Angie?"

"Oh, I don't know. I might go to the pub, have a few drinks and a sandwich, and take in the town."

"You're kidding me, right?"

"Not really. It's Friday night, it's a lovely evening and I know of a pub in Mayfair where you can sit outside."

She frowned. "You're not afraid of…"

"Come on, Sally," I interjected. "We've been through that. This guy has either gone home to Poland…or maybe he's moved districts. I suspect he's gone home, otherwise if he were still active we'd have heard about him through the other forces. So, don't worry; I'll be fine. Now, enjoy yourself, and stop thinking about me."

She went off in a taxi, dropping me off at what had now become our local. It was fairly crowded, but I was able to commandeer a corner table close to the bar. I had a few drinks, then a few more drinks. I was still hungry, so I thought I'd go to the local Chinese; the thought of going off to Mayfair seemed to be too much trouble.

I was on my way there when I thought of Rachel and wondered if she might like to join me. It was fairly close to the pub, a bit on the late side, but – what the hell? I climbed the stairs to her flat, a bit dizzy from the drink, and it was then that I noticed the front door was open. I stopped, wondering what the hell was going on. I knew Laura wasn't there; she was up in Blackpool with Sam. I pushed open the door further and waited to see if I could hear any sounds.

There was nothing.

I went in, remained silent and pulled out my mace gun.

The lounge was quiet; so was the kitchen. That left only the two bedrooms. The first door I came to obviously belonged to Laura. It was empty, and I recognised some of her belongings there. The door to Rachel's door was closed. I opened it slowly.

There was a guy lying naked on top of Rachel, who was struggling beneath him, her mouth gagged with tape. A knife was pointed against her throat.

"Oh, shit," I said out loud. The assailant didn't hear me – he didn't move. I grabbed him by the hair, forced him to look towards me and sprayed him with the mace right into his olive green eyes. He screamed and fell off the bed, rubbing his eyes and letting go of the knife. I didn't go to Rachel at first. Instead I called for back-up, and waited until I had the all-clear; they would be here in a few minutes. Rachel still had on her knickers, so it seemed evident he hadn't yet raped her. I tore the gag away, and she sank into my arms, sobbing.

"Is it the same man?" I asked quietly.

She nodded, still crying. I helped her to dress, then, having locked the bedroom door, I led her into the lounge and seated her in one of the chairs. The police arrived a few minutes later, and we went through the protocol of admin. I showed them my warrant card and informed them that I would give a statement later. They asked if anyone required hospital treatment; Rachel shook her head.

"Why don't you let the hospital check you over, Rachel."

"No. I'm fine – thanks to you. He didn't touch me."

The officers then led the naked and still blind young man away, after I had given them instructions on the charges. I stayed most of the night with Rachel, trying to reassure her that she was safe now. It was very late when I got back to my flat; there was no sign of Sally. She had obviously taken me at my word and found a partner. I had a feeling I wouldn't be seeing her again at the flat.

I had the same mixed feelings I had had before: part of me felt elated that I had caught the rapist, but on the other hand I was feeling dispirited that I was now back on my own.

I felt a sadness coming over me as I tried to sleep.

* * * * * *

A few hours later – I don't know just how long it was – I was awoken by someone shaking me on the shoulder. It was Sally.

I groaned. "What time is it?" I mumbled.

"Look at this," she said, excitement in her voice. She was holding up an early edition of one of the nationals.

"What…what are you talking about, Sally?" I groaned again. Why the hell couldn't she let me sleep?

"Wake up, sleepyhead. Have a look at the papers. You're on the front page!"

I opened my eyes and caught a glimpse of the headline.:

SERIAL RAPIST APPREHENDED: LOCAL DCI ARRESTS HIM IN CAMDEN

It went on to describe the episode and how DCI Crossley had caught him, naked, attempting to rape a local girl. There was more, but it didn't impress me; I was too tired.

"You're famous!" Sally exclaimed. "Fuck me, you might even get a promotion."

"Where were you last night?" I enquired.

"Well, you weren't here, as it happens. You were too busy arresting this bastard. Was it Rachel – only they didn't say in the press?"

"Whoa. Slow down, will you? Yes, it was Rachel, and, no, I was there just at the right time. I was going to invite her for dinner when I came on the rapist. She was half undressed and in the process of being raped again. He was naked and I let him have it with the mace gun. The back-up officers must have informed the press; it certainly wasn't me."

"Very fucking brave of you, Angie. I don't know if I could have done it."

"You still haven't told me where you were last night – or is it something I probably know about?"

She grinned, rather like the proverbial Cheshire cat. "You might not believe this but, actually, nothing happened. I met some really nice guys, had a good time boozing with them, but no one I'd like to spend the night with. Fell asleep on the sofa in the house of one of the guys."

"You obviously had a good time, then?" I don't know why but there was something about it that irritated me. Perhaps it was because I had been too long on my own; or was it that secretly I fancied her? Still, I was very glad to see her back; I had thought she might never return. I climbed out of bed, rubbing my eyes.

"We'd better be getting ready for work," I muttered.

"Angie. It's Saturday. We're supposed to be having a day off."

I looked at my watch. It was only 7.30. "You might have though of that before you woke me up."

"Yeah. But you're a hero. I thought you'd like to hear about it."

I grumbled again.

"Listen, why don't you go back to sleep, Angie? I'll make some breakfast."

"No, it's okay. I'm up now, and I want to know how Rachel is. She was pretty shaken up last night."

"Right. Then let me make some breakfast for the hero, and then I'll come with you."

* * * * * *

I was right. Rachel was still traumatised when we went round to her flat. Sally made her a cup of tea whilst I tried to comfort her.

"I tried to tell you he would come back – didn't I?" she said tearfully.

"Yes, and I'm sorry we didn't take you seriously enough," I said. "But, even so, Rachel, we couldn't watch over you night and day; we simply don't have the resources."

"It was just as well Angie came round to see you," Sally declared, almost emphatically.

"I know. And I'm so grateful. I wasn't complaining, I was just stating a fact."

"Have you had any sleep?" I asked.

"No. I couldn't get that monster out of my head."

"So why don't you have some breakfast, take a bath, and go to bed? Sally here will look after you."

Sally gave me a quizzical stare.

"I have to go to the police station to give a statement. They'll want one from you, but it can keep for now. Come on, Rachel. Let us help you…"

Sally looked at me as I prepared to leave. "Are you going back to the office?" she asked.

"Yes. As soon as I've finished at the police station. Why?"

She shrugged. "It's just that I thought we could go out for a drink tonight – perhaps take Rachel with us." She dropped her gaze to Rachel. "That's if you fancy it," she added.

Rachel tried to smile but ended up simply nodding her agreement.

"Good idea. Why don't we all go out first for something to eat? I know a nice Italian on Wigmore Street." They agreed, so I left for the police station.

CHAPTER FIFTY-NINE

I really didn't have anything to do at the office – just some tidying up and one or two folders to go through. It was simply that I didn't want to spend all day either in the flat or wandering around Camden. I suppose I could have gone shopping, but what would be the point when I hardly went anywhere socially?

Jim phoned me to congratulate me on apprehending the rapist. He was a bit perplexed when I told him it had nothing to do with the visions – just police work.

"Are you sure?"

"Jim, of course I'm sure. The truth is I went round to Rachel's flat – it's round the corner from where I live – to invite her for dinner. And I walked in on the rapist."

"So you saved her?"

"I suppose I did. But it was fortuitous."

"I'm glad you told me; otherwise I'd be thinking we had the world's top policewoman on our books. By the way, have you heard or seen anything of the paedophile?"

"Nothing. I'm under the impression he must have either travelled upcountry, or maybe he's gone home to Poland."

"Don't write him off so easily, Ange. That's how we make mistakes. How are you getting along with Sally?"

"Okay. Well, fine actually. It's good to have someone to talk to."

"Good. I'll see you on Monday – unless, of course, something comes up in the meantime."

I spent the rest of the day updating the computers – 'tidying up', as I called it – and I guess I was getting ready to transfer across to MI5. I had a sandwich in the canteen at lunchtime, on my own, and decided I wouldn't contact Katy; even a Spirit Guide should have a day off! I finished what I had to do around four o'clock and went back to the flat. Sally wasn't there. "Perhaps she's getting along well with Rachel," I thought to myself.

I sat down in front of the telly and dozed off; it had been a long night and I was exhausted. Even heroes get knackered!

* * * * * *

"Angie," Sally said, yet again shaking my shoulder. "Angie, do you know it's almost seven?"

"Oh, Christ. And I wanted to have a bath."

"Yeah, well, you'll just have to shower. We're meeting Rachel in half an hour."

I stumbled into the bathroom, stripped and almost fell under the streaming hot water. It was wonderful. I dressed carefully, applied a touch of make-up, and I was ready.

"You look very nice," Sally said, an admiring note in her voice. I was pleased; it wasn't often I'd been flattered.

We collected Rachel a little while later, and I admired the trouble she'd taken to get ready, especially after what she'd been through. She gave me a kiss on the cheek, which I thought was really nice of her.

"So, where are we going?" Sally asked. "Didn't you say Wigmore Street?"

"I did, yes. But I think we'll all be overdressed if we go there. Why don't we go to the Langham Hotel on Upper Regent Street? It's very nice, I'm told. And afterwards we can go to that lounge bar you've been enthusing about to me."

"Don't we have to book? It is Saturday night, you know."

"Yeah. I'd forgotten about that. So where do you suggest?"

"We could try Ceros in Soho. I'm fairly well known there, so we should get in. And it's close to the club."

"What is it?" Rachel wanted to know. "I mean, is it Italian?"

Sally laughed. "Come on – we'll enjoy it."

She was right. She was well known there, and they found us a table at the back of the restaurant. We spent a pleasant evening, with a good dinner and plenty to drink. Afterwards we went on to the club, and it was as Sally had said. It was an elegant cocktail bar with luxurious furnishings. There was no sign of the 'others', as they say, and we were able to relax.

By eleven I was getting a bit smashed and decided it was time for me to hit the road. There was a cab waiting nearby, so I said goodnight to the two of them and more or less staggered into the taxi.

I gave the driver the address in Camden and slumped back in my seat, and I was half nodding off when I thought I saw smoke coming into the back of the taxi. Soon it was beginning to choke me, so I tried to push aside the sliding window to tell the cab driver, but it wouldn't move. I couldn't open the doors either; they were locked – so were the windows. I began to panic. What the fuck was going on? Was this deliberate?   Or was I about to become the unintentional victim of poisonous gases?

I thumped on the window, but to no avail. By now my head was starting to spin and I was feeling faint. "Katy," I managed to shout. All I heard was "I'm sorry, Angie; I didn't realise".

There was a familiar aroma pervading my nostrils, and my mind flashed back to Krakow and the evil that I had encountered in Kowalski's bedroom. It was that same all-consuming stench of evil that was now a cloying sensation in my nose, threatening to overpower me.

Choking on the fumes I desperately tried to get out of the cab, and then darkness enveloped me and I remembered nothing more.

CHAPTER SIXTY

I came to in the darkness of an old tunnel. It looked like one of those inlets near to Kings Cross; in fact, it could have been a garage, except that there were no vehicles present. I tried to look around, then realised I was lying on a mattress and tied to poles at each of the corners. I shuddered as the realisation of what was happening to me sank in. It was obviously the paedophile who was responsible. The taxi waiting outside the pub must somehow have belonged to him; no doubt he had commandeered it. I couldn't think of anyone else who would want to kidnap me.

I struggled against the ropes but they had been tied too tight for me to have any effect on them. I fought against the panic starting to overtake me. I realised I was trapped in this cavern, at the mercy of a killer who had already threatened to kill me, and I knew instinctively what was about to happen to me.

Will he rape me first? I wondered. How will he kill me? Slowly, with a knife? Surely he isn't going to shoot me – is he?

These thoughts went through my mind, almost as if I were detached from these events, as if I were witnessing someone else who was tied up to supporting poles, instead of myself. I closed my eyes, determined not to show fear; I did realise I was sweating, though. Then a man appeared at the side of me, carrying a knife and dangling it over me threateningly. He moved towards me and took a nick out of my neck; this was the second time I had had that experience with a knife.

He was older than I remembered from the woods, probably in his mid-50s. He had a sallow face, with tight lips that were currently displaying scorn. His hair was thinning, almost balding, and his eyes... His eyes almost defied description; they were so intense they almost belonged to an altogether different person. The person I was gazing upon didn't look as if he was malevolent; it was his eyes that betrayed him.

"Told you, did I not, I will find you?" he sneered in a heavy foreign accent. "You stopped me with boy from school – now it is your...your turn."

"If you kill me," I said, "the whole of the police force will hunt you down. You will never have any peace."

"Peace? Why I need peace if I cannot have my needs with boys? After you are dead I return to Poland; there I am safe."

"No you won't, Kowalski. In Krakow they have a warrant out for your arrest; as soon as you arrive the police will be waiting for you."

He laughed, but mirthlessly. "So, you know my name. Very clever of you, policewoman. And before I kill you I fuck you, so I enjoy your body." He approached me with the knife and sliced the buttons off my blouse, one by one. Next he dragged it from me, exposing my bra, which he then cut through the front strap, and I watched it fall from me as he began to fondle my breasts.

I tried to struggle but my hands and feet were too tightly bound. A kaleidoscope of recent incidents flashed before me: the arsonist in Manchester; the sexual killer from the underground trains; the terrorist policeman; the bastards who had been murdering prostitutes in the Midlands. And was it all now to end with this malicious killer of young boys, who was intent on raping and then butchering me? I tried to close my legs but he had already spread them wide, tied to the poles. He grinned at my struggles as he unbuttoned my jeans and ripped them off my legs. I groaned, "Not this; please, Katy – not this!" There was no reply as he tore my knickers away, leaving me utterly naked.

"Now, you tell me how you know about me." He was almost literally snarling when he spoke. "How you know where I am from? How you know I had the last boy?"

"My powers are greater than yours, Kowalski." I was gritting my teeth as I said this; being stark naked with a knife held to your throat is hardly conducive for a relaxed conversation. But I knew he would listen; he had to know what it was that motivated me.

"Powers? What are these powers, Crossley? You mean, as I know where you live and how I can attack you? So, tell me, or I kill you."

"Don't be absurd. Of course you're going to kill me. You haven't brought me here simply to discuss how I know about you. So, get on with it."

He grinned and let out a rather maniacal snigger. "Yes, but now I rape you to make you feel – what is the word? – yes, I look it up: diminished." He began to undress, stripping off his shirt. It looked as though he hadn't washed in ages; his odour assailed me. Finally he dropped his trousers, and I noticed that his penis was flaccid; obviously, the sight of my body didn't arouse him.

"I thought you only buggered young boys, Kowalski," I said, with a firmness in my voice that I wasn't feeling.

"You are correct, Crossley. And after I am hard I will bugger you first before I rape you."

He knelt on the floor in front of me, holding his dick in his hand.

"Now you must excite me," he muttered. "Put this in your mouth and make me big."

"Fuck you!" I said. Nothing on God's earth, not even his knife, would make me give him a blow job. I felt the knife circling my vagina.

"Are you sure?" he asked, casually, as though this was the most normal thing in the world.

"I said 'fuck you', Kowalski. Do whatever it is you want to do;" – I nodded towards his penis – "you will never put that thing in my mouth. If you really want to fuck me you'll have to get yourself aroused."

He roared out loud with anger, and raised the knife above my head. I closed my eyes and waited for the end to come. Just then I heard a door creak, and then a sudden explosion. It was a firearm, and I saw Kowalski, his head blown apart, crash to the floor. I looked up and saw that it was Steve Jenson.

"Thank God" I said. "How did you get here?"

He looked at me quizzically. "You called me," he replied.

"Called you?" I glanced at my ropes. "How the hell could I have called you, Steve? Look at me. I'm tied up like a trussed-up chicken and there's isn't a mobile in sight."

He shrugged as he put his revolver away. "Well, let's just say I received a message. To be truthful, I'm not sure where it came from, but I was led here knowing you were in danger. Who is this guy?" He pointed his gun at Kowalski.

"He's the paedophile we've been hunting. His name is Kowalski – he's from Poland. Did you really have to kill him, Steve?" I felt myself shaking at the trauma. No matter what happened to me from now on, I knew this episode had changed me from the person I was. I believed that either I would adjust to this type of crisis or my mental restraints would collapse. I remembered what Jim had told me when I was in Manchester: that I wouldn't be able to confront the sharp edge of my job. Strange, though, that he hadn't repeated this when he co-opted me to the crime unit; perhaps he felt I had already adjusted. If so, he was wrong.

"No," I heard Steve saying, "I could have tried to restrain him as he was plunging the knife into you." He shrugged again. "One dead policewoman, but one criminal we could have put on trial. Is that what you wanted?"

"Sorry," I apologised. "You saved my life and I'm trying to criticise you. Forgive me."

He grinned; not the cold merciless smile a natural killer would have worn, but a sense of warmth that filtered through me. He helped me out of the garage – still trembling – to his car, and spent some time away from me phoning in the incident to his superiors, and then we sped off to Camden. "You can tell me how he was able to capture you on the way," he said.

"Sure. And you can tell your superiors how I was able to call you, trussed up as I was, and direct you to this place when I didn't have a clue where we were. Is that fair?"

He roared with laughter. "Okay. We'll call it quits. But you're going to have to replace those clothes; they're ruined."

"Thank you, Katy," I whispered for my own benefit.

"Sorry, did you say something?"

I smiled. "Nothing that would interest you."

Steve came into the flat with me – partly to protect me from observers viewing my nakedness and partly because I suspected he wanted to stay the night. I was right. When I came out of the bedroom – fully dressed, I might add – I found that he had sat himself down and was devouring a large glass of my malt whisky.

"You can pour me one of those," I said. I was still shaking after the ordeal. It seemed that the nature of my life had undergone a drastic transformation, from essentially being a detached consultant, as I was in Manchester, to dealing with death on an almost everyday basis. The only way I could deal with it was to blank it out of my mind, pretend it wasn't happening to me – although, in fairness to myself, I did feel I was already adjusting to these ordeals.

"I already have," he replied, pulling a glass from behind himself.

"How are you going to explain the death of the paedophile?" I asked, once I'd settled down with the malt.

"I already have." He echoed his previous comment. "When I called it in I informed Dame Elizabeth that you had somehow summoned me to that tunnel in Kings Cross; when I found you were about to be murdered by that bastard, I shot him. In other words, Angie, I told the truth."

I laughed, almost hysterically. "You're kiddin' me, right?" Then I looked at him and realised he most definitely wasn't kidding me; he had told Dame Elizabeth exactly what had happened to him.

"What did she say – I mean, I do believe you, but it's so bizarre to hear you talking about it like this… It's as if it were the most natural thing in the world."

He shrugged and took a sip of his whisky. "As far as the hierarchy at MI5 are concerned, when it comes to you and your personal endowments, then everything has to be normal. To think otherwise then we would all of us have to be crazy."

"I see. So, you've now accepted my clairvoyance?"

"I've had no fucking choice, Angie. I still haven't learned to live with it but I guess, after you've joined us at MI5, then I suppose I'll get used to it. Right," he said, standing up; "are we going to bed?"

"I'm not going to chase you out of here," I said, slipping into his embrace. "I need someone to keep me company through the night, so I suppose you'll just have to do."

He leaned down to kiss me. "I hope you won't be disappointed."

CHAPTER SIXTY-ONE

The next morning, as with the first occasion, he had left, leaving me a note: "You have a meeting this morning with Dame Elizabeth at 9.30. Don't be late; I will be there, so will Commander Robbins."

Oh no, I groaned. I wish he'd warned me. But the meeting faded from my mind as I recalled the experience of the night before with Steve. He was a gentle lover, and there was something about him that I warmed to; a killer he might be, perhaps a justifiable killer as part of his job, but there was a tenderness about him that I empathised with. I was rather glad that Sally hadn't come back in the night; now I could tell her that her services were no longer required. The paedophile was dead and the little boys in this part of the world would be safe from him.

I showered slowly, shampooed my hair – I gazed at it critically, deciding that I needed another visit to the hairdressers – and dressed, not in my social outfit but in something suitable for the occasion: my dark tailored outfit with a pink blouse underneath. I looked at myself in the mirror; overall I was quite impressed, and felt ready to meet my potential new boss. I actually looked quite efficient.

Surprisingly, there was a car waiting for me outside in the pouring rain, with a driver I didn't know. I hesitated; when you survive in a dangerous world you become very cautious. He held up his warrant card and I got in, relieved.

"Are we going to MI5?" I asked.

"No, ma'am, we're not. Dame Elizabeth wishes to meet you at a safe house. We're going to the home of Sir Nicholas – it's in Surrey. It'll take about an hour from here, so sit back and enjoy the ride."

We set off, with the wipers on full.

I wasn't nervous – or at least I pretended I wasn't. What puzzled me was what exactly it was that I was going to be offered. I mean, was this to be a permanent appointment or would it be on an as and when basis? I thought about the previous night: not the sex with Steve but the trauma I had gone through. I shivered when I thought about it. I hadn't had time to talk to Katy about it but now, in the car, I gave her some of my thoughts on what had happened.

"It was you, wasn't it? Who summoned Steve to rescue me?"

"Yes. It was. It was the only thing I could do under the circumstances, Angie. I told you, I wasn't able to penetrate his protective shield, and, when I saw you were in danger, Steve was the first one I thought of."

"You mean, you knew he would kill the paedophile?"

"I thought it might happen, and just as well I did; that monster would have killed you."

"Tell me, is he now residing in heaven?"

I felt rather than heard her chuckle. "You know I can't talk about that with you, my dear. Let's be happy that you were saved and that that ghoul will have his just desserts. I'd better leave you now – you've arrived home."

She was right. We pulled into an enormous drive and parked in front of a Surrey mansion. It extended over three floors, with ivy clinging to some of the walls; I estimated it must have cost more than my lifetime's earnings. I stepped out of the car, stunned at the vision in front of me. I was completely mesmerised by this magnificent edifice. Before I was able to climb the steps the front door opened and a butler emerged, standing to one side.

"Good morning, Miss Crossley," he announced.

I had never before seen a fully dressed butler and I had to suppress a giggle. This was too fucking OTT. "Good morning," I replied, an unctuous tone in my voice.

"Follow me," he announced. "Sir Nicholas and Dame Elizabeth are with the others in the drawing room."

It was some drawing room; the whole of my flat would have fitted into just one corner of the room. Dame Elizabeth and the host were sitting amongst an array of sofas in front of a huge unlit open fireplace, whilst the commander and Steve Jenson were seated, somewhat uncomfortably, in a couple of nearby chairs. The room was opulent, to say the least.

"Good morning" was all I could think of saying.

"Good morning, Angela," Dame Elizabeth replied. She gestured with her hand. "Come, sit by me; it will be more comfortable." As I sat down she said, "I'm sorry we had to bring you out into the country but I thought it best if the other executives were not to have sight of you – especially after we make our offer to you." She smiled at that.

I sat down and glanced around the room again; I still couldn't think of any suitable expressions to describe it.

I was finally about to try and say something when the door opened and coffee arrived with a youngish maid. I was astonished at how some people lived; it was a world I'd never visited before. The maid poured out the coffee and then disappeared.

"Now," Elizabeth continued, "you remember our last discussion – about terrorists?"

I could only nod. I was still speechless at the surroundings.

"Well, I now understand from Steve here" (she gestured towards him) "– our 007! –" (she chuckled again, as if killing people were a huge joke) "that your involvement with the paedophile is now concluded." She looked towards Jim, who appeared to want to say something.

"It might have been helpful if I'd been warned of this development," he said. "As it is, I only learned of it this morning. And the fact we now have a body on our hands compels me to launch an enquiry into the facts…"

"No, commander, that won't be necessary," Elizabeth interrupted. "As far as your territory is concerned the culprit will simply have vanished – which, in fact, is exactly what has happened. For all you know, he may possibly have gone back to Poland."

"But what about my remit?"

"It stands. You only heard about the body from MI5; as far as your division is concerned there is no body; there will be no enquiry, no investigation – in fact, no crime.

"Now, where was I? Ah, yes. Angie, we would like you to join us, initially on an as and when basis, but ultimately as part of a more permanent arrangement. For now you will work closely with Steve Jenson, here; we wish for you to – how should I put it? – to use your insight to confirm or otherwise that we are on the right track. Steve will point out to you suspected terrorists; that means you will quite likely have to travel – sometimes overseas – and you will determine what it is they are planning, either in this country or elsewhere."

"You're not asking a lot, ma'am, are you?" I said. When I finally found my voice I surprised myself at the sarcasm in it; but this wasn't an assignment I had asked for. "When and where will I have to travel?"

She gave me one of her level looks, of the type that must have discouraged her protagonists from probing too deeply.

"My dear, when you will travel and to where is not a subject for discussion this morning. We will call upon you as and when needed. In the meantime, I have discussed this matter with the Commissioner and he is quite agreeable to your joining the team. In the meantime you will remain at Scotland Yard, and you will be promoted to the position of superintendent." She looked at me again, a half-smile playing around her lips. "Do you find that acceptable, Angela?"

"I'm…I'm not sure, ma'am. What will I expect to be doing at Scotland Yard? I don't believe the team will accept my promotion – I mean, I haven't done anything to deserve it." I turned to Jim Robbins. "What do you think, commander?"

He was shaking his head in disagreement. "I think Ange is correct. By all means she can stay at the Yard, doing what she does best – but a promotion? No. I don't think so, ma'am."

"I see. And are you happy to remain as a chief inspector, Angela?"

"Yes, Elizabeth. I would feel more comfortable with that arrangement. And if and when you decide I can be more helpful by transferring, then we can discuss my promotion."

"Very well. I will speak again with the Commissioner and make the arrangements; however, I will insist that you be paid the remuneration of a superintendent. Are we all clear on this now? Commander? Bear in mind that, for Angela Crossley's services, we will have priority over your unit."

"I understand, ma'am. And, yes, I am agreeable. The only thing I would ask is that when you call upon her you will first do so through me."

"Agreed. Angela, your contact will be Steve Jenson. You will do nothing unless you hear from him first."

"Yes, ma'am. I understand."

* * * * * *

Jim ran me back to New Scotland Yard. He was quiet for a time; then he said, "So what do you think about that, Ange? Are you comfortable with the arrangement?"

I shook my head. "I'm not sure. I don't know any of these people – apart from…"

"You mean the 'licence to kill' guy?"

I chuckled. "I know what you mean. And I'm not entirely happy with a killer, even though he did save my life."

Jim turned his head and looked at me. "Did he really have to kill that pervert? Wasn't there any other way?"

"He says not. Kowalski was about to plunge the knife into me – I was tied up and unable to move, and I have to bear in mind that I was provoking him."

"Yeah? How come?"

"He wanted me to suck his prick; it was the only way he could get an erection."

He laughed. "So you turned him down."

"Too fucking right I did. And this infuriated him, so he decided to kill me."

"You still haven't told me how he managed to find you. I know you were trussed up, so there was no way you could have used a mobile."

"My Spirit Guide, Katy. It was the only way she could get help to me."

"You mean, she called Steve Jenson? And obviously he came. Did he know what he was walking into?"

"No. He still isn't sure how she enticed him. All he remembers is following an urge to get to the cavern, and shooting the guy when he saw what he was about to do."

" You live in a strange kind of world, Ange. I'm not sure how you manage to cope with it."

"It isn't something I'd expect anyone to understand," I sighed. "It's a very private world, Jim. Sometimes I feel very much on my own."

"Doesn't that worry you?"

"No. It did at first. But if I hadn't adjusted to this phenomenon I genuinely believe I might have killed myself." I shrugged, not really caring to amplify.

"Did you…"

"Could we change the subject, Jim?" I intervened.

"Sorry. Yes, of course. Have you heard any news about the Blackpool incidents?

"Who's looking after the case?"

"I've got Sam on it."

"Do you think he might make chief inspector – after you've left us, I mean?"

I shrugged again. What could I say? It wasn't my call.

"Yeah, I know," Jim said. "It isn't your call. But I'd still like your opinion."

"I think he's as good as you'll get."

I watched him grin. "Without your extra-sensory powers, you mean?!"

"For the Met, that's a blessing."

We were quiet for a while and I was dozing off, refusing to think about the offer from MI5. I really wasn't sure how I would fit in – or, for that matter, where I would be sent. I wondered about Steve Jenson. I couldn't make up my mind about how I could relate to a natural killer. Sure, he was good in bed, but that was lust; there was nothing emotional about it. I never thought for a minute I could feel anything for him.

And if I were to spend time with him would I have to share his propensity for violence?

"I've been wondering of late," Jim interrupted my thoughts, "as to how you might get on in MI5 if you're exposed to the sharp end."

"That's a strange thing to say. What do you think I've been doing for the past few months?"

"Yes. But in my own way I've been trying to protect you. That's why Sally is sharing your flat – to avoid the confrontations. That's why you have a team around you; it's a kind of protection."

"Sure. But they weren't there when the paedophile struck. I was on my own, Jim. If it hadn't been for Katy I would have died. And, as for the future, that is who I'll have to rely on: my Spirit Guide. She watches over me when no one is able to, and that's why I'm not afraid of the sharp end.

"I see."

"Is that all you have to say, Jim?"

"I'm not being dismissive, Ange. It was something I'd overlooked when I thought of the dangers you might be engaging. But I agree with you. You have someone or something there that is very precious to you. It's more or less like having a guardian angel to watch over you." He turned and glanced at me. "I wish you everything you wish for yourself, Ange. And I'm glad we've had this little talk; it's eased my mind."

EPILOGUE

And thus begins a new chapter in my life in the service of MI5. It has been quite exciting, when I think about it. I recalled the day I began as a novice WPC in Birmingham. I was young and naïve and I realised I had so much to learn. And now I had been offered, and turned down, a promotion to superintendent. I shivered at the prospect; it was something I had always dreamt of but never really thought it would happen to me. But I have to bear in mind that it is largely Katy that I have to thank. If it hadn't been for her I wouldn't even be alive now.

My immediate thoughts went back to Connie and the tragedy she experienced; those were my earlier years. Then my mind turned to Paula, my lover in Manchester, who also met with tragedy, but largely through her own doing.

Were I to dwell on these issues I would feel unceasing sadness, but these days, largely thanks to my personal experiences, I have been able to place them at the back of my mind and view them dispassionately.

As I went into the Yard, I heard a soft voice in my ear:

"Angie, no matter where you go in the future or what you may have to do, you know I will always be watching over you."

It was that kind of endorsement that helped me to find peace within myself.

"Thank you, Katy," I whispered back.

AUTHOR'S BIOGRAPHY

Vincent Cobb was born and educated in Blackpool and spent most of his working life in the travel industry. Eventually he moved to London, where he became 'joint managing director' of Thomson Holidays, the giant package tour company, before moving on to head up Club 18-30. His first book, The Package Tour Industry, was published last year and recounts his many personal experiences in the early days of travel – some humorous and some terrifying.

The author lives in the Home Counties with his wife, Pat.

OTHER BOOKS BY VINCENT COBB

The package tour industry
Leave a light on for Jesus
Nemesis
Contrition

www.ingramcontent.com/pod-product-compliance
Lightning Source LLC
Chambersburg PA
CBHW021314250626
47155CB00002B/531